BRENDA NOVAK

When Summer Comes

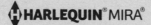

Recycling programs
for this product may
not exist in your area.

ISBN-13: 978-0-7783-1423-3

WHEN SUMMER COMES

Printed in U.S.A.

Dear Reader,

Welcome back to Whiskey Creek! This series has been fun for me to write. I love the group of friends these stories are based on. Truth be told, I'm a little jealous of them. I wish I'd been able to keep my high school friends a bit closer, but I moved the day after graduation and have never gone back, at least for any length of time. That's caused quite a bit of drifting in those relationships, which is too bad. There's definitely something special about knowing someone for so long and sharing so much.

This story was inspired by a friend of mine from college who was diagnosed with nonalcoholic fatty liver disease ten years ago. She was a wife and mother in the prime of her life and, being Mormon, never drank. I remember being so surprised that her only hope for life was a liver transplant. It seemed far too incongruous with how healthy she'd always been. But I'm happy to report that she received the transplant she needed. It's now a decade later and she's just as beautiful and energetic as she ever was. I saw her when I was visiting Utah recently and felt so gratified to see her thriving. Then I learned that another friend of mine (this one here in California) was recently diagnosed with the same thing. My California friend is currently on the national donor list, hoping and praying that a liver becomes available—and I'm hoping and praying right along with her.

In case you're not aware, there have been two other novels published in this series—*When Lightning Strikes* (released 9/12) and *When Snow Falls* (11/12). There's even a 150-page novella that kicks off the series (*When We Touch*). Information about these and my other titles can be found on my website, BrendaNovak.com. There, you can also enter to win my monthly drawings, sign up for my newsletter, contact me with comments or questions and join my fight to find a cure for diabetes. My youngest son suffers from this disease. So far, thanks to my generous supporters, my annual online auctions (held every May at BrendaNovak.com) have raised a cumulative total of $1.6 million.

Here's to your health and happiness!

Brenda Novak

1

The barking of her dog dragged Callie Vanetta from a deep sleep.

Rifle, the German shepherd her parents had given her for Christmas, was only two years old, but he was the smartest animal she'd ever known, certainly savvy enough not to make a racket in the middle of the night without reason. Despite all the critters that scurried around the place after dark, he hadn't awakened her like this once in the three months since she'd moved to the farm.

So if he thought she had something to worry about, there was a good chance she did.

Despite the warm June night, chills rolled through Callie's body as she lay on her back, blinking against the darkness. She'd always felt so safe in her grandparents' home. They'd passed away five years ago, but the comfort of their love and the memories created here lingered on. Sometimes, when she closed her eyes, she could almost feel their presence.

But not tonight. Fear eclipsed all other emotions, and she wondered what she'd been thinking when she gave up the small apartment above her photography studio downtown. She was out in the middle of nowhere, her closest neighbor over a mile down the road, with her dog sounding an alarm and scratching at the front door as if some menace lay beyond it.

"Rifle?" She whispered his name as loudly as she dared. "Hey!" she added, making kissing sounds.

He charged into her room, but he wasn't about to settle down. He circled in place, whining to let her know he didn't like something he heard outside. Then he darted back to the front door, singularly determined to show her where the trouble was.

She thought he might try to rouse her again. He obviously hoped to get her out of bed. But she was so frightened and undecided about what to do she couldn't move. Especially when he quit barking and emitted a deep, threatening growl—one that told her he'd laid back his ears and bared his teeth.

The hair rose on Callie's arms. Her dog meant business. She'd never seen him like this. What had him so upset? And what should she do about it? She'd watched too many true-crime shows not to realize what could happen. But, given her health, getting murdered would be too ironic. Surely, this couldn't be leading *there*.

She'd just decided to call the police when a heavy knock sounded and a male voice carried into the house.

"Hello? Anyone home? Sorry to wake you, but… could a man come out here, please? I need some help."

A *man?* Whoever was at her door wasn't from Whiskey Creek. Her family had lived in the area for generations. Everyone knew that this was the Vanetta farm, that the aging Theona and Herbert had died within months of each other and she was living here alone.

"Hello?" the man called again. "Please, someone answer me!"

Should she respond? Letting him hear her voice would tell him she was a woman, which didn't seem smart. But she had her dog to defend her. And she had a pellet gun she used to scare off skunks and raccoons and any other animals that might have rabies or get aggressive.

Problem was she couldn't remember where she'd put it. The screened-in porch that overlooked the outbuildings in back? The mudroom off the kitchen? She might even have left it in the barn. Until now, she hadn't felt any need for self-defense. All the wildlife she'd encountered seemed more afraid of her.

Still, she should've kept that gun close. What good was it otherwise? She wasn't going to scare anyone away with her camera.

"Open up!" *Bang, bang, bang.*

Drawing a shaky breath, she called 9-1-1 on her cell phone, which had been charging on the nightstand, and, speaking as low as she could and still be heard, told the operator that she had a stranger at her door. The operator advised her to sit tight, a squad car was on its way, but she slid out of bed and groped through the darkness for some clothes. Summer had come early this year. With the weather so mild, she hadn't worn anything to bed except a pair of panties. In case her visitor tried to break in before the police arrived, she wanted to get dressed.

"Can someone help me?" the man hollered.

Wearing a T-shirt and blue jeans, and armed with the knowledge that someone from Whiskey Creek's four-man police force would soon arrive, she crept toward the door. What was wrong?

Despite the ruckus her dog was making, her visitor

didn't seem to be giving up. His determination lent him a degree of credibility, even though she knew her reasoning was flawed. His persistence didn't necessarily mean he was telling the truth. If he had a gun and was capable of using it, he wouldn't have to worry about getting bitten.

So...was he really hurt? If the answer was yes, how'd he get that way? And how did he come across *her* property, tucked away as it was in the Sierra Nevada foothills? She couldn't imagine some random individual driving these back roads at one in the morning, especially midweek. She encountered plenty of strangers during tourist season, which was upon them, but always in town. Not out here.

"Shit," he grumbled when he got no response. Then something hit the door harder than a knock, as if he'd crumpled against the wooden panel and was sliding to the porch floor.

A flicker of concern warred with Callie's fear. Maybe he really *was* hurt. Maybe he'd run his car into a ditch or a tree and injured himself so badly he was about to die....

She snapped on the porch light. Although it went against her better judgment to let him know she was home, he'd managed to convince her that he might really need help. Some of the TV programs depicting real home-invasion robberies also showed innocent victims who were unable to get help because of other people's fear.

"What's wrong with you?" she asked.

A swiping sound suggested he was using the door to steady himself as he clambered to his feet. She peered through the peephole, hoping to catch a glimpse of him, but even with the porch light on she couldn't see much—just a man's head covered in a hooded sweat-shirt.

"Thank God," he said.

She might've thought it was one of the Amos brothers. Although they'd calmed down in recent years, a cou-ple of the younger ones still caused problems, from drunken-and-disorderly conduct to selling crystal meth to fighting. But they lived down by the river on the other side of town, they'd never bothered her before and she would've recognized the voice.

"Who are you and what do you want?" she called out over Rifle's barking. The dog was even more ex-cited now that he had the support of his master in tak-ing on this interloper.

"Name is Levi, Levi McCloud. I need a first-aid kit, some water and rags."

She ignored the second part. "I don't know a Levi."

"I'm just…passing through, ma'am."

He was leaning too close to the door for her to dis-tinguish his features. Was he doing that on purpose?

The idea that he could be made her more nervous than before. "But you decided to stop here?"

"No choice. My motorcycle…broke down a mile or two back."

"That's how you got hurt?"

"No. It was a…a couple of dogs. They ran out and attacked me…for no reason…while I was pushing my bike. Got me good, too."

The way he forced his words through his teeth sug-gested that he was in pain, but maybe he was faking it. Maybe he was planning to rob her, rape her, possi-bly kill her.

"*Where* did this happen?" she asked.

He attempted to laugh but the sound died almost immediately. "Hell if I know. I've never been around here before."

"Then what made you come now?"

"Heard it was pretty country."

That was it? He was out on a joyride? Alone? His response didn't seem particularly plausible, but the scenario he gave wasn't inconceivable. Out here in the country, dogs weren't always penned up or put on leashes. He could've been attacked, as he said.

She was tempted to open the door, if only to verify his story, see his injuries. But she couldn't take the risk. "How'd you get away?"

"Listen…" He dropped his head against the door, covering the peephole entirely. Now it was impossible for her to see anything. "I don't mean to frighten you. Is there…is there a man in the house? Someone else who…who might not…be afraid of me?"

She didn't want to let on that she was alone. But if a male didn't take command of the situation soon, he'd know, anyway. Perhaps he'd said that to confirm what he already suspected. "Tell me how you got away from the dogs."

"I…convinced them I wasn't…anything they wanted to mess with."

Meaning he'd hurt the dogs as much as they'd hurt him?

She wondered whose pets they were, and if the incident had really happened. "How badly are you hurt?"

"Hard to tell in the dark, but…it's bad enough to make me bother you, which isn't something I wanted to do."

She wiped sweaty palms on her jeans. "Okay, just… stay where you are. I've called for help. The police will be here soon."

"The *police?*" Instead of reacting with relief, as she'd expected, he cursed and shoved away from the door. "Are you serious? They won't do anything for me."

"They'll get you the medical attention you need," she said, but he wasn't listening. He was leaving. She could hear the porch creak under his weight.

"Where are you going?" she yelled.

He didn't answer.

After hurrying to the window, she dropped to her knees in an effort to catch a glimpse of him before he could move out of sight.

For just a moment, she could make out the broad shoulders of a tall, spare man wearing jeans with that hoodie.

Why was he taking off without the help he needed? And why had he acted so averse to meeting up with the police? Was he wanted? A known felon?

Possibly. He had to have *some* reason for avoiding the authorities. But seeing how obviously he favored one leg, she believed he really was hurt.

She checked the time on her cell phone, which she'd brought with her. How long could it take to get a cruiser out here? She didn't want to be any more vulnerable than she already was, but she also didn't want to be responsible for the death of a lonely, injured stranger.

"Come on, come on," she muttered, but each minute felt like an hour. When she couldn't wait any longer, she sprang to her feet and ordered her dog to silence.

Reassured by this show of strength, Rifle stared up at her, tongue hanging out and tail wagging eagerly. He seemed to be asking, "What now? What are we going to do now?"

"We're going to see where he went," she told him. She wasn't sure he could comprehend her words, but speaking calmed her, and he certainly understood her intention. He barked once to confirm that he was ready.

Holding him by the collar, she slowly, cautiously, opened the door a crack and peered outside. The porch was empty, just as she'd assumed. She couldn't hear or see any movement, didn't know where the stranger had gone.

Rifle struggled against the grasp she had on his collar. Then he nudged the door open wide enough to squeeze through and pull her along with him. He even tried to drag her down the steps. Clearly, he wanted to go after the man.

She wasn't up for that. But before she could insist they go back in and lock the door, she stepped in what her dog had probably smelled—something dark and wet smeared on the floorboards of the porch.

The second she realized it was there, she knew what it was. Blood.

The police had come and gone, and they hadn't found a thing—no tall, dark stranger hiding on the premises. Not in the old tack shed. Not in the barn. And not in the cellar. They attempted to follow the blood that led down the steps of Callie's porch, but the trail disappeared in the grass and dirt about ten feet away.

They poked around for over an hour, hoping to discover what had happened to her guest, but they didn't have any search dogs with them and Rifle wasn't trained to track. They tried using him for the first thirty minutes, but he was so distracted and excited by the two officers who'd come to help, she eventually had to shut him up in the mudroom, where she kept his food and water.

In the end, the police couldn't figure out where the injured man had gone, which left Callie as unsettled *after* they drove off as before. She couldn't help wondering if they hadn't found the stranger because he didn't want to be found. She didn't think he'd had time to go far, not injured as he was. So how had he just... disappeared?

Maybe he hadn't. Maybe he'd reached a neighbor's property. But if that was the case, why hadn't anyone else called to report a bloody, hood-wearing stranger? And why hadn't the cops been able to find his motorcycle? *Was* there a motorcycle? And was it really broken down?

Exhausted in a way she'd never been before she'd been diagnosed with non-alcoholic fatty liver disease, she finished cleaning up the blood—she didn't want to see it when she woke up—and went into the house.

Rifle barked and scratched at the mudroom door, whining to be let out. But even now that everyone was gone, he was too excited. She didn't want to deal with an agitated dog after what she'd already been through. She'd found her pellet gun in the barn, felt that would offer her some defense if the man came back. So she called out a good-night to Rifle, promising she'd take him for a long walk in the morning. Then she used the bathroom off the kitchen and checked all the doors.

Once she was satisfied that the house was as secure as she could make it, she took a final peek through the window, dragged the heavy pellet gun to her bedroom and peeled off her jeans. She was too rattled to sleep almost nude, like she'd been doing earlier, but she knew she'd never get comfortable in fabric as stiff and heavy as denim.

It wasn't until she'd propped the gun against the wall next to her headboard and crawled beneath the blankets that she heard a noise. She wasn't sure what it was; it had been too slight. But when it came again her fear returned.

She looked around—eyes wide, breath held—and realized her bathroom door was closed.

She rarely shut that door. It was in the master bedroom and she lived alone. There was never any reason to.

But that wasn't the only thing that made her heart race. The light was on in there. She could see it through the crack near the floor.

2

Several thoughts went through Callie's mind at the same time. She had the pellet gun and her cell phone, but her dog was shut in the mudroom. Should she slip out, free Rifle then call the police?

She had to have some way to defend herself until help could arrive. A pellet gun, even a high-powered one, wasn't the best weapon with which to stop a man. Thanks to a deluge of adrenaline, her limbs felt like rubber. She doubted she'd have the strength to effectively use any weapon, especially a heavy one.

That said yes to the dog. But she wasn't sure she could stomach what a struggle between Rifle and the intruder would entail. If she'd been told the truth, her visitor had already been attacked by *two* canines—and he'd beaten them off. She didn't want to risk Rifle's life, didn't want anyone hurt if she could avoid it. Life had become too precious to her. Since her diagnosis, she considered every moment a gift, and she felt that way not just about her own life but everyone else's.

At least now she understood why her dog had continued to strain at his leash and wouldn't calm down when they were searching. She'd chalked his behavior up to youth and inexperience, but that wasn't it at all.

He was the only one who could smell, probably even hear, that they still had company.

Sneaking into the house while she and the police were searching the outbuildings was a bold move—so bold she'd never seen it coming. Why had the stranger taken such a risk? Was he so badly hurt he'd had no choice?

Could be.

Or he was determined to gain whatever he wanted from her.

The memory of his blood on the porch, on her bare foot when she stepped in it, weighed heavily on Callie's mind. If he'd given her AIDS, there wouldn't be much point in continuing to search for a liver donor....

Sweat poured down her body as she once again slid out of bed and pulled on her jeans. She'd simply vacate the room, take her phone and her gun and barricade herself in the mudroom with her dog while she called the police.

But then she heard a curse, a clatter and a crash that was so loud, her dog started jumping against the door clear on the other side of the house.

What had happened? If Callie had her guess, the man had fallen.

"Hello?" she called out, hesitating midway across the room. She was holding her phone as well as the gun, which made it difficult to use either one.

There was no answer. No sound or movement, either.

Had he hit his head and knocked himself out—or worse?

"Oh, no," she murmured. In order to lift and aim the gun, she had to put down her phone. She hated to do that, but she was quickly growing more worried than scared, so she set it on her dresser close by. "I know you're in there."

"I pretty much…figured that…at this point." He sounded tired. No, more than tired. Drained. That was hardly what she'd expect from someone who meant her harm. But she'd never encountered a psychopath before—not knowingly, anyway. She had no clue how one might act.

"I've got a gun!" she warned.

"Unless you plan…on shooting me for no reason… I don't really care," he said. "Just tell me the police are gone."

Why would she admit she was alone? "They're not. They're right outside. I can call them in if necessary."

There was another long silence.

"Did you hear me?"

"Let them go and I…I'll leave. I just…needed some soap and water. That's all. Some gauze would've been nice. But you don't have that. What kind of woman doesn't have a first-aid kit?"

"I have a first-aid kit. But I don't keep it the medicine cabinet."

"Too bad. It would sure…make a nice send-off present, if you…could…forgive my intrusion."

What condition was he in? He was slurring his words. Talking at all seemed a struggle for him. "How'd you get inside my house?"

"Wasn't hard. You and those…two officers…"

"Yes?"

He made an attempt to rally. "You were so intent on trying to use your dog to follow my trail I just…circled around behind you. I could tell where you were at all times. Until you brought him in."

"How'd you keep from dripping blood all over?"

"I wrapped my sweatshirt around my arm…hoped that would help."

It had done the trick. The trail of blood had disappeared completely. "Sneaking in here takes a lot of nerve," she said.

"Lady, sometimes you…have to do…what you have to do. What else can I tell you."

Lady? That made her sound old. She thought of her good friend Cheyenne marrying Dylan Amos just four months ago, right before the doctor had given her the bad news about her liver, and winced. She'd wanted a husband, a family. She'd never had a hint of health problems, no reason to believe she wouldn't eventually have kids. Now chances were that she'd die before summer's end.

There were more noises. These Callie couldn't figure out. "What's going on?" she asked, worried again.

"I'm trying to get…the hell out of…your bathtub."

She was beginning to believe this whole night really had been about his injury. "What's wrong? You can't?"

"It'd be easier…if I wasn't so…damn dizzy."

What was she going to do now? She wasn't sure she had the heart to call the police on him again. It wasn't as if he'd waited in her bedroom and attacked her. "I don't understand why you wouldn't let me get you some help," she said. "I tried."

"No, you called the police."

"Same thing."

"Not quite."

She inched closer. She still held her gun at the ready but she was feeling more and more confident that she wouldn't have to use it. "Why are you so afraid of the authorities?"

He didn't respond for a few seconds. Judging by the noise, he was once again trying to get up. "Why do you think?"

"You're wanted?"

"Not for anything serious." He cursed as though he'd done something that hurt.

"Are you okay?"

He didn't answer. Instead, he reverted to the question she'd asked before. "I have a few...unpaid speeding tickets."

That sounded far too innocuous to explain his reaction. Surely it couldn't be the truth. "You're lying," she said. "Why would that make you afraid of the police?"

"We don't get along."

"Meaning..."

"I've had...a few run-ins with them. They don't like vagrants. Besides, a warrant is a warrant. Whether it's for a speeding ticket or...or whatever else, they'll take you in. I can't let that happen."

He'd called himself a vagrant, but he didn't sound like one. Although she could tell he was in considerable pain, he was mostly coherent. Articulate, too. "Where are you from?"

"Does it matter? Look, if you'll...help me a minute, I'll be...on my way."

"Where?"

"Wherever the road takes me."

She crept right up to the door. "I thought your motorcycle broke down."

"I'll fix it. Believe me...I want to leave as badly as

you want me gone. I have to get to my...my ride before someone else comes across it."

Including the police. No doubt they'd impound it.

She listened for movement but didn't hear anything. "Are you coming out or not?"

"I think...you're going to have to come in. Just... whatever you do...keep that dog of yours away."

"He's in another room. But I can get him in here pretty darn fast if I need to," she added.

"I won't hurt you. Give me some bandages. Then I'll go."

Lifting the barrel of the gun so she could reach the knob, Callie pushed the door wide.

Sure enough, the man she'd first spotted on the porch was in her tub. He must've stumbled and fallen while trying to clean himself up, because he'd broken the shower curtain rod on the way down. The curtain lay on the floor, stained with blood. Blood speckled the vanity, the floor and the bath mat, too. But that wasn't what concerned Callie. He didn't look good. He'd managed to get to his feet, but he was huddled, shivering in nothing but a pair of bloodstained jeans in the corner, where he could use the walls to hold himself up.

Callie felt her jaw drop. "*Look* at you."

He seemed to summon what strength he had left. "About that first-aid kit..."

"You need more than a Band-Aid." About her age, maybe a little younger, he had blood smeared all over him as if he'd swiped here and there to staunch the flow. The hooded sweatshirt he'd been wearing was tied around one arm; his bloody T-shirt lay on the floor not far from the shower curtain. She couldn't ascertain the injuries on the arm that was covered, but she could see he'd been bitten several times on the arm that was bare.

"You need painkiller, maybe food, a good doctor— and a heck of a lot of sleep."

He didn't respond. There was a gray cast beneath his tanned skin. That was probably new. But Callie suspected his gaunt, ravaged look wasn't. This man was accustomed to living a hard life. His cheekbones were pronounced, testament to the fact that he was too thin, especially since he had such wide shoulders and big hands. And yet...he wasn't unhandsome. Somehow his rawboned features gave him a rebel air and enhanced the impact of his hazel eyes, which regarded her with the wariness of a wild animal cornered because of injury.

He didn't trust her any more than she trusted him, she realized.

Lowering the gun, she set it aside. Maybe dropping her guard was the wrong thing to do. Maybe it put her own safety in jeopardy. But she no longer cared in the same, fearful way she had before. Without a functioning liver, she was going to die soon, anyway.

But maybe she could save him.

The woman was small, even for a woman, and curvy. With platinum-blond hair and big blue eyes, she had a certain...bombshell look about her. Thirty or so, she was wearing a pair of jeans and a T-shirt with no bra. The no-bra part was unmistakable.

"Come here." She stretched an arm toward him. "Let me help you out of the shower."

Levi shrank against the tile. There wasn't any reason for her to touch him. She'd only get blood on her clothes, and he'd caused her enough trouble for one night. "I just need—" he fought the dizziness that made it almost impossible to stay on his feet "—your first-aid kit."

Somehow he had to stop the bleeding so he could see how bad his injuries were. He could tell that both arms were chewed up, especially his right, which he'd swaddled in his sweatshirt. He'd also been bitten on the back of the neck, his shoulder and his leg in two places. He didn't know much about the dogs that'd attacked him, wasn't sure of the breed—it'd been too dark and things happened too fast. The only thing he could say for sure was that he hadn't been able to outrun them, even after he ditched his bike. When sharp teeth sank into his flesh, he'd been forced to fight. After that it had been a blur of snarling, lunging and gnashing teeth— on his part and that of the dogs.

Fortunately, he'd won. Or they'd all lost. One dog had finally taken a hard enough kick that he didn't want any more and the other had followed him when he limped away, whining. Levi had done his share of limping, too. It hadn't been a minor encounter for any of them.

The woman with the smooth complexion and soft, round features still had her hand out. "I'm afraid it can't be that simple, Mr. McCloud. You need a doctor. Come on, I'll take you to the hospital."

"No." He had no permanent address, no insurance and very little money. Everything he owned was stuffed into the backpack he'd left with his bike, except for the clothes on his back and the wadded-up bills in his pocket. Maybe twenty bucks at the most, it was just enough to buy food until he found his next odd job.

Worry tightened her voice. "How many times were you bitten?"

"Several." Closing his eyes, he rested his head against the wall. "I've never seen animals so intent on tearing someone to pieces." He winced at the memory. He'd been chased by a few dogs since returning from Afghanistan. Being out on the streets left him vulnerable. But he'd never been *attacked*. He'd made it through six years in the military, fighting in some of the worst hot spots in the Middle East without taking a bullet, only to be mangled by dogs in his own country.

"My arms took the brunt of it," he explained. "They wanted the front of my…neck, my jugular, but I kept blocking them. I would've been…better off with my leather jacket on. But I'd worked up a sweat pushing my bike and…had taken it off. Bad luck." He chuckled, but the thought of his bike, his jacket and his pack brought back the concern he'd been feeling earlier. He had to retrieve his belongings before someone stole them or the police came by. He'd had to leave his motorcycle right there on the side of the road, couldn't continue to push it after the attack. It was too damn heavy.

"Okay, well, at least sit down. You'll only hurt yourself more if you don't."

"I've gotta go." He tried to step out of the tub, nearly toppled over and had to let her help him down onto his ass. Muttering something he couldn't quite make out, she rolled up a towel she got from a cupboard and put it behind his head. Then she brought in a heavy blanket and covered him, right there in the tub. "Stay put," she ordered as she tucked it tightly around him. "I'll be back in a minute."

The decisiveness in her voice made him lift his head. "Where are you going?"

"To get the first-aid kit, since that's all you'll accept."

Relieved, he let his head fall back. If she was going to call the police again, she wouldn't have braved coming in. Surely that meant he'd soon be bandaged up and on his way. He'd walk his bike to the small gold-rush town a few miles back where he'd had dinner and find the necessary parts and tools to make the repairs. Maybe he could offer his services to an auto shop for a few days in trade for what he'd need. He'd done that before. He could fix any kind of engine, had been in charge of the heavy equipment for his platoon in Afghanistan.

Trying to keep his mind off the pain, Levi concentrated on the gas station with the repair bays he'd noticed in town before settling on a café. But he must've drifted off despite his efforts to remain lucid, because when he opened his eyes there was another man in the room. He was easily in his seventies, his hair completely gray, and he had a hook nose, full beard and paunch that hung over his belt. He'd removed the blanket that had kept Levi warm, which was what had disturbed him.

The woman who'd covered him was now wearing a bra under her shirt. She wrung her hands as she peered over the old man's shoulder. "Is he going to be okay?"

Levi didn't give him a chance to respond. "Where's the first-aid kit?" he asked, calling her on the deception.

She had the grace to look abashed. "I'm sorry. I was afraid you were going into shock. You need a doctor."

The other man glanced up at her. "*I'm* not a doctor."

She sent Levi an apologetic grin. "But he *is* a veterinarian."

"Who's mostly retired," the guy said with a note of exasperation.

"Still good at his craft." She patted his shoulder with obvious affection. "This was my grandfather's friend and next-door neighbor. Now he's *my* friend and neighbor. Godfrey Blume, meet Levi McCloud."

"So what do you think?" Callie shooed Rifle out of her way so she could pour the coffee she'd put on a few minutes earlier. Levi McCloud was asleep in her bed, but Godfrey was sitting at her kitchen table.

Every time her neighbor yawned she felt bad about waking him in the middle of the night. He was nearing eighty. But she hadn't expected providing Mr. McCloud with medical attention to take several hours. She'd been so caught up in helping to wash and bandage his wounds, she hadn't noticed the passage of time until she saw the break of dawn. Now her rooster was out in the yard, crowing for all he was worth.

She couldn't help smiling when she caught sight of the old bird strutting past her kitchen window. She loved early mornings. They reminded her of summers with her grandparents and awaking to the smell of frying bacon.

"I did what I could," Godfrey said. "But I wish he would've let us take him to the hospital. Or even to a real doctor. I've never seen an attack like that."

And her neighbor had worked with animals his whole life! She frowned as she set the sugar and cream on the table. "We did what we could."

"Mr. McCloud is a surprisingly stubborn man, given the extent of his injuries."

Once Godfrey had ascertained the large number of stitches their patient required, they'd both tried, once again, to get him in her car. Godfrey could only offer him a topical analgesic to ease the pain—and Tylenol. But there was nothing they could do to overcome

Mr. McCloud's resistance. He tried to leave on his own power when they insisted, and would've done so if they'd pushed it any further. At that point, Godfrey had relented and agreed that some care was better than none.

"We should report the dogs to animal control," she said. "They need to be restrained before they hurt someone else—a child, for instance."

"I plan on looking into it." Her neighbor had been the only veterinarian in town for most of his life. He'd officially retired three years ago, when the newly licensed Harrison Scarborough opened his practice. But some people still brought their animals to Godfrey.

"Do you have any idea whose pets they might be?" she asked while pouring herself some cranberry juice. She was on a strict diet that precluded alcohol, salt and coffee, among other things.

He smoothed his shirt over his belly. "My bet? There's a couple of pit bulls down the road, around the bend."

"Really?" Callie had never seen any, but she'd been pretty preoccupied of late. Adjusting to the shock of her diagnosis, especially since she'd never consumed much booze, hadn't been easy. She'd thought only alcoholics had to worry about cirrhosis. "You think it's them?"

"I can't imagine what other dogs it could be. I know all the rest of the animals in the area, and they wouldn't do something like what we saw."

"Whose pit bulls are they?"

"Belong to a couple of young men, maybe twenty-eight or twenty-nine, who are renting the old Gruper place. They're here for the summer, doing some prospecting."

Gold panning and dredging had become popular pastimes. A lot of tourists visited "the heart of gold country" to relive the history of the '49er. Coloma, where gold was first discovered in California, was an hour away, but the entire area had been rich in ore. At 5,912 feet, the nearby Kennedy mine was one of the deepest gold mines in the world.

"So you've met these men?" she asked.

"Just last week. I was selling my gold dredge. They saw my flyer on the bulletin board at the diner and came over to buy it. I guess they weren't finding anything using the panning method."

"Did you like them?"

"Not a bit." Godfrey spoke with his usual candor, but she'd already guessed his feelings from his sour expression.

"Why not?"

"They're unruly braggarts with big mouths and no respect. If I hadn't known better, I would've thought they were related to the Amoses."

The Amoses weren't as bad as they'd been immediately after their father went to prison. As a matter of fact, she really liked Cheyenne's husband. But she didn't mention that she now knew Dylan and cared about him. She didn't want to veer off topic. "I'm surprised they didn't hear their dogs growling and barking. You'd think they would've gone out to see what was going on."

He shrugged. "They were probably passed out, drunk."

"They're big partiers?"

"That's the impression they gave me."

"Great." She rolled of her eyes. "Just who you want

living so close—and with a couple of unsafe pit bulls, too."

He acknowledged her sarcasm with a tip of his cup. "Fortunately, it's only for three months."

Rifle brushed up against her, wanting some attention, so she bent to scratch behind his ears. "Short-timers or no, they still have to keep their dogs from biting people," she said. "Mr. McCloud could've been killed."

Godfrey sipped his coffee before responding. "I plan on heading over there later."

Knowing he'd do whatever needed to be done, she changed the subject. "Will Mr. McCloud be okay?"

Her neighbor's hands were oversize, like her injured guest's, except that Godfrey's were also thick. When he was stitching up Levi's bite wounds, Callie had been impressed by how dexterous his sausagelike fingers could be.

"As long as those bites don't get infected, he should be. He'll have a few scars, but I made the stitches very small. That'll help. In my opinion, he should get a tetanus booster, but he claims he was in the military, that his shots are current."

"They make sure soldiers stay up on that sort of thing, don't they?"

"They do. *If* he was really a soldier."

Apparently, Godfrey was taking nothing for granted. The people of Whiskey Creek could be suspicious of outsiders. But Callie believed at least that much of Mc-Cloud's story. He had a tattoo on one shoulder depicting an eagle with the word *Freedom*. A tattoo on the other arm said R.I.P. Sanchez, Williams, Phelps, Smith. The names were in different fonts, as if they'd been added as he'd lost friends.

She preferred not to consider how hard that would be to cope with.

"I can't tell you how much I appreciate your help, G.," she said, using the nickname her grandfather had given him. Poppy had coined a nickname for everyone. It was usually a shortened version of that person's first name but *Godfrey* became a little tricky. Only his wife sometimes teased him by calling him God.

"Happy to help. You know how much Mina and I care about you." Although his words were kind, he shot her a warning look from beneath his hairy eyebrows that indicated she might not like what was coming next.

"But…" she said, giving him the opportunity to speak his mind.

"But I'm going to stick my nose into your business and tell you that I think you should send this man on his way."

"I will, of course. As soon as he's better."

"I mean as soon as he wakes up."

Rifle wandered off as she sat down at the table. "G., he just got over a hundred stitches!"

"That's okay. In a few hours he'll be able to walk well enough to vacate the premises."

But how far would he have to go? Godfrey had mentioned infection as if it was a serious concern. Certainly heading off into the wild blue yonder wouldn't minimize that risk. And what if Levi couldn't find his motorcycle? For all she knew, the cops had impounded it. Even if the bike was exactly where he'd left it, it wasn't running. That was the whole reason he'd been in a position to be attacked in the first place. "He needs time to recover."

"We don't know anything about him, Callie. We don't even know if his version of what happened is true. Having him here might not be safe."

Callie sipped her juice. "But he has no home." And he had no mode of transportation. "Where will he go?"

"Wherever he was going before he met you."

His protectiveness wouldn't allow him to consider any mitigating factors, so she didn't argue further. "I'll send him off as soon as I can," she promised.

Godfrey finished his coffee and got up to bring his cup to the sink. "I'd better go. I'm sure Mina's wondering where on earth I am."

"Of course. Thanks again." When she ushered him out, she put Rifle into the fenced part of the yard so he could get some exercise. Then she returned to the house and stiffened in surprise. Levi McCloud was no longer asleep. He was coming out of her bedroom.

3

"Those clothes were in the tub for a reason," she said.

Careful not to tear out the stitches in his leg, Levi hobbled toward the door, eyeing the petite blonde who'd given him the help he needed. What was her name? She'd told him last night. Callie something… Anyway, he appreciated what she'd done for him. He also appreciated that she'd kept her word and hadn't called the police a second time. He doubted there were many women who would've taken such a risk and he admired her courage. But he didn't want her to get in his way now that he was ready to go. "I rinsed out the blood the best I could. I have to get my bike and my backpack," he explained.

"And if you manage to do that, then what?"

"I'm out of here." He never stayed in one place long. But how fast he could leave Whiskey Creek would depend on his bike. If the repairs cost more than elbow grease, he could be in trouble. He'd never find work in his current condition. With all the stitches in his arms, he looked pieced together, like Frankenstein's monster.

"Where's your backpack?" she asked.

He could smell coffee, wanted a cup but figured he could buy one along the way—provided he found his bike and was able to fix it. "I hope it's where I left it."

"What's in it?"

"Everything," he said simply. Everything he owned, anyway. That didn't consist of a lot, but he didn't need a lot.

She sidled over as if moving slowly would make it less apparent that she was cutting off his path to the door. "If you'll go back to bed and get some rest, I'll retrieve your bike."

She had dark circles under her eyes, looked as tired as he felt. But then, he'd kept her up all night, so that was to be expected. She was still damn pretty. She reminded him of Charlize Theron. Maybe even Marilyn Monroe.

"You don't know where it is," he said.

"You could solve that by telling me."

Her size relative to that of his bike didn't make her suggestion very plausible. "I had to drop it when the dogs attacked. Even if it's not in the ditch I was trying to avoid while I was pushing it—which it might be— you wouldn't be strong enough."

"But if you exert yourself, you could ruin everything we just accomplished with your stitches!"

She had a point. Medical help wasn't easy to come by, especially for someone like him. But, as he'd said, she couldn't lift his bike. "I don't have any choice."

She started to argue, to say nothing was worth risking further injury, but he cut her off. "What about the dogs that attacked me? They could still be around, licking their wounds. If they feel anything like I do this morning, they won't be in a good mood."

Her confidence seemed to falter. "I don't have to go alone. I have a friend who could help."

"A male friend?"

"Yes."

He hadn't gotten the impression she was in any kind of serious relationship. He was pretty sure it was just her and her dog living here. She had extra bedrooms but, as she'd mentioned to the vet who'd stitched him up, they were full of storage. The only bed was in her room, and there were no men's clothes or belongings in there.

That didn't mean she *couldn't* have a boyfriend, however… "Is he a mechanic?" he asked hopefully.

"No. But he has a truck and a trailer. We could load your bike up, bring it here. And I could wash your clothes. You can't be comfortable in those."

She obviously thought she'd overcome all objections, but Levi had reason to be worried about one more thing. "What is this male friend going to say when he finds me here—in your bed?"

Folding her arms, she raised her chin. "There's nothing he *can* say. This is my house. I make my own decisions."

That was good news, at least. The last thing he needed was to get into another fight. "Then maybe I should go with the two of you—"

"Rest." She made a shooing motion with her hands. "If you'll go back to bed, I'll make buttermilk pancakes for breakfast when I get back."

He was hungry. And it'd been forever since he'd had a home-cooked meal. His father had had a girlfriend once who could make the best pancakes he'd ever tasted. He missed her, like he missed some of the others who came and went. Pancakes shouldn't have been much of a draw, but Callie couldn't have offered anything that would've tempted him more.

Well, maybe there was *one* thing. It had been a long

time since he'd had that, too. "Buttermilk pancakes, huh?"

Her lips curved into a smile. "You've never had better."

He studied her, trying to figure out why she was being so nice.

"What?" she said, sounding a bit self-conscious.

"Why aren't you in more of a hurry to get rid of me?"

Her smile faded. "Maybe it feels good to focus on someone else's problems for a change."

"Let's go over your plan." Kyle Houseman, one of Callie's best friends and part of the clique she'd grown up with since grade school, drove his work truck slowly along the road where Levi said they should be able to find his bike.

"My plan?" Preoccupied with searching the shoulder and the ditch that ran alongside it, Callie wasn't paying a lot of attention. "What are you talking about?"

"Once we get this vagrant's bike back to your place. What then?"

She was fairly sure the motorcycle was gone. If not, she would've spotted it by now.

"Callie?" Kyle prompted when she didn't answer.

"Go slower, would you?"

"I'm barely creeping along as it is!" he complained but did as she asked.

"It *has* to be here." Pressed up against the harness of her seat belt, she gripped the window ledge as she searched. "If it's not…I don't know what he'll do."

"He'll pay a hefty impound fee," Kyle said.

Would some guy with only the clothes on his back have the money for that? "Someone other than the police could've taken it. Maybe it's been stolen," she mused. But she thought that would be the worse of the two possibilities.

"If so, his insurance will cut him a check. *If* he has insurance."

Kyle had spoken her concerns aloud. She doubted Levi carried any more insurance than was legally required, and liability didn't cover theft. "I don't want him to lose his bike."

Easing the truck over to the side, Kyle waited for a car coming up from behind to get around them. "Why are you so concerned about this guy?"

His surprise irritated her. Having a liver that no longer functioned properly made her look at certain issues differently. For the first time, she wondered how people could be so callous about certain things.

"Why are you not *more* concerned?" she countered. "We're talking about a human being who was attacked by dogs. He's already full of stitches. Doesn't seem fair that he should lose his only mode of transportation."

Kyle scowled at the censure in her voice. "There's no need to overreact. I just don't think you should get personally involved."

She blinked at him. "What should I do, then? Throw him out?"

"Why not? He isn't your responsibility. For all you know, he's an ex-con. Even if he's not, he could rob you blind—or worse!"

Before her diagnosis, both possibilities would've frightened her so much she probably wouldn't have taken the chance. But she didn't feel that way anymore. It wasn't that she didn't care to enjoy what time she had left. It was more that she wanted to take the opportunity to do good before she was gone.

"He's not dangerous," she said.

"You don't know that, Callie. Even if he isn't violent, or a thief in the usual sense, he could take advantage of you in other ways—play on your sympathies, sponge off you."

"He's not the type."

"You can recognize the type?"

Levi had been far too eager to handle his own problem with the bike for her to believe he expected her or anyone else to look after him. On the contrary, he gave her the impression that he was determined not to need anyone.

"I won't have trouble getting rid of him when the time comes," she insisted.

"You don't know that, either."

She met Kyle's gaze. He cared about her well-being. She trusted that—but there were other issues at play here, too, including, possibly, some jealousy. While trying to help him recover from his divorce a year ago, she'd gotten a little *too* close and wound up in his bed. After a few isolated incidents, they'd agreed to end all sexual activity. They didn't want to ruin their friendship. So far, that friendship had lasted twenty years.

But since moving to the farm, and knowing she was probably facing the end of her life, Callie had been so terribly lonely she'd slipped back into sleeping with Kyle a few times. "Stop acting like a jealous boyfriend, okay?"

"Is that what I'm doing?"

"Sounds like it."

"Some would say I have that right!"

She swatted him on the shoulder. "Oh, come on! You don't love me in that way, and you know it. You're still in love with Olivia."

"Since she's married now, it doesn't do me a lot of good."

Only the fact that she'd married his archrival—who was also his stepbrother—made it worse. "Regardless, *I* can't replace her. Even if we both wish otherwise, we're not in love. We've already gone over this."

"Fine. The motorcycle's not here. Let's go back."

She'd offended him. Sometimes he wanted more from her than other times. She understood. She waffled, too. They cared so much about each other that it was natural to question why they couldn't be even closer, why that added romantic element had never been there, especially since they'd turned out to be so sexually compatible.

"I want to keep looking. Could you please make another pass?" she asked.

Clearly not happy, he swung the truck around and began creeping down the road again. When they reached the Gruper rental, Callie peered into the yard, hoping to see the pit bulls Godfrey had mentioned and whether the animals showed evidence of having been in a fight. But the house looked empty of both man and beast.

Kyle broke into her thoughts. "How old is he?"

"Who?"

"This guy who showed up at your house last night. Who else?"

She'd been thinking about the renters. "His name's Levi McCloud."

"That's not what I asked."

"I'm guessing he's our age. Why?"

"Just curious." He turned down the radio. "What does he look like?"

He was handsome. There was no question about that. But Kyle wouldn't want to hear it. Not in his current frame of mind. He had to be going through a difficult period if he was acting so possessive of her. "He's about six-two, has blond hair slightly on the long side in front, hazel eyes and a few military tattoos. What does it matter?"

"I'm wondering if attraction is part of whatever you're feeling about him."

Another comment that seemed motivated by jealousy. She ignored it. "Can you pull over?"

"Here?"

"At that house we just passed." She indicated the rental.

"Why? What are you going to do?"

"I'm going to ask if anyone's seen a motorcycle on the side of the road."

"Who lives here?" he asked as he backed up.

"According to Godfrey, a couple of guys who've come to Whiskey Creek to do some prospecting for the summer."

"You'll just go up and knock?"

"Why not?"

"Because it seems to me that we've done enough."

She covered a yawn. The night was catching up with her. These days she didn't have a lot of strength to begin with. "This won't take long."

Kyle pulled into the driveway and let the engine idle. Before leaving the safety of the truck, Callie whistled, just in case. When no dogs came running, she climbed out and approached the dilapidated porch.

The blinds were down, so she couldn't see inside. Listening for sounds of movement, she knocked.

No one came to the door.

They were gone, as she'd guessed. She was on her way around back when Kyle called out to her.

"Callie, come on! No one's home."

She raised a finger to signal that she'd be just another second. She wanted to see if these men might have taken Levi's bike and rolled it out of sight. But she found no sign of that. She even checked in the detached, one-car garage.

Nothing, except the dredging machine they must have purchased from G. and buckets upon buckets of sediment and rock.

Disappointed, she was walking back when she spotted some bloody paw prints leading to the mudroom.

Aha! She'd found the offending dogs, after all—or where the offending dogs lived.

Eager to tell Kyle that she'd accomplished *something,* she almost missed the dirty, chewed-up backpack partially hidden by bushes. It appeared to be military issue, which made her think it had to be the one Levi lost when he dropped his bike.

"Are you coming?" Kyle called.

After scooping it up, she returned to the truck and tossed it in the bed. "Let's go."

He cocked an eyebrow at her as she got in. "Did you just steal that?"

"I'm guessing it belongs to Levi."

"But you don't know."

"We'll see soon enough. I can always return it."

* * *

The second Levi joined them in the living room Kyle could see that he had indeed suffered a traumatic dog attack. He had stitches in both arms, even in one leg. But Kyle couldn't feel much sympathy. He was too worried about the threat this man might pose to Callie. Judging by the wariness in Levi's eyes, those bites weren't the only injuries he'd ever sustained. Kyle was willing to bet he carried some significant battle scars on the inside, too.

Callie had said he'd been in the military. Maybe he'd seen some action. Kyle supposed he could be suffering from post-traumatic stress disorder. He wouldn't be the first vet to struggle with what he'd been through.

"Levi, this is Kyle Houseman." Callie gestured between them.

Lean but sinewy, Levi offered his hand. He was an inch or two taller than Kyle and, Kyle guessed, two or three years younger. He seemed brooding, watchful and a bit standoffish, even while wearing Callie's bathrobe, which should've made him look ridiculous. Instead, the pink terry cloth created a stark contrast between her size and his, her optimism and innocence and the cynicism of a jaded warrior. It also reminded Kyle of the wolf donning Grandma's mobcap in Little Red Riding Hood.

Would he have to play the part of the woodcutter?

"Nice robe," he said.

Levi lowered his hand when Kyle didn't accept it, but he didn't scramble to explain or apologize, as most guys who were so out of place probably would. "Would you rather I went without it?"

Kyle wasn't pleased with Mr. McCloud's response.

But he was the one who'd set the tone. What had evolved between him and Callie put Kyle in a difficult situation. Their relationship was so complicated that he often lay awake at night, trying to figure out what should happen now that they'd slept together. "I'm wondering where your clothes are."

Levi jerked his head in Callie's direction. "Ask your friend."

"They were torn and bloody!" Obviously rattled by what had already been said, Callie could hardly find her voice. "I'm washing them."

Kyle grinned as if he'd been joking the whole time. "Right. Of course. Then it's a good thing that robe fits as well as it does."

A muscle flexed in Levi's cheek. "I'm not after your woman, if that's what you're worried about."

His blatant honesty took Kyle off guard. "She's not my woman. But I care about her. I want to be clear on that." He also wanted to put McCloud on notice that she wasn't as defenseless as it might seem, even though she was keeping Rifle outside in deference to what her guest had been through.

"All I want is my bike." At that point, Levi turned to Callie. "Did you find it?"

When she shot him a dirty look, Kyle knew she wasn't pleased with how he'd handled the situation.

"No. Sorry to say I didn't," she told Levi. "We'll have to call the police, see if they impounded it."

"But you brought my backpack."

She stepped out of the way so he could get to the tattered canvas pack Kyle had set inside the front door. "Yes. It was at the house closest to where you said you were attacked. But it's filthy. I think the dogs took out their residual anger on what you left behind."

While bending to pick up his belongings, McCloud glanced at them from beneath the hank of blond hair hanging in his eyes and Kyle was again struck by the fact that this was not your typical vagrant. He was too handsome, too young—and he seemed very capable.

Kyle could only hope he wasn't capable of violence.

"I thought it had to be a neighbor's dogs," Levi said. "I couldn't have walked too far from where it happened."

"Those dogs don't belong to my neighbor, exactly," Callie said. "They belong to whoever is temporarily staying in that house. Godfrey told me two guys are renting it. He said they have pit bulls."

"That explains a lot—about size and strength."

"You certainly weren't dealing with poodles," she said.

The way she seemed to be pandering to him bothered Kyle.

"Did you see them?" Levi asked her.

"I didn't. But I discovered some bloody paw prints. That's what tipped me off."

There was blood on the bag, too. Kyle had ascertained that much when he carried it in. "Did you injure either of the dogs?" he asked.

Levi shrugged. "I tried. It was me or them." He unzipped his pack and pulled out a pair of jeans and a T-shirt. "Good news, Mr. Houseman." He held them up. "I can get out of your girlfriend's robe."

"I'm not his girlfriend." Callie's words reiterated what Kyle had already said, but Levi ignored them. When he turned, presumably to go change, she stopped him. "Why put those clothes on over your stitches? You'll just get ointment on them, and that stuff won't come out easily. You need to eat and go back to bed. You can dress later."

He gave her a pointed look. "Thank you, but I'll decide what I need to do," he said, and disappeared into the bedroom.

As soon as he was gone, Kyle guessed he was going to get harangued by Callie, so he went on the offensive. "That was rude what he just said to you."

Grabbing his arm, she dragged him into the kitchen. "What *he* said? You started it!" she whispered. "You were all but banging on your chest."

Kyle lowered his voice. "Maybe I could've been friendlier. But you're being friendly enough for both of us. That man has issues, Callie."

"Most vagrants do!" she responded. "That's why they don't have homes, why they aren't with their families!"

"Exactly! So don't tell me you're still going to let him stay!"

She released his arm. "What else can I do?"

"Have him go somewhere different…"

"Like?"

He considered his own circumstances. "I've got my sister and her kids at my place."

"I doubt he'd be willing to go home with you, anyway. It's not as if you were nice to him!"

"Beggars can't be choosers," he grumbled.

When she tilted up her chin, he knew he'd said the wrong thing. "He hasn't asked for anything—except some bandages to stop the bleeding. The rest has been my doing."

Kyle felt bad for not having more sympathy. He

should've at least shaken hands. But, homeless or not, McCloud wasn't the type of man who inspired pity. He was too remote, too mysterious and probably too angry. "He'll be fine."

"He has nowhere to go until he gets his motorcycle fixed."

"So I'll pay for a room at Little Mary's B and B for a few days. That'll solve it."

She got the buttermilk from the fridge. "He won't take your money."

"How do you know?"

"Try offering and see for yourself."

He didn't answer because he believed her.

"Anyway, there's no need to go that far," she said. "We can manage right here."

Kyle came up behind her. "He looks strong, despite his injuries, Callie. Doesn't that intimidate you?"

"I have to go sometime, Kyle."

Had he heard her correctly? She'd never said anything like that before. "That's a weird comment. How can you be so cavalier?" He slouched into a chair. "Do you realize how much damage a man like that could do to a woman like you if he decides to cause trouble?"

"A woman like me?"

"Someone who weighs barely one hundred pounds?"

"He's already had several chances to hurt me. He could've broken in last night instead of knocking on the door. He could've attacked me after I found him in the bathroom. Or maybe not—he was pretty hurt," she said. "But if he was intent on rape or murder, he could've stopped me before I called you this morning. He was feeling stronger by then."

"Just because he hasn't hurt you yet doesn't mean he

won't. Maybe he has a low frustration tolerance. Maybe you haven't done anything to piss him off."

"He's in pain. From the dog attack and possibly other things. Something sent him out on the road. I get the feeling that all he wants is to be left alone."

Kyle glanced over his shoulder to make sure they still had their privacy. "Fine. But it's summer, plenty warm out. At least have him sleep in your uncle's old room in the barn."

She nodded. "I'll have to. I only have one bed."

"And once you find his bike and get the damn thing fixed, send him on his way!"

Standing on tiptoe, she reached for the flour. "I don't think I'll have to ask him to leave."

A noise made them turn. Levi was there, wearing the clothes he'd pulled from his backpack, which looked clean. "I guarantee it," he said.

4

Breakfast was awkward. Callie wished Kyle would go home. She didn't like the skeptical way he kept looking at Levi, and she was sure Levi didn't like it, either. He bowed his head over his plate as he ate. Then he thanked her and asked if he could use her phone.

After she handed him her cell, he walked into the living room and she and Kyle cleared the table.

"Don't worry about the dishes," she said. Levi's voice carried back to them but they couldn't hear what he was saying.

"I'll help."

She guessed Kyle was feeling contrite for behaving so boorishly. "What's up with you today?" she asked. "You glared at Levi all through breakfast."

He squeezed her shoulders. "I know. I couldn't seem to stop. It's because I was already worried about you—and now this."

Pretending to be absorbed in her work, she averted her gaze. She hated lying to those she loved but wasn't ready to handle the alternative. "I don't know why you'd worry about me. I'm fine."

"Fine? You haven't been yourself since you moved here."

"Of course I've been myself." She'd done her best to go on as if nothing catastrophic had happened but, of course, there were bound to be changes. Hearing that she had only six months left, that this summer would be her last, still wasn't easy to cope with.

"No. You're quieter. Reflective. Withdrawn. You don't spend much time at the studio anymore, and you were there all the time before. I can't figure out what's wrong."

"Nothing's wrong," she said firmly. "My assistant is taking care of Reflections. That gives me a chance to live here, on the farm, like I've always wanted to, before my parents sell it. It's my way of saying good-bye to the place."

He obviously wasn't convinced. "You loved living in town, loved being in the middle of everything. And you were so determined to build your business. Then you went…AWOL."

"I haven't gone AWOL. I'm tired of doing weddings. I want to be able to photograph nature and help my parents, too. This is my opportunity."

He studied the black-and-white photograph mounted on canvas that hung on her wall. She'd managed to capture a large, hairy spider spinning a web out in the barn. The texture of the old wood came through so clearly. And she loved the shadow of the web on the ground. It was competition material. She knew it. Finally, she was taking artistic photographs—but she wasn't sure she'd be around to reap the rewards.

"So how are you making a living?" he asked. "I know your parents are giving you a little to get this place shaped up before they list it, but that can't be enough to cover your monthly expenses."

"Actually, the studio's booked for the season and I no longer have to pay rent on my old apartment. I'm better off than before."

"The business hasn't suffered without you there?"

"Not as much as you'd expect." Autumn might prove to be a different story, but autumn might not matter. *One day at a time...* "Tina's talented. I trained her well."

"If she's *that* talented she'll break out on her own someday."

She wouldn't have to. Callie planned to leave her the business. And she planned to leave Kyle her dog. Those were the only two things she had to give away, except her SUV, but that came with a monthly payment. "Maybe. Maybe not."

"So you're happy?"

The way he looked at her begged her to be honest with him, so she almost came out with the truth about her liver. She didn't want to hurt her friends and family by dying suddenly when she could've given them some warning.

But neither did she want to trade her final months for what sharing her secret would mean. Once everyone knew, she'd be the recipient of their pity. She'd have to live with their sadness as well as her own. And she'd have to respond to all that grief and concern with some polite phrase that showed courage in the face of bitter disappointment. She wasn't sure she was capable of being as brave as that required. Not yet.

Besides, her mother would want to take care of her, would pressure her to move home, and she wasn't ready. The doctors had given her until the end of summer. She wanted to enjoy as much of that time as possible.

Chances were good she wouldn't die suddenly, anyway. First she'd become too ill to take care of herself. At that point, she'd come out with it. But right now, the medication her doctor prescribed kept her fairly healthy, if she was careful to eat right, get plenty of rest and manage her stress. It even kept her from looking jaundiced.

"I'm happy," she insisted.

"So it's not me. It's not that we've…been together?"

"No." She smiled as she touched his face. "I know you'd marry me if I wanted you to. You already married another girl just because you slept with her." She was teasing. Their entire group teased Kyle about Noelle. First she'd used her pregnancy to get him to propose. Then she'd aborted the baby without consulting him when he wouldn't buy her the mansion she wanted. It was the most astonishing act of spite Callie had ever seen. She still couldn't bear to look at Noelle, who was once again working at A Damsel's Delights, a clothing and handmade-jewelry boutique in town.

Fortunately for Kyle, that episode of his life was over. Callie thought it was also fortunate for him that she'd given up on love and marriage; she had no expectations where he was concerned. She didn't have time to start a family. Even if she found the right man, she wouldn't want to get romantically involved, wouldn't want to hurt a partner by dragging him through what could easily turn out to be her death.

"The change in you…it happened about the time we first slept together," Kyle pressed.

No, it had happened precisely six weeks after. They'd both drunk a little too much and slept together on New Year's Eve. During the next four weeks she'd begun feeling poorly—tired, nauseous, feverish. She'd assumed she had the flu but the symptoms wouldn't go away. Then she became jaundiced and, before people could start to remark on it, she'd decided to drive to Sacramento and get checked out at a twenty-four-hour medical center. She must've had some inkling that it was serious, or she wouldn't have gone to such pains to avoid the local doctor. Still, it was a bombshell when, on Valentine's Day, a physician from that clinic called with the news.

When she didn't speak, Kyle said, "I can't help but assume it's what we've done that—"

"Kyle, you have nothing to worry about," she broke in. "There's no blame here. I want you to remember that, okay?"

She'd grown too serious. Her intensity made him even more suspicious, but before he could respond, Levi returned with her phone. Hearing his tread on the scarred wooden floor of the old kitchen, she whirled around to face him. "Any luck?"

When his eyes shifted from her to Kyle, Callie felt herself blush. She feared he already understood more about what was going on between them than the group they socialized with so often.

"The police have it," he said. "They picked it up probably an hour before you got there."

"Too bad I missed it. But at least it wasn't stolen." She didn't ask how much the impound fees would be. She doubted he had the money to pay them and didn't want to put him on the spot in front of Kyle. Besides, she felt partially responsible for his loss, since she was the one who'd told the officers about it.

"I've got to get back to work." Kyle looked at Levi. "Want me to drive you to the impound lot?"

Levi shook his head. "No need. I'm not ready to go

there yet. But if you're heading toward town, I'll hitch a ride as far as you're going."

He wasn't asking for any special consideration. That seemed to soften Kyle up. "I can take you wherever you'd like to go."

With barely a wince to give away what the movement cost him, Levi hauled his bag over his shoulder as if he might not be coming back. "I saw a gas station a few miles back."

"The Gas-N-Go?" Kyle said.

He nodded. "Anywhere close to that will be fine."

Finished with the dishes, Callie dried her hands. "What are you planning to do there?"

"Find work," he said, and turned away.

She stopped him. "You can't work! Not yet. You're covered in stitches."

He didn't seem to think that mattered. "I'll live."

"Wait." She sent Kyle a glance that warned him not to interfere. "I could use some help around here."

Levi's eyes narrowed skeptically. "Doing *what?*"

"My parents want to sell the place. I told them I'd get it in shape."

"Which would include…"

She could tell she'd caught his interest. "I've been meaning to repair and paint the barn, for one thing." Her parents had bought the paint; she just hadn't felt strong enough to get up on a ladder. She'd been considering hiring someone, anyway. The place had sat empty for so long there were plenty of other projects for her to do. Just keeping up with her gardening and photography seemed to be a full-time job. "If you'll provide the labor, I'll provide room and board until you finish.

I'll also front the money to retrieve your motorcycle and get it fixed."

He adjusted the bandages covering the stitches on his right arm. "How do you know I won't take advantage? That I won't fix my motorcycle and leave before I ever paint the barn?"

"Will you?" she asked, but she figured there could be worse things. Liver failure had a way of putting smaller disappointments in perspective.

There was a moment of silence. Then he said, "No. Where's the paint?"

She chuckled. "You're not in any shape to start quite yet. And the fees on that motorcycle are only going to go up the longer we leave it. Let's get that taken care of first."

Levi kept quiet while Callie drove to the impound lot in Kyle's truck with his trailer lagging behind. The silence stretched on so long it began to feel oppressive, so she made an attempt at small talk. "Last night you said you'd been in the military. Where'd you serve?"

When he glanced over, she could see him weighing whether or not he wanted to engage in this conversation.

"Is where you served classified information?" She grinned, trying to tempt him into lowering his guard, but he didn't even crack a smile.

"It's pointless to go through the usual rituals. We won't know each other long enough for any of it to matter."

"It'll take a week to finish the barn, and that's only if you're a fast worker. So humor me."

"Fine." He shrugged. "Afghanistan."

"That must've been tough."

No response, but she couldn't blame him for not wanting to talk about such a difficult post.

"Where are you from?"

"Seattle."

"Do you have family there?"

He wasn't looking at her. He'd gone back to staring out the window. "Some."

"A wife? Kids?" She'd seen no ring on his finger, but she knew that didn't necessarily mean he wasn't committed.

A muscle jumped in his cheek, giving her the impression that she'd just struck a nerve.

"Neither," he said, the word falling like an ax.

Curious as to why he'd be sensitive on this subject, she asked, "So you've been married?"

It took him a few seconds to answer, but eventually he managed another word. "No."

"Neither have I." She leaned forward to catch his eye. "In case you were wondering."

He made no comment, which led her to believe he *hadn't* been wondering—or wasn't willing to admit it if he was. He'd have to open up if he was going to ask any questions about her, and that would risk her asking even more questions about him.

"Wow, you're really easy to talk to," she said.

His eyes flicked her way.

"I'm afraid they won't release my bike."

"The impound lot? Why wouldn't they?"

"I don't have my license or registration."

Considering his situation, this didn't really surprise her. But it did create a problem. ID was usually required. "So what's your plan?"

"I don't know. It's *my* bike. If we pay the fine, they'd better give it to me."

Callie didn't want any problems. "You didn't…*steal* it, did you?"

He gave her a look that nearly shriveled her on the spot. "No. Just because I don't have the registration with me doesn't mean I stole it."

She wasn't sure why, but she believed him. He seemed too forthright to be a theif. "I have a friend who tows for this yard. Actually, it's the brother of a friend. I bet Joe can arrange it."

This seemed to ease some of his tension. "You think so?"

"It's a small town. We can work it out." She loosened her seat belt to give her a bit more breathing room. "So what brings you to California?"

"Figured this was as good a place as any."

She had so many loved ones she couldn't imagine taking to the road, trading her relationships with them for a series of roadside diners and two-bit hotels—even if she was well.

"Does your family know you're here?" Who'd been part of his life? And where had they gone? Did they miss him? Care about him?

Again, there was a slight delay in his answer. "I haven't talked to them in some time."

Why? She wanted to ask, but no amount of effort on her part seemed capable of breaching the walls he'd thrown up. Because he wouldn't engage in this conversation, it seemed more like an interrogation.

Convinced that she was wasting her time, Callie let it go. She wasn't necessarily looking for a friend. She had plenty of those. She was just trying to be one. But being a friend didn't have to include badgering him into revealing his situation. She could live and let live. After all, she had her own secrets.

Adjusting the volume on the radio, she fell silent and expected that silence to last—until *he* spoke.

"That guy, Kyle."

She tightened her grip on the steering wheel. "What about him?"

"You're sleeping with him, right?"

Fortunately, the impound lot was coming up. "Kyle's a long story," she said, and turned into the drive.

At the farm, the sun bore down on Levi, reminding him of Kandahar in July. In reality, this day, which was somewhere around ninety degrees, was mild by comparison. He'd never felt what the word *swelter* meant until he'd experienced one-hundred-and-fifteen-degree temperatures in the desert half a world away—while wearing an army uniform and fifty pounds of gear. Still…the blinding brightness of the afternoon sun brought back memories. Once again, he could taste the gritty dust that clogged his nose and throat, the salt of his own sweat, the fatigue of intense exertion. He could also hear the Pashto spoken in the market they policed. Afghanistan had been unlike any place he'd ever visited or previously imagined, but he hadn't disliked being there. Not in the beginning. Joining the army provided an escape from his father, which had considerably improved his life.

Besides, at nineteen and freshly graduated from high school, he'd been so idealistic and full of patriotism he'd been eager to face any challenge. He'd just had no idea what those challenges would entail—or how smiling at a pretty girl could turn out to be the biggest mistake he'd ever made.

"Are you thirsty?"

Grateful for the interruption, he raised a hand to block the sun. Callie was standing there, holding a glass of iced tea, but for a moment he thought he saw Behrukh in her *shami* dress and *hijab*—the way he'd first seen her in her father's store—and his chest constricted.

"Levi? Are you okay?"

The vision cleared. This wasn't Afghanistan. And Callie looked *nothing* like Behrukh, who'd been tall and thin with the characteristic dark hair and eyes of her people.

"Fine." In some ways, he was better than fine. The impound lot hadn't given him any trouble about releasing his bike. The guy there had chatted with Callie, flirted a bit and taken a call from her friend Joe, who vouched for him, and that was it. Hooking an arm around one knee, he sat up and accepted the glass she handed him.

"It's too soon for you to be working. I wish you'd get some rest."

"I'm okay." He took a long drink, letting the cool, sweet liquid soothe his parched throat.

"Have you figured out what's wrong with your bike?"

He motioned toward it with his glass. "Carburetor's jammed. I should also change the spark plugs."

"Will that be expensive?"

"Not too bad, since I can do the work myself."

"Do you need parts?"

He squinted against the sun. He was feeling a bit light-headed. Maybe it *was* time to knock off. While he'd been tearing apart the engine of his motorcycle,

Callie had been bringing fresh bedding from the house to the barn, where she said there was a room with a tiny bathroom in one corner. She'd apologized for the fact that he wouldn't have any heat or air-conditioning, but it was mild here this time of year, especially at night. He didn't mind making do. That had become his pattern for life. Right now, just getting out of the sun and into the shade would help.

"I need the plugs, maybe a few other things. I'll know more when I finish here. But…maybe we can go tomorrow?"

She nodded. "I'm glad to hear you say it can wait. I made some beef Stroganoff. My grandmother's recipe. Why don't you get showered and come in for dinner?"

There didn't seem to be any need to keep pushing himself. He wasn't in a hurry. He liked the farm. It was isolated enough that, besides Callie, he didn't have to run into other people.

"Okay."

"My uncle installed an instant water heater for the bathroom in the barn," she explained, "so you should have plenty of hot water, but the shower's tiny and not much to look at. I put some towels out there."

"Thank you." Fortunately, Callie, the one person he did see here, wasn't difficult to be around. After that conversation in the car, she'd stopped prying into his past. He got the feeling she understood that he didn't want to talk about himself and wouldn't push him again. Since they'd returned home, she'd left him to his own devices, and that felt almost comfortable.

"Let me know if you need anything else," she said, and started back to the house.

"Callie?"

She pivoted to face him.

"Why are you helping me?"

Her eyebrows slid up. "I want the barn painted, remember?"

"You could hire a handyman. It doesn't have to be some stranger who's been attacked by dogs. Your boyfriend could even do it on the weekends."

She didn't bother protesting the status he'd assigned to Kyle. She didn't seem to want to touch that subject, no matter when he brought it up. The way she'd answered his only question in the car led him to believe that she valued her privacy as much as he did. "You've got something I need, and I've got something you need. That makes it a fair trade for both of us." She tilted her head to one side. "Why? You don't trust me?"

"I don't want to owe anyone." He didn't want to feel any obligation or gratitude, either. He didn't want to feel *anything*—except the sun on his face and the wind in his hair.

"It's a fair trade, like I said. That means we'll be even."

When he nodded, she walked into the house and he got up to take a shower. She'd said all the right things—but he had a feeling that if he wasn't careful, he could wind up owing her a lot.

5

Dinner was delicious. Levi ate more than he had in a single meal for months. He probably should've stopped Callie when she kept ladling Stroganoff onto his plate, but he was enjoying it too much to protest. Unlike some of the other soldiers, he wasn't one to complain about the food served in the canteen. It'd tasted better than any he'd known previously. His father had been so determined to make an MMA champion out of him, and to use that success to build the reputation of his dojo, that comfort foods and junk food weren't allowed. No pizza, fries or greasy burgers. No gravies, no soda, no cookies or candy or cupcakes. He'd been in training almost since he was a toddler, had been raised on vegetables and lean protein. And steroids.

But Levi had flushed them down the toilet more often than not. Given the cost of those drugs, his father would've beaten him to within an inch of his life if he'd ever found out—there were certainly beatings for lesser crimes—but Levi definitely didn't want to turn out like his old man. He often wondered if Leo would've been a little less vicious without all the performance-enhancing drugs he'd taken to build up his own body.

Levi expected Callie to try and strike up another conversation. Normal people talked over dinner. But, apparently, she'd figured out that he preferred to be left to his own thoughts because she didn't say anything. Only the click of their utensils and an occasional "Would you like some more iced tea?" broke the silence.

"That was the best," he said when he'd finished.

She'd already gotten up and gone to the sink. Apparently, she hadn't expected him to say even that much. "Thank you."

When he didn't leave, she cast a glance over her shoulder. "Feel free to go out and get some sleep."

He was on his own? That easily?

At first, Levi felt relieved that she demanded so little. He was tired and sore, and he had a terrible headache. But he couldn't walk out without doing *something* to show his gratitude. Where would he be without her? His wounds had been stitched up, he had his bike, he had a full belly and a bed for the night. That was a lot to accept without giving in return. He hadn't even been good company.

He hadn't been good company to anyone for a long time....

"Is there anything I can do for you?" he asked.

Her eyes widened. "What do you mean?"

The setting sun cast shadows across the kitchen; she hadn't yet turned on the lights. "I'd like to repay you in some way, if I could."

"Painting the barn's enough."

He gathered up their glasses and silverware. He could at least do the dishes. She was looking pretty tired. When she thought he wasn't paying attention, she'd lean on the counter or hang her head as if she needed to regain her breath.

"I'll do it," she said, taking what he held. "It's not a big job. And you haven't had much sleep, considering what happened last night."

He couldn't quite figure out why she was going so easy on him, why she was allowing him to stay. "You're sure?"

She smiled. "Positive."

For a second, he wondered if something more than fatigue could be wrong with her, but then he decided it was the odd lighting that made her look so pale.

"Okay." He left the dishes to her but didn't go directly to the barn. He went into her bathroom so he could wipe up the mess he'd made there last night when he was bleeding. He'd been meaning to do it all day, but he'd been too drugged with whatever sleeping pills the vet had given him while stitching him up. Then he'd met Kyle, slept while they went looking for his bike because he could hardly stand, gone with Callie himself and, when they returned, started tinkering with his engine. Now he saw that it was too late. She'd already cleaned up.

The shower curtain he'd pulled down had been washed and was neatly folded on the back of the toilet. He must've bent the rod, since it was gone.

Making a mental note to see about fixing what he'd broken—so he wouldn't leave her any worse off than he'd found her—he headed out. But the place suddenly seemed too quiet. He glanced toward the kitchen to see why he couldn't hear Callie doing dishes anymore and spotted her through the doorway.

It looked as if she was clutching the edge of the table so she wouldn't topple over.

The creak of the floor must've given away his approach. She straightened and turned. "You're still here?"

He ignored the question. "Are you okay?"

"Of course!" She pressed a hand to her stomach. "I just…ate too much and…it gave me a cramp."

Not entirely convinced, he waited to see if she'd venture another explanation. What she'd said so far didn't quite match what he saw in her face. But when she left it at that, he could only accept her response. He couldn't see why she'd have any reason to lie, but he also couldn't see how whatever pain she felt could be related to too much food. From what he could remember, she hadn't eaten anything.

Rifle woke Callie for the second night in a row. Nerves jangled, she thought her dog was still reacting to Levi's presence. She'd been in bed for over an hour, although it was only ten o'clock. She'd barely drifted off. Maybe Levi couldn't sleep and had gotten up to work on his bike. There was a light in the barn if he chose to use it.

But she couldn't imagine he felt good enough to do that. And she couldn't understand why Levi's moving around would bother Rifle. So far, she'd limited contact between man and dog. The way Levi watched Rifle, as though he might have to defend himself at a moment's notice, confirmed that he was now, if he hadn't been before, leery of such a powerful animal. She had, however, introduced them, so that if they did come into contact there wouldn't be any problems. Once Rifle realized that she welcomed Levi's presence, he did, too. He'd even wagged his tail and tried to lick Levi's hand when Levi came in for dinner.

So what was going on?

Throwing off the covers, she got out of bed and dragged her pellet gun into the living room. She couldn't completely ignore Kyle's warnings. Levi, or anyone else, could be capable of far worse than she'd ever want to believe. He certainly wouldn't be the first person to turn on someone who'd merely been trying to help.

But it wasn't Levi who'd set the dog off.

Headlights bore down on the front of the house, and the engine of a truck continued to rumble as a door opened and shut. Although it was late for Godfrey to be out, Callie guessed he'd stopped by to tell her what he'd discovered on the pit bulls. She'd left him a message earlier, detailing what she'd found at the rental, so she'd been expecting him to get back to her with an update.

She almost opened the door, but then whoever approached called out to someone else. "Get your lazy ass out of the truck and come up here."

That voice definitely didn't belong to Godfrey....

The passenger door opened and slammed as Callie stood at the front window. Because of the glare, she couldn't make out who'd come to visit. It wasn't as if she had the benefit of streetlights. Out here, there was no lighting at all, except the moon and stars, and tonight the moon wasn't more than a thin silver smile.

The first man knocked as his companion joined him on the front stoop.

Gripping the pellet gun, Callie moved to the peephole and peered out. As she'd already surmised, she had two male visitors, neither of whom she recognized. "Who is it?"

"Denny Seamans and Powell Barney," came the answer.

"Who?" she muttered to Rifle. She'd never heard of a Denny or a Powell. "It's a little late to be out visiting," she called above Rifle's resounding bark.

"We're not out visiting."

"Then what can I do for you?"

"You can explain why the hell that old guy Godfrey Blume showed up at the vet's today and had my dogs taken away by animal control."

Denny and Powell were the Gruper renters.

Lowering the pellet rifle, Callie unlocked and opened the door.

The men were very obviously bodybuilders. About five feet nine inches, they had shaved heads to go with an overabundance of muscle and looked like twins, despite the differences in their facial features and last names.

"In case Godfrey didn't already explain," Callie began, "your dogs attacked a man who was pushing his motorcycle past—"

The first guy exploded before she could finish. "That's bullshit!"

Callie didn't know if it was Denny or Powell until he gestured at his companion.

"Tell her, Powell. Tell her Sauron and Spike would never do that."

"They wouldn't." Powell shook his head as if it was a foregone conclusion. "I've been around those dogs a whole year. They've never caused any problems."

Sauron's name suggested he'd be capable of anything. The only other place Callie had heard that name before was in *The Lord of the Rings*. Sauron was the villain, which she suspected Denny knew. But she didn't comment on that. He had the right to call his dog anything he wanted. Besides, the size of these men made her nervous. So did their attitudes.

She gripped her gun tighter, in case she had to raise it. She doubted a pellet would do much against the armor of all that beefcake—especially because she'd be lucky to squeeze the trigger once before the man who didn't get shot took the gun away—but she figured it was better than nothing. "Then you need to tell that to the authorities. You have no reason to be standing on my doorstep."

"According to Godfrey Blume, we do. *You're* the one who's saying otherwise. Seems your word is gold in this town."

She couldn't help reacting to his sarcasm. "Because they know I wouldn't lie."

"That's why we're here. It's you we have to convince. You need to stop what you started, or I'm going to lose my dogs."

"I'm sorry, but I can't change what they did. No one wins in these situations, least of all the animals. But I saw the results of what happened. You can't tell me they didn't attack."

"It isn't what you think!" Denny argued. "It's not like they went after that drifter without reason. He tried to sleep in our garage. That's trespassing. And my dogs just did what any guard dog would."

Levi had to find somewhere to sleep at night. Given his situation and the late hour, their story might've been plausible. Except the police found his bike on the side of the road, halfway in the ditch, right where Levi said he'd dropped it. And when she'd been at the Gruper rental earlier, she'd seen no blood in the garage—only on the driveway leading to the back porch, suggesting the incident had occurred off-site, and then the dogs had trotted home.

"That's not true," she said.

The way she'd challenged his explanation didn't sit well with Denny, who came off as the more aggressive of the two. "How the hell would *you* know?" His face, with its wide nose, jutted forward. "You weren't there."

These men didn't act at all concerned that their dogs had mangled someone. All they cared about was the possibility of their *own* loss.

"I was at your place this morning," she said. "I saw the bloody paw prints, Mr. Seamans. They weren't in the garage."

Denny's eyes narrowed to a razor-sharp point. "You went on to my property?"

"I knocked first. You didn't answer."

"That doesn't give you permission to snoop around!"

Rifle growled when Denny raised his voice, but Denny seemed too angry to care. Maybe he trusted her to hold the dog off. "Because of you, they're going to put down two innocent pit bulls!"

"Because of *me?*" Callie echoed. "You mean because you allowed your dogs to injure someone!"

"I didn't even know it was happening!"

"They're still your responsibility. A child couldn't have survived that attack. You didn't see the number of stitches it took to repair what your 'innocent' Sauron and Spike did!"

"The stupid bastard they bit shouldn't have trespassed on the property!"

Callie feared Levi would hear them. She didn't want

him to come out, didn't want this to get out of hand, so she lowered her voice. "He didn't trespass."

"You don't know that!" Powell shouted, despite her attempt to get him to speak quietly. "You don't know anything! You're just some small-town bitch who's sticking her nose in something that's got nothing to do with her."

The barn door slid open with a resounding bang. At that point, Callie knew Levi would be joining them. It was too late to hope he'd stay out of it.

"Time for you to go," he announced to the Gruper renters.

Because he wasn't within reach of Denny's head-lights or the dim circle thrown by her porch light, Callie could only make out his shape, but it was enough to tell her he was striding purposely toward them.

Denny and Powell swung around. "Who the hell are you?" Denny asked.

Powell grabbed Denny's arm as Levi stepped into the light. "That's got to be the guy. Why else would he be in the barn so late? He tried sleeping in our garage last night, didn't he?"

In deference to the cooler temperatures once the sun went down, Levi was wearing a thermal shirt with his jeans. He must've gotten it from his pack because Callie hadn't seen it before. She liked it on him, but she wasn't too encouraged by how lean it made him look in comparison to the two bruisers on her porch.

With Denny and Powell distracted by the interruption, Callie raised her gun. She was afraid she might have to head off a fight. But she hesitated to speak up too soon, didn't want a show of force to cause this situation to escalate if there was still a chance of avoiding it.

"Calm down," she warned Rifle who, taking his lead from Levi's appearance, was growling at Denny and Powell.

Levi came close—close enough for Callie to see the fury in his eyes. Together with the anger chiseled in the hollows of his cheeks, the firm set of his jaw and the thinness of his lips, he looked dangerous despite the fact that he weighed a lot less than the two Gruper renters.

"I don't want any trouble." She had to lower her gun to grab hold of her dog. She wished she could toss her weapon to Levi. Maybe it only shot pellets, but she couldn't imagine him taking on two men without some kind of defense, especially *these* men. He had too many stitches, for starters.

To her dismay, he didn't allow her the chance to give him the gun. He answered her, but he didn't even look over.

"There won't be trouble, provided these two get back in their truck and drive away."

Denny seemed so surprised that this "vagrant" would stand up to him he didn't react immediately. He glanced at Powell as if confirming that this was just the invitation they'd been waiting for, and Powell seemed to interpret that as a signal to take charge.

"Look, if you want to get your ass kicked, we'll be happy to take care of it," he said.

"Is that what you came here for?" Levi responded. "A fight?"

"A *fight?*" Powell laughed out loud. "I'm talking about teaching you a lesson, *loser,* about trespassing on other people's property. Because it looks to me like Sauron and Spike didn't do half what they should have."

The porch railing creaked under his weight as he

swung his body over it, but before Callie could even process the threat and let go of Rifle, Powell was lying in the dirt. It all happened so fast she couldn't tell how Levi had accomplished such a feat. It'd looked as if he'd landed only one punch, but the big guy wasn't getting up.

Denny, who'd started down the steps, was now backing away from Levi instead of heading toward him. "What's wrong with you, man? Are you crazy?"

"I'm sure there are psychologists out there who would say I am," Levi replied.

"Now I know what happened to my dogs, why they got the worst of it."

He had no idea what his dogs had done. Levi's clothing covered the stitches, but Callie kept her mouth shut because Levi was already talking.

"Your dogs attacked me, and I did what I had to in order to survive."

Powell was coming around. "What the hell...what'd he hit me with?" He blinked, shaking his head.

"Just get up," Denny told him. "Get up right now."

Powell managed to find his feet, but he staggered before he could begin making his way to the truck. Denny waited for him, then hurried around to the driver's side.

"This isn't finished," he called back to Levi as he climbed in. "I hope you know that. I won't let some piece-of-shit drifter destroy my dogs. And you'll pay for what you just did to my friend, too."

"You want more, we could finish it right here," Levi said, but he sounded more tired than threatening. Maybe that was because he knew Denny wouldn't take him up on the offer.

The door slamming shut was his only answer. Then

Denny threw the truck in Reverse, swung around and charged down Callie's driveway.

As his tires churned up the dust, Callie gaped at Levi, who was shaking the pain from his hand. "Did you break it?"

"No."

"You're sure?"

"Positive."

"Would you know if you had?"

"I'm pretty sure I would. I've broken it before."

Rifle whined and sat down, letting Callie know there was no need to continue restraining him. She sighed as she straightened, feeling weaker than ever now that the excitement was over. "What'd you *do* to him?"

He stared after their red taillights. "You saw it."

"But it happened so fast."

"Just because a guy can lift weights doesn't mean he can fight," Levi said with a shrug.

"Where did *you* learn to fight?" She put the pellet gun aside. "In the military?"

"There's no need for martial arts when you have a lethal weapon."

She thought of Kyle and how rude he'd been earlier— and was glad he hadn't pushed Levi too far. "You had to learn somewhere."

He didn't explain. "If you want me to leave instead of painting the barn, I'll understand."

"There's no need for you to leave. They were the ones who got out of line, not you."

"But as long as I'm here, they could come back."

"They could come back, anyway. And it looks like I'll be safer if you stay," she added with a grin. "I doubt my pellet gun could've done what you just did."

"Rifle could've handled them."

She watched her dog lick Levi's injured hand and wag his tail as if he'd just found a new hero. "I'd prefer he not have to."

A dark spot was growing on Levi's sleeve. "You've torn out some of your stitches."

He glanced down. "It'll be okay."

"We can't leave it like that." She waved him forward. "Come on in."

She applied a couple of butterfly Band-Aids to act in place of the torn stitches. Then she changed the dressing and got a blanket out of the linen closet.

"What are you doing?" he asked when she made a bed on the couch.

She was providing them with a little insurance that Denny and Powell wouldn't be able to jump him while he was sleeping. "I think it's better if you stay inside tonight."

"You don't have to worry about me."

"I won't if you'll do me this favor," she said.

It was late when Levi woke up. He could tell by the color of light streaming through the windows. The exhaustion of the past few days had caught up with him, but where was Callie? Was she still in bed?

He lay without moving, enjoying the peace and quiet while listening for her. At first, he heard nothing. But after several minutes, she whistled to her dog outside.

Yawning, he scratched his head, then winced at the pain caused by such a small action. Thanks to the miles he'd had to push his bike, the dogfight, the stitches, the lack of sleep and the confrontation with the two body-builders, he was banged up. Every muscle was sore.

But it wasn't the first time he'd ever woken up like this. When he'd lived at home, feeling as if he'd been hit by a truck had been a common occurrence.

Pain is weakness leaving the body.

How often had his father said that? And how many times had he made Levi prove it?

Unwilling to think of Leo and all his talk about becoming the best, he sat up and waited for his head to stop pounding before getting to his feet.

When he finally walked outside, Rifle came racing toward him. Levi couldn't help tensing at the dog's approach, but he'd lived with the threat of physical danger his whole life—if not in the ring, then at home, with a father whose hair-trigger temper could explode for almost no reason. Levi wasn't about to let one incident with dogs make him cower in fear, especially because he'd always been a dog lover. After his mother took off with his sister, it was his dog who'd given him enough love to get him through the next ten years.

Fortunately, Rifle merely barked a hello. Then he circled, acting eager to lead the way to his master.

Levi motioned for the dog to start off. "Fine. Go."

With another bark, Rifle loped toward the barn, but he didn't stop at the entrance. He trotted through the middle and out the other side to where Callie was lying on the ground with a camera.

"You're taking pictures of dirt?" Levi asked as he approached her.

Lowering her camera, she looked up at him. She was wearing a pair of khaki shorts and a white T-shirt top, which was no longer clean, due to all that scooting around. "See? I've found an anthill!"

The excitement in her voice surprised him. "An anthill."

"Yeah." A bead of sweat rolled from her temple as she smiled. "I've been getting some *great* shots."

He indicated the camera. "This is your hobby?"

"My profession. I have a studio in town. Reflections by Callie. We do a lot of weddings. But lately I've been shooting nature."

He recalled the impressive photograph hanging in the kitchen. "That spider by the table."

"Is mine, yes."

"It's nice."

She seemed gratified. "Thanks."

"So how often do you go into your studio?"

"I used to go every day. But…I'm taking the summer off."

"To photograph nature."

"And to say goodbye."

He studied her carefully. "To whom?"

Sitting up, she tilted her head so that the sun could hit her face. "To this place. It belonged to my grandparents before they died. I spent a lot of summer days and weekends here when I was growing up, have a lot of fond memories."

"That's why you're living out here alone?"

"That's right. Why?"

He hesitated to put what he was feeling into words. He sensed that something was wrong, something beyond having to sell a piece of property that had been in the family for years. But he didn't really know Callie and could easily be mistaken. He hoped he was. As much as he was determined not to feel anything, hc appreciated her kind heart. He'd never experienced much gentleness. Not until he met Behrukh.

Maybe that was why he'd been foolish enough to get involved with her. He'd returned to her father's store again and again, to buy gum, candy, bottled water, anything he could think of. He'd never been with a woman before and his hormones were running rampant.

"Who's taking care of the studio?" he asked. "Or did you close it for the summer?"

"We couldn't miss bridal season. So I have an assistant—more like an apprentice, I guess—who's handling things for me."

"While you work out here, taking pictures of nature and getting the farm in shape."

"Basically."

She wasn't wearing any makeup. He got the impression she'd climbed out of bed, pulled her hair up and headed outside. But he liked her this way. She looked fresh and dewy and soft.

Suddenly, he craved some of that softness. A moment of tenderness. A respite from the bitterness that had left his own heart so hard. It felt like forever since he'd lost himself inside a woman.

But the only woman he'd known in that way was dead because of him. So was the baby she carried—*his* baby.

He tried to steel himself against the memory he avoided more than any other, but nearly swooned beneath the vision that broke on his mind. Being around Callie made it almost impossible to forget what happened. Although she looked nothing like the woman he'd loved, the two had a similar spirit.

"Are you okay?" Callie's voice was soft, practically a whisper.

He opened his eyes. He hadn't even realized he'd closed them. This wasn't Behrukh, he reminded himself. And what had happened in Kandahar? There was nothing he could do to change it.

"Fine," he managed to say. He wanted to get away from Callie, *needed* to get away.

Soon, he promised himself. As soon as he fulfilled his obligation. "Where's the paint?"

Although she didn't look convinced that he was as fine as he said, she didn't inquire further. She dusted off her knees and got to her feet. "I'll get it for you. After we have breakfast."

6

Callie turned on some music while she made fried potatoes, omelets and toast. She'd always enjoyed cooking, but having someone to fix a meal for was even more fulfilling. Had she been on her own, she would've settled for toast and juice, since she often felt nauseous after a big meal.

"You don't have to go to so much trouble." Levi spoke from where he was cleaning up his bedding in the other room.

She didn't bother to come up with a response. She'd awakened this morning feeling inexplicably happy just to be alive. Part of it was the sunshine pouring into the old farmhouse. She loved it here, was glad she'd moved. But Levi was another reason she felt so good. Trying to help someone else gave fresh purpose to her own life. It also dragged her attention away from her various worries and complaints—and the inevitable, should she be unable to find a liver donor.

"Did you hear me?" he called.

"I heard you," she replied.

"Why didn't you answer?"

"Because I'm going to make what I'm going to make."

"Okay, forget I said anything."

She smiled at the pique in his voice. She had no idea what his story was, or if he'd tell her before he left. Most likely not. She didn't care either way. He had a right to his privacy. She simply liked thinking that she'd made a positive impact on someone, if only in a small way—giving him a place to stay, some food to eat, a few days of peace.

"We need to go into town so I can get a new rod for your shower," he said.

"Why not take the one from the other bathroom?" she suggested.

"We have to get parts for my bike, anyway." Having folded his bedding, he was now standing in the doorway. She could tell by the sound of his voice, but she didn't turn.

"Callie."

She was pretty sure it was the first time he'd called her by name. She cast a glance over her shoulder. "Hmm?"

"What's really going on with you?"

The gravity in his voice told her this wasn't a casual question. He could sense that something wasn't ideal. But she didn't want him to know about her diagnosis any more than she wanted anyone else to know. She couldn't say why. Maybe she was afraid he'd see her as flawed or defective. Why would he choose to spend even a few days with a woman who wouldn't be around in a couple of weeks or months? And she didn't want him to go. She was intrigued enough to hope he'd finish out the week.

"What's really going on with *you?*" she asked, turning his own question back on him. "There's got to be a reason a handsome, capable guy goes rambling around America."

When he grunted, she took it to mean *"Touché,"* and chuckled to herself.

"You're not like other women," he said.

She got a plate out of the cupboard. "Are you like other men?"

"I like the same things they do."

There seemed to be added significance to this statement, as if he was talking about liking women, liking *sex,* but she chose to ignore that—just as she chose to ignore the way he was looking at her. "Good. Then you should enjoy your breakfast." She carried his omelet to the table before returning to the counter for his toast and hash browns.

"Where's yours?" he asked when she sat down with only half a glass of juice.

She'd been so eager to see him eat that she hadn't prepared anything for herself. "I'm not hungry."

"You didn't eat much last night."

"I was too tired."

"And now?"

"I ate earlier."

He glanced around the kitchen, but said nothing about the lack of evidence.

She nodded toward his food. "Go ahead while it's hot," she said. Then she stood. "I'll shower so we can drive to town when you're finished."

"I'd feel better if you'd eat."

She couldn't imagine why it would matter to him. "I'm fine," she insisted, and felt his gaze follow her out.

Levi hadn't felt much physical desire in the past year. He hadn't cared whether he lived or died, let alone whether he satisfied his sexual appetite. After Behrukh, he'd figured he'd never want a woman again. He certainly didn't deserve to go on without her, especially in that way.

But sitting in Callie's house knowing she was standing naked under the shower, gave him his first erection—that wasn't a dream—since Kandahar. He kept picturing the spray running between her full breasts, cascading over her flat stomach to roll between her legs, where he wanted to touch her, to feel her slick, wet body close around him.

Listening to the whine of the pipes in the old house, he stopped chewing and put down his fork. His heart was pounding, and he was finding it difficult to breathe. Did such a sudden, unexpected rush of lust mean he was recovering? Or that he was an even worse person than he'd thought?

A phone rang. Callie's cell phone. She'd left it on the kitchen counter.

To distract himself, he got up to see who it was. A picture of Kyle filled the screen. It was her boyfriend, or whatever she wanted to call him, no doubt checking in to see if she was okay.

Kyle's intrusion reminded Levi that he had no business thinking about Callie in that way. He didn't know her. And, other than her one throwaway statement about his being handsome and capable, she'd certainly given no indication that she'd welcome his advances. Why would she want to be touched by a vagrant? Someone who'd essentially abandoned any kind of normal life?

He couldn't act on his desire, even if she extended an invitation. He'd feel far too guilty.

Taking a deep breath, he returned to the table, where

he finished eating in slow, deliberate bites. From that moment on, he was extradiligent about keeping his mind blank, but it didn't help. He was still rock-hard when the water went off, so he quickly cleaned up the kitchen and fled to the barn.

"Your boyfriend called while you were in the shower."

Callie was driving. Levi sat in the passenger seat. She'd noticed the missed call when she'd picked up her phone, but she hadn't wanted to speak to Kyle while she was with Levi. She knew he wouldn't be happy about the encounter with Denny Seamans and Powell Barney. He'd say that Levi's presence had compromised her safety. But it was Denny and Powell, and only Denny and Powell, who were to blame for what happened last night.

"You mean my friend," she said. "I saw that."

"You're not going to call him back?"

"I will when I have a minute to focus."

"You might want to do it sooner rather than later."

She arched her eyebrows. "Because..."

"He'll only come over if you don't."

"True." He had an excellent point. Having these two men in the same room made her uncomfortable. She preferred to avoid that in future. But if she called Kyle while driving, she'd have to use her hands-free, which essentially put him on speakerphone, and she wasn't about to let Levi hear their conversation. She had no idea what Kyle might say. So she waited until she pulled into the auto parts store.

"I'll be right in," she told Levi, and dialed Kyle's number the second he got out.

"Hey," she said when Kyle answered,

"Hey yourself," he responded. "Where've you been?"

"Sorry I missed your call. I was in the shower."

"All morning?"

"Levi and I were in a hurry to get to town."

"So he's with you?"

"Sort of. He's in the auto parts store."

"I see. And once he fixes that bike of his he'll be leaving?"

She clenched her jaw. "After he's painted the barn, Kyle. You know the deal."

"That doesn't mean I have to like it," he grumbled. "But I'm relieved you're okay. He didn't hurt you or do anything weird?"

"No."

"The owner of the dogs who attacked Levi brought them to the vet yesterday."

She slipped her keys into her purse. She could see Levi heading down an aisle inside the store. He wasn't at the register yet, but she'd have to go in soon so she could pay for the parts he needed. "How do you know?"

"Cheyenne was there. Her dog has a sore foot."

"Why didn't she call me?"

"Why would she? She didn't know you had anything to do with some vagrant getting bitten by pit bulls—until I told her."

Great. Now Cheyenne knew? She was part of the group Callie and Kyle had grown up with. It was only a matter of time before the whole gang found out, which meant Callie would be hearing from more and more of them. "I still don't get why she called *you*."

"She wanted to tell me that she'd seen Noelle with another guy on her way home."

Noelle had to be the most hated ex in all of Whiskey Creek. She hadn't been particularly popular *before* marrying Kyle. Everyone had known he was making a terrible mistake. But, at the time, there'd been a baby involved and his sense of decency demanded he see it through. "That's *good* news, right?"

"*If* she marries him. Then I won't have to continue paying spousal maintenance." He cursed under his breath. "I still can't believe how much that judge ordered me to pay. He saw a pretty woman weeping in front of him and it didn't matter what I said after that."

"You could've fought harder."

"It wasn't worth it to me to drag the damn thing out. Money is only money, I guess. At least I don't have to live with her anymore."

"So how badly were they hurt?"

"The dogs? One had a couple of broken ribs. The other a broken leg. And they each needed stitches. Cheyenne said she thinks they must've hurt each other in the fight, because one's ear was cut."

The attack must've been horrific. It was a wonder both dogs and Levi had come out of it basically okay. Callie doubted someone without Levi's ability to defend himself would've been able to fend them off. "They would've killed a lesser man."

"A lesser man?" Kyle repeated.

She straightened at the wry note in his voice. "Someone who can't fight like he can."

"How do you know he can fight?"

"Because I saw him. The owner of those dogs— Denny Seamans—brought his buddy Powell and showed up on my doorstep last night."

"And you didn't call me?"

The thought hadn't even crossed her mind, but she didn't want to admit that. "I wasn't expecting it to go the way it did."

"What happened?"

"Denny tried to convince me that his dogs weren't at fault, that they only attacked because Levi trespassed on their property."

"Maybe that's really how it went down," Kyle said. "You don't know. You weren't there."

"Levi wasn't in their garage." She was so glad she'd had a chance to peek inside it. She suspected no one would believe the truth otherwise, not with Denny and Powell protesting to high heaven.

"You were looking for his *bike* when you checked, Cal."

"Yeah, but if those dogs attacked Levi in the garage and not out on the street, there would've been blood." Just look at the amount he'd gotten on her porch....

"Maybe Denny Whoever cleaned it up before we got there."

"When they had two dogs who needed to see a vet right away? No. I'm guessing he and Powell woke up to find the dogs injured, loaded them up and took off. That's why they weren't home when we went by." She shifted in the seat, trying to get comfortable. "They didn't bother cleaning up the blood on the driveway, did they?"

"So what are you now? A forensics tech?"

She could tell her loyalty to Levi irritated him. He didn't want to deal with some interloper, especially one who had nothing—no reputation, job or known background—to recommend him. Kyle had been through too much with his divorce. Not only that, but he'd been stressed out before Levi appeared. His sister was going through her own divorce. She and her kids had been staying with him for two months.

"It doesn't take a forensics tech to realize there'd be a mess," she said.

"I'm guessing you told Denny and Powell this."

It was getting too hot to sit in the SUV. Once again checking the store to make sure Levi wasn't waiting for her, she opened her door to catch the breeze. "More or less. Then our exchange woke Levi and he—"

"Snapped," Kyle broke in.

Why did he automatically assume it was Levi's fault? "No, he didn't snap. Not exactly. I think he would've done a lot more damage if he'd really let go."

Kyle barked out an incredulous laugh. "Against *two* guys? Come on! Cheyenne said they were built like army tanks."

"That's true. They are—and last night they were itching for a fight. But when one of them went after Levi, Levi knocked him out with a single punch."

Her recap sobered him. "What did the other guy do?"

"Fortunately, that discouraged Denny from getting involved. But he wasn't happy. He helped his friend to the car, said it wasn't over and drove off."

Silence.

"So what do you think?" she asked.

"You should've listened to me and sent McCloud on his way when you had the chance."

She slapped the steering wheel. "Levi hasn't done anything wrong!"

"He caused Denny's dogs to be impounded and knocked out his friend!"

"As much as I hate to say it, since I love dogs, those

two are dangerous. So are their owner and his buddy! I have to stand up for the truth, Kyle. If I don't, it'll be my fault if those pit bulls are released and hurt someone else. Is that what you want?"

The question seemed to take the edge off his anger. "No. Of course not. I just… If Levi's going to be moving on, it's better if he does it sooner rather than later. That's all."

"Better for whom?" she demanded.

"Better for you."

"No, better for *you*." She hung up, then sat staring at her phone. She couldn't remember the last time she'd gotten into an argument with Kyle. They could get a little irritated with each other, and at that point they usually parted company. But she'd never hung up on him before.

Was what she'd feared happening? Had sleeping together ruined their friendship? Doomed it to failure?

She hoped not. She'd only been trying to give him a shoulder to cry on, had never intended to end up in his bed.

She thought of their other friends—Gail, Cheyenne, Eve, Noah, Baxter, Ted, Sophia, Riley—and was embarrassed. A rift between two of them risked the enjoyment they *all* received from being part of the group.

"You coming in?"

Callie jerked her head up to see Levi standing in the doorway. Thanks to her conversation with Kyle, she'd stopped checking to see if he was ready for her. "Uh, yeah," she said, and dropped her phone in her purse before climbing out.

Levi watched her closely. "Kyle said something you didn't like?"

She refused to meet his eyes. "I'm not sure what's going on with him."

"He wants me gone," he said simply.

"I don't think he knows *what* he wants."

Levi could've said more. No doubt he understood why their relationship was so complex. But he didn't press her to answer any more questions. He merely held the door and she went in to pay.

After the auto parts store, which was located in the next town, they returned to Whiskey Creek and bought a shower rod from the hardware store. With the Old West–style boardwalk in front and the antique gold lettering on the window, the place resembled a mercantile out of the 1800s. Most of the other businesses on Sutter Street looked similar. They were definitely a blast from the past, including Callie's photography studio, where they stopped next. When Levi had passed through Whiskey Creek, he hadn't paid a lot of attention to it, except to eat and buy gas. Two days ago, this town was just another spot on the map. He'd never expected to see it again.

A young woman with long dark hair sat working on a computer. She glanced up when the bell over the door rang, then jumped to her feet.

"I didn't realize you were coming in," she said to Callie.

Callie shrugged. "I was in town, so I thought I'd come by, see how things are going."

Her eyes drifted to Levi.

"This is a friend of mine," Callie explained. "He's visiting for a week or so. Levi, this is Tina, my assistant."

Tina offered him a shy smile. "Hello."

He acknowledged her greeting with a nod.

"I was just finishing up the Barrado album," she said, returning her attention to Callie.

"How's it turning out?"

"Great."

"Farrah Johnson called. She was wondering when her pictures will be in."

"I don't know why she bothered you. I've already talked to her. I have an appointment with her next week."

"Maybe she's miffed that I didn't do her wedding myself."

Their words faded to background noise as Levi circled the studio, studying the photographs that hung on the walls—a pregnant woman standing partially in shadow, two toddlers playing with a bunny, a family wading in a river, several brides and graduates and chubby babies. Callie was good at chronicling life, he thought. She seemed to capture just the right nuances of lighting and expression—if these were all her work and not Tina's.

In a small covelike display area, he found a picture of ten people, who all looked to be about the same age. Callie hadn't taken this shot; she was in it. So was Kyle.

"You ready?" Callie asked

Levi glanced over at her. "Who are these people?"

"My best friends."

"There're a lot of them."

She smiled. "Except for Chey, we've known one another since grade school."

"Only in a place like this," he murmured.

"Probably." She fished out her keys. "There's too much shifting around in the bigger cities."

"You didn't lose *any* of the group? None of them ever moved away?"

She pointed to a moderately attractive redhead at one end. "Gail did. She's still gone, but she comes back to visit when she can. Do you recognize her?"

"No. Am I supposed to?"

"She's married to Simon O'Neal."

"The *movie star* Simon O'Neal?"

"One and the same."

"How did she meet him?"

"She started a PR company in L.A. about eleven years ago. Used to do his publicity. She still does."

"Didn't he recently go through a very public meltdown?" He remembered getting bits and pieces of Hollywood gossip, even in Afghanistan.

"It's been a couple of years, but yes. Definitely not his finest hour. That was before they fell in love and she got him turned around," she added with a wink.

"I haven't heard anything about him lately." But he didn't spend much time in front of the TV. Once he returned home after his third tour, he took to the road almost immediately. At that point, what one movie star or another was or wasn't doing seemed to have no relevance to his life.

"The fact that you haven't heard anything is good news. It means he's recovered." She drew his attention to a dark-haired woman with olive skin and a severe widow's peak. "This is Eve. She runs Little Mary's B and B down the street, which her parents bought shortly after their marriage." She rested one graceful-looking hand on her hip. "It's rumored to be haunted by the ghost of a six-year-old girl who was murdered in the basement in 1871."

He slid his hands into his pockets. "Do you believe that's true?"

"The murder's documented. I don't know about the haunting. Some strange things have certainly happened there. Eve's not the superstitious type, would never make this up. And she's not the only one who's experienced strange noises and movement. Some people even claim to have seen the child's ghost."

"But not Eve."

"She hasn't, no."

"Who killed the girl?"

"No one knows. The truth never came out."

"Sounds like the twentieth-century equivalent of the JonBenét Ramsey case."

"I guess you could say that. *Unsolved Mysteries* came here the first of the year and did a show on it. They hired investigators and forensic profilers and had Simon do a cameo appearance. In the end, they tried to say it was most likely the gardener, but I wasn't convinced."

"What about her father?"

Callie seemed mildly surprised by the question. "He was an older wealthy man who married late in life. Mary was his only child. You think he might've killed her?"

"I'm thinking he would've had access and opportunity."

"But his own daughter?"

"Maybe she made him angry. Maybe he was trying to punish her and got carried away, went too far." He understood how that went, didn't he? If his father wasn't beating on him physically, he was pushing him in the gym.

"The show suggested that exact scenario as their second favorite solution. But they couldn't uncover any proof. I assume that's why they went with the gardener. Who wants to believe a father could be so heinous?"

No one. Only the mother was likely to know what the father was capable of. But if she was as cowed as his mother had been, it wouldn't matter. The child would be left with no protection.

Callie went through the rest of the group, telling him who everyone was and what each person did for a living. Noah Somebody owned a bike store. Baxter North commuted to San Francisco, where he worked as a stockbroker. Kyle manufactured solar panels.

"So he's rich?" Levi asked.

"Kyle?"

He nodded. In the picture, he wasn't standing by Callie. He had his arm around someone else.

"He's not as rich as Simon and Gail," she said. "But almost no one's as rich as they are. Still, Kyle does very well for himself."

Levi looked back at the portrait. "Who's this?"

She'd already told him, but repeated the name. "Cheyenne. Pretty, isn't she?"

Not as pretty as Callie. None of the other women were as pretty as Callie.

"But don't get your hopes up," she teased. "She just got married."

"And this person?" He pointed to someone else.

"That's Ted Dixon. He's a thriller writer. Has a handful of books out. Maybe you've heard of him?"

"No." He'd never done much reading, not even

when he was in school. Homework and preparing for college—that hadn't been nearly as important to his father as making sure Levi was lifting weights and learning new martial-arts moves. Leo had needed a prizefighter to put his dojo on the map. His own street cred had depended on it; so had the amount he could earn.

Tina interrupted with a question for Callie, and Callie walked over to the computer to help. When she returned, she touched his arm. "You ready to go?"

Levi pulled himself away from the portrait. He hadn't expected it, but the unity and tranquillity of this town appealed to him.

7

Callie felt a hard lump in her stomach the moment she saw a police cruiser turn down her drive. She'd been out photographing the anthill again while Levi repaired the hinges on the back door of the barn. The roof would need even more work, but due to their trip to town, which had included some grocery shopping on the way home, they hadn't gotten an early start. He fixed his motorcycle first, so he'd only been working on the barn for an hour. She was already walking to the house, planning what to make for dinner, when she saw that the cop was Tim Stacy, chief of Whiskey Creek's four-man police force.

Window down, arm hanging out, he didn't seem to notice the dust being kicked up by his tires. He waved as if this was a friendly visit, but she suspected it wasn't all *that* friendly. Although Chief Stacy was about ten years her senior, they'd known each other for years. She'd taken his children's baby pictures. But if she had to guess, he wasn't here for personal reasons. He'd come to get to the bottom of the dog incident. She wouldn't have minded that, except it was probably at Denny and Powell's insistence.

And she knew Levi wouldn't be pleased to learn the police were now involved....

Masking her concern with a welcoming smile, she greeted Stacy as he got out. "Hi, Chief!"

"Gorgeous evening, isn't it?"

"There's no summer like a Whiskey Creek summer," she said, although to her mind, fall was even more beautiful.

He acknowledged her words with a jerk of his hat. "No, ma'am."

Leaving her camera on the wicker love seat by the front door, she stepped up to meet him as he reached the stairs. "What can I do for you today?"

The way he studied her gave her the impression that he was weighing every reaction. "Word has it you have a guest."

"That's true."

Thumbs hooked in his belt, he turned to survey the property until he heard Levi's hammer ring out from the vicinity of the barn. Then, seemingly satisfied to have located the object of their conversation, he faced her again.

"A *drifter*—that right?"

The censure in those words, suggesting she was crazy to take Levi in, bothered her but she couldn't blame Stacy. She knew her parents would feel the same. "I don't know much about his personal situation," she admitted. "But his name is Levi McCloud."

"Do you know where he's from?"

She felt as if every line he spoke had an alternate interpretation. This time he was asking if she'd looked into his background, at least to that extent. "Seattle," she told him.

"And you met him..."

He already knew this. He was taking her through the basic facts to drive home a point. "Here. Night before last. He showed up at my door."

"Covered in blood. So you called emergency services."

"That's right. Officers Willis and Jones came out, but he was gone by the time they got here." And they couldn't find him, even though they'd searched, because Levi had slipped into her bathroom. But she wasn't going to volunteer that. It certainly wouldn't make her actions look any more sensible—or his any less suspect.

"That's how I understand it, too." He squinted at her. "So when did he come back?"

"After they left."

"Because…"

"He had no choice," she explained. "He'd been attacked by two dogs and was in no condition to go elsewhere."

"See…this is where I get confused." He pushed his hat up to scratch underneath it. "How'd he manage to elude my men if he was so badly hurt? Or maybe a better question would be…*why* would he go to the trouble?"

She shook her head. "I don't know." It was the truth, but she wasn't entirely comfortable with it.

"Yet this man is staying here with you."

Denny and Powell had paid Stacy a visit, all right. Otherwise, how would the police chief know where Levi was?

Or maybe Kyle or Godfrey had asked him to keep an eye on her.

"Until he can get his motorcycle fixed, yes," she said.

"I see." He sighed before glancing in the direction of the intermittent hammering. "You mind if I have a talk with him?"

"Not at all," she replied but, in a way, she did mind. If there was anything terrible in Levi's background, she didn't want to know about it. She wasn't sure why. Maybe it was because she believed he needed a new start—that regardless of what had happened in the past, he'd suffered enough.

"Levi?" she called. "Could you come to the house for a minute?"

The hammering stopped. Callie felt certain he'd heard her. But he didn't appear.

"Levi?" she called again. "Chief Stacy would like a word with you."

Nothing. No answer.

Finally, they walked to where he'd been repairing the door. Rifle was lying near the ladder, but Levi was gone. And when they searched the farm they couldn't find him anywhere.

By the time Levi knocked at the farmhouse door, it'd been a good hour since the police had left. Levi had been wrestling with himself all of that time. He knew he should drive away and leave Whiskey Creek behind. It wasn't wise to stay here. But, wise or not, he couldn't go without fulfilling the promises he'd made.

Maybe Callie would change his mind. Maybe she'd refuse to let him in. But she didn't. She stared up at him for a second, then stepped back so he could walk past her. "Your dinner's cold," she said. "Come and sit down. I'll heat it up."

"I can heat it up," he responded, but either she didn't hear him or she wanted to do it herself because she didn't change course.

"They'll just come back later. You realize that," she

said as a plate of chicken, mashed potatoes and gravy turned in the microwave.

He'd chosen the seat on the far side of the table, where he'd sat for breakfast. "I do."

"By then you'll have your bike fixed. Is that it?"

"My bike's already fixed. By then I'm hoping to have the barn finished."

She took some utensils out of the drawer and placed them in front of him, along with a glass of wine. "What are you afraid they'll do?"

"I told you."

"You're afraid they'll arrest you."

He stretched out his legs. "Basically."

"Over an unpaid speeding ticket."

There was also a warrant out for his arrest in Nevada, which was far more serious, but he couldn't say anything about that. "*Two* unpaid speeding tickets."

"What's the worst that can happen?" she asked.

"Don't know. And I don't want to find out."

"Community service? Fines? Jail time?"

"Probably jail time." *Definitely* jail time, since the speeding tickets were the least of his worries.

"Maybe they won't realize you have those outstanding warrants."

"They will eventually." If they ever figured out his real last name...

The microwave shut off with a ding. "Right. They're too curious about you," she admitted as she retrieved his plate. "With Denny and Powell making you sound shady in an attempt to save their dogs, everyone will want to know who you are."

"It'd be best if I'm gone by the time they dig up too many details."

"That might not be long."

He understood that. But he didn't want to go without keeping his end of the bargain. She'd put herself at risk to help him, and he wouldn't forget her generosity. "We'll play it by ear, see how much we can get done in the next few days."

"If you say so."

He certainly didn't want to leave right now. The food smelled so good his stomach growled. He couldn't remember ever enjoying meals as much as he'd enjoyed them since coming to Callie's. He'd been to many roadside cafés in the past six months, but they couldn't compete with her home cooking. What made it even better was that she seemed to like feeding him. At least, she smiled as she watched him eat whatever she put in front of him.

"You haven't asked where I went," he said when he was about halfway through.

"What are you talking about?" She was back at the counter.

"When the police chief came."

She blew out a sigh. "Because I don't want to know."

That made sense. Not knowing enabled her to be honest if he ever had to hide there again, which protected them both.

"Want more?" she asked.

"No, thanks." He paused to look up at her. The dark circles under her eyes were *more* marked instead of less. "Have *you* eaten?"

She started tidying up. "I had dinner earlier."

The memory of her, leaning on the table last night as if she didn't have the strength to stand, popped into his mind. There was probably plenty she wasn't telling him.

But there was plenty he wasn't telling her, too.

"Eat just a few bites."

She raised her eyebrows. "Why?"

"Because you need the nutrients."

"Fine." Taking his right hand, she ate the piece of chicken he had on his fork. "There you go," she said with a laugh.

The fact that she was willing to eat from his fork told him she wasn't afraid he carried some sort of disease. It also drew his attention to her mouth.

"You know how pretty you are, don't you?" he asked quietly.

She didn't blush or glance away as he thought she might. Her eyes remained steady on his. No doubt she'd had her share of compliments. "I think this is the first time you've ever really looked at me."

"No," he said. "It's definitely not."

That night Levi dreamed of a woman. He couldn't see her face, but he was driving into her supple body, climbing toward orgasm, feeling the clench and pull of her body as she met each thrust. But a second before achieving that much-needed release, he woke up, heart pounding and muscles taut.

"Shit." He lay there, breathing as hard as if it had all been real and wondering why he couldn't have awakened a few seconds later. He was supremely unsatisfied but unwilling to ease his own discomfort. After causing Behrukh to lose her life, he didn't deserve that kind of pleasure, didn't deserve anything.

How long until morning?

He had no idea. He didn't wear a watch, didn't have a cell phone. Time didn't matter when a person had nowhere to go. But he didn't want to lie awake for hours, waiting for dawn. He'd done that enough those last few months in Kandahar.

After several minutes, his heartbeat began to slow but his erection remained, probably because he couldn't stop thinking about Callie. He wasn't positive she was the woman in his dreams, but it hadn't been Behrukh. The feel of Behrukh would've been different. She was leaner, physically stronger, because she'd led a harder life. She would've smelled different, too—like the curry she cooked so often. After her death, he hadn't been able to dream of her, anyway. He hadn't been able to dream at all. The insomnia that'd plagued him the year before he joined the army had returned; he'd lain awake, sweating in the heat while staring at the dark tent above him. He'd listen to the coughs and snores and rustles of the other platoon members and wish he could be like them. But he couldn't. Some days he had to roll out of bed to make muster, feeling so sleep-deprived he could hardly stay on his feet.

Ironic though it was, he'd won a roomful of martial-arts trophies growing up but was proudest of simply *enduring* those final months in Afghanistan—something he couldn't have done without the training he'd received from his father. Well before any army sergeant had gotten hold of him, Leo had drilled certain rules into him. Levi knew how to use every ounce of self-control he possessed. He knew how to adhere to a regimen. He knew that sometimes he had to withstand pain and keep fighting even in the face of sure defeat. Without Leo, Levi would not have finished his last tour so he could be honorably discharged—but that was the kindest thing he could say about his father.

A sound brought his head up. He couldn't identify it, but it didn't seem to fit with the noises he'd been hearing. He thought maybe someone was creeping toward the barn.

Had he missed picking up on the hum of a motor?

Maybe the police or the men who owned the pit bulls were back, hoping to take him by surprise. Neither group wanted him hanging around....

The creak of the barn door, along with a subtle flash of moonlight, told him he'd guessed right. Someone was approaching. He had no idea who, but he refused to allow himself to be caught in a vulnerable position.

He pretended to roll over, so the sound of his movements would draw whoever it was immediately to him, but got up instead. Then he waited for the right moment, for the intruder to come close.

A second later he heard footsteps near his bed and grabbed whoever it was from behind, cutting off his air with one arm and rendering him immediately defenseless.

Only it wasn't a him. The soft body against his gave Callie away long before she could even attempt to speak.

Panic turned Callie's knees to water as she felt the raw power of Levi's quick, sure movements. She opened her mouth to scream but couldn't get enough air.

For the first time, she was afraid of him. *Really* afraid. In that moment, she knew without a doubt that, despite her diagnosis, she still cared about living, about sticking around for as long as possible.

The fear didn't last, however. As soon as he realized it was her, he eased his hold and turned her in his arms. "I'm sorry," he murmured. "I hope...I hope I didn't hurt you. I didn't know..."

His words fell off, but she understood. He hadn't known it was her. She should've announced herself. She would have, except that she'd been waiting to get close enough to touch his arm, in case he was sleeping. "It's okay," she said. "I...I shouldn't have surprised you."

"What are you doing out here?"

He released her but she couldn't quite let go of him. She was still trying to overcome the effect of such a fright, worried that she might crumple to the ground. "I—I wanted to see if you'd come inside."

"Why?"

His deep voice rumbled in her ear, but he must have felt her unsteadiness because his hands no longer hung at his sides. They were sliding up her back. She could feel the warmth of his splayed fingers through the satin of her pajama top as he drew her into a solid embrace that reassured her but did nothing to slow her galloping heart.

Instinctively, she rested her cheek against the soft cotton of his T-shirt. *Don't read anything into this. He's just being kind.* But she couldn't deny that the chemistry between them had suddenly changed. She liked the feel of his firm chest, the security she felt in the circle of his arms, but there was also a sexual element— probably because he wasn't completely dressed. She'd already felt the band of his briefs and, since her pajama bottoms were panties, the crisp hair on his legs as he brushed up against her.

She swallowed hard as his hands settled between her shoulder blades. "I couldn't sleep."

"Why not?"

"I was...I was worried that maybe Denny and his idiot friend would come back and cause trouble."

"They might. But they're the kind of trouble I can handle."

"Not if they bring a weapon. And not if you want to avoid the police." She stepped away because the embrace had gone on too long. She didn't know this man. Not really. Although they'd spent two days together, he'd revealed very little about himself. And there was Kyle. They weren't in a romantic relationship; they both knew that. But they'd slept together as recently as last week, which made her feel disloyal in spite of their understanding. "Anyone can be taken unawares."

He didn't respond.

"So what do you say?" she asked.

"About what?"

She wondered what he was feeling, if he'd enjoyed their contact as much as she had. "Will you come in? I think…I think it would help me relax if I knew you were safe, that we were both in the house."

He didn't seem eager to accept. He was suddenly so standoffish that she expected him to say he was fine where he was and let it go at that.

But he didn't. "I'm sorry if you're lonely," he said. "I wish things were different but…I have nothing to offer you."

"I'm not asking for…for *sex,*" she clarified. "I just want…I just want you to come in the house."

She was pretty sure she wouldn't be *opposed* to having sex with him, however. Right now, more contact with him was all she could think about. He seemed to understand that but, after a brief hesitation, he said okay and grabbed something.

"What's that?" she asked.

"My pack. It has my clothes."

She wondered if it also contained condoms.

8

Maybe if Levi had been able to go back to sleep, he wouldn't have realized something was wrong. The noises that tipped him off were slight enough he might've credited them to the dog. Except that Callie had shut Rifle up in the mudroom. He whined occasionally, but the noises that worried Levi weren't coming from that direction. They were coming from Callie's bedroom.

Relax. If she was up and around, it was none of his business. Dawn was turning the night sky a deep shade of purple. Perhaps she was an early riser. Soon, he'd get up and start his day, too, and with any luck he'd finish repairing the barn so he could paint tomorrow.

A weak-sounding cough had Rifle scratching at the door, as if he didn't like what he heard, either. What was going on?

Levi sat up. "Callie?"

There was no response from her, but Rifle barked. A second later a toilet flushed.

She was up, all right. She had to be. But when he twisted around to look at her door, he couldn't see a light underneath it. Like him, she probably couldn't sleep and was tossing and turning.

Then he heard another sound, a sound of distress, and that got him up and moving.

"Callie?" He knocked at her bedroom door. She didn't respond, but the door wasn't locked. Apparently, she wasn't worried that he might attack her. Almost from the beginning—at least since she'd found him bleeding in her bathroom—she seemed to trust him more than their short acquaintance should warrant. He wouldn't have advised her to take the same approach with any other stranger, but he appreciated how her confidence made him feel. He didn't want her to be wary of him. He'd hated how the women who'd passed through his father's life had flinched at any sudden movement—even though they'd reacted that way for good reason.

Callie's bed was empty. In the light bending around the bathroom door, which stood slightly ajar, he could see the rumpled covers. She was no longer beneath them.

"What's wrong? Are you okay?"

A soft moan scared him enough that he crossed the room and shoved the bathroom door wide—and there she was, lying on the tile floor, her face chalk-white, eyes closed.

"Shit, what is it?" As he crouched to see what was wrong, her eyelids fluttered open. She made an attempt to get up but couldn't quite manage it.

"I'm...fine," she said. "Go...go back to bed. Please."

Please? Why? She obviously needed help. She seemed so drained she could hardly move. And he could tell from the pungent odor that she'd been throwing up.

"Go..." She attempted to shoo him away. "I...I'm better off...alone."

She didn't like him invading her privacy. He could

understand that. Not only was she sick, she was in her underwear. So was he, but the sheer black fabric of her panties revealed quite a bit more than his briefs, especially since she wasn't even strong enough to pull her T-shirt down to cover them.

"Where's your cell?" he asked. "I'll call an ambulance."

"No." After rising slightly, she slumped back to the floor. "I...I know what's wrong. There's nothing... nothing they can do for me. I just...I need to rest. You... go back to bed."

"And leave you like this?"

She didn't answer. She seemed to be conserving her strength.

"We should get a doctor," he argued.

"No." The word came out as a whisper, an emphatic one.

"How do you know? We've got to try. You look... you look *really* sick."

"I'll be fine...in a little while. It was just...the shock...earlier. It...it upset my system."

The shock? Did she mean when she came out to the barn? He'd grabbed her because he didn't know who it was, but he hadn't hurt her. How could that have resulted in *this?*

"Come here." He bent to help her up, but she fended him off and lunged for the toilet.

"Go out," she said, her words feeble, broken, as she retched and sputtered and coughed. "Go...out."

Levi wanted to leave her in peace, but he couldn't. He was afraid of what might happen to her. After smoothing the hair out of her face, he supported her by the shoulders while she finished throwing up. Maybe she didn't want him to be part of this, but he'd seen a lot worse in his day. He was just glad her vomit wasn't filled with blood.

He flushed the toilet. Then he got a cool damp washcloth so he could wipe her mouth and face.

"It's freezing on this floor. That can't be good for you," he said, and gathered her in his arms.

She didn't fight him. She didn't seem capable of it. She did try to protest, however. "I can't…go to bed yet. What if…what if I have to…throw up again?"

"I'll get a pan, just in case."

When he returned from the kitchen, he found her curled up in the middle of the bed. She'd made a half-hearted attempt to cover herself, but even that seemed to require too much effort.

"Look." He lightly rubbed her back to get her to open her eyes. "Your pan is right here."

She gave a barely perceptible nod as he wedged it between a pillow and the headboard.

"Now let's get you warm." He pulled down her shirt to cover her panties and rearranged the covers, but he couldn't leave her even then. She was too cool and clammy, too weak. He'd never seen someone look this fragile—not someone who'd lived. He was still tempted to call an ambulance. He would have if she hadn't been so certain he shouldn't. His own reservations about not involving public authorities made him sensitive to that.

"Can I call your vet friend at least?" he asked.

"No! Please, no one." She caught his hand and attempted a smile. "Thanks."

"What's wrong with you?" he whispered, curling his fingers around hers so she wouldn't have to use any strength to hang on to him.

"Just…the flu," she said, but she was shivering so violently he could barely understand her.

What the hell was going on?

Releasing her, Levi started to walk out of the room. He didn't want to feel the empathy he was feeling, didn't want to watch Callie suffer, even through the flu. He'd had a front row seat to so much suffering already.

She'd be fine, he told himself. The flu didn't last long. But he couldn't force his feet to move past the bedroom door. He was too worried. He paced for a few seconds, arguing with himself. Then he gave up, took off his shirt and slipped beneath the covers, hoping his body heat would quickly warm her.

She didn't respond when he pulled her against his body, but it seemed to help. She never had to reach for the pan he'd brought, never spoke, hardly even moved. Slowly, she stopped shivering and clasped one of his hands in both of hers, tucking it under her chin before she fell asleep.

When Callie woke, she felt almost like new. Sometimes the slightest thing could make her ill. Too much stress. Too much or too little of her medication, which was why her doctor kept adjusting the dosage. The kind of shock that resulted from bad news or a sudden scare. Lack of sleep. She was embarrassed that Levi had seen her retching over a toilet bowl. That couldn't have been a pretty sight. For some reason, she cared more than she wanted to about what he thought of her; she supposed it was basic female vanity. But regardless of all that, she was grateful for his help and couldn't fault how he'd handled the situation. He'd been kind, gentle, supportive. He was still in bed with her, his muscular body more effective at keeping her warm than an electric blanket.

She didn't move right away. She was comfortable wedged up against him, didn't want him to take her awakening as a signal that he should leave her bed.

Something must've told him she was no longer asleep, however, because he spoke. "You okay?"

"Yeah."

"Good. You scared me."

She smiled when he snuggled closer. They barely knew each other, but here they were—one with a damaged body and the other, from all indications, with a wounded soul—offering each other the solace of physical comfort. She'd never realized how much being held during such a low moment could mean. Maybe, because of her situation, she was putting too much store in it, but she'd been as content during the past few minutes as ever before in her life—probably more so because now she knew how to appreciate simple things.

"What?" he said as if he could tell she was busy thinking and wanted her to share her thoughts.

"Nothing. It's just…if you'd told me last week that I'd be spending the night with a tall, blond stranger, I wouldn't have believed it."

"Because there are no strangers in your world," he said with a laugh. "You know everyone."

He didn't laugh often. She liked the sound of it. "Exactly."

"Even *I* wouldn't be here if it wasn't for my bike—and those dogs."

The idea of his leaving didn't appeal to her. He'd given her a new focus, someone to worry about other than herself. She liked having him here. "I know."

"I hope…"

"What?" she prompted.

"I hope I didn't cause what happened."

At first she didn't understand what he meant, but then she remembered telling him it was the scare that had made her sick. It probably was. But normal people didn't get deathly ill from an encounter like that. "No. I wasn't making sense last night. It was just the flu. Anybody can get the flu."

"So you're better?" He didn't seem convinced.

"I am."

"Good. Then I'm going to make you something to eat so you'll stay that way."

"*You're* cooking?"

"Unless you don't want me in your kitchen."

She'd rather have him in her bed. But she was also eager for a few minutes of privacy to brush her teeth. "The kitchen's up for grabs," she said, hiding a yawn. "Knock yourself out."

When he got up, he inadvertently gave her a good view of his backside in those briefs. As thin as he was, he had a nice build. But last night hadn't been about beauty or physique. Only now that she felt well enough to appreciate the sight did his attire, or lack thereof, matter.

Her excitement over his near-nudity withered instantly when Kyle's voice boomed through the house. *"Callie?"* He sounded as if he was on a tear. "Where are you?"

She sent Levi a startled glance, but there was no time to say anything, no time for Levi to grab a shirt or a pair of pants. A second later, Kyle stood in the doorway of her bedroom, his jaw hanging open at the sight of Levi in his underwear.

"I was going to ask why you're not answering your phone, but I think I can guess." He seemed more shocked than angry.

Levi's eyes narrowed, but he didn't respond, and Callie was glad he was allowing her to handle Kyle's surprise visit. "This isn't what it looks like," she said. "I was sick last night. It's fortunate that Levi was here to take care of me."

"He did that in his underwear, did he?"

"He was sleeping when I started throwing up."

Kyle's chest lifted as he took a deep breath. "How could he have heard that from the barn?"

"He wasn't in the barn. I—I'd asked him to come in because—"

"You could've called me," Kyle broke in. "I would've helped you."

"I know. But I had no warning, and I didn't realize it would get as bad as it did."

"What made you sick?"

"The flu."

"Wait…" He blinked as he shook his head. "Why was he inside again?"

"I didn't want the two guys who own the dogs that attacked him to come back. They gave us some trouble night before last, remember?"

She purposely didn't mention that the prospect of the police returning also worried her. She knew how it would make Levi look to say he wanted to avoid them.

Kyle didn't seem to be listening, anyway. If she had her guess, he was feeling too many conflicting emotions. Shock. Outrage. Possessiveness. Chagrin at the knowledge that he had no right to be possessive.

Once again they were in that no-man's-land they'd created when they'd slept together.

"Shit," he said at last.

Levi raised a hand. "Look, I'm leaving in a few days. You have nothing to worry about."

Kyle eyed him, gave a deep sigh. "I'm not worried about me. Don't you get that? She deserves someone who's capable of loving her. Someone who's stable and can help her build a good life. She wants marriage, kids. Is that what you have to offer?"

"I have nothing to offer. I'm leaving, like I said."

"Then do it before you hurt her," he snapped, and walked out.

A second later, Callie heard what she hadn't noticed before he let himself in—the sound of his truck engine. It flared up, then dimmed as he drove away.

Levi shoved a hand through his hair. "How'd he get in?"

She'd locked the door. Levi had watched her do it after she'd brought him into the house. "He has his own key."

Lowering his head, he started to leave the room, but she didn't want him to go just yet. She felt the need to explain.

"Kyle and I have slept together. You were right about that."

He looked at her but said nothing. She couldn't even ascertain what he was feeling.

"It's happened a few times—five or six. But…it's not what you think. It's not about love, and it's not about screwing around just to get off."

"Then what's it about?"

She got the impression that he didn't want to ask but couldn't resist. "We're both tired of being alone, I guess."

He seemed to consider her response. "I can understand that," he said, and went to get dressed.

Callie had a doctor's appointment. She didn't want to admit that to Levi, didn't want him asking any questions. But she was also nervous about leaving him there alone. Not because she thought he'd steal from her or harm anything. She was afraid he'd be gone when she came back.

That was really an odd reaction to have to a drifter, someone she'd always known she couldn't maintain a relationship with. But she couldn't help it. All morning she kept remembering how it had felt when he'd snuggled up with her. Different from Kyle. Different from any other guy she'd been with—not that there'd been very many. She'd also been unable to get the image of Levi standing by her bed in his briefs, with certain body parts more apparent than usual, out of her mind.

"So do you want me to put Rifle in the fenced yard while I'm gone?" she asked as she stood beneath the ladder Levi was using, holding her purse and her car keys.

Levi focused on the dog pacing at her heels. Rifle had been running loose on the property—she let him do that when someone was out with him—and there hadn't been any trouble between the two of them. Still, before she drove off, Callie wanted to be sure Levi felt safe. She didn't want to come home to see either him or her dog hurt. The stitches that snaked across the golden skin on his arms were a constant reminder.

"He's fine. He doesn't go more than a few feet from me." Levi's biceps strained as he adjusted a piece of heavy metal he was attaching to the roof.

"You're sure?"

He shifted the metal until he was satisfied he had it in place. "Positive."

He'd made a lot of progress since breakfast. Not long ago, she'd heard him start his motorcycle, knew he was double-checking his repairs. Now he was working on the barn.

She gazed around the property, seeing all the other jobs he could do. But he wouldn't want to stay, even if she could offer him work. Whatever had sent him out on the road seemed to be chasing him, especially when he let down his guard. He refused to allow himself to form any attachments. For whatever reason, even friends were too much of an emotional risk for him.

She wondered what had happened in Afghanistan, guessed it was the tragedies of war that had left him so scarred.

"When will you be back?" he called as she walked toward her car.

"It'll be several hours."

"You'll be at the studio?"

She cleared her throat. She'd said she had some errands to run. Apparently, he assumed that stopping at the studio would be one of them.

She didn't correct him. "That's right."

"Can you pick up a handful of these nails from the hardware store on your way back?"

He got off the ladder to show her what he had in his pocket, and she took one with her, just to be sure she got the correct kind.

"Don't worry about dinner," she said. "I'll bring something."

He squinted against the sun as he stared at her.

"What?" she said when he didn't go back to work.

"You sure you're okay? Last night was…last night seemed bad."

"The flu always seems bad. I'm fine."

"Good." His gaze moved down. "By the way, I really like that dress."

A tingle of awareness made her curl her fingernails into her palms. She'd chosen the dress with him in mind.

Callie chewed her bottom lip as she tried to read her hepatologist's expression. Had her situation worsened? Would her placement on the national organ-donor list change?

She hated going to the doctor's alone. She was most tempted to tell someone about her condition whenever she faced an appointment. One of her friends would gladly have driven her the hour it took to reach the University of Davis Medical Center.

But then she'd have to confront the reality of her situation every time she looked into her friends' or family's eyes, and she wasn't ready. She kept coming back to that, to putting off the moment of truth so she wouldn't have to deal with other people's emotions while struggling with her own. Maybe it'd be different if she had any chance of finding a live donor. With live-donor transplants doctors took a portion of a living person's healthy liver and put it inside someone like her. Both pieces regenerated, which made the procedure sound very attractive. But it wasn't quite that simple. Only a small number of these operations were performed and it was usually done between family members. As an only child, she wasn't likely to find a match. Her mother had multiple sclerosis and required a wheelchair to get around, and her father had type 2 diabetes, which ruled them out.

Briefly, she thought of Levi's comforting presence last night and wished she'd brought him with her today. Very soon he'd be out of her life. What would it matter if he knew the truth?

That was what her head told her. But her heart said something else. Maybe he'd be moving on come the weekend, but while he was staying at her place she didn't want him to know she was critically ill. She found him attractive. That made her hope to be attractive to him, too. And she couldn't imagine it would be remotely appealing to hear that she had non-alcoholic fatty liver disease, even if it was, as her doctor said, idiopathic, meaning no one could say why her liver had suddenly stopped functioning properly. She didn't have hepatitis or anything, wasn't contagious.

"So?" Breaking a silence that had felt stifling, she wiped her sweaty palms on her sundress. "What do the latest tests reveal?"

The doctor was sitting on a rolling stool, studying her chart. After everything she'd been through, she couldn't believe she still found it difficult to wait for the latest results. While being evaluated by the center's transplant team, she'd undergone a biopsy to confirm her diagnosis and a computed tomography to determine the size and shape of her liver. She'd also had an echocardiogram to check her heart, numerous blood tests to search for infection and determine her clotting ability, an upper endoscopy to examine the state of the veins in her ab-

dominal wall, some pulmonary function studies to ensure that her lungs were exchanging oxygen and carbon
dioxide properly and several ultrasounds. She'd been at
this center so often over the past two months it sometimes felt as if she lived there. That was another reason she'd decided to entrust her photography business
to her assistant. She couldn't do certain shoots. Even if
she felt well enough to work, there were days when she
had to be gone. What would she have said every time
she had to run to Sacramento for new tests?

"Well…" Her doctor set her chart aside. "Unfortu-
nately, I see some degradation of your condition."

After feeling so terrible last night, she'd prepared
herself for this. But how much degradation? Would he
classify her as status one? Status one meant she'd be
given the highest priority for a new liver. It also meant
she wasn't expected to live longer than a week.

A week! Maybe she'd be gone before Levi….

She swallowed. "How bad is it?"

"It's affected your MELD score by a fairly significant margin."

The Model for End-stage Liver Disease or MELD
score was how the United Network for Organ Sharing
determined where she belonged on the national donor
list. A computer-generated number between six and
forty, based on blood tests, indicated how likely she
was to die in the next ninety days without a transplant.
The higher the number, the more serious her condition.

"How much of a margin?"

"Three points. You were at seventeen. Now you're
twenty because your bilirubin count is up. The good
news is that your international normalized ratio and
creatinine—"

"Creatinine?" She'd forgotten what that was. She knew bilirubin measured the amount of bile pigment in her blood, and the PT-INR measured her blood's clotting ability, which came from proteins secreted by the liver. But what was the creatinine?

"It measures renal function," he explained.

"You mean kidney function."

"Right. Along with your PT-INR, your creatinine levels are not too alarming."

When liver failure became acute, a patient also had severe kidney problems and could wind up on dialysis. She was hoping to receive a transplant before that.

"So it's the bilirubin that concerns me the most," he was saying. "Are you being careful about what you eat?"

"Very. I haven't had *any* alcohol. No salt. Plenty of fruit and vegetables. Whole grains. Lean protein." If she ate at all… It was almost easier *not* to eat. But she needed the strength.

"Glad to hear it. I'll update your standing on the donor list and we'll pray for a match."

Pray. Weren't doctor's supposed to act as if *they* were in control?

She was actually glad Dr. Yee didn't pretend. She preferred to face the truth—that he was just a man and could not ultimately decide her fate.

He stood to smile and shake her hand but, for some reason, this appointment was more difficult than the others here at the center. Her chest constricted and her eyes filled with tears—and the weird thing was that she felt it had something to do with wearing the pretty sundress she'd chosen for today and the look in Levi's eyes when he told her he liked it.

9

Callie wasn't sure how Levi would react when she returned home with new clothes for him. She doubted he'd be pleased. He'd made it clear that he didn't want her to do him any more favors. If she cooked, he insisted on doing the dishes or fixing something around the house—like the screen door in back that had been sticking for ages—in exchange for his meal. This morning, he did the cooking himself. He also joined her when she'd gone out to weed the garden and, with his help, she made much quicker work of it than she would have otherwise. He felt as if he was already in her debt and, technically, he was. She'd spent two hundred and eighty dollars on his motorcycle. But it would've cost her a lot more to have the barn fixed and painted, so she figured she was getting a bargain.

Regardless, he wouldn't want her spending any extra money on him. But thinking about someone she liked as much as she liked him counteracted—just a little—the bad news of her MELD score. She *enjoyed* having him in her life. She wasn't sure why. She'd never felt quite the same about any other man.

But she'd never been dying of liver disease before, either. She had to admit that changed her perspective.

"Can I help you?"

She turned to see a sales associate. She'd driven to Arden Fair Mall so she'd have a selection. "I need a shirt and a pair of jeans for a man who's maybe six foot two and one hundred and ninety pounds."

"You want something casual, for summer?"

She nodded. Levi wasn't the type to dress up. He looked perfect in a plain white tee and worn blue jeans. But she hadn't managed to get the shirt clean that he'd been wearing when he was attacked, and the jeans he'd had on were torn well beyond what was stylish.

"How about this?" The woman held out a stone-washed, reddish shirt, basically a V-neck tee. It was rugged, simple. Callie could easily imagine how good Levi's well-defined chest would look in that and thought it was just masculine enough that he might like it.

"Great. I'll take a large."

The saleswoman brought the shirt to the register, then beckoned her over to a large display of jeans. "Are you interested in dark or light denim?"

"Dark." She might as well get him something slightly dressier than the ones he had.

"What about these? They're a loose fit."

She considered them but ultimately decided they weren't right. "With his build he could afford to go a little tighter."

"Gotcha." Lips curved into a conspirator's smile, the woman plucked up a different pair. "These?"

"Definitely." They weren't "skinny" jeans, nothing metrosexual or too trendy, but they'd make the most of his physique.

"What size?"

"I'm guessing...thirty-two by thirty-six?"

"You're in luck. We have one pair left." She pulled some jeans from the bottom of the stack.

Callie had paid for her purchases and was walking out of the mall, carrying the sack, when her phone rang. It was her neighbor Godfrey. She'd forgotten that he'd tried to reach her earlier, when she was at the transplant clinic.

"Hello?"

"Callie?"

An older gentleman held the door so she could walk out into the bright afternoon sunshine. "What's up, G.? Do you have an update for me on those pit bulls?"

"I'm afraid the situation's not good. I could have them euthanized. That's the only way to ensure they won't hurt someone else. But if I do, the owners are claiming they'll sue the city."

She hated the idea of killing any animal but, under the circumstances, she didn't think they had a choice. "If you *don't,* and someone else gets attacked, the victim or the victim's family will also have cause to sue, because now we all know those dogs are dangerous."

"The details are…kind of murky."

She waited for a break in the traffic so she could cross to her car. He hadn't thought they were murky when he stitched up Levi's wounds. "Because…"

"Because we weren't around when it happened. We don't know exactly what occurred."

"Levi told us what occurred."

"But is it the truth? Even if it is, he's a drifter. He won't be around to testify if or when this goes to court."

She was winded just from the exertion of walking to and from the mall. The fatigue was almost the worst of what she was going through. "So? He deserves the same consideration as any other citizen. Drifting isn't against the law." She put her bag in the backseat of her BMW X3. "So what's happening?"

"The dogs are currently at the shelter. I wanted to see how convinced you are about what should be done before I go any further."

She sighed. If these pit bulls were dangerous, she couldn't allow her love of animals to come before human safety. What if they attacked a child?

She didn't want to be responsible for that. And after meeting Denny and Powell, and seeing how they behaved, she doubted they'd take the situation seriously enough to put a stop to the threat.

"I believe Levi," she said. "You saw what those dogs did."

"But did he trespass? Egg them on in some way?"

She could've reminded him about the lack of blood in the garage where Denny was staying, or the placement of Levi's bike, but she knew it came down to credibility. She and G. had credibility in Whiskey Creek. They'd lived here all their lives, knew everyone. Levi and the renters did not.

"Like I said, I believe Levi."

"Okay," he said, as if that decided it. "Consider this handled, but…"

"But?" she repeated.

"There's one other reason I've been dragging my feet."

"And that is…"

"I don't trust Denny Seamans or Powell Barney. I'm afraid of how they might respond, afraid they might blame you instead of me."

"They shouldn't blame anyone, except their dogs—

or, more to the point, themselves, if they didn't train those dogs properly."

"They aren't the type to accept responsibility. They've been trying to place the blame elsewhere ever since this happened. So...you should be careful. I wouldn't be surprised if there wasn't some sort of... backlash."

Denny and Powell had already stopped by, but no one seemed to know that. Apparently, they weren't telling—probably because coming to her house and getting into an altercation would only make them look as combative as their dogs. Also, Callie believed a guy who prided himself on his size wouldn't want to admit that he'd been so easily taken by a drifter weighing fifty pounds less.

"I'll be careful." She tried to sound confident, but in her current condition, she wouldn't be able to put up much of a defense once Levi left.

It was close to seven when Levi saw Callie's SUV turn down the drive. He'd finished working for the day, had just showered in the small, makeshift bathroom in the barn and was playing a game of fetch with Rifle. Fortunately, now that she was back he wouldn't have to figure out how to occupy himself next. He was hungry, but he hesitated to invade her privacy by going inside her house while she was gone, even though she'd told him he could make himself at home.

He stood to one side as she parked.

"Hey," she said as she got out. Her smile suggested she was happy to see him. It was so infectious he couldn't help smiling back.

"Hey yourself. That took all day."

"I had lots to do."

"Get it done?"

"I think so." She leaned in for a small paper sack that was sitting on the console. "Found the nails you wanted, but it was like looking for a needle in a haystack."

After taking the bag, he compared what she'd bought with one of the nails still in his pocket. "You did great."

She crouched to say hello to her dog, who was so excited to have her home his whole hind end was wagging. "There's my baby. How are you today?" she cooed, scratching and patting and hugging him. Then she squinted up at Levi. "Looks as if you two have been getting along."

"Rifle's a good dog."

"You hear that? He likes you." With a final pat, she straightened and collected the bags piled in her backseat. "I don't want you to get mad at me for this, but I bought you a couple of things at the mall."

"Me?" he said in surprise.

"I thought you could use them."

He cocked his head to see around her, at what she was digging out of her SUV. "What'd you get?"

"A pair of jeans and a shirt." She shoved a Macy's bag at him. "Go try them on."

Reluctantly, he accepted her offering, but he scowled to let her know he wasn't pleased. "Callie—"

"Oh, stop," she said with an impatient wave. "You're going to end up doing a lot more work than what I've paid you for. I'll owe you—and Lord knows you could use a change of clothes, so…do we have to make a big deal out of this?"

Her expression seemed almost childlike in its entreaty.

"I guess not."

"Wonderful!" Her smile returned. "Will you try them on? So I can see if I got the right sizes?"

"Sure." With a sigh, he helped bring in some take-out that smelled good enough to make his mouth water, as well as several other bags that had come from various shops other than the department store where she'd bought his clothes.

"I think I'm safe with the shirt," she said. "But the jeans. I had to guess."

He gave her the food and dropped the other bags on the couch before proceeding to her bedroom, where he changed. When he came out, the food was gone—she'd probably put it in the kitchen—and she was resting on the couch.

"You okay?" The paleness of her face reminded him of the harrowing hours of illness she'd suffered the night before.

She opened her eyes. "Just tired."

"You need to get in bed early."

"Nice," she said as she noticed his clothes. "I did well."

Everything felt comfortable, fit perfectly. "I like what you bought," he said. "Thanks."

"You come across as very conservative. I thought I couldn't go wrong with a pair of jeans and a dark shirt." She laughed. "You ready to eat?"

"I'm starving."

"It's on the table."

He paused halfway to the kitchen. "What about you?"

"I'm going to lie here for a bit."

She'd bought tri-tip, roasted vegetables, corn on the

cob and some thick-sliced bread from a place called Just Like Mom's. Hoping to encourage her to eat, he brought her a plate before dishing up his own, but it was too late.

"Damn," he said when he saw that she'd drifted off. He set her food on the coffee table so he could carry her to bed.

"How was dinner?" she murmured as he lifted her up.

"I'm sure it'll be delicious." He thought she might tell him it was too early to go to bed. But she didn't. She seemed willing enough to let him carry her, too.

"Where are you going to sleep tonight?" she asked.

"In the barn, where I'm supposed to be sleeping."

"No, stay inside, okay?"

He was beginning to want things he hadn't wanted for a long time, so he wasn't sure that would be a smart move. "It's probably better if I don't, Callie."

She'd closed her eyes and turned her face into his chest. "Better in what way?"

He wasn't about to explain it to her if she hadn't already guessed. "Fine. I'll stay in."

"Thanks."

After depositing her on the bed, he covered her and returned to the living room. He was in a hurry to have his dinner before it got cold and he'd have to reheat it, but he noticed something that stopped him before he could go very far. One of her shopping bags had a very distinctive color and logo.

Pink. Victoria's Secret.

What had she bought there?

Maybe it was just a bra or panties for everyday use, but he couldn't help checking. Pushing the tissue aside, he pulled out a sheer white number with a lace-up front and a matching pair of barely there panties.

"Holy hell," he muttered as his body reacted.

A sound from behind him told Levi she'd followed him out. Embarrassed to be caught handling her lingerie, he turned to find her watching him.

At first she didn't speak. They stared at each other for a moment. Then she cleared her throat and said, "I was just coming to get my stuff."

That was his cue to shove the sexy scraps of fabric back into the bag and walk away. But he couldn't pretend that what he'd found didn't affect him.

"Pretty," he said.

"I don't know why I bought that." She went bright red. "It was just…something I'd want to buy if…"

"If?" he prompted.

"If I had a reason."

He couldn't give her that reason. Tossing the bag onto the couch, he pivoted toward the kitchen. Food. He needed to concentrate on something else, because he knew that if he looked into those big blue eyes any longer, he'd carry her into the bedroom and break his promise to Behrukh.

10

Standing with her back to the closed door of the bedroom, Callie covered her mouth. *Oh, my gosh! Oh, my gosh! Oh, my gosh!* she screamed, but only inside her head. She'd remembered that Victoria's Secret purchase just as she was about to fall asleep and forced herself to get up so she could retrieve the bag. She'd wanted to hide the contents before Levi could stumble across it, but she'd ended up surprising him instead—and creating a terribly awkward moment for both of them.

He'd had no right to snoop. But she could understand why he might be interested. She shouldn't have bought such a thing to begin with. Why had she wasted the money?

Actually, she knew the answer to that. No doubt Levi did, too. But there was more to it than merely wanting to be with a man. When she looked at that bustier, she didn't think about *dying,* she thought about *living.* About loving. About passion and beauty. At thirty-two, there were so many things she had yet to do and see and feel. She didn't want to die without ever experiencing a night of real passion.

She couldn't forget Gail describing how it had been the first time she'd made love with Simon. Just think-

ing about her friend's happiness made Callie smile, especially since Gail and Simon were now married and
having a family, and that happiness was lasting.

Rifle had been lying on the rug by the bed. She nor-
mally left her door open and let him roam through the
house at will, but she didn't want to leave him alone
with Levi for too long too soon. When she didn't continue into the room, he cocked his head and whined as
if asking what was wrong.

"With all the odds stacked against me, I'll never
have the luck Gail had," she told him. Gail had married a movie star.

But an out-of-this-world encounter with the tall,
handsome man who'd walked into her life three days
ago didn't seem like too much to ask.

Even if sleeping with Levi *wasn't* everything she
imagined, it wouldn't be too difficult to surpass what
she'd known so far. Kyle was by far the best of the
few lovers she'd had, but physical fulfillment wasn't
necessarily emotional fulfillment. Before she died, she
wanted to see what it was like to *drown* in desire and
thought maybe the attractive, mysterious Levi could
provide that experience—*if* he was still capable of having sex. It was possible that what he'd been through had
robbed him of that ability.

She remembered feeling a certain solid object pressing into her backside at various moments last night.
That suggested he *could* perform. And yet he'd made no
attempt to act on his arousal. It was only because she'd
been sick that he'd gotten in bed with her. So even if the
problem wasn't physiological, there was some avoidance
there. Maybe it was a mental or emotional problem.

Either way, she'd been stupid to buy such expensive lingerie.

Planning to take her purchases back to the store after Levi left, she shoved them in a drawer and picked up her cell phone. Lately, she'd been too afraid her friends would notice her failing health to hang out with them as often as she used to; she was always traipsing back and forth to the transplant center, anyway. She hadn't been diligent about returning their calls.

But now that she'd had a chance to acclimate, as much as one could acclimate to the possibility of dying, she missed them.

Baxter answered on the first ring. Callie wasn't sure why she hadn't chosen to contact one of her female friends first. Gail or Eve or Cheyenne would've been a more natural choice. Even the married Sophia. But if her suspicions about Baxter were true, he was also unlucky in love. Given that she believed he was as gay as her first boyfriend and in love with Noah, who was also part of their group, she thought he'd be the most likely to understand how conflicted she was feeling.

"Hey, don't tell me this is *Callie*—Callie who was too busy to visit me in San Francisco and have lunch last week."

She couldn't have gone to the city. She'd had too many doctors' appointments in Sacramento— appointments she didn't dare cancel. She was fighting for her life, hoping against hope that the people who ran the national donor list would be able to come up with a liver in time.

"Sorry about that," she said. "I'll come another day." Baxter commuted to a brokerage house in San Francisco four days a week. As long as her health held out, she would have other opportunities.

"I can count on that? You haven't been returning my calls," he said.

"I've been busy."

"Getting your grandparents' place ready to sell? Is the job really that all-consuming? I mean, it's been five years. I hate to sound harsh, but maybe I could understand your complete absorption in this if they'd just died."

"I miss them."

"To the point that you can't take a few hours for your friends? You haven't joined us at the coffeehouse in a month. For some reason, you're shutting us all out. Except *Kyle*."

She heard the undercurrent in those last two words. He suspected she and Kyle were more involved than they'd been letting on. Some of the others did, too. Eve had once asked, point-blank, if they were sleeping together. But that was before they'd become intimate, so Callie had felt comfortable saying no.

"You know where I live," she told Baxter. "It's just that Kyle comes over and you don't."

"Because *I've* never been invited."

The TV went on. Apparently, Levi wasn't ready to sleep. "Kyle doesn't sit back and wait for an invitation."

"Why do you think that is?"

There it was again. What she'd done with Kyle was another reason she'd been pulling away from the group. She was embarrassed by her own behavior.

She considered admitting that she'd slept with Kyle. If nothing else, the revelation would throw Baxter off the trail of what else was going on in her life. But she quickly decided against it. She had no right to divulge anything without Kyle's consent.

Besides, what had happened between them—it was just a blip on the radar, an anomaly, a...lapse. And it was over. Somehow, since Levi had appeared on her porch, she hadn't even thought about getting naked with Kyle, except to be mortified that she'd let the situation interfere with her good judgment in the first place.

"Is it because he likes me more than you do?" she asked, putting a teasing lilt in her voice just in case.

"I'd say he likes you in a different way."

She cleared her throat. "We all have our secrets, right?"

When he immediately let it go and changed the subject, she felt more confident than ever that she'd guessed one of his.

"So what's up?" he said. "How are things going with your guest?"

Relieved by the shift in the conversation, she drew a deep breath. "Kyle told you about Levi?"

"*He's* still returning my calls. We had a drink together last night."

She ignored the jab. "And?"

"He's worried."

But not just about Levi. Kyle had been the only one to spend much time with her in the past three weeks, the only one to see her begin to feel worse and worse as her bilirubin count went up.

"There's nothing to worry about," she said. "If Levi was going to murder me, he would've done it by now."

"It's not like you to take in some drifter."

"This isn't *some drifter*."

"Who is he, then?"

"A man who needs a helping hand. A vet who's served our country."

"I admire the patriotism. But from what I've heard, he's also a loner who might be damaged beyond repair. Have you considered that?"

She'd thought of little else. But instead of being frightened or repelled, she wanted to help him. That desire was taking over her life, and she was grateful she'd found such a compelling cause. Before he'd shown up, each day had been harder than the last. He'd made what she was going through easier just by being around.

Last night, for example. What would she have done on her own? Spent hours upon hours on the bathroom floor without the strength to stumble to her bed?

"Doesn't matter," she said. "Whatever his situation, I want to do what I can for him."

"Selfless and admirable. Or…is there more to it?"

"By that you're suggesting…"

"Is he also someone you find attractive?"

Callie pictured Levi as she'd seen him earlier, on the ladder with his sweat-dampened T-shirt clinging to his muscular torso. *"Definitely."*

"Ah…riddle solved."

"What do you mean?"

"I mean, you have ulterior motives."

She almost denied it but laughed instead. "Maybe— to a certain extent. Would that be so bad?"

"Yes. Because then he could hurt you in a whole new way."

She doubted Levi could hear her above the program he was watching, but she lowered her voice just in case. "I'm not expecting a commitment from him. He'll be leaving soon."

"So we're talking about…sex?"

She supposed they were. For whatever reason, she felt a compulsion to get closer to him, but she'd convinced herself that it stemmed from her desire to "fix" him, since she couldn't fix herself. "That's part of it."

"Oh, jeez," Baxter said. "Whatever you do, make sure he's clean."

"Don't act like he'll…contaminate me!" she whispered harshly.

"*Someone* needs to caution you. You don't know him, so you'd be taking a huge risk—and you're not really the risk-taking kind. You *still* regret that one-night stand you had after Peter broke up with you, despite the fact that you went out looking to get laid!"

"The memory is revolting! I regretted it even while I was doing it."

He chuckled at her passionate response. "How do you know this would be any different?"

She didn't think she could adequately explain, but she made the attempt. "*He* excites me. I close my eyes and…he's who I dream about. I wasn't attracted to that other guy. I just wanted someone to reassure me that I was desirable, that it wasn't my fault Peter preferred men."

"Sexuality doesn't work that way."

"A fact I understand *now*. I was twenty, remember?"

"I get all that. But…you changed *before* Levi showed up. So none of this really relates."

"Of course it does."

"*Callie*…what's going on?"

He wasn't letting her cajole him. Squeezing her eyes shut, she cradled her head in her hand. "What would you say if I told you I was dying of non-alcoholic fatty liver disease?"

"What?"

The words were out. They'd been trapped inside her for so long she could scarcely believe she'd released them.

"Could you say that again?"

"You heard me." She couldn't bring herself to repeat what she'd said.

There was a silence during which Baxter dropped, almost as if it were a physical object, the "you need to get your head on straight" attitude he'd wielded throughout the conversation so far.

"I hope..." He couldn't continue, which led her to believe he'd choked up—and suddenly she was crying, too.

She held her breath so he wouldn't know. She'd promised herself she'd be calm, cool and collected when she made this announcement, didn't want to cause *more* sorrow by not handling it well. But there was no stopping the tears. They rolled down her cheeks and dripped off her chin as she stood at the window, wondering why, after maintaining her silence for so long, she'd blurted out her news to Baxter.

He was trying to talk again but was obviously struggling with his emotions. "I—I hope that was...just a cruel joke," he managed to say, but she could tell he knew it wasn't. The bomb she'd dropped explained too much. Everything he'd been questioning a few minutes earlier made sense.

But she hadn't done enough to prepare him, and for that she felt terrible. She was bad at goodbyes. That was another reason she'd been putting off telling her loved ones the truth. From the moment word got out, she'd be facing one long goodbye.

When she didn't confirm that it was a joke, he said, "How long have you known?"

She had to speak past the lump in her throat. "I found out on Valentine's Day."

"That was four months ago! It's taken you *four months* to tell us? Or—" his voice grew louder, indignant "—was I the only one who didn't know?"

In one way, revealing her condition was a huge relief. She no longer had to feel guilty for keeping it to herself. But Baxter's reaction was just one person's. Like the ripples caused by a rock thrown into a pond, the circles would widen and widen as more and more people found out. "I haven't told anyone else. Not a single soul."

"What about your parents? That doesn't include them, does it?"

"I'm afraid it does."

"Holy shit! I can't believe it. But…maybe you won't have to tell them. We'll get you help, do whatever we have to."

With a sniff, she wiped her cheeks. There was no use pretending she wasn't feeling sorry for herself. The heartbreak of losing all the years she'd expected to have was too obvious to hide. "That's just it. The doctors are already doing everything they can."

"So why haven't they been able to fix what's wrong?" Suddenly, he sounded angry. "In this day and age, there have to be answers, options."

"There's *one* option." She patted Rifle, who'd followed her to the window. "It's called a liver transplant."

He choked up again, so he had an even more difficult time speaking. "How do you get one?"

"You put your name on the list at various donor registries, and then you wait."

"Maybe, if we pay the right people, we can make it happen faster."

"Pay whom? Someone on the black market?"

"Whoever's in charge of doling them out!"

"Your place on the list isn't determined by ability to pay. It's according to need."

"Then we'll find our own donor!"

"How?"

"We'll all be tested to see if one of us is a match."

"They do very few live transplants, Baxter. They're complicated surgeries that can be life-threatening to the donor."

He muttered a curse. "There has to be an answer. You said non-alcoholic fatty liver disease?"

"That's right."

"If alcohol didn't cause it, what did? Is it genetic or—?"

"Some people develop a condition where their body stores too much iron or copper, which destroys their liver. If it's copper, I believe it's called Wilson's disease. I'm not sure about iron, but both of those conditions have genetic factors. That's not what happened to me. No one knows what went wrong in my case. My liver just…quit functioning properly."

"I can't accept that there's nothing we can do," he said. "There has to be *some*thing."

She stared out at the barn. Without much of a moon tonight, it was a hulking dark shadow but, for some inexplicable reason, she felt better when she remembered Levi and how great he'd looked up on that ladder. "I guess we just enjoy the time I have left."

"Shit…" A pause. "Kyle doesn't know?"

She could tell it surprised Baxter that he'd been the

first she'd told. But he felt safer, in some respects, than her girlfriends. Or Kyle. Baxter was less likely to tell the others. That made this sort of a practice run. "No."

"I'm sorry."

The window showed the reflection of her sad smile. "Thanks."

"You have to tell your parents, though. You can't… you can't let it go any longer. They don't know that they need to be more vigilant about the time they spend with you, don't know that—"

"I'll break it to them soon." She'd been bearing the burden of her secret long enough to understand how heavy it was. She just wasn't convinced that telling the truth would make the load any lighter. She'd be changing one set of worries and concerns for another. "But… not quite yet. It's been hard enough telling you."

"What about Eve and Cheyenne and the others?" His words were muffled, as if he'd dropped his head in his hands.

"I was waiting, in case…in case I had positive news about a transplant before I came out with my condition."

"But then you'd be whisked into surgery with barely any notice. They can't keep that…type of thing on ice indefinitely."

What he said was true. She was listed with several different transplant centers. Her doctors said that should help her get the liver she needed. But there were no guarantees, not when twenty thousand people a year needed a transplant and only about five thousand received one. "Right."

"How'd you know you had a problem? What were your symptoms?"

"Besides looking jaundiced and feeling shitty? I got these weird red spots on my chest—spider angiomata, they're called. I also had redness on the palms of my hands."

"That's from liver disease?"

"Those are some of the symptoms, yes. Once I went in, they found that my liver was enlarged."

"What are the chances of surviving a transplant?"

She crouched to hug her dog. "That'll depend on whether or not my body rejects the new liver. But the statistics are hopeful. The majority of liver transplants are successful."

"The majority…"

"About eighty-five percent of recipients survive one year," she clarified. "Something like seventy percent survive three. I don't know after that, but I'm young and otherwise healthy. With the right match, I'd have a good prognosis. I'd just have to take immunosuppressant drugs for the rest of my life."

"And that's okay?"

"They have some potentially harsh side effects. The steroids can cause skin cancer and other problems, but they'll watch me closely. Except for taking a lot more pills on any given day than the average person, I'll be able to live a normal life."

"That means all we have to do is make sure you get a new liver."

"I wish we had more control over that than we do." She rubbed her face against Rifle's as he licked her cheek. "We're having coffee with the others in the morning. Maybe I'll tell them." In light of Baxter's reaction, the guilt of not having done so was bothering her.

"Right there in the coffee shop?" he asked.

She straightened. "No?"

"Family first, Callie. Hard as it is, you have to tell your parents."

"Don't pressure me! I think that's why I've been holding off. I don't want to feel what others are feeling."

"You're not an island. You need to do it soon."

"I'll do it in my own time. Tell me you'll respect that."

"Of course I'll respect that! But—"

"No buts. I'll come back and haunt you if you let me down."

"That's not funny," he said.

She felt like crying again and couldn't come up with anything to say in return. Silence settled between them. Then he asked, "Does the man who's staying with you—Levi—know what's going on?"

She glanced at her closed door. "He doesn't. And I'd rather he didn't find out." He wasn't part of her usual world, so she felt no obligation to tell him. "He'll be gone before I'm at my worst."

How long do I have to live? she'd asked her doctors. *You might make it through the summer, but...you'll probably be feeling pretty poorly by August...* If last night was any indication, the doctor was absolutely right. "There's no reason for him to know."

"Your worst," Baxter repeated. "This is nuts. I'm at a total loss, don't even know what to say. It just...can't be happening."

Thinking of the nausea that often plagued her, she turned away from her reflection. "Trust me. It's for real."

"Now I'm *glad* you have someone living with you. If you'd picked up when I called before, I would've told you it wasn't safe. But I like the idea that you've got company. At least you're not out there alone."

When she climbed into bed, Rifle lay down on the rug where he'd been resting before. "I'm glad, too."

"One more thing."

"What?"

"Shouldn't you tell Kyle? I mean…you two are closer than the rest of us."

"Oh, my gosh! You're not giving up until I admit it!" She chuckled but she didn't really find it funny.

"I'm just thinking of all the people who'll be hurt by this. I don't care who you sleep with, Callie. I hope you know that. I'd be the last person to judge."

"I feel the same way about you," she said.

There was a slight pause. "I appreciate that more than I can say."

"I'll tell Kyle soon," she promised. "But will you ever tell Noah what you've been keeping from him?"

"No. Absolutely not. I can't."

This was the closest Baxter had ever come to admitting his feelings for Noah.

"I understand why," she said.

"Are you the only one who's guessed?"

She had to be honest with him. "No, Eve's guessed, too. And Cheyenne. But not Gail or Sophia, so far as I know. And none of the guys."

"I keep telling myself to move to the city, where I can be who I am."

"But…"

"That would mean leaving you and everyone else behind. Including him."

"We want what's going to make you happiest."

"Problem is…there's a cost either way."

11

"I'm going to have coffee with my friends this morning." Wearing a robe over the T-shirt and panties she'd slept in, Callie scooped scrambled eggs onto Levi's plate. "Would you like to come with me and meet them or—"

"No, I think it's best if I stay out of town." He kept his eyes on his food even when Rifle nudged him, hoping for a pat. "I'll get to work on the barn."

"Okay. Is there anything you need? Like those nails I bought yesterday?"

"I don't think so."

"There's got to be something you want." They sold giant cinnamon rolls at Black Gold Coffee. Delicious muffins, too. She'd been about to mention those, but when he finally glanced up, the words seemed to congeal in her throat. In that moment, she understood how he'd interpreted her words. She also understood that there *was* something he wanted, but it had nothing to do with food. His discovery of that bustier last night had created some added tension between them. He hadn't acted any differently when she'd walked out to find him in the process of getting dressed. He'd merely buttoned his jeans and pulled on a shirt. But now... She could feel the change.

Instinctively, she wet her lips, but then he tore his gaze away, and she knew, for whatever reason, he'd never actually touch her. He wanted to but he wouldn't.

"Levi?"

He was eating again, as if that brief exchange of energy had never occurred. *"What?"*

The gruffness of his answer implied that he wasn't pleased to be feeling what he was feeling—or maybe he wasn't pleased by what he'd just revealed. It wasn't like him to be so transparent, to drop the indifferent mask he wore, even for a second.

"You..." She swallowed hard. "You confuse me. I was embarrassed when you found that bustier because I assumed, from your reaction, that you weren't interested in me...in that way."

"You're beautiful. What single man wouldn't be interested? Especially if he hasn't had a woman in a long time."

"Is that you?"

Finished with his eggs, he got up to rinse his plate in the sink. "You're better off with Kyle."

It wasn't easy walking into Black Gold Coffee. Friday mornings with the gang had always been Callie's favorite time of the week, but these casual get-togethers grew increasingly uncomfortable the longer she kept her diagnosis a secret. Knowing that Baxter would be there—a witness to everything she said and, more to the point, *didn't* say—only made it worse. She was tempted to tell them all and get it over with. She was feeling stronger, healthier, today. Maybe she could face the emotional fallout. She had to do it sometime.

But Baxter was right. She had to tell her parents first. She figured she'd keep her mouth shut for now and go to their place directly afterward.

"Hey, look who showed up this week!" Noah stood to embrace her, a sardonic smile on his darkly tanned face.

He had his coffee. So did Baxter, who hugged her next. Not only had they grown up as best friends, they'd been neighbors until they moved out on their own, so it wasn't unusual for them to sit together. These days Noah lived behind Crank It Up, the bike shop he owned. Baxter had recently purchased a Victorian at the edge of town, a house he'd wanted for years. The look he shot her as they sat down told her how pathetic he felt to be in love with his best friend, who didn't even know he was gay. That enabled her to smile and relax a little regarding her own circumstances. Everyone had problems.

"Good to see you, too," she told Noah.

"Aren't you getting something?" He gestured toward the counter.

"No, I've eaten." She'd made herself a couple of eggs when she fed Levi. "No races this week?"

As a professional cyclist, Noah was often out of town during the summer, training or competing in Europe.

"Nope." He grimaced as he stretched his right leg. "Pulled a hamstring. Gotta let it heal before climbing back on a bike."

"Bet you hate the inactivity."

"I've been kayaking lately, but…yeah. I'd rather not lose everything I gained in training."

Kyle strolled in. His eyes gravitated to her first, but he waved to Noah and Baxter from the line forming at the counter as Cheyenne and her husband, Dylan, entered behind him. Eve, Sophia and Ted trailed in last.

They each placed an order before taking a seat at their customary table in the back corner. "Where's Riley today?" Sophia asked as she settled her expensive Gucci bag at her feet.

"He had to be in Jackson for a job," Ted answered but he didn't look at Sophia when he spoke. They'd once been an item—until she'd broken up with him to marry Skip Debussi instead. According to town gossip, she did this for Skip's money. He came from money to begin with, so he stood to inherit—and he'd made millions on his own. But everyone believed Sophia regretted the marriage and stayed in it only because she had a daughter with him.

"He'll be here with us next week," Kyle added.

The barista called Eve's name. "I thought maybe Phoenix had gotten out of prison and he was dealing with that," she said as she stood to collect her latte.

Because of her own problems, Callie had lost track of the latest with Riley and Phoenix, but it was definitely a sensational topic, one that invited a lot of conjecture. Riley had dated Phoenix during their senior year—just long enough to get her pregnant. But he hadn't known about the baby when he moved on. Neither had he ever expected her to run down the next girl he liked. Phoenix had been serving time for vehicular manslaughter since shortly after graduation. She'd even had the baby in prison, at which point the authorities had shuttled Jacob out to Riley and his parents.

"No." Baxter shook his head. "Phoenix got into a fight in the exercise yard. Claims she was jumped by three other women. But there was no way to tell who started it. So they extended her stay."

"Until when?" Cheyenne asked.

"Kyle said end of August," Noah told her.

Callie couldn't help feeling sorry for Phoenix. It was irrefutable that she'd swerved. There were witnesses. But had she meant to *kill* Lori Mansfield? That was hard to believe. Phoenix had always been a bit... different. She came from a challenging situation. But Callie had had a class with Phoenix and found her to be nice enough.

"I can't imagine she'll come back *here,*" Ted said. "She doesn't have anything to come back to. We all know what her mother's like. It's a miracle she hasn't been featured on an episode of *Hoarders.*"

Callie scowled. "Hoarder or not, Lizzie is still her mother and she's only getting older and more...off. Someone's got to take care of her. It's not as if Phoenix's brothers will step up to help."

"And Jacob's here," Sophia added. "Phoenix hasn't seen her son since she gave birth to him."

"Sophia's right," Eve agreed. "Phoenix has been writing Riley all along, asking for pictures of Jacob."

"I didn't know that," Cheyenne said. "Does he respond to those letters?"

"Most of the time he ignores them. He can't encourage her or he'll make the situation worse." Noah paused to take a sip of his coffee. "You don't want someone like that to have any influence over your child."

"He's told her plenty of times that he doesn't want anything to do with her, that Jacob is better off without her," Ted chipped in. "She should just stay out of their lives. Start over somewhere else."

Of course, Riley wouldn't want this woman, this convict, showing up on his doorstep and laying claim to the child he'd raised for thirteen years. But what about Jacob? What if he wanted to know his mother?

Callie wondered if she'd be alive to see what happened the day Phoenix returned to Whiskey Creek....

"Maybe she's not as bad as we all think."

This comment came from Sophia, which seemed to surprise more than just Callie. Sophia hadn't been one of them in high school. She'd had her own group, most of whom were as mean as she'd been.

"She caused Lori's *death*," Eve said, obviously exasperated.

"I know but—" Sophia turned her cup in a circle as if she was hesitant yet driven to speak up "—she'd been drinking. Sometimes people do *really* stupid things when they're drunk."

There was no arguing with that, but everyone was so firmly on Riley's side that this comment didn't bring her the positive attention she'd been looking for since trying to become part of the group. Gail was about the only one who'd been able to forgive her. Maybe it would be easier for the others to do that, too, if she hadn't done so many catty things. Actually, at times she'd been *more* than catty.

"Regardless, what happened happened," Ted muttered. "Like I said, she should leave Riley and Jacob alone and build a life elsewhere."

Sophia shot Ted a steely look. "When you're a mother, accepting the loss of a child is easier said than done."

Putting his elbows on the table, Ted leaned forward

to make his point. "If Phoenix hadn't killed Lori, she wouldn't be in this situation."

"You don't know what was going on inside her head when it happened!" Sophia retorted. "How can you judge? It's easy to think you know who's right and who's wrong when you're looking in from the outside."

Ted slammed down his cup. "So what are we really talking about, Sophia? What you did to *Scott?*"

There was a collective gasp as she blanched. Then her face reddened and she stood. "I—I'm sorry. I don't seem to be very good company today. Excuse me."

They all gaped at Ted as she left.

"Wasn't that a little harsh?" Noah asked after the door swung shut.

Given how much time had passed, Callie thought it was. They hadn't mentioned Scott's name since Sophia had started coming to coffee. Once the best basketball player to attend Eureka High, he'd been killed in a drunk-driving accident that most people blamed her for causing. Even though she wasn't in the vehicle with him, it was her actions that had led him to take the risk.

"She's the only mother among us," Cheyenne said. "Of course she's going to feel bad for a woman whose actions have cost her her child."

"Forget about her. She has no business coming here, anyway," Ted grumbled, but he slumped morosely over his coffee, as if he regretted what he'd done.

"Gail says she's not so bad anymore—" Cheyenne started, but Noah grabbed her arm.

"Let it go," he murmured, and she did. They all knew that Ted was probably still in love with Sophia. That was why he couldn't get past how she'd wronged him.

"There are better things to talk about than Sophia or Phoenix," Baxter said.

"Like?" Eve asked.

He wiggled his eyebrows. "Callie's got something interesting going on in her life."

A flicker of fear raced through Callie—until she realized that Baxter wasn't about to give her away. He was referring to the fact that she had a guest at the farm.

"Oh, yeah!" Noah said. "Tell us about this drifter."

Obviously, Baxter had mentioned Levi to Noah. Or Kyle had. Maybe they'd all talked about him, because no one asked, "What drifter?" Anything of note spread quickly among them.

"There's not much to tell," she said, when all eyes turned to her. "His name's Levi. He needs work—and I need labor." She shrugged, hoping to convince her friends that his being in her life wasn't a big deal. "So we've worked out a trade."

"How long will he be staying with you?" Dylan typically didn't do much of the talking. Until he'd married Cheyenne, he hadn't been a member of the group. But he'd been a far more welcome addition to coffee on Fridays than Sophia, even though she'd been coming a lot longer. Their first loyalty was and always would be to Ted.

Callie met Dylan's gaze. His eyes were too pretty to belong to a former MMA fighter, she thought, but his crooked nose betrayed him. "A week or so."

Kyle's scowl grew so dark, several people shifted as if he was making them uncomfortable.

"You don't like that he's there, Kyle?" Cheyenne asked, calling him on his reaction.

A second rush of panic, this one for an entirely different reason, had Callie curling her fingernails into her palms. If Kyle wasn't careful, he'd give them away. She already felt as though she had the word *guilty* emblazoned on her forehead.

"I'm just worried," he replied. "She doesn't really know him, doesn't know what he's capable of."

Eve looked perplexed. "Hasn't he been there a few nights already?"

"Doesn't mean anything," Kyle insisted. "It takes longer than that to earn trust."

Callie rolled her eyes. "He's not going to hurt me."

When Baxter spoke up, Callie was grateful to him for drawing some of the scrutiny away from her. "I think having a man on the farm might be a good thing."

"Why do you think that?" It was Kyle, of course, who challenged him.

"You never know." He cradled his cup. "That means she's got help on hand, if she needs it. From what she's told me, this dude can fight."

Dylan might've spoken up. He knew all about professional fighting. But Kyle was having none of it. "She's got Rifle to protect her."

"True," Baxter said, "but the owners of those killer pit bulls are blaming her for the fact that they've been impounded."

"Those guys are renters," Kyle argued. "They won't be in town long. And they'll calm down and forget about her once he leaves."

"What if they don't?" Baxter asked.

"Then we'll protect her. I don't care how good this guy can fight. No one can fight better than Dylan."

"What's his name again?" Dylan asked.

Someone told him "Levi McCloud" and Dylan said

he'd never heard of him, but Callie had stopped paying attention. Her chair scraped the old wooden floor as she shoved it back. Kyle was driving her crazy. "Look, I'll do what I want, okay? We're not taking a vote."

Startled by the edge in her voice, everyone looked up, including Kyle. She'd sounded far too impassioned, but she couldn't stem the emotions that threatened to come bubbling out of her. For some reason, she wasn't really enjoying this morning. She had too much on her mind. She just wanted to get back to Levi.

"I've got to go." She hurried to her car and pulled out of the parking lot before anyone could catch up with her. She wanted to return to the farmhouse, but she drove to her parents' instead.

"Mom?" Callie let herself in the front door and stood in the entry.

"There you are!" Her mother rolled down a hallway that had recently been widened to accommodate her wheelchair. "Too bad your father's not home. He's been asking if I've heard from you."

Boone Vanetta sold life insurance. Although Callie had a fifty-fifty chance of finding him at home on any given day, his truck wasn't parked in its usual spot out by the flagpole. Callie guessed he was at his office in town. At sixty-six he still worked but he'd gone part-time since her mother's health had begun to deteriorate. Fortunately, he was the only State Farm agent in Whiskey Creek and had a very loyal clientele.

"You've been so quiet lately." Her mother didn't sound pleased; her next few words explained why. "It seems like you hardly ever call."

The guilt Callie was already feeling became more

intense. She checked in fairly regularly, but she'd meant to do it more often. She'd just been so preoccupied after Levi arrived. And Diana's pointed questions made it hard to lie—about anything. Since being diagnosed with cirrhosis of the liver, Callie had squirmed through every conversation.

Forcing a smile despite the anxiety slamming through her like a million gallons of rushing water, she bent to kiss her mother's cheek. She hated seeing Diana in a wheelchair. A relatively new addition to their lives, it was proof that her mother would have more difficulties to face as her own disease progressed. "I'm sorry. I've been so busy."

"At the studio?" The chair's motor whined. "I thought you were taking the summer off. That's what you said when you moved out to the farm. That's why I thought we'd see more of you."

"I'm still helping at Reflections when I can. I have my garden and some other photography to keep up with. And it's taking time and effort to put the farm to rights." She considered mentioning Levi. She had to tell her parents about him, too. But she figured she'd save that for later. She had more pressing news.

"I hate to sell that place," her mother said. "I loved growing up there."

Callie adjusted her purse strap. "Maybe we should keep it." She came back to that again and again, even though the amount of care a farm required didn't make owning one very practical for someone who didn't plan to work it. And what would her parents do with the property after she was gone? They'd just have to sell it. So why not do it now?

"It'll be smarter to liquidate. Then we'll have the

money we need for our retirement, and you'll inherit the rest." Her mother rolled back a few inches to take a good look at her. "You've lost weight."

Callie cleared her throat. "A few pounds."

"Come on. Some homemade lasagna will fatten you up."

"But it's not even noon yet." And there was no way that was on her diet.

Her mother was already rolling into the other room. "Then you can take some home with you."

Reluctantly, Callie followed Diana into the kitchen and sat at the table. She wanted to tell her mother what she'd come to say, to get it off her chest, but she didn't know how to start. "You been feeling okay?" she asked instead.

"About the same." Her mother maneuvered around the kitchen with surprising dexterity.

"How's dad been managing his diabetes?"

"His glucose numbers haven't been as good as they should be." She tossed Callie an exasperated grin. "I think he's sneaking sweets."

If he was eating her lasagna, he was getting plenty of carbohydrates without sneaking sweets.

"He doesn't seem willing to change his diet as much as the doctor says he should," her mother complained.

More likely, Diana was cooking the way she'd always cooked. But she didn't see the correlation.

"He needs to stick with lean proteins and vegetables," Callie said. "That's what you need to make for him, okay? Not pasta or potatoes or breads."

"When you get as old as we are, you deserve *some* enjoyment out of life," she said, slightly insulted.

But they had to take care of themselves since Callie likely wouldn't be around to do it. "So…" She hesitated, trying to decide how to segue into her diagnosis.

"What?" Her mother gave her a strange look.

"I came by today because—" she could hear her pulse thumping in her ears, which was as annoying as it was distracting "—there's something I need to tell you."

An expression of alarm settled on her mother's face, but the sound of a car pulling up outside distracted both of them.

"Oh, good. Your father's here."

Callie wiped sweaty palms on her denim shorts. "What's he doing home so early?"

"He's taking me to get my hair done." She checked the clock. "We've only got fifteen minutes before we have to leave."

Of course. Her mother had a standing appointment with Lola Leidecker at Shearwood Forest every Friday. How could Callie have forgotten? Fifteen minutes wouldn't give Diana enough time to recover from the blow she was about to be dealt. Once she broke the news, Callie doubted her mother would feel up to leaving the house.

"Callie?" Her father came through the garage door bellowing her name.

"Hi, Pop." Obviously, he'd seen her SUV out front. She hugged him but he was so eager to talk he barely squeezed her in return.

"What's this I hear about you taking in some drifter?" he demanded.

Her mother's eyebrows immediately assumed their "I'm displeased" position. "I hope that isn't what you were about to tell me," she said. "You haven't taken in a stranger, have you? You know better than that!"

"He needs help," she hedged.

"So you're risking your life to give it to him?" Her father's voice nearly shook the glass in the windows. A bear of man, Boone could be intimidating. But Callie knew he had the softest heart imaginable and hardly flinched when he raised his voice.

"He was attacked by dogs, Dad. I *had* to help him. You should've seen the blood. You would've done the same."

"I'm not a single woman!"

"It's not like he was some stalker or peeping Tom. His motorcycle broke down and he got bitten. Now he's fixing the roof on the barn to pay me back for fronting the money to repair his bike."

The fact that she wasn't giving ground made her father pause. But he soon rallied. "Chief Stacy doesn't like him. Says that boy's up to no good."

Chief Stacy had talked with her father? At least Godfrey hadn't ratted her out.... She appreciated her neighbor's discretion.

"What are you thinking?" her mother asked.

"Chief Stacy's suspicious of any stranger," she said. "You know how distrusting this town can be when it comes to new faces. But Levi's lived at the farm for three days. He just wants some space to be able to get his head on straight." She focused on Boone. "You fought in Korea, Dad. You know what war is like."

He leaned a hip against the counter. "He's a vet?" he asked, already showing signs of bending.

"Yes."

"What some of those boys go through," he said with a click of his tongue.

"It's terrible," Diana agreed.

Callie rested a beseeching hand on her father's folded arms. "Levi needs a temporary safe haven, Dad."

When he shifted his weight and harrumphed, she knew he'd accepted her explanation. And that reminded her of one of the many reasons she loved her father so much. Maybe he could appear ferocious, but he was every bit a gentle giant. She'd seen him take similar risks, stopping to assist folks stuck on the side of the road, or picking up a hitchhiker. Whether he wanted her following in his footsteps or not, he understood that helping someone in need sometimes called for a certain amount of risk.

"It scared me when Chief Stacy made it sound so foolhardy," he said. "I don't know what I'd do—what *we'd* do—" he gestured at her mother "—if something ever happened to you. Lord knows it was hard enough to get you here."

His words caught Callie like a bullet to the chest. She stood there, instantly disarmed. All the things she'd planned to say, the admission she'd put off for so long, swirled through her mind, but she couldn't bring it to her lips, couldn't break her parents' hearts. It'd taken them ten years to have a baby. Only after months and months of fertility treatments had they conceived. Callie knew, had always known, that she meant a great deal to them. Her father was already facing the decline of the woman he'd married forty years ago, the only woman he'd ever loved. That was bad enough.

"I'm glad I let him stay, Dad," she managed to say. "It…it's helped me."

He might've asked what she meant by such a strange comment but her mother interrupted.

"We've got to go, Boone. I can't miss my hair appointment. You know how busy Lola is." Diana moved her wheelchair closer to Callie so they could touch. "You be careful with that man around. Keep your eyes open," she warned, gripping Callie's hands. "And call us nightly."

Callie stifled a sigh. "I will."

"You don't think…you don't think he'd ever—" her mother lowered her voice as if she couldn't bear to say the word "—*rape* you, do you?"

Considering the bustier episode, which could've been taken as an invitation to have consensual sex, Callie might've laughed. But nothing about this situation was funny. "Definitely not."

"Okay." Seemingly satisfied, her mother nodded. "Don't forget to check in."

"Maybe he should stay here," her dad mused, still reluctant to trust her safety to an unknown person.

Callie shook her head. "No. You and Mom have enough going on. And I need his help on the farm. I feel safer with him there. I promise."

"Okay." When he pulled her into his arms, he almost swept her off her feet. "Love you, Callie girl."

Callie choked on the lump rising in her throat. She couldn't tell them she was going to die. Something had to change.

"I love you, too," she murmured against his shirt. Then, after they left, she sat in her car crying as she watched their taillights disappear down the street.

12

Callie bought Levi another shirt. She'd needed to distract herself so she could calm down and get her emotions under control before returning to the farm. And she liked shopping for him, liked picturing him in the clothes she found. Telling herself that she was fulfilling a need—he had practically nothing—and that he'd be wearing that shirt long after they parted company, somehow brought her peace. Maybe he'd think of her occasionally when he wore it....

She knew he'd find it odd that she was so keen on devoting her resources to him, since he was leaving in a few days and they'd probably never see each other again. But so what? She was going to do whatever she had to in order to cope with life as she currently knew it. If shopping for Levi buoyed her spirits, she'd shop for Levi. It might cost her a few bucks, but it wasn't as if she was buying him a sports car.

Of course, the fact that she'd also bought condoms—and gone to the next town to do it so she wouldn't have to look someone she knew in the eye while paying—was a little revealing. But no one had to know about that. She'd already hidden them in her purse.

As soon as she cut the engine, he strode toward her, Rifle at his heels.

"Well, would you look at that!" she said as she opened the door.

He glanced behind him. "Look at what?"

More pleased to see him than she probably should've been, she grinned. "Rifle is dogging your every foot-step—so to speak. The two of you have become friends in spite of your ugly encounter with Spike and Sauron."

"Who're Spike and Sauron? The pit bulls?"

"That would be them."

Bending slightly, he scratched behind her dog's ears. "This is a good animal. Smart. Loyal. Eager to please."

"I just hope he doesn't try to go with you when you leave," she said with a laugh. Rifle had never shown much interest in another human. She'd always come first. But he seemed to be quite taken with Levi. Although she understood the attraction, Callie couldn't avoid feeling a twinge of jealousy. Levi possessed some indefinable quality that made him even more appeal-ing than his handsome face and well-toned body would warrant on their own.

Levi straightened. "Doubt he'd fit on the back of my bike."

"It looks like he'd follow you anywhere."

Rifle seemed able to tell that he was the subject of their conversation. The tags on his collar jingled as he trotted over to lick her hand. But then he returned to Levi's side.

"Traitor," she grumbled.

Levi didn't comment further on the dog's behavior. His mind was clearly on something else. "So...you're okay?"

She'd tried to wait long enough that the evidence of her tears would be gone, and she'd thought she'd done that, so this surprised her. "Of course. Why wouldn't I be?"

"You left hours ago. I was beginning to worry."

"That you might have to cook your own dinner?" she teased.

His hands rested on his hips, above the tool belt he'd put on. "That you might've run into trouble."

"What kind of trouble?" She hoped he wasn't going to mention her pale face or her noticeable fatigue. Now that she was home, she wanted to forget about her condition, at least for a few hours. Why ruin whatever time she had left by constantly fretting? Facing reality as she'd faced it this morning had been emotionally exhausting. She couldn't continue to carry such a heavy load. She had to rely on hope, which was what she'd been doing so far. Surely her doctor would call with good news at some point—some point *soon*.

"Denny and Powell came by."

She'd just turned to get the chambray shirt she'd purchased at the Western clothing store in town. She was eager to show it to him. But at this, she froze. "They spoke to you?"

"Briefly. I think they were startled to find me here. It was obvious they expected me to be gone."

A trickle of unease ran through her. "What'd they want?"

"They were looking for you, had something for you to sign."

"Did they try to start anything?"

"No. They kept their distance."

Apparently, they weren't as dumb as they looked.

But she feared they might be as mean. "What was it they had for me to sign?"

"I didn't see it and I didn't ask. I think it's safe to assume it's something that'll save their dogs."

"Why didn't they have *you* sign it?"

"They probably knew better than to ask."

"I can't sign it, either."

His biceps bulged as he folded his arms. "Maybe you should."

Grabbing the sack she'd been reaching for earlier, she climbed out. "Why?"

"I don't want them bothering you after I'm gone."

"But those dogs are dangerous." She pointed at his right arm, which had more stitches than his left. "I'm not likely to forget that, not after spending all night helping Godfrey stitch you up."

"Maybe it was a freak incident. Maybe a noise or a smell evoked an old memory that set them off and it'll never happen again. Dogs don't usually attack like that unless they come from some irresponsible backyard breeder or they've got owners who train them to be vicious."

"Both of those things are probably true in this case. And even if they're not, it doesn't change the fact that they *did* attack you. Did it happen on the street, without provocation, like you said?"

"Yes."

She hugged her bags to her chest, dropping her keys in her purse as she did. "Then how can we take the risk?"

With a sigh, he squinted into the distance before returning his attention to her face. "I'm uncomfortable where Denny and Powell are concerned. They have no respect for women. They won't let you be the only obstacle standing between them and what they want. They feel they should be able to overcome something as…inconsequential as a small-town girl who's stuck her nose in their business."

Outraged, she stared at him. "That's what they said?"

"Basically they said that the night I hit Powell. If you don't give them what they want, I'm afraid they might… retaliate. And if I'm not here to—"

She waved his words away before he could finish. "They wouldn't be so stupid as to make a bad situation worse."

"Prisons are full of people who are just that stupid," he pointed out.

Her day had been bad enough. She didn't want to think about this. "You're worried for nothing. If they were that concerned about their dogs, they should've been more careful with them."

"They don't see that they have any responsibility in this."

"Doesn't change the fact that they do." She jerked her head toward the house, indicating that he should follow her. "Come on in and get showered."

"I can shower in the barn."

"It's okay. You can use my bathroom." She smiled, somehow happy in spite of everything. "I bought you another shirt, by the way."

"You…*what?*"

Because she'd expected this kind of reaction, she kept walking. "It was on sale. You won't be able to wear it much until later in the year, since it has long sleeves, but it's going to look *great* on you."

"Callie, I'm not some stray animal you've found that you need to take care of...."

She raised a hand. "You're reading too much into it. I had fun picking it out, that's all."

The shirt really didn't hold any significance, she told herself. Buying it for him was a pleasant diversion, her way of helping him.

But what about the condoms?

Dinner wasn't difficult to throw together. Callie already had her mother's lasagna, which she couldn't eat, so that meant there'd be plenty for Levi. She couldn't have the garlic bread she served, either, but planned to fill up on the salad she'd made to go with everything else.

Levi, hair damp from his shower, appeared in the kitchen smelling like her beauty soap.

"Vanilla, huh?" She grinned as she heard his tread behind her but didn't look back. She was too busy pulling the bread from the oven. "Smells good on you."

"If I wanted to get clean, perfumed soap seemed to be my only choice."

"You could've asked me for something else." She set the pan on top of the stove.

"It's okay. It's not like a flowery scent. Why *can't* a guy smell like homemade cookies?"

She could tell he was teasing. "At least you're comfortable with your masculinity."

"It seems pointless to be any other way. So...what do you think?"

After closing the oven with her foot, she turned to see that he was wearing his new shirt. She thought it was perfect. But she didn't want to act *too* pleased. "It fits. Do you like it?"

"I do. But it's too hot to wear tonight."

They were experiencing higher temperatures than normal, even for summer. She had the windows open and a fan whirring in the living room, like her grandparents had always done in the warmer months. "It'll keep."

Rifle approached Levi, tail wagging. Her dog craved his attention as much as she did, she thought wryly.

"Hey, boy." Levi crouched to acknowledge him. "Do I smell like Callie?"

"Maybe *that's* why he likes you."

"He liked me before."

When he began to strip off the shirt, Callie paused to stare.

He raised his eyebrows when he noticed, and she shrugged. "Doesn't hurt to look," she said with a laugh, but then she made herself turn back to the counter and start dishing up the food.

By the time she faced him again, he was wearing the clean T-shirt he'd brought in with him and was sitting in his usual place.

"I'm starved," he said.

The longer she was home, the better she felt. He seemed relaxed and content, too—far more relaxed and content than he'd been when he'd awakened here last Tuesday.

"You get much done today?" she asked.

"Nearly finished the roof. That old wood was more deteriorated than I realized. I had to remove a huge section of it."

"I'll pay you for the extra hours."

"There's no need for that. I'm satisfied with our

trade. I just wanted to let you know why it's going to take longer than I expected."

For a change, Callie was hungry. Sitting across from him, she ate instead of just watching.

"Finally," he said.

"What?"

He motioned to her plate. "That's the first time I've seen you eat."

"Glad I could make you happy."

"I'm easy to please."

She thought maybe they'd fall into the silence that had marked their earlier meals, but tonight he wanted to talk. He avoided certain subjects—or perhaps she just imagined he was avoiding them because she was sensitive about asking certain questions—but he seemed willing enough to share details about the places he'd visited since returning from Afghanistan. He'd been to almost every state, appreciated something about all of them. But he was particularly enamored with southern Utah.

"Have you ever been there?" he asked.

"No. What's so great about it?"

"There's Zion National Park, Arches National Park, Moab and the surrounding area, which they call Canyonlands."

"I've been to the Grand Canyon in Arizona. We went on a long driving vacation the summer I was fourteen."

"I like the Grand Canyon. But I already knew it would be spectacular. Southern Utah came as a surprise."

"Did you get to do much traveling as a kid?"

"Not really."

"You grew up in Seattle, right? Is that where your folks are?"

She knew this was a personal question, the kind she recognized as more or less off-limits. But Callie couldn't resist. He'd helped her the entire night she'd been sick—even slept in her bed—yet she didn't know the most basic facts about his life or background.

His hesitation made her self-conscious about having asked, but then he answered, "I don't know where my mother is."

"Because…"

"She took my baby sister and got out while she could."

The food in Callie's mouth sat there, suddenly tasteless. She took a drink of water so she could swallow it. "How old were you?"

"Ten."

"How old was she?"

"Ellen? Or my mother?"

"Both, I guess."

"Ellen was four. My mother must've been about… my age," he said as if he was slightly surprised to make that connection.

"And you are…"

"Twenty-seven."

Five years younger than she was, like she'd guessed. "She had you when she was *seventeen?*"

"Yes. My father was eighteen. They married right out of high school, when I was one."

"But the marriage didn't work."

He chuckled bitterly. "No."

She moved some of the celery from her salad around

on her plate. "Why didn't your mother take *you* when she left?"

A muscle flexed in his cheek. "Because she knew my father would hunt her down and kill her if she did."

Callie set her fork to the side of her plate. She hoped he didn't mean "kill" in its literal sense, but she got the impression he did. "Was he violent?"

"He could get physical. He was also controlling." He shook his head. "Impossible to live with."

"How did she get away with taking his daughter?"

Levi stopped eating, too. He seemed to be looking at his past life like something he'd buried long ago and just unearthed, something he hadn't particularly treasured but about which he felt a mild curiosity. "He wasn't all that excited about having a girl."

"You meant more to him?"

"Only because I'd already shown an aptitude for martial arts."

"Why would he care so much about that?"

"He'd always wanted to be a champion, a recognized force in the industry. But an old injury kept him from going very far in competition. So he decided to make his mark a different way. He opened his own dojo and started to train others, was determined to turn out some of the world's best fighters."

"And you were one of them."

"I was winning and providing him with the championships he needed, yes." His smile took on a bitter slant. "He was never prouder than when I took home another trophy. We barely had enough for groceries, yet he spent thousands having special cases built at the dojo just so he could display them."

"You must've made him look like a great sensei."

"He *was* a good sensei. He just wasn't a good dad."

Callie wished she could touch Levi, let him know he wasn't as alone as he probably felt. He seemed so isolated, sitting there mired in such dark memories. "Did you like competing?"

He shrugged. "For the most part."

The sun was going down. She leaned forward to light the candle she'd put on the table. "So why'd you join the army?"

"To get away from him."

The flame on the end of the candle flickered and cast moving shadows on his lean face. "Was he abusive with you, too?"

"Absolutely. Nothing too bad, like broken bones, but he certainly got violent. That's not why I left, though. I was afraid I'd turn on him someday, hurt him—maybe even kill him. I had to get out before that day came."

Obviously, he was dealing with a great deal of anger and resentment. She'd guessed that from his situation. She just hadn't known the cause of it. "I see."

He nursed the glass of chardonnay she'd served him. Because of her condition, she had to avoid alcohol as avidly as she avoided salt, but she liked to keep a bottle of wine on hand for her friends. She knew they'd guess something was up if she didn't. They'd always shared a bottle when they had dinner in the past.

"What about your parents?" he asked.

His bottom lip, wet from the wine, drew her attention. He had a nice mouth—not that she was wise to notice. That fell into the same category as buying rubbers.

"They're great." She got up and carried her plate to the sink. "Very loving. Just saw them today."

"Any siblings?"

"Nope. I'm an only child. Due to fertility problems, my parents had me late in life. I'm their 'miracle,' the answer to their prayers." She indulged in a sentimental smile. "They've doted on me my whole life."

"Doesn't seem to have spoiled you."

"I don't think you can ruin anyone with love."

For a few seconds, only the water running in the sink and the thump of Rifle's tail hitting the floor where he lay in the corner broke the silence.

"So…what's the hardest thing you've ever dealt with?" Levi asked.

She almost laughed. He'd said that as if he expected her to struggle for an answer. He'd grown up without a mother, and he'd had an abusive, controlling father. Then he'd gone to war and, if those names on his arm were as significant as she assumed, he'd watched several of his friends die. But at least he'd survived. At least he was finished staring death in the face and now had his whole life ahead of him.

"You can't think of anything?" Levi prompted when she didn't reply.

Not that she wanted to share… "I guess I'd have to say…what I've done with Kyle."

"You wish you hadn't slept with him?"

She shut off the water and turned toward him. "It was a mistake."

"Because…"

"It didn't happen for the right reasons."

He seemed to consider that. "Why'd you do it?"

"A number of factors led up to it."

Leaning back as if he was all set to listen but skeptical he could be convinced, he folded his arms. "Like…"

"A lack of options, for one. This is a small town."

"That means you have to sleep with your friends?"

She flushed at his facetious tone. "No, but there aren't a lot of romantic options here. So we've got two close friends, male and female, spending a great deal of time together in a town where there aren't that many people to date. The guy has just come through a nasty divorce and is reeling from it. The woman knows he needs love and attention and that he's everything she should want."

Levi balanced his chair on its back legs. "Basically, you considered him."

"I *what?*"

"You thought you might like to become more than friends."

She dried her hands on a dish towel before tossing it aside. "I think he and I both felt that way at various points. It would've made life so easy if we could fall in love. We're ready to settle down. We want children before we get too much older. We know the other is a good person, a trustworthy person. The only problem is that the nature of our love didn't change just because we went to bed together."

"So why can't you forget it? You tried. It didn't work. Move on."

Typical guy. Practical in the extreme. "Because every time we see each other I'm reminded. I'm also afraid he might expect another…encounter, and that it'll be hard to explain why my answer has to be no when it was 'yes' just a few weeks ago."

"Can't you avoid him?"

"No." She knew he was teasing, but she explained, anyway. "He's one of my best friends. Hence, the problem."

He dropped his chair on all fours long enough to scoop the last of his lasagna into his mouth. "Was he your first?"

"At thirty-two?" She chuckled. "I've lived a sheltered life but not quite *that* sheltered. No, he wasn't my first. But I wish he had been."

"He was that good?"

"My first was that bad."

"Tell me about him."

"Peter was…a surprise. And definitely not a pleasant one."

"This is getting more interesting by the minute." Levi poured himself another glass of wine. He lifted the bottle to offer her some, but she shook her head. "Man, you eat healthy," he said. "When you eat at all."

"I'm doing the best I can."

"Anyway, what was so surprising about Peter?"

"At first, I didn't think there was anything unusual about him. He was two years older than me. Very suave. Very popular. Great tennis player. I fell head over heels."

"Until…"

"He told me he was gay."

He gaped at her. "You're serious?"

"Completely."

"And you had no clue?"

"None. I mean…I knew he wasn't that interested in making love. He'd be very affectionate in public, which would make me think all was well. But once we got behind closed doors he'd withdraw. I had to instigate almost every encounter, and he didn't do a very good job of participating when we did have sex."

Holding his glass loosely in both hands, he propped his elbows on the table. "Meaning…"

"You can't guess?"

"Spell it out for me."

She thought she detected a hint of humor in his voice, but answered, anyway. "It was difficult to arouse him."

"What did he say when he couldn't get it up?"

"He'd blame it on me. He'd complain that I didn't know what a man liked. That I wasn't skinny enough. That I was too forward. He hinted I was oversexed. You name it."

"Most men would consider themselves lucky to find a woman who's oversexed," he joked. "How old were you when you were with him?"

"Twenty."

"And how long were you together before you learned the truth?"

"He came out when he broke up with me. We'd been dating nine months."

He hooked an arm over the back of his chair. "That must've been a terrible day."

"Then why are you laughing?" She tried to act mad, but his laugh was so rare she couldn't help responding with a grudging smile.

"I just can't imagine someone who's gay getting with someone who…"

"Who what?" Curious now, she quit smiling.

"Who looks like you, has a body like yours. It's what fantasies are made of."

Even *his* fantasies? Because he didn't seem particularly interested. She doubted his reasons for not wanting to touch her were the same as Peter's. The way Levi looked at her was completely different. But there was *something* holding him back.

"Maybe that's why he told me I should be flattered," she said. "When I asked him why he got with me in the first place, he said he thought if any woman could turn him on, it would be me." Tempted to break down and have a drink, she eyed the wine bottle. If she was going to die, anyway, it seemed pointless to abstain. But she couldn't extinguish that small hope....

"That was how he justified lying to you for so long."

She nodded. "And...it didn't feel like a compliment at the time."

"No wonder. Since he was your first, you might not have realized that it isn't normal to have to work so hard to keep a man aroused—certainly at that age."

She wondered how difficult it would be to keep *him* aroused.... "I heard my friends talking about how their boyfriends behaved, but I figured everyone was different. I didn't want to break up with him just because he couldn't maintain an erection."

"You say that like it's a minor thing," he said with another laugh.

"I wanted a more fulfilling sex life. But, like I said, he had me convinced it was *my* fault." She smacked her head. "Ugh, I was so naive! And what made it worse was that I felt this terrible sense of failure because I hadn't been attractive enough to succeed, the way he thought I could."

"Callie, you can't change someone's sexual orientation."

"I understand that *now*. But this was my first love, remember?"

"Where is he these days?"

"Last I heard, he was living with a partner in San Francisco."

Twirling the stem of his glass, he watched the liquid swirl inside. "Have you ever been with anyone else?"

"Other than Kyle? No. Only a one-night stand that happened a few days after Peter's big announcement. I decided I was going to get laid by someone who knew what to do with a woman."

"How'd that go?"

"Not so great."

"You figured you deserved an orgasm after everything you'd been through."

"Mostly I just wanted to feel attractive. Desired."

"And?"

"That actually turned out to be the worst experience of all."

"Why?"

She tried to make a joke out of it. "Number one, there was no orgasm."

He gave her a pouting look. "Poor you."

"And number two, making love with a stranger isn't all it's cracked up to be." She grimaced. "I just couldn't get into it. It made me feel cheap and foolish. Degraded."

"I think number two explains number one. Who was the guy?"

"I don't remember his name. I've blocked it out."

He got up and brought his plate over. But after he put it on the counter he didn't move away. She could feel the heat of his body directly behind her, knew if she stepped back by even an inch she'd brush up against him, which was exactly what she wanted to do.

"So you didn't buy that lingerie for Kyle," he said, his mouth close to her ear.

"No," she whispered.

When she felt his lips slide along the sensitive skin at her neck, she caught her breath and let her eyes close. She kept telling herself that she didn't know Levi well enough to want him so badly. But right now that didn't seem to matter. There was none of the confusion she'd experienced with Peter, none of the revulsion she'd experienced with Rebound Man and none of the misgivings she'd experienced with Kyle. That made her glad she'd bought condoms....

But just as she was about to turn so she could meet his mouth with her own, he withdrew.

"I'm sorry, pretty Callie. I'm not the right man for you," he murmured and, to add insult to injury, had to order Rifle to stay inside when he went out to the barn.

13

Sitting on the bed in the narrow bunkhouse, Levi stared at the four walls surrounding him. No doubt he'd just confused Callie even more. He'd acted as if he wanted her—physically, he did—but he couldn't take her to bed. It was too great a betrayal of Behrukh.

He closed his eyes as he remembered what sex had been like with the only woman he'd ever loved. Heady. Sensuous. All-consuming. The memories alone made him weak with longing. *If only...*

There were a million *if onlys* that went through his mind whenever he thought of Behrukh, and each one brought its own particular brand of torment. *If only,* after growing up under his father's thumb, he hadn't been so starved for everything a woman could offer. *If only* he hadn't been so drawn to the softness of her body, the gentleness of her touch, the sweetness of her kiss. Maybe he wouldn't have made such a terrible mistake.

I don't think you can ruin anyone with love.

Callie had said that. She believed it. But it wasn't true. You *could* destroy someone with love. He knew because he'd done it—and had destroyed himself in the process.

* * *

When Callie's phone rang, she hesitated to pick up. Several of her friends had tried to reach her, some more than once. She felt terrible for not being more responsive. But she was finding it harder and harder to pretend that everything was okay. And before she revealed the truth to them, she *had* to tell her parents.

Just how was she going to do that? Her visit today had been so…poignant. There was her mother rolling down the hall in her wheelchair, looking more fragile than ever, her father hugging her with the unabashed love of a doting parent. She couldn't think of those things without flinching.

But it wasn't only the secret about her health that kept her from answering her phone. She didn't want to deal with any accusations regarding her involvement with Kyle. After Kyle's behavior this morning, Cheyenne and Eve and the others had to suspect, since there'd been earlier evidence that had resulted in questions.

Maybe she should simply tell the truth about Kyle and apologize. Maybe that would rid her of the guilt and shame. It would lighten *part* of the load she was carrying, wouldn't it?

But did she really want the others to know?

Absolutely not. Especially if she was going to die. She hated the thought that news of her indiscretion might become one of their last memories of her.

Besides, was her and Kyle's secret any of their business? Not in some ways and, as he'd said, perhaps those were the ways that really mattered. She and Kyle were adults. They'd both consented to their encounters, just as they'd both agreed to keep their mouths shut.

She checked to see whose call she'd just missed.

Eve's. The list was getting extensive. Kyle had tried her three times. Cheyenne, Sophia and Baxter had each called once. Even Noah and Ted had reached out to see if she was okay. They could all sense that something was wrong.

If she told them about Kyle, they'd never guess she was fighting a much bigger battle. That could buy her some time, enough for her doctor to come up with the liver she needed—or, barring that, for her to find a way to tell her parents. Her doctor kept asking her to bring a family member to the clinic. He wanted to be sure she had the proper support at home. Fortunately, she'd been so consistent in saying she had the best parents and friends in the world that he'd let this stipulation slide.

"What do I do?" she asked Rifle, who paced with her along one side of the bed.

Ears perked up, he barked in response and licked her hand, which made her smile.

"I love you," she told him. "Even if you *are* willing to throw me over for Levi."

He tilted his head as if he didn't understand why she'd accuse him of betrayal. She laughed; he could always make her feel better. But then her phone rang again and, since she had it in her hand, she could easily see who it was. Kyle.

He was the last person she wanted to talk to. But he also felt safer than Eve because he already knew one of her secrets.

"I've put myself in such a situation where he's concerned," she confided to Rifle. Then she took a deep breath and answered. She had to call all the rest of her friends back tonight. She might as well take this call now.

"There you are!" he said. "You had me so damn worried I was getting ready to drive over there."

Good thing she'd answered. "I'm fine. I keep telling everyone that. I'm fine, I'm fine, I'm *fine!* Why do you keep asking?"

When he didn't respond, she knew she'd been far too emphatic. Somehow she had to calm down. She didn't have the right to feel sorry for herself. Until Valentine's Day, she'd had a perfect life. She'd had wonderful parents, a happy childhood, devoted friends. Maybe she hadn't had a particularly great sex life or fallen head over heels in love, the way she'd dreamed of doing while watching *Sleeping Beauty* and *Cinderella* as a little girl, but what was that compared with all the rest?

Some people *never* experienced the peace and contentment she'd taken for granted.

Kyle cleared his throat, no doubt trying to figure out what to say. "Callie, I—"

She broke in before he could offer yet another apology. "I think we should tell."

"What?"

"You heard me. We should tell the others. About us."

"Hell, no! What's there to be gained from that?"

When she pivoted in front of her dresser, she barely avoided tripping over her dog, who seemed reluctant to settle down for the night until she did. "I hate feeling as if…as if we've wronged them in some way."

"How have we wronged *them?*"

"Our actions have threatened the cohesiveness of the group, changed the chemistry. You know that."

Rifle barked as if he agreed.

"Our actions haven't threatened anything," Kyle insisted. "Because we're not going to let what happened come between us. We've talked about this already."

"That's easier said than done, Kyle."

"Why can't you just let it go? Or are you angry with *me* about what we did?"

With her foot she smoothed a wrinkle in the throw rug covering the hardwood floor. "I'm not *blaming* you, if that's what you're asking. I'm angry with myself for allowing the situation to get out of control."

"We got caught up in what was going on between us at the time. I think we both wondered…*what if,* thought it might lead somewhere. At least, *I* did. And, if it helps, I take full responsibility for dragging you into it. Just please tell me that's not what's eating you up inside!"

She squeezed her forehead. She didn't want to put Kyle through this. She wasn't sure what she was doing, why she was making such an issue out of a handful of sexual encounters that they'd both enjoyed. Maybe it was because she'd experienced so few sexual encounters in her life.

"Are you afraid we might let it happen again?" he asked.

That had been the problem over the past few weeks. Once they'd crossed that line, it was too easy to slip over it again. They were young and full of the hormones that went with their stage of life—and now they were comfortable getting naked together.

But there'd been no danger of sleeping with Kyle since Levi had shown up. Callie hadn't even thought of it, except to regret what she'd done.

Kyle guessed the truth before she could answer. "Not anymore, right?"

"Kyle, I care about you. I'm just going through a hard time."

"Are you *that* attracted to Levi?"

She felt ready to melt just *remembering* Levi's lips on her neck, and it had been the slightest touch. It shouldn't have had such a profound effect on her. But it did. "Yes."

Kyle muttered a curse. "Listen," he said, "being with this…*drifter* wouldn't be any better than being with me. I'm not saying that because I'm…trying to…to get back in your pants. I enjoyed our time together, don't get me wrong—"

"You don't have to be so diplomatic, Kyle."

"It's true, or I wouldn't have come back for more. But you were right when you said I'm still in love with Olivia. I'm not sure I'll ever get over her."

She was beginning to feel sorry for him again. "Don't say that."

"Fine. Maybe that's not true and I'll hardly remember her name in a few months—even though I have to see her at every family event. Either way, Levi worries me. For one thing, he's quite a bit younger than you."

"Five years is quite a bit?" Perhaps it was to some people, but as long as he was an adult, what did age matter to someone in her situation? She couldn't establish a permanent relationship with him, anyway.

"It's not just his age. He doesn't have a job. And he obviously has some mental problems."

"What do you mean?"

"Normal people don't go wandering around like that."

She raked a hand through her hair. "Look what's happening, Kyle. Look what sleeping together has produced. You've never tried to tell me who I can get involved with before."

"I'm not doing it because I'm being possessive! It's because I feel I sort of…left you vulnerable. I don't want to be responsible for getting you hurt."

"You didn't leave me vulnerable."

"Then what's going on?"

She toyed with the jewelry holder sitting on her dresser. "I can't explain it. He…does something to me. I'm *drawn* to him."

"Sexually?"

"Yes! That, too." *Especially* that. "Bottom line, I like that he's here."

A moment of silence indicated a change in tone. "Do your parents know you have a stranger staying with you at the farm?"

"We talked about it today."

"They don't mind?"

They hadn't been *happy* about it, but they seemed willing to trust her judgment. "No."

"Maybe I wouldn't, either, except…I can't help thinking that he's hanging around hoping to get lucky. Once he obtains what he wants, he'll take off."

He wasn't hanging around for sex. Callie knew that already. "Stop. He hasn't made one attempt to take my clothes off. If getting lucky is what he's after, I'd know it by now."

A beep signaled that she had another call.

It was Godfrey. She told Kyle she had to go.

"We'll get past what we did," he said before she could switch over.

"I hope so."

"I promise. Try and forget about it, okay?"

After she'd agreed to do that, he hung up and she connected with the incoming call. "Godfrey, how are you?"

"Fine. You?"

"Good." She forced a smile so it would reflect in her voice. "What's going on?"

"Just calling to give you an update on the pit bulls."

"Thank you. What's the latest?"

"Once we proved the dogs had all their shots, the county decided to fine Denny and let them live."

She stopped pacing. "That's it? He'll get them back?"

"That was the original plan. He's not a permanent resident. We thought he'd take the dogs and go, leave the area. No one around here likes killing animals."

That was certainly the case with Callie. But those stitches on Levi's arm created a horrific picture of what had occurred. "You said that was the *original* plan."

"It was…until one of the dogs tried to take off the hand of a volunteer who was attempting to feed it."

Callie hated hearing this—but she wasn't surprised. It confirmed that another attack would likely occur if the dogs were released. "So now animal control is going to put them down?"

"That's what'll happen to Sauron. Denny can still save Spike. He might only have attacked Levi because he was following the lead of Sauron, who's more aggressive. He seems to behave as long as he's kept separate."

"So pack mentality got him in trouble."

"That's my guess. But once a dog like that gets a taste for blood he might not settle down. It's a risk to release him, like I said, but no one, especially me, wants to be responsible for euthanizing an animal that could live if only it had a more responsible owner."

"How did Denny take the news?"

"He's mad as hell. Said his dogs wouldn't even be

in the shelter if it wasn't for Levi trespassing on his property."

Too worn down to keep moving, Callie perched on the edge of her bed. "How does he explain this latest show of aggression?"

"Claims Sauron acted up only because he's in unfamiliar territory, that he got spooked." He sighed. "Believe me, he has all kinds of excuses. But there's nothing he can do at this point. When Sauron attacked again… that sealed his fate."

"As much as I don't care for Denny, I feel bad. I know that in his own way he loves those dogs. It would kill me to lose Rifle." Who was sitting in front of her, wagging his tail every time she looked at him.

"He'll have Spike—if he pays the fine and Spike doesn't act out before then."

Keeping one was better than losing them both….

"How's Levi doing?" Godfrey asked.

She summoned the energy to get up so she could saunter over to the window and gaze out at the barn. Light gleamed around the edges of its wide, heavy doors. Levi was still up. "His wounds seem to be healing. But he's been working hard, despite those stitches."

"He can take it—he's young and strong. If he's around in a few more days, give me a holler. I'll stop by and remove his stitches. It's not like they're the fancy disappearing kind. I had to make do with what I had."

"We're grateful. Thanks for everything," she said. Then she shook her head as she hung up. *We're* grateful? She'd said that as if they were a couple….

Rifle jumped on Callie's bed and howled at the ceiling, waking her from a deep sleep.

"What is it? What's going on?" she gasped, struggling to come to full awareness.

He didn't wait for her to gain her bearings. He barked, howled, then barked again and jumped down, after which he dashed out of her bedroom.

"Rifle! What's wrong with you? Come here, boy!" She managed a short whistle despite her grogginess, but the dog wouldn't obey. He was going berserk out in the living room—running and barking and throwing himself against the front door, from the sounds of it.

Her heart pounded as her mind raced. Did they have another visitor?

That was her first guess. But Rifle wasn't acting the way he'd behaved when Levi showed up—or even how he'd behaved when the steroid-crazed Denny and Powell paid her a visit. Her German shepherd wasn't trying to scare off an intruder or make her aware that they had company. He was upset.

No, he was frantic. Why?

A crash—the sound of shattering glass—made her blood run cold.

Had someone just broken in? If so, they'd managed to silence Rifle. She could no longer hear him barking.

"Oh, God!" As she scrambled out of bed, she considered pulling on a robe but didn't dare take the time. Already dressed in a pair of silky pajama shorts and a matching spaghetti-strap top, she figured that would have to be good enough. She was afraid her dog had been killed—and that she might be next!

"Rifle?" she called while searching for her pellet gun. If her dog was dead, she was going to need some way to defend herself. There was no telling if Levi even knew they had trouble. It wasn't as if he had a cell phone she could call.

She found the pellet gun leaning against the wall in her closet, where she'd put it yesterday. But before she could reach the living room she caught a whiff of smoke and paused. Something was burning! The house?

Fires were supposed to be loud, but…she couldn't hear any crackling.

Maybe someone had thrown a bottle rocket through the front window and it was setting the carpet on fire….

"Rifle!" Now she felt completely frantic. But she forced herself to proceed with caution. She didn't want to be stupid, didn't want to walk into trouble.

Gun raised, she crept out of her room and scanned the shadowy furniture, searching for her dog, for any sign of fire, for an intruder. Besides the broken window, she couldn't see anything amiss. Her dog was simply…gone.

Then she heard Rifle bellowing and realized he was outside.

What the heck? Relieved but perplexed, she kept her gun at the ready and slid over to the window to peer out.

Her jaw dropped and her arms sagged to the point her weapon nearly slipped from her hands. Bright orange-and-gold flames leaped from the barn, sending up a roiling black smoke.

She'd found the source of the smell.

And something else became clear. There was no glass on the carpet. No one had broken her window, attempting to get *in*. Her dog had jumped through it, desperate to get *out*.

Rifle was going for Levi. She could hear his howl as he reached the barn. But the structure appeared to be consumed by flames, and Callie feared it was already too late.

14

Levi felt a tug on his arm, then several sharp teeth sank into his flesh. He assumed he was being attacked again—and yet he couldn't fight. He didn't have the strength. His mind ordered him to react, to defend himself, but his body was sluggish and resistant.

It wasn't real, he decided. He was having one of those dreams, the kind where he ran and ran but never went anywhere. This dream involved dogs because he'd recently had a bad experience with them.

As soon as his mind conjured up that answer, which seemed to make sense, he began to sink back into sleep. That was all he wanted to do...drift away into peaceful nothingness. He didn't have to muster the energy to fight if the threat wasn't real—

But those damn teeth.

Something dragged him halfway out of bed before letting go. Then the animal—it had to be a dog because of the barking—jumped on top of him, leaped off and barked some more before trying to drag him farther.

When fresh pain lanced through his arm, Levi finally got mad enough to battle the lethargy. Damn it! He wasn't going to be mauled again!

He came up swinging, which sent the dog flying, but

the determined animal crept toward him again. Only this time, he didn't come so close. He made a racket while dancing around, just out of reach.

It wasn't until Levi tried to shout at the damn thing to get away and couldn't draw enough breath to do so that he recognized Rifle. At the same moment, it occurred to him that the night was far hotter than any he'd ever experienced. The heat pressed in on him from all sides.

What was going on?

Then it hit him. This might be surreal, but it wasn't a dream. Neither was it another dog attack. He was in his room in the barn at Callie's, and Rifle was trying to wake him because the barn was on fire.

Shit! Panic gave him a burst of energy. As he glanced around, taking in the flames devouring the old wood, he couldn't believe his eyes. The fire had sucked most of the oxygen out of the enclosed space, leaving carbon monoxide and Lord knew what other noxious gases. No wonder he couldn't seem to come around. That was what he'd been breathing—what he was *still* breathing.

"Go!" He managed a hoarse cry to the dog and stumbled to his feet. The back door hung slightly ajar. He pointed at it while lunging forward. "I'm up! Get out!"

The dog started to obey, but once he got to the door he doubled back to prod Levi on.

Levi wasn't sure he would've reached the yard without Rifle's badgering. The dog provided him with a focus as well as a constant reminder. *Crouch low. Keep moving.* He thought that over and over—because the darkness that hovered at the edges of his mind could've overtaken him at any time. He had to push it away, resist its strange allure, or he wouldn't come out of this alive.

What was probably only a few seconds seemed like

an eternity, but he finally staggered through the door—
and almost knocked Callie to the ground. She was just
entering the barn, obviously looking for him and her
dog.

"Get back!" He dragged her with him into the cool,
clear night, but it wasn't easy. His skin felt as if it was
melting off, and his lungs were seared. He struggled
to get enough oxygen even now that he was away from
the worst of the smoke.

But luckily, no one seemed to be hurt. His bike was,
for the moment, safe in the clearing. And he couldn't
see any flames coming from the house. Those things
bolstered his strength. The fire seemed to be concentrated in one place—but it wouldn't be long before it
began to spread....

Callie changed out of her pajamas before heading
back outside. She also gathered up the clothes Levi had
in the laundry to take out to him, since he was in his
underwear and couldn't go into the barn to reclaim what
he'd removed when he went to bed. Fortunately, adrenaline lent her the strength she needed to remain on her
feet. Otherwise, she doubted a person in her condition
would be able to hold up under such a strain. But she
was determined to battle through the fatigue for the
sake of the farm.

Levi had her gardening hose, which was long enough
to reach almost anywhere in the clearing. He was using
it to wet the buildings closest to the fire so that one of
the sparks floating in the air wouldn't cause something
else to ignite.

But he needed to get off the premises. The fire department was on its way. No doubt the police would fol-

low. They'd want to know what had started the blaze. *She* wanted to know the same thing. After hearing Godfrey tell her how upset Denny was, she suspected this was the retribution he and Powell had promised a couple of nights ago, but she wasn't about to make any accusations. Not until she learned more about the origins of the fire.

"Let me take over," she said. "You need to put these on and get out of here."

He resisted her attempt to give him his jeans and grab the hose. "Stand back, I've got it."

"The fire department will arrive any minute!"

"You look like you're about to keel over from shock. I'm not going to hand this off to you."

The way she looked had nothing to do with the shock—or not that much. But she was glad she didn't have to lie. He'd supplied his own answer. "You're the one who came coughing and stumbling out of the barn only a few minutes ago."

"I'm fine. Take Rifle and go in the house so the two of you don't get hurt."

Rifle was darting back and forth, barking at the fire as if he could scare it away.

"If the fire department doesn't get here soon, we won't be able to keep this from spreading," he said. "I'll come for you if it gets anywhere close to the house."

Callie was afraid it would destroy the entire farm. Fortunately, Godfrey lived far enough away that it wouldn't threaten his property. He had no clue there was trouble, or she knew he'd be here, doing what he could to help. Anyway, this was her problem, not Levi's, especially when protecting it put him at risk. "Don't you understand? Chief Stacy or someone else will come, too." She had to shout to be heard over the fire and the splat of water hitting wood. "They'll question you, maybe discover something that'll lead them to those speeding tickets."

When she tried to take the hose again, he held it away from her. "I'm not leaving this to you!"

"But I'm worried." She didn't want his gallantry rewarded with jail time. "They could lock you up if…if what you're running from is serious enough."

"Some things are worth doing time for."

His response brought Callie a measure of relief. Whatever he'd done in the past couldn't be too bad or he wouldn't take that chance.

"You like this place as much as I do," she said.

"I was talking about *you*," he responded matter-of-factly. Then he asked her to hold the hose so he could jerk on his clothes and went to get another ladder from the garden shed. The one he'd been using to fix the barn roof was too close to the blaze, and he couldn't retrieve it. This was shorter, but tall enough that he could reach the tops of the smaller buildings he was hoping to save. Her grandfather had used it to pick grapefruit and oranges.

Since the only other hose was connected to a spigot inside the barn, Callie could do nothing but watch him work. He was efficient and strong, and she was glad to have his help. She barely felt capable of staying on her feet; she couldn't have carried that hose and climbed up and down that ladder.

But there wasn't a lot he could do to put out the fire on his own. They needed more hands and more water. If the fire department didn't arrive soon, the barn, at least, would be completely destroyed.

She was about to go inside to call the dispatcher again when she heard the sirens and checked her phone. It'd taken them twenty-nine minutes, which wasn't bad for a country department made up almost entirely of volunteers.

Wringing her hands, she tried to wait as patiently as possible, but watching the flames leap higher and higher wasn't easy. It was important to her that the farm survive and go on, even if she didn't.

The dry, sun-bleached wood of the barn made such perfect tinder that putting out the fire turned into a real battle. After two hours, they managed to save part of the structure, but the back section had burned almost completely to cinders, including the room Levi had been using. Seeing the charred remains of the bed where he'd been sleeping when the fire broke out left quite an impression on him.

But he couldn't focus on that. Not right now. Chief Stacy had just approached him, asking if he'd come inside the house so they could talk.

Levi was tempted to put him off, to act as if he was still trying to salvage some of his belongings from the ashes. He might be able to slip away among the departing firemen, many of whom had shown up in their own vehicles. He'd fixed his bike, so he had transportation. Only his promise to paint the barn stood in his way, and there was no longer anything he could do to fulfill that commitment. It would take a minimum of two weeks to rebuild what had been damaged. And the labor would cost far more than the few hundred bucks he owed Callie.

He could send her the money for the impound fees

and those bike parts when he landed his next job. He had to leave, move on before his past caught up with him.

But he couldn't abandon her on the heels of such a traumatic event. If it was arson, as he suspected, there was a good chance Denny was behind it. Who else would do this? Besides Kyle and Godfrey, Levi hadn't interacted with anyone in Whiskey Creek. And Callie couldn't name one other person who might have a grudge against her.

Levi wanted Chief Stacy to look into the possibility of Seamans's involvement and, if he'd done it, hold him accountable. Levi wouldn't, couldn't, leave Callie alone until he knew she'd be safe—not when it was helping him that had endangered her in the first place.

"Well?" Stacy prompted.

Levi figured he was probably making the wrong decision, but he wiped his sooty hands on his jeans and agreed.

Stacy started toward the house with the expectation that Levi would follow, and Levi did. If he wasn't going to move on right away, he could only hope to get through the coming interview without divulging too much.

As soon as they walked in, Rifle dashed out of the kitchen where Callie was making breakfast. He hadn't liked being shut up, away from all the action. But he had a several cuts on his forelegs from when he'd jumped through the window, and Callie had wanted to clean them and keep him inside so he wouldn't sustain any more injuries.

"You two hungry?" She'd followed her dog as far as the doorway between the two rooms and was looking from one to the other as if eager to ascertain the tenor of their business.

"No, thanks. But a cup of coffee would be great." Stacy removed his hat and placed it on the table at his elbow as he took a seat in one of the wingback chairs.

"Levi?" she asked.

"Nothing for me." He carried the wooden bench from its location near the door over to the couch. His clothes were too dirty to sit on the upholstered furniture.

Callie disappeared and came back with Chief Stacy's coffee. She brought sugar and cream, too. Then her cell phone rang. With a final anxious look in their direction, she said, "It's my parents. I'm afraid they've already heard about the fire, so…I have to take this."

Levi nodded, and she went into the kitchen to answer it, but Rifle stayed by his side. "What can I do for you, Chief?"

Stacy had been busy fixing his coffee. At this he glanced up. "Let's begin with the fire."

Levi inclined his head. That seemed like a good idea to him.

"Can you tell me how it got started?"

"No."

He paused to take the first sip from his cup, grimaced as if it was too hot but swallowed, anyway. "You don't smoke? You weren't burning candles or setting off firecrackers?"

Firecrackers? What was he? Twelve? "No, sir. Everything was calm and quiet when I hit the sack. Next thing I knew, Rifle was trying to drag me from my bed."

"How'd he do that?"

"The only way he could." Levi stretched out his arm to show the fresh bite marks.

"Wow." Stacy set his coffee aside, clicking his tongue. "They aren't anything compared to all those stitches, though, are they?"

"Rifle wasn't trying to tear me apart."

"I heard about the pit bull attack, of course. Godfrey told me he took care of you. But I had no idea your injuries were so extensive." He rubbed his hand over his jaw with a rasping sound. "I'm afraid Whiskey Creek hasn't been a lucky stop for you."

Levi could tell that wasn't the throwaway remark Stacy pretended it was. "Depends on how you look at it, I guess."

"Excuse me?"

"If Rifle hadn't risked his life to wake me, I wouldn't be sitting here now. I'd breathed in so much carbon monoxide I was halfway unconscious, so it's a miracle he got to me in time. I guess that makes me pretty lucky."

"Oh…right." Stacy chuckled, then whistled to Rifle. "What a good boy," he said, giving the dog a pat when Rifle walked over. "Callie told me he jumped through the window to reach you. That's impressive."

"He's got the cuts to prove it."

Stacy jerked a thumb toward the broken window, which had to be boarded up until Callie could get it fixed. "Sailing through a window like that? Believe me, his injuries could've been a lot worse."

Levi raised his eyebrows. "See what I mean about luck?"

"I'd call that devotion. He must like you a great deal to go to such lengths to keep you safe."

As if to prove that he did indeed like Levi, Rifle returned to his side and lay at his feet.

Stacy motioned to the dog. "Would you look at that! You've won him over in record time."

Levi managed a self-deprecating grin. "No accounting for a dog's taste, I guess."

Callie was still on the phone. Levi could hear her in the other room, working hard to convince her parents that she was safe and had things under control. Someone had alerted them to the fire, all right.

Stacy could, no doubt, hear her, too, but he twisted around as though looking for her. Then he lowered his voice. "And what about Callie? How much does *she* like you?"

"I'm not sure I follow," Levi said.

"I just asked if there's something between you and Callie. That's simple enough, isn't it?"

It was his *reason* for asking that bothered Levi. Their relationship wasn't a matter of police business. "Does that have anything to do with the fire?"

Stacy had been reaching for his cup, but he straightened without picking it up. "Maybe."

Levi blinked at him. "I'm afraid I don't see the connection."

The police chief made a show of brushing a piece of lint from his uniform. "Then I'll spell it out for you. I know her parents quite well. I knew her grandparents before they passed, too. And many of her friends are my friends."

Levi's heavy-lidded look was meant to suggest he didn't give a shit. "You're trying to say you've got a personal stake in how we feel about each other?"

A muscle flexed in Stacy's cheek. Forgetting his coffee, he slid forward. "I'm trying to say I've sworn to protect the people of this town, and I plan to do that."

Levi leaned forward, too. "From what?"

"From whatever threat they might face!"

"Too bad you weren't around tonight."

Stacy obviously recognized the sarcasm in his voice. He gave Levi a dirty look as he reclaimed his cup. "Don't worry. I'm going to get to the bottom of what went on here. I promise you that. And I'll make sure Callie's safe from any *other* threats, too."

"You mean…like the threat posed by an unsavory drifter?"

Stacy's cup hit the saucer with a loud clack. The glitter in his eyes told Levi that he didn't like meeting with any resistance. But Levi didn't like what he was hearing, either. After growing up with an overbearing father and coping with the rigid structure of the military, including one or two superior officers who should never have been given authority over other soldiers, Levi could no longer tolerate those who overstepped their bounds. What had happened to Behrukh only made it worse. The men in her life thought they had the right to tell her whom she could love.

"If necessary," Stacy said.

Suddenly, Levi itched to hit the road, to leave this arrogant son of a bitch behind—so he wouldn't do something he might regret, like rearranging Stacy's face. "And how do you propose to do that?" he asked. "By getting involved in Callie's personal life, even though she wouldn't thank you for it?"

"Mr. McCloud, I'll decide what's too personal and what isn't. Do you understand?"

"Better than you realize."

"I don't think that's the case. So let me make things

a little clearer. You've been here almost a week. That's long enough to recover."

"Are you asking me to leave?"

"I'm merely pointing out that you might be wearing out your welcome. Where do you plan on going from here?"

Knowing his delay in responding would make as much of a statement as his words, Levi waited a second before replying. "Wherever I want."

"That's easy, isn't it?" Stacy said with a humorless chuckle. "When you don't have a job like the rest of us?"

"Is that why we're sitting here, Chief Stacy? Because I don't have a job? That's somehow breaking the law in your book?"

Red suffused the other man's face. "I'll admit there could be worse things. There's nothing on you in the system, Mr. McCloud. No traffic citations. No previous arrests."

It required effort not to curl his hands into fists. "Isn't that good?"

"It would be if it was accurate. But I have reason to believe it's not."

An uneasy feeling skittered down Levi's spine.

"Godfrey mentioned that you were in the military. Is that true?"

He said nothing.

"It is, isn't it? But the background check I ran doesn't show that, either. No Levi McCloud from Seattle has ever served in the armed forces."

Stacy knew he wasn't using his real name, or his military record would've come up.

"Do you have an ID you can show me?"

"Sorry. It got burned in the fire." That wasn't true.

After that night in Nevada, he'd thrown his wallet into a lake. He knew he'd never be able to use it again, had simply picked a new name, but hadn't gone so far as to buy false ID. He had no idea where people even came up with that shit.

"That's too bad," Stacy said. "Now you have no proof that you are who you say you are."

"It's unfortunate," Levi agreed.

"There *is* one way to solve it...."

"And that is?"

"I'd rather you were someone else's problem. Since you arrived, we've had a dog attack and a fire. *Two* serious incidents. Whether you're to blame or not, trouble seems to follow you. So let me ask you again—how long are you planning on staying?"

A noise over by the kitchen drew Levi's attention. Callie was off the phone. He had no idea when she'd started listening in, but judging by the blush of anger on her cheeks, she'd overheard enough to know that all wasn't well.

"What are you trying to say, Chief?" she asked, coming into the room. "Are you saying he's not welcome in Whiskey Creek?"

After taking a final swallow of coffee, Stacy put his cup and saucer on the table. "No need to get upset, Callie. I think Mr. McCloud and I understand each other," he said, and wished them both a good day before he left.

15

"What did all that mean?"

Reluctant to look at Callie, who was crouched in front of his chair, staring up at him, Levi pinched the bridge of his nose. "You don't want to know."

"Chief Stacy said your service in the military didn't show up in his background search."

"That's what he said."

She nudged his leg. *"Why?"*

Blowing out a sigh, he returned her gaze. "Because my name isn't McCloud, okay?"

Eyes wide, she rocked back. "Then...who are you?"

For some reason, her crestfallen expression made him angry. He didn't want to see her so shocked and upset, didn't want to be the cause of it. "Does it matter?" he snapped. "You knew I was wanted by the police."

"You said it was for speeding tickets! But Stacy said you had no speeding tickets. And, even if you really do, a couple of speeding tickets is no reason to assume a false identity."

"It's as good a reason as any. Why go to jail? Anyway, I'm just helping you out for a few days. We're never going to see each other after I leave. So how is my name even important? Would Smith or Jones or Hall be any better than McCloud for some man who once painted your barn?"

He was being a jerk, but he couldn't say why. He had no excuse to be unkind to Callie. It was the police chief who'd hit him with reality and made him want to strike back. Callie hadn't done anything except try to help him.

Fortunately, she didn't make matters worse by appearing wounded. She came right back at him. "Are you that determined not to care about anyone? And not to let anyone care about you?"

"I told you from the beginning not to expect anything from me!" Desperate to put some space between them, he got up and approached the mantel, where a large gilded mirror showed him the conflicting emotions on his face.

Rising to her feet, she spoke from behind him. "Then go, if that's what you're dying to do! Nothing's stopping you."

"Except my word. I'll pay you back before I leave."

"You've already done enough. You don't owe me anything. Consider the money I spent on your bike a…a gift—from one stranger to another."

He whirled to confront her. "And what about Denny Seamans and his buddy? They probably set the fire in the barn tonight. You know that. They could come back."

"I can handle them myself," she insisted. "I don't need you any more than you need me."

"Fine." He no longer had his leather coat, his backpack, his extra clothes and shoes—just what he had on his back and the boots he'd worn the night he was attacked by those dogs. He'd cleaned off the blood and left them by the back door to dry. But that was enough. He'd always been able to fend for himself. It was when others depended on him that life got complicated.

So she was right—it was best that he leave now, before whatever had started here grew any messier.

But his steps slowed as he reached the door. "Just tell me one thing." She didn't agree to do that, but he continued, anyway. "How does my name change any of the interaction we've had? I'm still the same man, regardless of what you call me."

"Your *name* isn't the problem," she said.

"Then what is?"

"Does it matter?"

"I want to know."

"Fine. I'm crazy about you, even though I shouldn't be. And you hate that. Maybe you hate *me*. So move on, Whoever You Are. Be alone and make sure you stay alone. Have it your way."

When she moved toward the bedroom, he told himself to let her go and walk out. Her words seemed to echo through the house. *Make sure you stay alone.* Was that how he wanted to live? Not really. He just hadn't seen any other way to cope with the turmoil inside him, any other way to keep from hurting the people he cared about.

Suddenly, he didn't know why it was so important that he not touch her. Behrukh seemed far away, part of another lifetime. She'd *died* because of him. How could he make what he'd done any worse?

"Callie."

"Go." She didn't look back at him, but he could tell she was crying. Catching her before she could disappear into the bedroom and slam the door, he turned her around and drew her up against him. "I *do* hate you," he murmured, "but only because I want you so much."

He saw the confusion in her eyes, but he couldn't explain something he didn't understand himself. All he could do was try to forget the past. And losing himself in making love with her seemed to hold the most immediate promise.

Callie knew she was crossing a line she shouldn't cross. Levi wasn't the only one who hadn't been completely forthcoming. What she'd held back was possibly worse. But she didn't feel she needed to stop him from touching her long enough to bare her soul. One romantic interlude didn't mean he'd be sticking around. Chances were he'd be gone by morning.

And she'd let him go, maybe even encourage him to leave sooner rather than later. She didn't want to drag him through what was about to happen to her. She preferred to hang on to this memory, to treasure the next few minutes like a pretty seashell in her pocket, one she could take out and examine when she needed something to bolster her for the challenges ahead. Then she could smile, knowing he was out there on his motorcycle, driving God knew where, oblivious to her struggle.

"You feel exactly how I imagined you would," he said as he slid his hands up her shirt. "You're *so* soft. Everywhere."

She grinned at him. "Just like you imagined? When did you imagine putting your hands on me?"

He smoothed the hair out of her face. "What do you think I've been dreaming about out there in the barn— or here on the couch?"

"It sounds like we've been having the same dream.

But—" she wiped the rest of her tears away "—don't worry, okay? About anything. You can leave tomorrow. No guilt."

He stared at her. "What'd you say?"

"I'm telling you that I understand this doesn't constitute a—a commitment. It's not like I think…you know, that you're falling in love with me…or that you'll stay." She laughed as if both of those possibilities would be too far-fetched to even consider. She actually hoped they were, for his sake. "The barn's burned down. Nothing's keeping you here."

He frowned. "Do you mind if we enjoy this before you start saying goodbye?"

"Of course. No goodbyes. Not yet. We can save that for tomorrow. I just…I thought you'd want to be… reassured."

"I don't," he said. "It makes me feel as if…I'm Kyle."

"Excuse me?"

"A stand-in."

Maybe she'd been a little *too* zealous in getting her point across. But she felt as if she had to do *something* to protect him, just in case he wasn't as impervious to their attraction as he seemed. Setting up the right expectations would help. "You're definitely not a stand-in," she said. "You're what I've been waiting for—a man who makes me weak in the knees just to look at him. But I'm not taking this seriously, so don't let that spook you," she quickly clarified.

"I'd really like you to stop talking," he said, and that was okay because she'd been having a hard time *thinking* since he'd unfastened her bra.

"Right. No more talking."

"That solves one problem."

"We have another?"

"I'm covered in soot. Put on that sexy thing you bought from Victoria's Secret while I have a shower."

Was he really going to take time for a shower? "I was going to return that bustier."

"No way. I'm not missing out. Give me five minutes," he said, and pulled off his shirt as he headed to her bathroom.

Callie hadn't been this nervous in years. She put Rifle in the yard and covered the broken window with cardboard. Then she donned the bustier and panties and covered them with a short, silky robe. She also smoothed lotion over her arms and legs and sprayed on some perfume. But by the time she heard the shower stop, she'd just about talked herself into calling off the whole thing. She was exploiting Levi's ignorance when it came to her situation, and she had no right.

What do I do? That question whirled through her head a million times. But when he emerged from the bathroom completely nude, hair wet and uncombed and curling slightly around his ears, she still had no answer—just a rush of hormones to contend with.

"You look a little unsure," he said, his eyes narrowing. He caught on quickly.

"And you look even better than I expected," she whispered.

When he grinned at her words, every nerve in her body tingled in anticipation. This was going to be the experience she'd long imagined, where she wanted to make love so badly she could hardly breathe. She had to take advantage of the opportunity, before she got too sick to feel desire, didn't she? Liver disease could cause impotence in men; she was glad it hadn't yet affected her libido. At least not on good days like today.

She managed to put up a hand before he could get too close. "Maybe…maybe we're being foolish. We should think about this. I haven't been making the best decisions of late."

Considering his state of arousal, she was no longer worried about his ability to perform. Whatever had been holding him back certainly wasn't physical. That was apparent.

He didn't seem to hear her, didn't acknowledge her halting words. "I admit that robe is pretty, but I'm far more interested in what's underneath," he said. "How about you take it off? Let me see you in that…whatever you call it."

She edged around the foot of the bed. "Bustier."

"That's it."

Tempted in spite of her reservations, she toyed with the ends of the belt. "Wouldn't you like to…to talk about this first?"

"Haven't I already made the answer to that question clear? What I'd like is to feel you against me."

He continued to advance on her, but she backed away an equal number of steps. "You were hesitant," she pointed out. "You didn't want me."

"Not true. It's complicated. But I'm not holding back anymore."

She swallowed hard. "You must've had a reason for holding back in the first place."

"I don't want to think about that."

"You will later, whether you want to or not."

"I'll deal with it in my own time."

"See? I'd feel terrible if you regretted it later. I prefer

to imagine you happy as you drive off into the sunset—
and to think that you'll smile when you remember me."

"How about you put a smile on my face right now?"

Obviously, he wasn't picking up on everything she
was saying. He could only concentrate on meeting the
demands of his body, which made her doubly conscious
of how she was misleading him. But maybe she was
overthinking it. After all, he couldn't be taking this too
seriously. He hadn't even told her his real name.

"What do I call you?" she asked.

He reached her and held her against the wall, hands at
her waist, eyes on mouth. "What are you saying now?"

"Levi feels silly since I know it's not your name."

"It *is* my name."

The feral gleam in his eyes gave her goose bumps.
"Levi what?"

"Who cares?"

See? She had nothing to worry about. He wasn't even
willing to tell her his last name. He'd be gone by morning. "I guess no one," she admitted.

"Are we done with the nervous jitters?"

"I think so."

"Great. Let's get rid of this," he said, and tugged
off her robe.

Callie's mouth was hot and wet and parted just when
Levi wanted it to. Behrukh hadn't been able to kiss
him with such abandon for months. She'd never kissed
anyone else, and she was so frightened of what she
was feeling, and of getting caught with him, that she'd
resisted learning. He'd never forget how stilted and
wooden she'd been when he first touched his lips to
hers, how many times he'd had to kiss her before she

grew warm and pliable and responsive. But he'd understood. She'd been told Americans were infidels, that he'd drag her down to hell if she even spoke to him. It was remarkable that they'd been able to overcome all that. It'd taken him months of stopping in at the store where she worked, of smiling at her until she'd at least meet his eyes, of flirting with her when her father was gone. And then it took several more months before he could convince her to meet him somewhere else so they could talk, touch. Kiss.

Ironically, now that she was gone, he missed all those early experiences as much as everything else about her.

The fact that Callie was nothing like Behrukh wasn't as easy to overlook as he'd first thought. She was beautiful and sensuous and as pliable as Behrukh had been stiff and unyielding. But she smelled all wrong and moved all wrong. He didn't want a substitute—he wanted to make love with the woman who owned his heart, with Behrukh. When he closed his eyes he could almost feel the swell of her belly beneath his hand, feel the excitement of knowing his baby grew in her womb.

But Behrukh was gone. So was their child. And he couldn't seem to overcome the loss.

Unable to continue, he pulled back. "I'm sorry," he said. "I...can't. I just...can't."

Callie was panting slightly as she looked up at him. "Did I do something that triggered a...a bad memory or—"

"It's not you." He closed his eyes as he stepped away from her and pressed his fingers to his forehead. "It's me. I shouldn't have started this."

"Because..."

He met her gaze. "I'm in love with someone else, Callie."

She flinched as if he'd slapped her, and he cursed his own stupidity. He should've told her before, but there'd seemed so little point in talking about a woman who no longer existed. He'd thought he could finally get beyond the past.

Just seconds ago, he'd been determined to do so.

But he couldn't persuade his heart to betray Behrukh, not even her memory.

"I see." Callie smiled, but he could tell by the emptiness in her eyes that her pleasant expression was a front. "I understand. To be faithful to someone…that's an admirable thing."

She scrambled to reclaim her robe as though she was suddenly embarrassed to let him see her without it, and he regretted that he couldn't make her feel as attractive as she was.

"I support you one hundred percent," she added, filling the silence as she jammed her arms through the sleeves and averted her gaze. He was still naked, but he didn't care about that. He *wanted* to be naked. He wanted to make love. He wanted to find himself again. But it was impossible. He couldn't overcome the resistance in his heart and his head.

"I didn't know or…I wouldn't have…bought this," she was saying. "I feel silly, of course."

He couldn't move. Even now he was torn between touching her and just getting the hell out, before he made matters worse. "Don't feel silly. It's me, like I said. And it's not that I'm cheating. The situation isn't what you think."

She chuckled without mirth. "*I* don't even know what I think! I mean, you're not gay—"

"No!" He shook his head. "This isn't history repeating itself. What your intuition's been telling you—that I'm attracted to you, that I want you—it's true. If only I'd met you before."

"You're really in love."

"Yes."

"So…why aren't you with her? Is she married or—"

He cursed as the memories began to pile up. "She's dead, Callie."

It felt as if someone had knocked the wind out of him, but Levi cared enough about this new person in his life to want to offer *some* explanation.

Her jaw dropped. "How?"

"I met her in Afghanistan."

"She was in the army?"

"No. She was a civilian. Her father pretended to be friendly to Americans because he wanted our business. He owned a little grocery store. I actually thought he liked me." He grimaced as the bitterness threatened to overwhelm him. "But he was secretly aligned with the insurgents. Someone in her extended family—her brothers wouldn't tell me who for fear of reprisal—shot her in the head when she admitted that she was carrying my child. They said she'd defiled herself by lying with a filthy American. I wanted to bring her home with me, wanted to marry her, but…her father didn't care."

He hadn't told anyone about Behrukh. He shouldn't have told Callie, either, because now he couldn't look her in the eye. It had been a mistake to touch Behrukh. And it had been a mistake to touch Callie. But she was the best thing to happen to him since Afghanistan. For the first time in months, he'd felt human—instead of like some kind of robot, just going through the motions of living.

It was time to get out of her life before he hurt her, too. But he couldn't leave her vulnerable to Denny. First, he had to know she'd be safe.

"I'll start cleaning up the mess in the barn."

He was exhausted after being up all night, but he wanted to get away from her, needed the escape.

Turning he put on his clothes and, without another word, left the house.

16

"Callie? Callie, are you okay?"

Rolling onto her back, she forced her heavy eyelids to open. Kyle and Baxter were leaning over her, their faces pinched with worry. Earlier, after Levi had hammered some boards over the broken window, she'd put on an old flannel nightgown, crawled into bed, and that was the last thing she remembered. She didn't know how much time had passed, but it felt like a lot. It was getting dark outside.

"What...what are you doing here?" As if to underscore how long she'd been sleeping, her voice sounded gravelly from disuse.

"We came as soon as we learned about the fire," Kyle said.

The fire was just this morning but it seemed like ages ago. "Who told you?"

"Some of the volunteers who helped fight it were talking at Just Like Mom's."

Because it'd happened out of town in the middle of the night, she hadn't expected a burning barn to generate much interest. No one had been hurt, and the fire hadn't spread. But there was some question as to the cause and that, naturally, invited conjecture. Or maybe the firefighters knew. Maybe that was what they'd been discussing.

"Was it arson?" she asked.

"One guy said it had to be," Baxter answered. Kyle was too busy scowling.

Dragging a hand up to push the hair out of her face, she finally awoke enough to see that the bustier she'd bought for Levi's benefit was lying in the middle of the floor, along with her silky robe. Kyle and Baxter had to step over them to get to her.

Shit…

"Levi didn't have anything to do with what happened, did he?" Kyle's voice and manner were just shy of accusatory.

"Of course not!" she replied. "He tried to put it out. Without him it would've done more damage."

"Then where is he?"

This question gave her a start, a moment of panic when she realized that, if he'd left, she might never see him again. She knew she shouldn't be surprised—or sad. This had been coming all along. But she felt so unprepared. "He's not here?" she managed to say.

"When you didn't answer the door, we walked around back. Rifle's in the yard, but Levi's motorcycle is gone."

Suddenly desperate to fade back into sleep, to avoid this reality, even though she should've expected it, she drew a steadying breath. "I guess he decided to move on."

"You didn't *know?*" Baxter asked.

She scrambled for an answer that would cover at least some of her embarrassment, given what they'd seen on the floor. "Things have been chaotic because of the fire."

"So that's it?" Kyle said. "He's out of your life for good?"

The relief in those words bothered Callie. Whether Levi stayed or went shouldn't make any difference to Kyle. They were finished sleeping together. They'd spent months trying to feel just a fraction of the excitement and attraction she'd experienced so naturally with Levi, but trying to turn friendship into love hadn't worked. As a matter of fact, it was such a poor substitute she knew she could never settle for something so diluted again, even if she had another fifty years to live. Which she didn't.

"I told you he wouldn't hang around forever. With the…with the barn burned, there's no way he can paint it." But he could've said goodbye….

Kyle encouraged her to scoot over so he could sit beside her on the bed. "What exactly happened last night?"

"I wish I knew." She propped the pillows behind her back as she explained the sequence of events to him and to Baxter, who was standing to one side.

"Is there any chance Levi was smoking when the fire broke out?"

Baxter asked this. Callie shifted her gaze to him. "Levi doesn't smoke. As you probably heard, the cause wasn't obvious. Chief Stacy said he'd get an arson investigator out here."

Kyle and Baxter exchanged a glance. "Why would anyone want to set fire to your barn?"

"I'm hoping no one did. That there's another explanation. But…there is *one* person who has a grudge against me."

Baxter barked a laugh. "No, there isn't! Everyone in this town loves you."

"Not Denny Seamans and Powell Barney," she said.

"Who are—" Baxter started, but Kyle interrupted.

"The two guys who own the pit bulls that attacked Levi."

"Oh, right."

Kyle stood. "Damn it, Callie. This is what I was hoping to avoid! If you'd only stayed out of it—"

"I wasn't trying to get involved!" she broke in. "What else could I have done? Turned Levi away when he was bleeding all over my doorstep? Told him he had to leave when his bike wasn't working?"

"He's a big boy," Kyle grumbled. "He can take care of himself."

Baxter nudged Kyle. "Come on, that was her choice."

"Exactly!" she agreed.

"But look what's happening because of it!" Kyle said.

Callie straightened the bedding. "Denny's upset and he's blaming me. That doesn't make it my fault."

Kyle shoved his hands in his pockets. "Maybe Baxter, Noah, Ted and I should go over and have a talk with Denny."

"Don't! I'd rather not have all my friends become their enemies, too," she said, but Kyle wasn't willing to back off quite that easily.

"They'd better not be responsible."

She held up a hand in the classic stop position. "Let's wait and see what caused the fire before we go off accusing people."

"When's the arson investigator coming?" Baxter asked. "Or has he already been here?"

"He hasn't shown up to my knowledge. Stacy didn't mention a time."

Baxter took Kyle's seat on the bed. "How are you feeling?"

There was an earnest quality to his voice that indicated he wasn't only concerned about how she'd been affected by the fire. As the one person who knew about her liver disease, he was asking after her health. "I'm fine. Just…tired. I was up all night."

Kyle stooped to recover the bustier and threw it in her closet, out of sight. "Have you eaten?"

She twisted around to see the clock. It was nearly eight. She'd slept all day. "Not yet."

"You should have some dinner. I'll go make something." With that, he went to the kitchen, but Baxter stayed behind.

"What happened?" he asked, his voice low.

"I told you," she said.

"I'm not talking about the fire."

She wasn't sure she wanted to talk about anything else. "What, then?"

He arched his eyebrows. "Are you going to pretend you didn't have sex with your guest?"

"I didn't."

"Come on." A skeptical grin tugged at his lips. "A girl doesn't break out a bustier unless she's got plans."

She smiled that he could name that particular type of lingerie when Levi couldn't seem to remember it no matter how many times she told him. "*I* had plans. It was Levi who called it quits."

"*What?*"

"It's true." And now he was gone....

Baxter made a sympathetic sound. "You have the worst luck when it comes to men, don't you?"

She couldn't help chuckling. "That's no joke," she said, then sobered. "But I haven't lost anything, right, Bax? I knew he was going to move on. And now he has. So..."

"So?" he prompted.

"Why am I sad?"

He shrugged. "There's just something about this guy."

That was true. She'd felt it almost from the start. "I wish we could choose who we want to love."

"So do I!"

His expression suggested this was the understatement of the year and she knew that for him it was. She reached out to squeeze his arm, and he responded by lying down with her. "We're pathetic, the two of us," he said as they settled close.

"How long have you been in love with Noah?" she whispered. They could hear Kyle banging around in the kitchen as he cooked. It wasn't as though he was listening in, but the seriousness of the subject seemed to warrant extra care.

Baxter hesitated so long she thought he wasn't going to answer. But then he took a deep breath and murmured, "Since forever."

"What do you think he'd do if you told him?"

"I don't want to find out."

"He can't get *too* mad. It's a compliment."

"You're kidding, right? He'd probably start throwing punches."

She rose up on her elbows. "Really?"

"You don't agree?"

"I know he cares about you."

This didn't seem to please him. "*Caring* sounds so weak compared to my side of things." He ran a hand over his face. "He'd feel betrayed," he mused. "As if I was only pretending to be his friend all these years. As if I've been living a lie. And I have been. I make it worse every time he talks to me about a woman and I pretend to understand and agree and support him."

What other options did he have? "I can see why you're tempted to move away. Why not live in S.F. and find someone else, someone who can fulfill you?"

"Because I'd have to leave you and the rest of our friends. I could never replace what we have."

She snuggled closer. "I feel the same."

"And I'm afraid of what'll happen to me there, how I'll change."

"You'd come out of the closet, wouldn't you?"

"I wouldn't be able to stay in it, not in an environment where it feels safe to be who and what I really am. Maybe I could pull off a double life for a while, but…" His words faded before he regrouped and finished. "Noah would find out eventually. So would my parents."

"Would that be so bad?" she asked. "Surely, they'd have to accept it."

"Would they?" he challenged.

She couldn't say for sure. She hated to encourage him to do something that wouldn't turn out well, and yet she understood how difficult it must be to pretend.

"Noah would hate me," he said. "So would my dad."

She wished it didn't have to be that way. "I'm sorry."

He kissed her temple. "I know."

* * *

As soon as Callie heard the sound of a motorcycle, she dropped her fork. The clang of it hitting her plate made Kyle and Baxter pause in the middle of their dinners.

"What is it?" Kyle asked.

She picked up her fork. "Nothing," she said, but she felt giddy with relief. Levi wasn't gone. She had no idea where he'd been all day, but he was back, and that made her far happier than it should have.

The motor she heard outside died. Then there was a quick knock and Levi poked his head into the living room. "Callie?"

"In here!" Instinctively, she shoved her chair back. She wanted to go to him, but he was already on his way, and she preferred not to reveal her own eagerness.

He stopped in the doorway of the kitchen. The fact that he was covered in grease and wearing a blue Whiskey Creek Gas-N-Go shirt surprised her.

"You've been...at the gas station?" she asked.

He eyed Baxter. He had to have seen Kyle's truck, but he would've had no reason to expect a third person. "All day. I was going to start cleaning up the mess left by the fire but figured that might not be wise—to touch anything before the arson investigator arrives."

"Oh, right," she said. "Of course. But you couldn't have slept more than a few hours last night. Surely, you've got to be tired."

He pulled his gaze away from Baxter. "I am now. But I needed to work." He handed her a stack of bills. "That's part of what I owe you."

"They paid you in cash?"

"That was our agreement. It's just day labor, whenever Joe needs me."

Of course. At least he was still in Whiskey Creek. "Levi, this is my friend Baxter. He's a stockbroker in San Francisco."

"Nice to meet you." Baxter played it serious, but then he flashed Callie an insider's smile, as if to say he could see why she was so taken with this guy.

In an effort to keep Levi and Kyle from noticing, Callie hurried to divert them. "Have you eaten?" she asked, and stood to scramble some more eggs. Kyle had cooked egg burritos. She could easily assemble the ingredients for another one.

"I can't eat yet. I'm too dirty."

"The only soap I have that might be strong enough to get the grease off your hands is dishwashing liquid, which is right here. Go ahead and use that side of the sink. You can shower after."

As he ran the water to get it hot, she cracked four eggs into a bowl.

"So...*Joe* hired you?" Kyle asked. "On the spot?"

Levi spoke above the running water. "He wasn't too keen on the idea at first, if that makes you feel better."

Kyle scowled. "It doesn't make me feel anything. I'm just surprised."

"Why, is he one of your friends? Was giving me a job some kind of betrayal?"

"Not really."

"Joe is Gail's brother," Callie explained. "She's the woman from that picture at my studio, remember?"

Understanding dawned. "The redhead who married the movie star."

"That's her."

Baxter leaned back, holding his water glass. "If Joe wasn't excited about the extra help, how come you've got his logo on your chest?"

"It's Saturday. He was slammed. And he had a BMW that was giving him problems. Owner brought it back while I was talking to him, said there were still times it wouldn't start, even after several attempts to fix it. I had a few ideas on how to solve that problem."

"How'd you do it?" Baxter asked.

"They'd already replaced the fuel pump. It wasn't the starter or the alternator. Far as I'm concerned, that leaves the central computer."

Kyle pushed his plate away. "And was that it?"

Levi dried his hands on the towel Callie provided. "We've ordered one. We'll see when it comes in."

After hanging the towel on its hook, Callie poured the eggs into a skillet. "I thought…I thought maybe you'd gone." She couldn't look at him when she said this. She was too afraid he'd read the embarrassment she felt about what had happened between them earlier. Now that he was back, she wasn't going to let things drift in that direction again. If she was careful, she could still enjoy the time she had left with him.

"I can't go anywhere," he told her. "Not until we find out how that fire got started."

"You think it was Denny Seamans." Kyle said this.

"I do," Levi responded without a heartbeat of hesitation. "Makes no sense that a random fire would break out when and where it did. There was nothing in the barn that could've caused it. Nothing flammable. No one smoking. No lightning."

"Sometimes fires start for odd reasons," Kyle said.

Levi took a seat at the table. "This wasn't one of those times."

Kyle slid the pitcher of lemonade toward him as Callie brought him a glass. "Then I should thank you."

Levi seemed confused as he poured himself a drink. "For what?"

"For caring enough to stay with Callie. For making sure she isn't here alone."

The two men stared at each other for a second, then Levi nodded and Kyle smiled. It was a small concession, on both their parts, but the exchange meant a lot to Callie.

"See what a good friend he is?" she said to Levi, and was glad that Kyle had proved it once again.

Maybe they really could forget the mistakes they'd made this year.

Callie was careful not to touch Levi when she passed him. She made a point of not letting their hands brush as she started making his bed on the couch and he came over to help spread out the blankets. She even avoided meeting his gaze, because she could tell he had something to say, that he was searching for the right words, and she was fairly confident she didn't want to hear it. She'd already had another difficult conversation with her parents, one in which she'd had to assure them— several times—that the barn could be rebuilt and she'd be safe. She certainly didn't want to talk about anything else that would be painful, especially what had happened when she'd put on that silly bustier. She'd been foolish to buy it in the first place. If Levi was interested in her, he would've let her know. And even if that *was* the case, it would be heartless to draw him any closer. Why would she set him up to suffer through yet another traumatic event? She could very well die while he was still around.

She was satisfied with having him back, she decided. With being able to spend a little more time with him. She wasn't going to do anything to scare him off. The leaving would come soon enough. He'd made his intentions clear, yet again, during dinner, when he mentioned that his work at the Gas-N-Go was only temporary.

"Do you think you'll need a heavier blanket?" she asked. "It's cooling off a bit tonight."

"No, that's fine," he replied.

"Okay." She called Rifle, whom she'd brought inside after supper. Then she curved her lips in a polite smile, one she might bestow on any guest. "Get some sleep. Hopefully, we won't have any trouble tonight."

"We could be in a world of hurt if we do. The way I feel right now, I'm not good for anything." He returned her smile with a tired one of his own.

"You'll feel better in the morning. We'll be fine until then. I've got my pellet gun, after all," she added with a chuckle. Then, with Rifle at her heels, she turned and fled toward her room—but Levi stopped her before she could get very far.

"Callie?"

She clenched her hands as she looked back. "Yes?"

"I'm sorry about earlier."

"Please, don't apologize." She conjured up that same polite smile. "I respect your…your position on that. Actually, I don't know what came over me. I'm embarrassed that I've been so forward." Her laugh sounded a bit awkward to her own ears, but she hoped *he* wouldn't notice. "I have no excuse except…I haven't really been myself lately. There's…there's a lot going on in my life."

"You have nothing to be embarrassed about, Callie. I'm flattered to think you might want to be with me."

"That's kind of you to say. Thank you for…for being such a gentleman." She started to hurry away again, but he continued to talk, and courtesy demanded she stop and listen.

"It isn't that you're not…attractive to me," he said. "You realize that, right?"

She raised one hand. "Really, you don't have to say any more. I was *completely* out of line. I just…misread what you were feeling and assumed too much. So *I'm* the one who owes *you* an apology for…for putting you on the spot like that. Let's forget it ever happened. I have a better understanding of the situation now, if that makes you feel more comfortable."

When he muttered a curse, she didn't know how to respond. But no way was she going to question him about it. She desperately wanted to drop the subject. "See you in the morning."

"You didn't misread *anything*," he called after her.

She'd reached her bedroom door, so this time she didn't turn around to face him. "Levi, please believe me. Everything's fine. We don't have to talk about it. Nothing like that will ever happen again. Okay?"

He made no comment.

Grateful for the reprieve, she closed the door. Then she went into the bathroom, cut up that bustier and threw it and every last condom in the trash.

17

Because it was Sunday, Callie thought the arson investigator wouldn't come until the following day, but he showed up bright and early. Callie didn't recognize him. He was a small man, compactly built, who came from the county. He didn't say much to her. Chief Stacy insisted she and Levi stay out of the way, so they had almost no interaction with the man at first. The police chief was the one who showed him around. But they didn't have to wait long for his opinion. It took the investigator only a couple of hours to decide what had started the fire. Then he sought them out to say that an accelerant had been used, probably gasoline, which could've been ignited with a match.

"Arson," Callie repeated, shocked in spite of her assumptions.

"Without a doubt," he said. Then he asked them to recount exactly what had occurred last night. As soon as they finished, Chief Stacy pulled him aside again and they spoke in low voices. She and Levi were left standing near the charred remains of the barn.

"I had a feeling," she murmured. "But I still don't want to believe it." How could someone do such a thing—even someone as angry and vengeful as Denny

Seamans? What if Levi had been killed in the blaze? Had Denny *really* intended to take a human life? He knew, from when he'd been over before, that Levi was staying in the barn....

Levi squinted as he looked over at the other men. "What I want to know is whether they'll be able to prove who did it. Gasoline and matches are very common substances. Everyone has access to them, so that hardly narrows the list of suspects."

"Maybe someone saw Denny's truck last night."

"Out here? Who'd be up at that time of night?"

"It's possible," she said.

"But not likely."

"Which means he'll go unpunished."

"Which means he'll be free to try something else."

"One fire is bad enough." She rubbed the goose bumps from her arms. "What do we do?"

"Keep our eyes open."

Callie nodded. She was chilled by the thought of further trouble. But there was one bright spot—as long as Levi was worried about her safety, he'd probably stay.

When someone knocked on the door in the late afternoon, Levi figured it might be the arson investigator, back with a few questions or wanting to take a second peek at the barn. Or Chief Stacy. Had he finally discovered Levi's true identity? Was he here with an arrest warrant?

It was neither. He held Rifle back as he opened the door to find a big, barrel-chested man, salt-and-pepper hair buzzed short, on the stoop, scowling in the direction of the damaged barn.

"Look at that," he said the moment Levi opened the door. "Just about destroyed the whole thing."

Levi didn't know what to say. He had no idea who this was, until the man looked directly at him. Then something about his face reminded Levi of Callie—probably the dimples on either side of his mouth.

"You must be...Callie's father?" he guessed.

"That's right." He squatted to acknowledge Rifle, who was obviously excited to see him, then focused on the stitches snaking down Levi's arm. "And you must be the fellow who was attacked by those dogs."

"That would be me."

He straightened. "A terrible experience. Sorry about that."

After Chief Stacy had made it clear that Levi wasn't welcome in Whiskey Creek—that he wasn't even good enough to stay for a week or two—Levi hadn't expected Callie's parents to be friendly. If anyone had a right to doubt him, to be leery of him, it was them. But Levi quickly decided that her father never had a bad thought about anyone. It just wasn't in his nature to be skeptical or withholding, and that was apparent from his very first words.

"Boone Vanetta." He stuck out his big paw so they could shake. "Nice to meet you."

"Nice to meet you, too," Levi responded.

He leaned to the left so he could look around Levi and into the house. "My daughter here somewhere?"

Levi shook his head. "No, sir. I'm afraid not. She had to run into town. Her assistant at the studio needed a hand." Actually, Callie hadn't said much about where she was going. She'd told him she had a few errands, but he'd heard her on the phone with Tina and knew she was stopping by there. Tina didn't usually work on Sunday, Callie said, but Monday was full of appointments, and she had to get ready for them.

"Wouldn't you know we'd pass each other. Isn't that the way?"

"Would you like to come in?" Levi ordered Rifle to stay inside and opened the door wider, just in case. He couldn't imagine that this man was happy to have a complete stranger, a vagrant, at his daughter's home, but he didn't seem to be particularly concerned. Levi got the impression that Boone trusted as easily as Callie. Or maybe he was better at reading a man's intentions than the arrogant chief of police. Maybe he could tell that Levi would never hurt her.

"For a minute. Damn hot today, isn't it? Could I get a glass of water?"

"Of course." He stepped aside as the big man squeezed into the house.

"Would you prefer some juice?" Levi asked.

"If she's got some."

Levi led the way to the kitchen, where he got a glass out of the cupboard.

"What are you fixing here?" Boone indicated the tools spread out on the floor.

"There's been a slow leak under the sink for a while. It's causing a bit of dry rot. Thought I'd take care of it while I've got the time."

He nodded. "Nice of ya."

"It was nice of your daughter to help me out after the attack."

"She's a gem, that one." He beamed with pride as he scratched behind Rifle's ears. "You won't find a nicer gal anywhere."

Levi smiled as he took the pomegranate juice from the fridge; it was about all Callie had to drink. She didn't stock soda or any alcohol, save the bottle of wine she'd opened for him. From what he could tell, she kept herself on a diet even stricter than his father's.

"Thanks." Boone accepted the glass, downed the juice then pulled a paper towel from the hanger and began mopping the perspiration from his forehead.

"Have you heard what the arson investigator had to say about the fire?" Levi asked.

"Callie called after he left. That's why I came. I wanted to see the damage for myself. Hard to figure out why anyone would purposely set fire to a building."

"It happens far too often."

"Not here."

Levi took a deep breath. "I'm afraid I might be responsible for that."

Boone handed him back the glass. "You didn't set the fire, did ya?"

"No, sir."

"Then as far as I'm concerned, you're not responsible for it."

Levi almost couldn't believe his ears. "I appreciate the sentiment. But I doubt it would've happened if she hadn't stepped up to help me."

"She did the right thing. It's this Denny fella who's in the wrong. I told her the two of you should come stay with us until Chief Stacy can put that yahoo behind bars, but she won't hear of it. She said she doesn't want to bring trouble to our door." He lowered his voice. "And she has a point. We'd be hard-pressed to get her mother out of the house if someone set fire to our place. That's why I'm glad you're here. I'd hate to think of Callie alone now that someone might wish her harm."

"Her mother is…ill?"

"She's in a wheelchair. Was diagnosed with multiple sclerosis a few years back. That disease is a tough one, you know. Some days are better than others."

"I'm sorry to hear about it."

"I wish to hell it was me instead of her." As he heaved a deep sigh, Levi had no doubt he was absolutely sincere. "But we all have problems," he went on.

"Yes, we do," Levi said.

Boone sized him up. "You're a nice-lookin' fella. No wonder my daughter likes you."

Levi chuckled. "She's not bad herself. But don't worry, I'll be moving on soon."

"Why would I be worried?"

Boone had surprised Levi again. "According to Chief Stacy, I'm not to be trusted. He isn't pleased that I'm even in town."

"Chief Stacy is a man with a lot of responsibility on his shoulders, and he does his best to manage it. But he doesn't know everything. If my daughter likes you, there's got to be good reason."

Guilt for all he'd done—for putting Behrukh in a position that had cost her her life and for the way he'd behaved in Nevada—sank deep. Stacy's suspicions merely angered Levi, tempted him to keep striking back at the world. But a few words from Boone, and Levi wanted to be a better man. "You wouldn't care if she took up with a vagrant?" he asked.

Boone's dimples flashed as he grinned. "If you settled down you wouldn't be a vagrant."

"So what are you going to do?" Baxter asked.

Callie had gone to his house, one of a handful of

restored Victorians not far from the heart of town, on her way home from Sacramento. Her doctor had called earlier, just after the arson inspector left, and said he wanted to start her on rifaximin, an antibiotic used to prevent the encephalopathy that could be caused by her disease. She wasn't sure why he'd be thinking of her on a Sunday, but she knew he took his practice very seriously and hardly ever stopped working. She felt sorry for his family, if he had one. It couldn't be easy for him to deal with so many critically ill patients.

After they hung up, she'd had to make up an excuse for Levi so she could drive to the pharmacy where she had her prescriptions filled. She couldn't use the one inside Nature's Way—a locally owned grocery store not far from Whiskey Creek—unless she wanted everyone to know about her condition before she found the nerve to tell them. It wasn't as if she could claim the diuretic spironolactone, or the lactulose, which she had to take four times a day to inhibit the buildup of ammonia in her blood, were for a harmless condition like premenstrual cramps. She was just lucky that she didn't need beta-blockers. So many people with cirrhosis of the liver developed enlarged veins in the esophagus and bled internally as a result.

"There's nothing I can do." She sat on the edge of the chair swing he'd hung from the ceiling of his old-fashioned porch. "If Denny set that fire, I have to hope the police will be able to prove it and prosecute him, or...I'll continue to live in fear."

Baxter was generally dressed in either an expensive, hand-tailored suit, which he wore to work, or something equally classic and stylish for casual. But in honor of a lazy Sunday afternoon, he was wearing designer jeans, a button-down shirt and house shoes. "Indefinitely?"

If she lived at all. Wondering about the side effects, she frowned at the medication she'd brought in so she could take her first dose. "What other choice do I have? It sucks, but they can't charge him with a crime just because I believe he's guilty."

"You could move back into town."

"What good would that do?"

"It would get you out of the sticks and farther away from where Denny lives!"

"He won't be staying in that house for long. He's only leased it for the summer. Anyway, why should I let him chase me out of where I want to spend my final months?"

A hand went to his chest as if she'd just stabbed him. *"Don't say 'final months'!"*

"I'm sorry." She shoved the medication into her purse so she wouldn't have to look at it. "Anyway, where would I go?"

"Your parents'. Or..." He gestured at the hundred-year-old house behind them. He'd spent an inordinate amount of time picking flooring and paint and accoutrements so Riley, their contractor friend, could restore it, and it was lovely. "Heck, you could even come here. I have an extra bedroom."

"And give you a front row seat to what's going to happen to me?" She shook her head. "No, thanks."

He clasped her hand. "I'd take care of you, Callie."

"I don't want you to *have* to."

"Come on. That's what friends are for."

"I know." She curled her fingers more tightly through his. "But I wouldn't want to bring my Denny trouble into anyone else's life. And I like being at the farm. That way I've got the privacy I need to cope with my illness."

"You mean Levi's there," he said with a laugh.

She grinned. "That, too."

Baxter gave the swing a push, and it started to sway. "I like him," he said as they watched the cars, many of them tourists coming to see a genuine gold-rush town, pass by on the street.

She broadened her smile. "He's hot, huh?"

"Not as hot as Noah, but…"

They laughed together. Then he sobered. "When are you going to tell him?"

"About what?"

He widened his eyes. "What do you think?"

"That I'm about to die? Why would I *ever* tell him?"

Baxter stopped the swing. "Callie—"

"Levi and I are just hanging out until the police can get to the bottom of this arson. Why would I need to let him know I'm a terrible investment of his time? That there won't be any return?"

"Knowing you is a privilege," he insisted. "No matter what."

"Come on! It's too intense for a new acquaintance. We're not even sleeping together."

He let go of her hand to tie the leather thong that was coming undone on one of his shoes. "I get the feeling things are drifting that way."

"Well, they're not. For your information, I dumped all my birth control last night."

"Not a good idea."

She tucked her feet under her. "What don't you understand about…*he's not interested?*"

"He might tell you that, but it's not necessarily the

truth. I wasn't the only one who could feel the sexual tension between the two of you yesterday." He bent his head to make his next words more meaningful. "Kyle mentioned it."

"He did?"

"As soon as we left."

"Is he...upset about that?" She missed Kyle. They'd spent so much time together in the past year and now that she'd put the brakes on sleeping with him, trying to reestablish the old boundaries felt so strained and awkward. But with everything that'd happened, what he knew about and what he didn't, it wasn't as if they could carry on the way they had before.

"He's playing it straight," Baxter said, "acting like he'd be happy if you could find a good guy."

She toyed with the chain holding the swing. "Levi *is* a good guy, but he's not *that* guy."

"He's obviously wrestling with some inner demons, Cal. Doesn't mean they'll win. Maybe he won't wind up going anywhere. Maybe you'll get that liver transplant and he'll stay."

"You're dreaming!" she said with a roll of her eyes.

"He came back yesterday when you thought he was gone, didn't he?"

A gentle breeze stirred the chrysanthemums that lined his porch. "Only because he feels responsible for getting me into the mess I'm in. If he'd shown up on someone else's doorstep after that dog attack, it would probably be their barn that got burned."

"Maybe he realizes what he has in you."

"Let's face it." A door slammed and she lowered her voice because Baxter's neighbor had come out to water his lawn. "That would be the worst scenario. I don't want him to suffer any more loss." She considered telling Baxter about the woman who'd been killed in Afghanistan, but since Levi had entrusted her with something that personal, she wanted to respect his privacy. "So the most I can hope for is a couple of great weeks with him before he takes off—and before this damn disease gets the better of me and I'm no good for anything."

Concern etched deep grooves between his eyebrows. "Do you feel sick?"

"Surprisingly, I don't. I mean…I have my moments." Like the night she'd started throwing up and couldn't seem to stop, and Levi had carried her to bed. "But most of the time I feel like the old me, except for a sense of lethargy. Many people have no symptoms at all, not until the very end."

"Then, since you still feel good enough to want a man, I say you go buy more birth control."

She gave his shoulder a shove. "Quit that. I'm determined to settle for being his friend, for knowing I helped him at a time when he needed someone."

The neighbor waved and Baxter waved back. "I've been thinking," he said.

"About your situation or mine?"

"Don't try to change the subject."

"Why not?"

"Because there's nothing I can do. I wish I could change my sexual orientation, but I can't."

"When did you figure out you were gay?"

"In the fifth grade, when I realized that girls didn't mean the same thing to me as they did to Noah."

"You've known that long?"

"I certainly wondered. But we're talking about *you.*

I think you should tell Gail right away. Maybe she can help."

"How?"

"She's married to one of the biggest movie stars on the planet. Simon has contacts and money the rest of us don't."

She scowled at him. "I told you. The donor lists don't work that way. Besides, his money isn't mine!"

"For Gail's sake, he'll do whatever he can. What good is having money if it can't make a difference when it's most important? We'll all pitch in, although he hardly needs to ask for donations."

"You think she might be able to get me moved to the top of the transplant list by *bribing* someone?"

"I'll bet she can get you a liver by tomorrow."

"I would hope the people who manage this type of thing aren't that corrupt."

"You can hope, just don't bet on it. Money talks."

"But that would just nudge everyone else down the list."

"So?"

"So?" she echoed. "Who are we to say I have any more right to survive than the other people waiting for a transplant?"

She could tell he didn't want to look at it that way. "There're no guarantees for anyone as it is," he said.

"I couldn't live knowing I took someone else's chance of surviving. That just feels too creepy to me, like we're playing God."

The swing tilted to her side when he got up and began to pace. "You have to fight for your life, Callie! That means throwing everything you have at this. You just happen to be best friends with Simon O'Neal's wife. Take whatever help they can give you!"

She wanted to live so desperately that, for a moment, she considered letting him convince her. She wasn't sure Simon would be able to do anything; his contacts weren't in the medical field. But he was treated like a god by just about everyone. His level of fame made such a difference. And on top of that, in a world where money mattered so much, paying the right people probably *could* improve her chances of receiving a liver before it was too late.

But what about those who were waiting and hoping, who might not know a celebrity of his stature? What if one of them was a single mother? A father with a family to support? A child?

She shook her head. "I couldn't. Living is important, but—"

"What could be *more* important than that?" he interrupted, clearly exasperated that she would argue when he was so certain he'd come up with the perfect solution.

It was a tough choice. She'd give just about anything to reclaim the promise of a future, to know she could avoid the terrible fate that loomed ahead.

Anything except her integrity. "Living right."

That seemed to take the fight out of him. Tears filled his eyes and he glanced away. "I don't want to lose you," he said, his voice strangled.

This was what she'd have to face if she told the others. Maybe Gail would even act on her own. "There's always a chance I'll pull through." Gathering her purse, she got out of the swing. "I have to go, Bax."

He blinked away his tears. "So when will you let everyone else in on our little secret?"

He didn't like hearing the burden of it alone. But if she divulged the truth, word would get back to Levi. Since he'd made arrangements to help Joe at the station, he'd be coming into town whenever Joe called him. The repair shop wasn't open on Sundays, but it would be tomorrow and the next day and the day after. That meant she'd no longer have control over what he heard and what he didn't. So why take the risk? Why tell anybody? There was no need for Levi to be burdened with the knowledge of something she could easily tell her friends after he left.

She was going to enjoy what little time she had with him.

"When Levi's gone," she said.

Baxter gripped the railing. "Seriously? You're putting it off again? But we talked about this!"

"I've waited four months. What's another few weeks?"

Another few weeks could be everything, could be The End. And yet it *still* meant more to her to spend the coming days with this new person in her life.

"He's that important to you?"

"For some reason, he is."

Baxter cursed but eventually sighed. "Fine."

"You'll respect my wishes?"

"Of course, but…"

"There's a 'but'?"

"At least sleep with him!" he said, and waved her off.

18

The Gruper rental, as Levi had heard Callie refer to it, wasn't one of the nicer homes in Whiskey Creek. Not only did it lack the sturdy construction of the farm-house, it possessed none of the nineteenth-century charm of the Victorians closer to town. Such a cheap, unimaginative structure didn't even seem to belong in the area. The gray stucco walls had cracks, indicating it had been cheaply built to begin with. And, judging by what Levi saw, no one had bothered to take care of it since. Dog piles—or bleached grass where dog piles had disintegrated with time—dotted the dry, brittle lawn. The paint was peeling under the eaves. The screen door hung at an awkward angle.

The only remotely interesting thing about this house was two holes, chest-high, in the screen door. Levi thought they looked as if someone had fired a couple of bullets through it....

That made him leery. But not leery enough to get back on his motorcycle and drive away. He'd tried to talk himself out of coming here. But, for better or worse, he wasn't going to let others threaten his life or the life of someone he cared about. In his opinion, a man should have the right to defend himself against pricks like Denny and his friend.

The truck Denny had driven to the farm sat in the driveway. Levi eyed it while listening for sounds that might suggest Denny had reclaimed Spike. When he didn't hear barking, he felt confident that Denny hadn't yet raised the money for the fine. At least he wouldn't have to fight off another pit bull.

He lifted his hand to knock, and the door swung open almost as soon as his knuckles could strike wood. Sure enough, no dog came charging out.

"Powell, come here! Quick!" Denny yelled. "It's our homeless friend."

A toilet flushed and Powell came hurrying into the living room, zipping his pants. "What's he want?"

"That's a good question." Heartened by Powell's presence, Denny stood a little taller. "What are you doing here?"

With the blinds drawn and only a television throwing off any light, the house was so dark inside Levi couldn't see Denny or Powell very clearly. He could smell alcohol, though, and wondered if they'd been sitting around, stewing and drinking.

Men with a few beers under their belts were often more impetuous, or just plain stupid, than others. But Levi had known coming here would be a gamble. He was willing to accept the odds.

Scowling, he focused on Denny, who was right in front of him. Powell stood closely behind and to one side. "Take a wild guess."

"You looking for trouble?"

"If trouble is what it takes."

"What the hell's *that* supposed to mean?" Powell demanded.

"It means I know you guys did it," Levi said. "I know you started the fire at the farm night before last."

"No, we didn't," Powell argued, but the expression on Denny's face led Levi to believe he was dying to take credit for what he'd done, to convince Levi that he was as big and bad as he liked to act.

When Denny's lips curved into a taunting smile, Levi supposed ego had won. "Even if we did, there's nothing you can do about it, asshole," he said. "Not unless you can prove it."

Levi grinned and kept grinning until Denny exchanged an uncertain glance with his buddy.

"What?" he said. "Why are you smiling like that?"

"I'm just waiting for you to realize your mistake."

"I haven't made a mistake," Denny said, but the satisfaction he'd exhibited earlier was gone. These words came out sullen and dark.

"Yes, you have," Levi told him. "There's nothing *Chief Stacy* can do. He's the one who faces the burden of proof. Not me."

"Go to hell!" Denny shoved Powell out of the way and started to slam the door, but Levi stopped it with his foot.

"I've already lost everything I care about," he said.

"So?" Denny sneered.

"So I'm not the kind of guy you want to provoke. Now do you understand the situation a little better?"

"Get your foot out of my damn door!" Denny cried.

Levi didn't remove it. "Not before I have my say. You set any more fires, or harm Callie or anything that belongs to her, I'll make you sorry you were ever born." He shifted his attention to Powell. "That goes for both of you."

Powell ripped the door out of Denny's hands. "Are you threatening us?"

Levi didn't bother denying it. "Yes, I am."

He blinked as if he hadn't expected an admission. Now that he had one, there was nowhere to go. He immediately began to backpedal. "Denny was just messing with you, man, making you think we set that fire. But we didn't. We didn't do anything."

Levi shook his head. "We both know better than that, so don't insult me by lying. Tell me I've made myself clear. That's all I'm looking for today."

"You can't come over here like this, trying to pick a fight," Denny said, but Powell spoke at the same time. "I'm going to call Chief Stacy!"

Levi chuckled. "Damn, those are great costumes."

They glanced at each other. "What are you talking about?" Powell asked.

"Those bodies you've worked so hard to build. They put up a nice front."

Denny finally rallied. "Get out of here before we kick your ass."

It was a weak threat, but Levi wasn't about to let him get away with any more than he'd already done. "I'm not opposed to letting you try."

"You son of a bitch—" Denny started to come after him, but Powell jerked his friend back.

"He's not worth it, man. For all we know, the hillbillies in this town will take *his* side and we'll wind up in jail."

"By way of the hospital," Levi said. "I may not be

good at too many things, but I do have talent in certain areas."

"And if I have a gun?" Denny muttered. "What can your talents do against that?"

Levi lowered his voice. "Either one of you comes at me with a weapon, that takes this to a whole new level."

"Meaning..."

"I'll do everything I can to make sure you're the one who doesn't survive," he said, and walked back to his bike.

Chief Stacy called while Callie was driving, so she had to use her Bluetooth to answer. "Hello?"

"You think that friend of yours is a law-abiding citizen, do you?"

Callie gripped the steering wheel a little tighter. Had Stacy come up with Levi's true identity? If so, what did it reveal?

"Which friend?" she said, trying to play it as if she wasn't worried. "I've got a lot of them."

"None of them concern me like the man who's currently living under your roof."

"I've told you not to worry about Levi."

"It's my job to worry. And he's giving me plenty of reason."

Slowing, she pulled to the side of the road. She didn't want the stress of driving on top of having this conversation. "How?"

"He threatened Denny Seamans and Powell Barney."

She wasn't surprised. Not really. Levi wasn't the type to sit by and allow Denny to behave the way he did without reacting. "Who told you that?"

"Denny just filed a complaint."

"Are you going to arrest him?" she asked with a laugh that said doing so would be preposterous.

This seemed to take Stacy off guard. "Why wouldn't I?"

"Because it's his word against Levi's!"

"Powell's backing him up. Said he was there and heard the whole conversation."

"But Powell would say anything Denny wants. And Denny's a known liar."

The volume of Stacy's voice went up. "I think Levi's been doing his share of lying, too, Callie. You heard what I told him at your place. My background search turned up zilch on a Levi McCloud from Seattle. No parking tickets, no speeding tickets, no military service, nothing."

"So? There could be a mistake."

"There's no mistake. He's not being straight with us. I'm convinced of it."

She nibbled at her bottom lip while watching the other cars on the road. "Post-traumatic stress disorder affects a lot of our soldiers, makes them do things that might seem crazy to us."

"Using a false name isn't crazy. It's a willful deception, an attempt to hide his past."

"Maybe it's nothing like what you're thinking."

"What else could it be?"

She'd already created an alternate scenario. She'd needed *some* way to justify continuing to associate with him. "I know he has an abusive father. Maybe he wanted to leave his past behind to prevent his father from ever contacting him."

"Is that what he told you?"

"No. But it's plausible."

"If that was it, he would've said."

Not necessarily. Levi wasn't at all forthcoming. What she'd learned about him had come out in bits and pieces. "Everyone's different. I think you're missing the bigger point here."

"Which is…"

Her friend Riley passed by with his son, Jacob. Under normal circumstances, she would've flagged him down so she could ask him whether or not he knew for sure when Phoenix would be getting out of prison. Callie realized that day would be difficult for him. It would be difficult for Phoenix, too. How would she ever make the transition to regular life, especially since she'd be returning to a community so united against her?

But Callie didn't honk or wave. Instead, she hunkered down in her seat and hoped he wouldn't notice her. Lately, she hadn't been good about returning his calls, either, couldn't cope with any more accusations of neglect and questions about what was wrong with her.

Fortunately, her car was a popular make and model, and there were enough tourists streaming through town. He drove by without even slowing.

"Denny lied about the night of the attack," she said into the phone. "We know that for sure. We also know he blames me for the loss of his dog and that he's been making noises about doing something to punish me for it. That leads me to believe he's got to be the one who set fire to the barn. There isn't anyone else who has it in for me. So…how does a liar and a possible arsonist have enough credibility to convince you that you need to arrest *Levi?*"

There was a long pause. "You won't listen to me on this guy, will you?"

She didn't respond to that directly. "Even if Levi did threaten Denny, you can't blame him for wanting to defend himself."

"Are you sleeping with him?"

This was the last question she'd expected from the chief of police. "Does that have anything to do with the barn-burning or anything else we were discussing?" she asked.

"It could explain your behavior, why you're so blind when it comes to him."

The air-conditioning was too cold. She adjusted the vents so they wouldn't blow on her. "I think I'm seeing well enough, Chief. I know Levi has problems. But he's a good person, someone who's worth helping. I've already noticed how he's begun to relax since he's been here, that he isn't walling everyone out anymore."

She could've expounded on that statement, could've told him she didn't know many people who would've taken care of a two-day acquaintance as well as he'd cared for her the night she was sick. He was also a man of his word, or he would've moved on the second his bike was fixed. Even with the barn burned, he was sticking around, trying to look out for her. He had a tender heart. What would he be like with consistent kindness and a stronger sense of safety and security? There was no telling. But she was afraid revealing all of that would only confirm what the police chief had already inferred—that she cared about him and, therefore, saw only the best.

"Callie, I've known you since we were kids," Chief Stacy said. "Maybe I've got a few years on you, but we grew up together. I don't want to see you hurt."

She felt guilty for being so defensive. He was just

trying to do his job, a job he was good at. "I appreciate the sentiment. Really, I do. But Denny is the only threat to me. If you really want to help, make sure *he* keeps his distance, okay?"

He spoke over the blare of a radio in the background. "I've got a cruiser going by your place every hour, starting at eight in the evening."

Putting her X3 back in Drive, she waited for a break in the traffic streaming past her. "I'm grateful. Thank you."

"I have to admit, though…"

"What?" she said when his words drifted off.

"I never expected you to fall for someone like Levi. A woman like you…you deserve more. A guy with a job, at least," he added with a chuckle.

She had a chance to merge onto the highway, but the chief's words—or rather, the telltale self-consciousness in his voice—shocked her so badly that she missed it. "I'm flattered," she said. "I really am."

"My divorce will be final soon."

Where was he going with *this?* If it was what she thought, what any woman would think, she regretted saying she was flattered.

"Will you keep that in mind?" he asked before she could respond to the divorce statement.

Callie shoved her transmission back in Park. Was he serious? So what if he had a steady job? She'd never looked at him as a possible love interest. He seemed much older, had been married since she was in high school. But the divorce changed nothing on her part. She didn't find him remotely attractive.

Since when had he decided he'd like to date her? Was

it just because he'd recently become more aware of her, thanks to the dog attack and Levi?

Obviously, he assumed that if she'd be interested in a vagrant, he should have a much better chance.

Intending to let him down easy, she opened her mouth to say that she appreciated the kind of person he was. It was the beginning of her own version of the clichéd "I just want to be friends" speech. But then she realized she might not need to state her feelings one way or the other. If she didn't get a liver soon, dating *anyone* would be a moot point.

"I'll keep that in mind," she promised.

The first thing Callie saw when she arrived home was a worn leather jacket tossed over Levi's bike, which was parked out front instead of in the back, as usual.

He'd been over to Denny's, all right. He must've found his jacket there. She couldn't see any blood on it, but the dirt ground into one sleeve suggested it'd been in a ditch or a field.

"Hello?" she called when she entered the house. "Anyone home?"

A tantalizing aroma drifted out of the kitchen.

"Hey!" Levi answered as Rifle trotted into the living room to greet her. "It's about time you got here. Dinner's almost ready."

"Smells great."

"You hungry?"

"Famished." She'd skipped lunch for fear it would make her nauseous. She was afraid of eating, but her hunger prevented her from avoiding it now.

"Come on, then."

"Be right there." First she wanted to hide the advanced directive she'd printed off the internet when she stopped by the studio after Baxter's. Since Tina had finished getting the slide shows of her recent shoots ready for the clients who were coming in tomorrow, Callie'd had the place to herself. Her doctor had advised her to fill out a directive several weeks ago, but she hadn't been able to make herself face the decisions involved. What did she want her parents to do if she ended up on life support? At what point should they pull the plug? What other decisions would she want them to make if she could no longer decide for herself?

At thirty-two it seemed macabre to even consider those questions. The panic she felt at the thought of losing control over such basic things, even to people she trusted as much as her parents, nearly made her break into a cold sweat. But she figured she should be clear about her wishes while she had the chance, otherwise, she'd leave herself vulnerable to having *no one* in control.

"Can I pour you a glass of wine?" he called.

"No, thanks." She dropped her purse on her bed, slipped the directive into her top drawer and hurried to the kitchen to see that he'd grilled salmon, steamed asparagus and prepared wild rice. "Wow, fancy."

"Healthy. That's how you eat, right?"

She wondered if he'd added any salt. Because of her liver problems, she had to be careful not to build up ascites, or excess abdominal fluids. She didn't want to have to get a shunt to drain her abdominal cavity. She'd been warned about the danger. The excess fluid invited infection, which made it doubly bad. "You didn't use much salt, did you?"

"No. Why?"

"I avoid it as much as possible." She could rinse her asparagus and scrape off the fish....

"I went easy," he assured her.

"Great. Thanks."

He carried two plates to the table. "Anything exciting happen today?"

She smiled at how domestic it felt to have him cooking in her kitchen and serving her dinner. "Not really. I hear yours was eventful, though."

"Who told you?"

"I got a call from Chief Stacy on my way home."

A muscle flexed in his cheek. "Those bastards reported me?"

She nearly smiled again even though that wasn't the appropriate response. She was just happy to see him. Somehow he helped her forget what she'd dealt with today. "You didn't expect them to?"

"Actually, I did," he admitted. "But what I said had to be said." He shrugged as he got them both some utensils. "What's Stacy going to do?"

"At this point, I don't think he's going to do anything."

"Then why'd he call?"

She sipped the water he had waiting on the table. "To tell me that I shouldn't be hanging out with you."

He hesitated before taking his seat. "He still believes I'm dangerous?"

"He's still concerned about your murky past."

"Of course."

"And...there might be a little more to it."

His eyebrows arched in question.

"He hinted that he'd like to date me."

That same muscle moved in his cheek. "He's got to

be over forty. There's probably a fifteen-year age difference."

"From me it's only ten," she pointed out.

"A decade's significant."

"It wouldn't be if I was interested in him."

He sat down across from her. "So what'd you tell him?"

"Nothing yet. He's letting me ponder the fact that he has a good job."

"Ah. One with a pension and everything. Tempting, huh?"

"Not really. A pension's not what I need right now."

He held his fork loosely in one hand. "What do you need?"

To get well, she thought, but smiled to camouflage the gravity of her reality. "A tasty dinner."

After washing up, they decided to watch a movie. They were both exhausted. But Levi couldn't relax when he sat on one end of the couch and, instead of sitting on the other end, Callie chose a chair off to the side. He might not have cared, except the decision seemed so premeditated. He knew she couldn't see the TV as well over there. She'd selected her seat with other considerations in mind, and he was fairly certain he could guess what those considerations were. No matter where he walked or sat or stood, she put distance between them.

"Still holding a grudge?" he asked.

She was combing her fingers through Rifle's fur while waiting for the movie to start. "What do you mean?"

He thought about trying to get past the encounter that obviously loomed so large in her mind, but decided against it. Today, when he'd taken out the trash, he'd found a bunch of unopened condoms Callie must've thrown away. Judging from that, she'd accepted his limits. He should be glad. That was what he'd intended, right?

Of course. So why couldn't he stop picturing her in that sexy lace-up number she'd bought from Victoria's Secret? And why had he rescued those condoms and shoved them under one of the couch cushions?

He certainly wasn't hoping to use them with anyone else.

"I met your father today," he said.

She'd just leaned back, but at this she sat up straight. "He came by?"

"For a minute."

"What'd he want?"

"To take a look at the barn."

She grimaced. "Did it upset him?"

"Not too badly. I got the impression he doesn't let anything get under his skin."

"No," she said with a wistful smile.

Levi studied her. "I liked him."

Her smile broadened. "Everyone does."

The movie started so they grew silent, but Levi couldn't get drawn into what was happening on the screen. He was too aware of Callie trying to make herself comfortable in that straight-back chair. She'd pull her knees in and lean to one side. Then she'd drop her feet to the floor and shift to the other.

"Why don't you come over here, where you can lie down?" he asked.

She acted surprised that he even mentioned it. "Why? I'm fine."

"If *I* go over there, will you come over here?"

"That's not it," she said.

He stared at her disbelievingly. "Prove it."

"Sure. No problem." She got up, stepped around Rifle, who was on the floor, and walked to the couch, but she sat as far away from him as possible.

"That's not so bad, is it?" he asked.

"Of course not," she replied as if she hadn't been avoiding him in the first place. It wasn't until she started to fall asleep that she allowed him to lift her feet onto his lap.

19

The second Callie felt Levi's hands on her she was tempted to withdraw. She knew letting him touch her, even in a nonsexual way, would only make her crave more contact. But the swirling motion of his thumbs felt so good on the arches of her feet. She'd had very few foot massages in her life, had no idea they could be so enjoyable—or so erotic.

Her breathing grew shallow as she fought against the deluge of awareness washing over her. She tried telling herself that this little television interlude and foot rub should affect her no more than a date with...with Chief Stacy! She couldn't be with either man.

But some people were easier to refuse than others....

When his hands began to travel up her legs, to knead her calf muscles, she opened her eyes and watched him from beneath her lashes until she was sure she'd caught his attention.

"I can feel that," she said.

His hands continued their soothing work. "I was hoping you could."

Forcing herself to remove her feet from his lap, she sat up. "It's late. We should get some sleep."

Nothing. No response from him.

"See you in the morning."

He reached for her when she got up, but let her slip from his grasp when she seemed intent on it.

"Good night," she said.

Cheyenne Amos tapped her fingers on the table as she waited for her phone to ring.

"Aren't you coming to bed?"

At the sound of her husband's voice, which she heard over the TV he was watching, she walked to the doorway of her bedroom to see that he had Lucky, her three-legged dog, as well as his two dogs with him. He'd stacked some pillows behind his back and was wielding the remote. He slept in his underwear, so his chest was bare. She found that an appealing sight. He was eager enough to have her join him that the rest of him might be bare, too....

The possibility made the temptation to crawl in with him that much stronger. She loved nothing more than making love with Dylan, curling up and falling asleep together, then waking up and sharing another day with him. But she couldn't succumb to the promise of what he offered just yet.

"There you are. What are you doing?" he asked when he saw her standing in the doorway.

She was just watching him, thinking about how happy she'd been since she'd met him, but she told him that often enough. "I'm expecting a call from Eve, Riley, Baxter and Noah. We're getting Kyle on the phone, too. We're worried about Callie. She's been acting strange for a long time and we need to get to the bottom of it."

"If anyone knows what's going on, it's Kyle."

"Exactly."

He was watching an MMA fight he'd recorded on their DVR. He'd once supported his younger brothers by getting in the ring and he still had a lot of interest in the sport. He usually watched the matches with his brothers. But since he'd bought her a two-bedroom home in town, complete with a white picket fence he'd built himself, he didn't see his brothers after work quite as often as when they'd all been living down in the river bottoms.

"She wasn't herself on Friday," he said. "But what about Sophia? You didn't mention her or Ted."

Folding her arms, Cheyenne leaned against the door-jamb, her attention on the fight as they talked. "I've tried to reach Sophia. I can't get her to pick up. I'm afraid she's still upset by what Ted said to her. That wasn't necessary."

"You don't think she was responsible for Scott's crash?"

"I really can't say. But who are we to punish her for it? Besides, it happened a long time ago."

"Makes sense to me." He scratched behind Lucky's ears, and she whined her thanks. "And Ted's not joining the call because…"

"We didn't invite him. We're a little ticked off by how he treated her. I love Ted, but he can be harsh."

"He's too damn smart for his own good. But you once told me he has reason to dislike her."

Until he was forced to drop out, Dylan had gone to the same high school they had. He'd just been too busy raising hell to notice what was going on with their group. They hadn't interacted with him much back then. Cheyenne might not have gotten to know him at all if her sister hadn't started hanging out with him and his brothers. "He does," she said, "but it's time to get past old grievances. He knows she's not happy. He's seen the bruises on her arms and face. That should be punishment enough."

"Maybe he still wants her. Maybe that hasn't changed."

"You might be right. Otherwise, he'd be able to let it go."

He adjusted the blankets, and Lucky and the other two dogs shifted before settling down again. "Did you get the message that Presley called?"

"Yeah, I talked to her."

"Everything okay?"

"Fine." Cheyenne could hardly believe it, but her sister had been out of rehab for three months. That meant she'd been clean and sober for six—which was a relief on many counts but none more critical than the fact that she was almost seven months pregnant. The baby belonged to Aaron, Dylan's younger brother, but no one besides Presley and Cheyenne knew that. Cheyenne hated keeping such a secret from her husband. She was afraid of how he might react if he found out, hoped that day never came because she had no choice in the deception. That baby was the only thing Presley had to cling to, the only reason powerful enough to get her to give up the drugs that had almost destroyed her life.

Aaron wasn't ready for a child, anyway. He hadn't lasted in rehab, was *still* using. Dylan saw him at Amos Auto Body, the collision repair shop they owned, every day. He witnessed the results of Aaron's actions and worried about him constantly.

"She tell you about the ultrasound?"

"No." Cheyenne came forward to perch on the edge

of the bed. "Did she tell *you* something about an ultrasound?"

"She knows the gender of the baby."

That Dylan was the one who'd learned this surprised Cheyenne. Other than to say the father was some guy she met when she was in Phoenix at Christmas, Presley had been tight-lipped about the baby, especially with him. She didn't want any of the details of her life leaking back to Aaron. She knew if he contacted her, she might break down and see him, and that would be the worst thing for her *and* the baby. "What is it?"

He grinned. "A boy."

Of course it was a boy. That seemed to be all the Amoses could create, not that she was going to remark on it. "Oh, my gosh! I can't believe she didn't tell me! A boy! And...and did she say if everything looked... okay?"

Because the pregnancy had started out while Presley was drinking and doing drugs—and nearly ended in an abortion—they'd been concerned about how the fetus might be developing. Presley had enough challenges just fighting her addictions and keeping a steady job. Cheyenne feared she wouldn't be able to cope with a child who had serious medical issues.

"Everything's fine. Presley's told you that before."

She couldn't help double-checking. "That's great."

He laughed. "God, I love that silly smile on your face."

"What silly smile?" She grabbed one of the decorator pillows he'd pushed off to one side and threw it at him, which caused the dogs to scramble off the bed.

Catching it, he tossed it back, and Lucky barked at them both. "The one that says you couldn't be happier."

"It's a miracle she's reached this stage, Dyl. Those days after Anita died…when she took off and I thought I might never see her again… They were terrible. I'm thrilled that she's doing so well."

"It's too bad she doesn't live in Whiskey Creek anymore. Stockton's a dive."

"Not everyone thinks so. Anyway, it's a bigger city, where she's been able to find a cheap apartment and a decent job."

"You call working at a thrift store a decent job?"

"She likes it."

"You'd be more involved the pregnancy if she was here," he pointed out.

But then she might fall back in with Aaron. Cheyenne knew Presley was still in love with him. The two of them couldn't be in close proximity, or they'd start seeing each other again, and Presley would slide downhill. "It's better if she's not around her old friends."

"You mean Aaron. I know that. He wouldn't be a good influence." He put the TV on pause and turned to look at her.

"What?" she said.

"Speaking of babies…"

Something in his expression made her cheeks flush with warmth. "Yes?"

He caught her by the wrist and pulled her toward him. "I was wondering if you might be interested in making a baby with me."

Her heart lodged in her throat. She'd been waiting for him to ask. She knew if she brought it up, he'd say yes just to ensure that she wasn't denied anything she really wanted. But it was important to her that *he* crave a child just as much. "You've raised your brothers," she said, "Are you *sure* you're ready to start a family? What about your father?"

"What about him?"

"He gets out of prison next year. We could hold off until after that…until he's back and settled in, doing whatever he's going to do with his life. Then you'll feel more settled yourself."

He smoothed the hair out of her face. "I'm not going to plan my life around his release. At this point, I don't even know if we'll have a relationship."

"But you want a child."

"Absolutely."

"Because…"

"Because I love you." He kissed her tenderly. "Get in bed. Let me show you how much."

The phone rang. But Cheyenne ignored it. She'd have to catch up with her friends later because right now nothing mattered more than Dylan.

Baxter knew what this call was about and wasn't entirely comfortable participating. He couldn't break his word to Callie, but he didn't want to lie to everyone, either.

"Cheyenne's not picking up. She must've fallen asleep," Eve announced as soon as everyone else was on the call.

"We could do this tomorrow," Baxter said. Hopefully at a time when *he* wasn't available.…

"No, everyone's got to work," Eve responded. "I'll fill her in later. I don't think we should put this off any longer."

"Put *what* off?" Noah asked.

"Something's going on with Callie," she replied. "Haven't you noticed?"

"She hasn't been showing up for coffee much," he mused. "Is everything okay with her business?"

"She doesn't seem to care about her business anymore," Eve said. "From what I can tell, she's turned it over to Tina."

"Because she's getting the farm ready to put on the market," Kyle explained.

"You think that's it?" Eve again. "You saw the way she acted on Friday."

"Have you tried asking her?" Noah wanted to know.

"We've all tried," Eve said. "She avoids us when she can, gets off the phone if we start to push, rarely returns a call. I'm just…so worried. Has she said anything to any of you that might offer some clue as to what's going on?"

Baxter cringed but remained silent.

"She's said nothing to me," Kyle told them.

"Are you sure?" Eve pressed. "I feel that if anyone can unravel the mystery, it'd be you."

"I don't know what's wrong with her," Kyle insisted.

Baxter wondered if Kyle was squirming with guilt. He had to be asking himself if he'd had a hand in how she was behaving.

"I couldn't be there Friday—" Riley entered the conversation "—so I don't know how she acted, but I agree she's been more aloof than usual."

"*More* aloof?" Eve said. "She's *never* aloof. She's not that kind of person."

"We know she has some guy staying at the farm with her." Noah didn't sound particularly worried, but he wasn't the worrying kind. "And there's been trouble with the renters nearby and their dogs. I think how she's acting could be related to her guest and what's happened because of him. Don't you agree, Kyle?"

"This started before that," Kyle said.

"So what's going on with our friend?" Eve asked. "And what can we do about it?"

Baxter cleared his throat. "I think…I think she might be going through a difficult time, but we need to give her the space to deal with it."

"Space," Eve repeated.

"Yeah," he said, but Eve was having none of it.

"We've given her space, Bax. She's not snapping out of it. Like Kyle said, this has been going on for some time. She's lost weight. She's withdrawn."

Riley made a suggestion. "Her mother's health has been getting worse. Maybe that's it."

"Instead of guessing behind her back, let's go out there and have a talk with her," Noah said.

"Tonight?" Riley asked.

Baxter did what he could to kill that idea. "No, it's too late."

Noah pushed harder. "Tomorrow, then. Or the next day."

"I don't know if she'll like that." Eve sounded hesitant.

"We're her friends," Noah said. "We don't always need an invitation."

Baxter was about to say they shouldn't surprise her, but Kyle jumped in before he could form the words.

"It's because of me."

"Kyle—" Baxter wanted to warn him that what he was about to say might not help, but didn't get the chance.

"Callie and I have been sleeping together," he announced. "And I feel terrible about it because I know she regrets it."

Stunned silence met this announcement. Maybe they'd had their suspicions, but no one had expected him to confess.

Baxter admired Kyle for being willing to own up to what he'd done. It proved that he was worried, too, and that he cared more about Callie than about covering his tracks. "I doubt that's it," he said, hoping to ease some of the surprise and awkwardness that had sprung up.

"You've been with *Callie?*" Noah said.

"Just a few times," Kyle replied, "but she hasn't been the same since. I feel like shit that I let it happen. I don't know what's wrong with me. Ever since Olivia and I broke up...I'm just not the man I used to be. I keep messing up everyone's lives."

"I *really* don't think that's it," Baxter repeated.

"I wondered," Eve admitted.

Noah muttered a curse. "So what do we do now?"

"We forget about it," Baxter replied. "I'm sure she'd be embarrassed that we know. It's really none of our business."

"It helps us understand what she's going through, at least," Eve said.

"Maybe she's...having a crisis of sorts, feeling guilty." Riley lowered his voice to just this side of exasperated. "Women can be like that."

"*Women,* Riley?" Eve snapped. "Really? All of us?"

Riley grew defensive. "Relax. It was a generalization."

"I bet it only happened because she was afraid she'd never meet the right guy," Eve said.

"Meaning what?" Noah asked.

"Meaning she took what was available."

"Wow, that really makes it sound as if she cares about me," Kyle complained.

"Oh, stop," Eve said. "That's your ego talking because we all know you're still in love with Olivia."

He didn't refute it.

Baxter switched the phone to his other ear. They were going down the wrong road, but he couldn't stop them. Not without revealing that he knew more than they did.

"She keeps talking about Cheyenne and how happy she is," Eve told them. "I get the feeling she really wants to find someone and settle down."

"If that's the case maybe we should be more worried about the drifter she's got living out there," Noah said.

Kyle jumped in again. "I *have* been worried!"

"No, that's called jealousy," Riley joked.

"It's not jealousy! I practically chased her into this guy's arms, but he doesn't have a thing to offer her. How can he possibly make her happy? He'll probably stay just long enough to break her heart."

"Maybe he's exactly what she needs right now." Baxter could see it, in the context of what she was going through. She felt that Levi was temporary, so she could enjoy him and he'd go before she had to face her future, whatever that might be.

There was a moment of silence. Obviously, this wasn't a popular opinion.

"What makes you say that?" Noah finally asked.

"She's a smart girl," Baxter said. "We need to trust her judgment."

"That's what we've been doing so far, and it's not fixing anything," Eve complained.

Baxter left his recliner to pace in front of his hundred-year-old windows. "Let's give her some more time."

"I agree," Noah said. "I wouldn't want you guys having this conversation about me."

"We just want to be sure we're doing all we can for her." Eve sounded stung.

"Noah, we talk about you all the time," Riley teased.

Noah ignored him. "I know you mean well, Eve, but—"

Riley broke in, now serious. "Why don't we go over there sometime this week, let her know Kyle told us about…what happened between them and that we understand."

Baxter thought that might help. At least it would ease *some* of Callie's worries. "I could support a visit if that's the purpose. If we were careful about the timing."

"So…is everyone in?" Riley asked, and they all agreed.

Levi groaned as the shower went on. Apparently, Callie wasn't going straight to bed. Maybe she needed to cool off.

He could certainly use a cold shower. But he wasn't sure it would do any good. He wanted Callie too badly to stop the thoughts flowing through his head.

He imagined her lips parting beneath his as they had yesterday morning and felt his body tighten in response. Two years was a long time for a man to ignore his sexual appetites. He was learning just how relentless those appetites could be.

But he'd already screwed up with her once. He'd had

her put on that lingerie, then pulled back almost the second he touched her. He'd rejected her when she was most vulnerable—when any woman would be most vulnerable—and he doubted she'd be willing to trust him again. She wouldn't want to run into the same problem.

For that matter, neither did he.

If he went to her tonight, would he be able to follow through?

He'd make himself, he decided. But how would he feel after?

He had so many hormones coursing through him he could hardly think. His brain kept showing him tantalizing snippets of what it would be like to have Callie beneath him, to feel her hips rise to meet his. Part of him, the part that kept driving him to take her regardless of all else, didn't seem to care that he was still in love with Behrukh, that he'd promised to *always* love her.

Where had his conviction gone? His remorse for what he'd caused by coaxing her to become his friend, his lover, his fiancée?

Ashamed that he could be so easily tempted away from what he knew to be a just and deserving punishment, he dropped his head in his hands. He'd meant everything he'd told Behrukh, hadn't he?

Of course he had. Then why did those promises seem so impossible to keep?

Rifle, who'd stayed with him instead of Callie for a change, lifted his head and perked up his ears as if asking why he was so agitated.

"Hell if I know," he told the dog. "I can't have her. But I can't stop wanting her, either."

The dog yawned, clearly not impressed by the gravity of this human problem, and rested his snout on his paws.

"Thanks for your support, buddy." Levi wished he still had a room out in the barn. Maybe, if he could put enough space between them, his heart would quit pumping like a piston and his erection would go away. But staying inside like this, cooped up with her—he was too close to the object of his desire.

He was fighting the inevitable.

Convinced he'd succumb eventually, he went into her bedroom and shut the door to keep Rifle out.

It was just a physical release, he told himself. It wasn't as if he was really cheating on Behrukh because it wouldn't mean anything.

20

Sophia heard the doorbell. She was reading in the library, but she could've been in the shower, or even blow-drying her hair, and she still wouldn't have missed those deep gongs. The doorbell Skip had chosen was the best money could buy. Everything in her house fell into that category. Her husband insisted they had a reputation to uphold, a responsibility to provide Whiskey Creek with a couple anyone could look up to. Exhibiting their wealth convinced others of his success, which helped build his credibility and bring him new investors, which in turn brought him more success.

But she couldn't imagine why he'd need any other investors. He was flying all over the world as it was, could hardly keep up with the number of projects he had. Not only that, but just about everyone who had any money in Whiskey Creek was already participating in one of his many joint venture partnerships. How much more could one man need—or manage?

Sophia was tired of the facade, tired of the pretense. Their relationship had deteriorated so quickly, she longed to walk out on it all. To admit she'd made a mistake when she married the high school senior voted Most Likely to Succeed in the class six years ahead of hers. He'd grown verbally abusive as soon as she'd conceived Alexa, and physically abusive after that, too full of his own power, but she'd never really loved him in the first place.

There were moments, moments like now, when she wanted to tell him so, wanted to watch the truth register on his pale, bespectacled face.

Except she could do nothing of the sort. If she did, she'd never see her daughter again. Skip would take Alexa away, even if it meant he had to steal her and go into hiding in some foreign country.

Skip was nothing if not vengeful.

Knocking followed the sound of the doorbell and still she didn't move. She couldn't. Skip had blackened her eye this morning before he left for Houston. With her eleven-year-old daughter at cheer camp he hadn't needed to worry that she might overhear, hadn't needed to worry that this time Alexa might not believe she'd run into *another* door. So he'd let himself get more carried away than usual. She'd have to stay inside the house for several days this time, probably for as long as Alexa would be gone.

Maybe that was the real reason he'd done what he'd done and not the fact that she'd argued with him, again, over having another child, something she definitely didn't want to do. He liked knowing she'd be a prisoner inside their house while he had all the freedom he could desire.

Whoever was at her door wasn't giving up. The gongs of the doorbell repeated themselves, sounding deep and hollow in the expansive house.

Resting her head against the supple leather of her chair, Sophia let the book she'd selected from her own shelves fall into her lap. "Go away," she murmured. "I don't know who you are or what you want, but it doesn't matter."

It was most likely a friend of Alexa's. Few people came to the door for Sophia. Skip insisted that she appear at every community event and make a big deal of the contributions they made, but the person she had to be when she was with him didn't attract friends. She'd thought the *real* her—the woman she was when he was out of town—had been making some inroads with Gail DeMarco's circle. Sophia had wanted to belong to that group for years, had always felt that they had something special, and she envied their closeness.

But last Friday at the coffee shop showed her just how ineffective she'd been. They didn't give a damn about her, either.

When the doorbell rang for the third time, she shoved the ice pack she'd set on the side table to the ground with an irritated curse. Why wouldn't whoever it was just leave her in peace? It was getting too late for company, anyway.

She wished she had a housekeeper who could tell the person to go. Skip had once suggested hiring someone—no one in town had that kind of help, so it would make quite a statement—but she'd rejected the idea. If he took the housework away from her she'd have *nothing* to do, since he wouldn't let her get a job.

Fortunately, he hadn't pushed the idea. No doubt he'd had second thoughts. He wanted the people of Whiskey Creek to think he was perfect, admirable in every regard. He couldn't risk destroying his carefully built image by letting what went on behind closed doors go public.

"Sophia! Answer the damn door!"

Hearing her name made her curious enough to overcome the lethargy that had kept her pinned to the chair for hours. Who would be that insistent?

She stood and steadied herself with a hand to the wall before moving gingerly, in deference to her pounding head, out of the room and down the long, winding staircase to the marble entry. There, she peered through the peephole in the massive door Skip had had shipped over from Indonesia.

With a gasp, she covered her mouth. Ted Dixon, her old flame, stood beneath her porch light. She'd never dreamed she'd see the day when he showed up on *her* doorstep. He hated her.

And he had every right.

"Sophia, I know you're in there," he called. "Let me talk to you!"

No way. She couldn't. Her eye was so swollen she could barely open it and what makeup she'd put on before Skip got up she'd long since cried off. When Alexa was here, she didn't mind sequestering herself inside her husband's mansion. At least with her daughter around she had *some* company. Alexa meant more to her than anything in the world. But when her daughter was gone, the emptiness overwhelmed her, and she started thinking about the bottle of sleeping pills in their medicine cabinet....

"Sophia? Come on. I'm sorry about how I behaved at the coffee shop. I don't blame you for Scott. He's—he's the one who chose to get behind the wheel."

Fresh tears filled her eyes as she pressed her cheek to the carved wood. She couldn't think of Scott. Not now. And even if she hadn't been wearing proof of her husband's abuse, she couldn't answer Ted, couldn't be alone with him. She was too afraid of what she might say. Her emotions, where he was concerned, remained poignant, despite all the years they'd been apart.

With a final bang on the door to show his frustration, he turned and headed down the walkway to the circular drive where he'd left his Lexus. Craving his forgiveness as she did, she found it difficult not to go after him. She thought since he'd come to her somewhat penitent, she might have a chance to achieve what he'd denied her from the moment she'd broken up with him.

But she couldn't go after him. It wouldn't lead anywhere good, even if he did forgive her, even if she could believe he didn't hate her quite as much as before. There could be no closure. A half measure would just increase her desire for what she couldn't have, make her want to draw him inside, so this night wouldn't have to be as lonely as all the others. Already, she pretended it was him and not Skip whenever Skip wanted to make love. That was the only way she could tolerate her husband's touch.

She'd made a mistake when she chose Skip.

And now she had to live with it.

Callie thought she heard a knock at the bathroom door but it was hard to tell. She'd been trying to use the force and noise of the water to block out what she was feeling, wasn't particularly interested in returning her attention to anything going on outside the bathroom. Especially if it involved Levi. He was the reason she'd wanted to escape in the first place.

Was he now at the door?

Holding still, she listened more carefully and, sure

enough, the *tap, tap, tap* sounded again. But this time it was followed by Levi's deep voice.

"Callie? Can I come in?"

She grappled for the best way to respond. "Um, I'm in the shower. I'll be out in a few minutes. You can use the bathroom then."

"I don't need to use the bathroom."

Of course he didn't. She'd just thought that purposely misunderstanding might be enough to send him back to the living room. "What do you want, then?"

"I'm looking for a second chance. Can you give me that?"

No, she couldn't—for several reasons, not the least of which was what he'd told her yesterday. His feelings for the woman who'd come to such a heartbreaking end could not have changed so soon. She didn't want to make love with him feeling he'd only regret it later.

"I don't think you're ready. But that's okay. There's no rush. There'll be other women." *When you've healed and I'm gone....* Not that she wanted to imagine him with anyone else....

"Other women," he repeated flatly.

She had to clear her throat in order to continue speaking. "When the time is right."

"The hell with that," he snapped. "I want you."

Callie felt her nipples tighten at the need in his voice. She was searching her brain for a response she could live with when she heard the doorknob rattle. She'd locked it, but in this old house, that wasn't much of a deterrent. If he jiggled the handle long enough, it'd open. He knew that as well as she did, since he'd been using her bathroom, too.

It only took a second. Then he was coming in. If she

really wanted to stop him, she had to be more decisive, more forceful. Let him know that "no" really meant *no*

But she couldn't drag a single word to her lips. She stood under the spray, scarcely feeling the water on her skin as she waited to see what he'd do next.

When the shower curtain slid open and she saw him standing there, fully clothed, she covered herself as best she could with her hands.

"Look at you," he said.

The appreciation on his face made the breath catch in her throat, but she shook her head. "Levi, don't start this again...."

"Shh," he said. "Let me see you."

He wanted her to drop her arms. But she was too frightened of what she was feeling. At the hunger in his eyes, she found it difficult to think, to remember why she couldn't be with him, even temporarily.

"Come on," he coaxed. "It's okay."

She couldn't uncover herself. She didn't have the trust that it required, not with him dressed and in love with a memory.

He seemed to understand she wouldn't be able to act on her own. After kicking off his shoes, he stepped into the tub, completely unconcerned that he'd soak his clothes.

"Let me help," he said, and gently pulled her hands away.

Goose bumps jumped out on her skin as he gazed down at her.

"You're beautiful. But that's no surprise."

"Beauty doesn't matter if—"

He cut her off before she could finish. "It certainly doesn't hurt."

She was shaking. She wasn't sure why. She just felt so vulnerable, so torn between what she was dying to have and what she knew she should refuse. "I don't have any birth control."

He pulled a condom out of his back pocket. "I do. Funny thing. I happened to find some brand-new Trojans in the trash."

She gave him a guilty smile. "I wonder who could've put them there."

He chuckled at her facetious tone. "I think it was someone who wants to get laid."

If that was all she wanted, she could've continued sleeping with Kyle. But she didn't point that out. She'd rather he didn't realize that he was somehow special.

"Glad you completed the rescue mission." She doubted she could conceive in her condition, anyway. Liver failure eventually caused the failure of other organs. Not only that, but she was on so much medication. Still, she figured it was better to be safe than sorry. She was already facing an epic battle. She didn't need to make another life dependent on her own.

He set the package in the soap dispenser. Then he stripped off his wet T-shirt, tossed it behind him and, with one finger, followed a drop of water between her breasts. "I can hardly stay on my feet," he admitted.

"You said it's been a long time."

When he finally pulled her to him, she could tell that he was shaking, too.

"It *has* been a long time. In fact, it feels like an eternity. I'm afraid I might disappoint you in round one."

"That's okay. Maybe it is better if you—you use me for this round. Then it'll be easier with the next woman."

Lifting his head, he scowled. "Why are we talking about other women again?"

He sounded annoyed, but she was trying to let him know not to invest too much in what was about to occur. It was the only way her conscience could allow her to continue. "I'm just saying."

"*Stop* saying. That's not what I want to hear right now."

She blinked the water out of her eyelashes. "What would you like to hear?"

His hands came up to cup her breasts and his thumbs flicked lightly over the tips. "How much you want me would be nice."

The world seemed to shift beneath her feet. She drew a deep breath, hoping to steady herself. "If I tell you how much I want you, you might not realize you can stop, if—if you need to."

"I'm not planning on turning back."

"But the regret might not be worth it for you—"

"I can see I'm going to have to shut you up my own way."

"I'm sorry, but—"

She didn't get the rest out because he covered her mouth with his and kissed her until she could no longer remember what she wanted to get across.

"We're going to set down a few rules," he murmured against her lips when they stopped to gasp for breath. "You understand?"

"*Rules?*" she repeated numbly. "What rules?"

He kissed her again, immediately and deeply, adding more tongue and more urgency as his hands slid down her body. "Let's go over them."

Her skin was so sensitive she could hardly focus. All she wanted was for him to go on touching her. "Later."

"That's better," he said, accurately reading her impatience to forget any kind of conversation. "But just in case, this is what you can say."

His finger was running down the crevice of her behind. "I don't know what you're talking about."

"We're going over approved content for when we're making love."

She smiled at his playful expression. "I see. How about 'just shut up and kiss me'?"

"Not bad. I've used that one myself," he said, his mouth so close to hers they exchanged breath.

"Do you have a list?" she asked.

"Just some suggestions."

"Like…"

"'Give me more' is fine. 'God, that feels good' is even better. And 'Ah, yes, fuck me' in broken gasps is pretty much my favorite. But I'm in a precarious state when it comes to control, so you might not want to use that one too soon."

She laughed; she'd never seen this side of him. He'd always been so serious. "What about '*nice* ass'?"

He nipped at her lips. "I give you 'fuck' and you give me 'ass'? That's grade school stuff."

"I'm not too good at being crude."

"Try again. This is the one time crude works."

"Um…" She felt herself blush, but she liked this. "'Don't come yet'?"

"I'll admit that's useful but I'm hoping I'll be able to tell where you're at in the process. I'm also hoping I can last until I get you there. We may have some difficulty in that regard."

"That's the second time you've warned me. Are you

telling me you have a problem with premature ejaculation?"

"Not usually. But—" When his mouth closed over one nipple, she groaned and he grew too distracted to continue.

She let her head fall back as darts of pleasure shot through her. Still, she was curious enough that she managed to hang on to the thread of the conversation. "But…"

He lifted his head. "You should know I'm about to come just looking at you."

The levity of a moment before disappeared. "You *are* better at bedroom talk than I am," she whispered.

"We'll practice together." His hand found the sensitive spot it'd been seeking, but she stopped him almost as soon as he touched her there.

"I've dreamed of having you inside me from the moment you first staggered out of my bedroom on Tuesday morning," she said.

He moved a hank of wet hair off her forehead. "See? It's not that difficult."

Again, she held him off. "Take off your pants."

"Wow! You *really* got it." His smile slanted to one side as he unbuttoned his jeans and peeled them off— not an easy feat given that the denim was heavy from the water.

She made a point of dropping her gaze to his erection. "Impressive. You're bigger than a horse!"

"Okay, okay, you should quit while you're ahead," he said, and they both laughed as he found her mouth again. Then there wasn't any more talking at all.

Callie wasn't like Behrukh. Levi couldn't help noticing that—again. But this time he didn't find it so hard to cope with. He wasn't sure what had changed from yesterday, except that he was more prepared to kiss a woman who didn't taste like Behrukh, more prepared to touch a woman who didn't feel like her. Maybe it helped that he'd had over twenty-four hours to recognize how unrealistic he'd been when he thought he could resist Callie.

He could even appreciate some of what made Callie unique to him. Behrukh had been so literal. She would not have understood all of the conversation they'd just had. Too much would've been lost in translation. With the vast differences between his culture and hers, they sometimes had difficulty communicating about basic things. Callie was as American as he was. That made certain nuances accessible to both of them from the start.

He also liked how transparent she was. Her obvious enthusiasm for what they were doing added a level of eroticism he hadn't yet experienced. It didn't hurt that, with her, there was no need to fear a backlash, no need to keep glancing over his shoulder as if he was taking something he had no right to take.

"This isn't comfortable. Let's get the hell out of here," he said, and scooped her into his arms. They'd already tried making love in the shower but this one was too old and small. So far he'd succeeded only in donning a rubber and pulling down the damn shower rod he'd just fixed.

He wanted Callie in bed. *Now.*

They were wet, and he didn't stop so they could dry off. He hoped she wouldn't care. He couldn't wait another second to feel her close around him.

If she minded, she didn't complain. She stared up at him, her eyes finally saying far more than her lips.

"What you lack in bedroom talk, you make up for in other areas," he said as he pushed inside her.

She raked her fingernails down his back and arched into him. "I meant that horse comment."

He flashed her a smile. He appreciated the joke, but they were both too wound up to laugh. The compulsion to thrust overtook him, and she responded with a guttural moan that said she liked it.

He loved the feel of Callie, but he also liked watching her as they moved together. She looked up at him as if...as if this was somehow momentous, which was oddly gratifying. But he'd been right to issue a warning. He had no stamina. It'd been too long since he'd had any kind of sexual release. The sudden rush of climax hit him almost instantly.

He tried to stop himself, to hang on so he could provide more enjoyment for her, but she shook her head.

"It's okay," she murmured, and tightened her legs, drawing him so deep there was nothing he could do but let go.

"Give me a few minutes," Levi said as he attempted to recover. "I'm really not so bad in bed."

Callie combed her fingers through his hair, which was still wet but drying quickly. "There's no rush," she said. "I'm tired, anyway."

Lately, she was always tired. She wanted to fall asleep with him lying on her shoulder, as he was now, but she had to go take some of the medication she'd hidden above the fridge, behind an odd assortment of her grandmother's rose vases and pitchers. She hadn't wanted him to see her swallowing pills at dinner. Then she'd gotten so caught up in the tension between them she'd forgotten.

"Where are you going?" he asked as she slipped out of bed.

"To dry my hair or it'll be wet all night."

"Okay, wake me when you get back."

"I will," she promised. But when she returned, she was careful not to disturb his sleep. She lay awake for some time, listening to him breathe and saying a silent prayer that she hadn't done something she'd regret.

21

When Callie woke up, it was only two-thirty in the morning. She hadn't been asleep for more than a few hours.

At first, she couldn't figure out what had disturbed her. Levi hadn't budged. His breathing was soft and even, and she felt warm and comfortable beside him. Rifle wasn't stirring, either; he was dozing peacefully on the carpet by her bed. And there were no strange noises coming from outside, nothing that led her to believe Denny and Powell were back....

Then she realized. She didn't feel well. As a matter of fact, she felt *terrible*. Weak. Nauseous.

Shit. She was going to throw up again. But she didn't want Levi to hear her. Then he'd know something was wrong. She couldn't claim she had the flu twice in such a short time. She had to get up and out of the bedroom.

Moving as carefully as possible, so she wouldn't disturb him, she slipped out of bed and tiptoed from the room. The jingle of Rifle's collar told her she'd awakened him. He was following her. But Levi remained dead to the world. He'd missed a lot of sleep the past week, and she was glad he had the chance to catch up.

She had to move faster if she expected to get her-

self somewhere she could throw up without being noticed. She considered going outside, to the barn. But
there wasn't time to walk that far. She made it to the
half bath off the kitchen before everything she'd had
for dinner came back up.

She tried not to make a sound until she could close
the door, a feat she managed with her foot since she
couldn't leave the toilet. Rifle squeezed through first,
however. He watched her, tongue hanging out, eyes
seemingly sympathetic. That was enough to make her
grateful for his presence.

"I'm going…to be okay," she told him. She wouldn't
succumb to liver failure. She was going to get well. If
meeting Levi had taught her anything, it was that falling in love was every bit as wonderful as it was supposed to be. Experiencing this in her condition and with
someone she didn't know anything about wasn't ideal.
But she wanted to enjoy it as long as possible, as long
as Levi was willing to stay.

She leaned over the toilet as she struggled to regain
her breath. If she didn't want to end up on the floor, she
had to conserve her strength. But she retched again a
few minutes later. And a few minutes after that. Only
this time when she lifted her head she saw a red sub-
stance in what had come up.

Fresh fear lanced through her. She was vomiting
blood.

Levi woke to an empty bed. He listened for Callie,
but couldn't hear her moving around the house. Thinking she might be in the kitchen, eating breakfast, he
climbed out of bed and pulled on her pink robe, since
his only clothes were still wet. But the kitchen was as

empty as all the other rooms. She didn't even seem to have eaten.

The clock hanging on the wall caught his eye. It was just before six; the sun had barely come up. Where could she be?

Rifle whined. Callie had shut her dog in the mudroom. Levi didn't know why she'd done that. She generally let him wander throughout the house.

Maybe she was afraid the dog would disturb him....

"What's going on, boy? Where's your pretty mistress?" he asked as he let Rifle out.

The dog looked up at him as if he had the same question.

Levi supposed Callie could be out with her camera, taking pictures. He was sure the anthill that had intrigued her so much before the fire had been destroyed. But if she was happy with an anthill, there were a lot of other bits of nature she could photograph. Maybe she'd found a caterpillar, a butterfly, a particular flower or another spider.

He was about to go outside and see when he spotted a note on the fridge. It looked as if it had been written with a shaky hand—he guessed she'd been in a hurry—but he could read the message.

"Had to run out. Will probably be late."

Levi scratched his head. What started before six?

For the first time in a long while, he wished he had a cell phone. He wanted to call the photography studio. He could only guess that Tina was behind and Callie had gone in to help her get ready for the day.

He wished he'd been able to see Callie before she left. Last night had ended far too soon. He felt as if he'd let her down.

* * *

Baxter had taken Callie to the hospital that was part of the transplant clinic. He sat beside her bed, looking overwrought and reading a magazine he'd grabbed from the waiting room, which was pretty much how he'd passed the entire morning. She'd thrown up into a bowl the whole time they'd been on the road. Seeing her, hearing her, had upset him so badly he'd driven with tears streaming down his cheeks.

Now he just seemed irritable. And tired. His thick, curly hair was smashed down on one side, since her call had dragged him out of bed in the middle of the night and scared him enough that he threw on his clothes without taking time for anything else.

She didn't think she'd ever seen him when he wasn't well-groomed.

Of course, he'd never seen her like this, either.

"You can leave, you know. If you have to go to work," she said, biting her bottom lip as she studied him.

He closed the magazine. "I'm not going anywhere."

She smoothed her bedding with one hand. "Why? I can handle this on my own. I've done it before." Sort of. She'd been to the clinic for many, many tests, but she'd never been admitted via the emergency room. The fact that she'd had to do it today wasn't a good sign.

"The point is…you don't *need* to handle it on your own," he said. *"You have people who love you!"*

True. But there was someone new in her life, and she was positive she'd lose him the instant he found out about her disease. She was going to lose him soon enough as it was. Why couldn't she put off the Big Revelation just a little longer? That wasn't asking too much, was it? If she had to die, she was at least going to do everything possible to enjoy the intense interest, desire and euphoria Levi created—without letting the reality of her situation affect him.

"I'm aware of that," she said.

"Then why won't you let them support you?"

She couldn't tell him why. It would only lead to an argument. He'd say that any man who'd walk out on her while she was going through something like this wasn't worth her time in the first place. But that wasn't a fair assessment. He'd be speaking as someone who'd grown up with her, not someone who'd just entered her life. Levi had no reason to involve himself in the sadness of watching her die. She wouldn't blame him if he took off as soon as he heard. There were so many other women out there he could choose from. And he'd feel whole enough to love again soon. He was beginning to heal, to get beyond what he'd suffered in Afghanistan. She could sense it.

"I have my reasons."

"Yeah, well, they aren't *valid* reasons." Baxter jiggled his knee while they waited for her doctor to return with the results of her latest tests. Certain enzymes helped the liver perform its many functions. But when a liver became damaged, these enzymes leaked into the blood and could be picked up on a blood test, giving an indication of just how damaged her liver was. Her doctor had already started her on beta-blockers to control the bleeding from her esophagus.

"I slept with him last night," she announced.

At this, Baxter dropped his magazine. "You did?"

She gave him a shy smile.

"What was it like?"

She groped for the best way to explain it to him. "Like...like you'd feel if you were with Noah."

"That good, huh?"

"It was exactly what I wanted." She would've clarified that it wasn't because the sex itself was so great. There'd just been that one brief interlude and then he'd slept so deeply he hadn't awakened for more as he'd planned. Technically, she'd had greater physical pleasure with Kyle. But that didn't matter. Bad sex with Levi was better than good sex with anyone else. She just couldn't say so, not without revealing information she was too protective of Levi to share.

Baxter sighed and rubbed his face. "Of all the times to fall in love, Callie."

Remembering the intoxication she felt in Levi's arms, she leaned her head back on the bed. "Falling in love now beats never falling in love at all."

Some people had to take what they could get....

Where was she?

Levi had washed and dried his clothes, fixed the shower curtain rod again, made up the bed and filled Rifle's food and water bowls. He'd also answered the door to Godfrey, who'd removed his stitches. Then he'd weeded and watered the garden and stabilized the empty chicken coop that was listing to one side. He would've started tearing down the barn after that, but the insurance adjuster hadn't yet been by to take a look. So he spent the rest of his afternoon repairing a broken fence at the back of the property. He kept thinking Callie would pull up any minute, but when he finished working after six, she still wasn't home.

Sticky with sweat after so much physical exertion,

he paused and squinted toward the road. Today he'd gazed in that direction many times but saw no sign of a car turning in. A car with Callie inside it...

Where had she gone?

The obvious answer was the studio. She must've had work to do. But if that was the case, why hadn't she driven there? Her SUV was parked where she'd left it when she got home last night.

She had to be with someone else. He just hoped it was Kyle or one of her other friends, because the more time dragged on, the more concerned he became.

Surely, Denny or Powell hadn't gotten hold of her....

He already knew what he'd do to them if they'd hurt her. But he couldn't think about that or he might tear them apart without any proof.

Telling himself to calm down, to fix some dinner and wait a little longer, he went inside. It wasn't as if she'd just disappeared. She'd left him a note, hadn't she?

She was probably fine.

Probably... But he found it strange that she hadn't mentioned having to be somewhere so early when they were together last night. It was also odd that she hadn't taken her car.

When he got out of the shower and there was still no sign of her, he ran out of patience. Digging his motor-cycle keys out of his pocket, he put Rifle in the house and drove his bike past the Gruper rental.

Denny and Powell weren't home. At least, Denny's truck wasn't in the drive and no one answered Levi's knock. So he went to the photography studio.

No one was there, either. Reflections by Callie was dark and locked up tight. He banged on the door, just in case someone was in the back where he couldn't see the light, but there was no response.

What now? he asked himself. He didn't have her cell phone number, or even a cell phone of his own to call her with. But this was a small town. Everyone knew everyone else. He figured he'd ask around.

He went to the Gas-N-Go first, since that was the place he was most familiar with. Joe had just finished for the day, but Levi managed to catch him before he could climb into his truck.

"Hey!" he shouted above the noise of his bike as he rolled to a stop.

"What's up?" Joe asked. "You gonna be able to come in tomorrow?"

Levi killed his engine. "Tomorrow?"

"You didn't hear? I left Callie a couple messages, trying to get hold of you. I've got a busy week coming up and one of my techs will be out on vacation. I could use a hand through Saturday if you're around."

"I'll be here first thing in the morning."

"Eight or nine is fine."

"Okay, but…speaking of Callie, when you called, did you actually talk to her?"

"'Fraid not. Got transferred to voice mail both times. Why? Something wrong?"

Levi didn't want to throw everyone into a panic. This could be nothing. "I doubt it. I just…I expected her home by now, thought I'd check on her."

"Where is she supposed to be?"

"She didn't say. Would you mind trying her cell again?"

Joe seemed mildly surprised by Levi's concern, but he pulled his phone out.

Levi waited, hoping for the best, but he knew he wasn't going to learn anything new when Joe shook his head.

"Voice mail." Joe held the phone out so Levi could take it and leave a message if he chose to, but Levi waved him off. He didn't see any point in telling Callie he was worried and wanted to know where she was, not when she'd have no way of calling him back.

"What about Kyle?" Levi asked.

"You think she might be with him?"

"Could be, right? They're friends. Do you have his number?"

"No, but I could get it from my sister—"

"Maybe you could just tell me where he lives and I'll go by there."

"This time of day he's probably still at the plant," Joe said, and gave Levi directions.

It turned out that Kyle was gone for the day, but the house on the corner of the property hardly looked as though it belonged to an employee, even a manager. The place was too nice. Levi guessed Kyle owned it, so he took a chance and stopped there.

Sure enough, Kyle answered the door—and was visibly shocked to see him. "What's going on?"

"Do you know where Callie is?"

Kyle hesitated as if all the doubts he'd had about Levi were flooding back, but he seemed to put some effort into reserving judgment. "No, why?"

"She left early this morning and hasn't come home. You haven't heard from her?"

"Not a single word."

Kyle didn't add, "Since you came to town everything has been different," but Levi got the impression that was implied.

"You're worried that Denny might've…hurt her?" Kyle guessed.

"I am. Something feels off." Considering Kyle's previous relationship with Callie, Levi couldn't explain some of the nuances that figured into his concern. Like the fact that they'd made love last night and he thought if she had to get up early and leave, she would've mentioned it. Or that he was impatient to see her again because they had unfinished business. He hadn't meant to sleep for hours, hadn't meant to leave her unsatisfied as if he didn't care about her fulfillment. That was a small thing compared to her overall safety, but the way their time together had ended contributed to his sense of unease. Maybe she was so disappointed she wasn't in any hurry to come home….

"Do you think it's too soon to go to the police?" He hated the idea of contacting Chief Stacy. Their last conversation hadn't gone well. But he knew he'd do whatever he had to.

"Have you tried her parents?"

"I don't know where they live."

Kyle opened the screen door and held it wide. "Come on in. We'll give Diana and Boone a call."

Callie couldn't get the doctor to release her. She was feeling better, wanted to go back to the farm. As confident as she was that she wouldn't have any more problems, the doctor said he preferred to keep her overnight so the hospital staff could monitor her progress. If she experienced any more internal bleeding, there was a chance she'd need a transjugular intrahepatic portosystemic shunt. Then it would be a few days before she could go home, and only if she remained free of infection.

"So what are you going to tell everyone again?" she asked Baxter.

Despite her protests, he'd insisted on staying the whole day, had sat by her bedside even while she slept. Occasionally when she woke up, she'd find him frowning at all the equipment, the tubes running into her body, instead of thumbing through his magazine, as he did when he knew she was watching. Reading was all he could do. He'd left home in such a hurry he didn't even have his computer. But now it was after dinnertime. He needed to go eat, shower and get some rest.

"You know what I'm going to say—exactly what you had me tell your parents earlier."

"Great."

He rolled his eyes. "But I'm not sure anyone will buy it."

"Why not? It's summer. Your work schedule isn't as rigorous as usual. They don't know what we had planned."

"One of them might see my car at the house tonight or early tomorrow."

"The chances of them noticing are slim. It'll be after eight before you reach Whiskey Creek. And you generally leave early for work."

"True. Still…"

She didn't want to think about the off chance that someone would realize he hadn't stayed in San Francisco with her as he'd claimed. "So are you sure you're okay to drive me home tomorrow? It'll take you away from work again."

"I don't care about that. I have the freedom. Whatever you need. Call me and I'll come."

She smiled at the reassurance his support gave her. As soon as she got word from her doctor, she'd have Baxter pick her up and bring her to the farm—and she'd get through the long hours in between by thinking of that moment.

Her cell phone rang. Although she'd either ignored or slept through several earlier calls, this one she had to take. She raised a finger to let Baxter know not to open the door.

"Hi, Mom. How are you?"

"I'm fine. How are *you?*"

"Great, why?" She wondered why her mother would be calling. They'd talked just a few hours ago. Diana was the one person Callie had contacted herself. She'd been checking in religiously since she went to visit last week.

"I heard from Kyle a minute ago," her mother said.

Callie sent Baxter an uneasy glance. "What'd he have to say?"

"I guess that Levi fellow who's been staying at the farm is at his place."

Bracing her weight on one hand, Callie propped herself up. *"What for?"*

"He's worried about you, said you've been gone all day."

"I *have* been gone all day. I told you earlier. I'm in San Francisco with Baxter, remember?"

"I explained that, but he didn't seem convinced. He said he had no idea you were going to leave town."

Callie eased herself back. Her stomach was still tender. She didn't want to do anything to make her condition worse. "I forgot to mention it to him. Then I didn't want to wake him. But I left a note."

"From what I can tell, it didn't say much."

"I was in a hurry. Would you like to talk to Bax? He's right here with me."

Baxter's eyes went wide. He didn't like the idea of lying to her mother, especially about this. But Diana stopped her before she could hand him the phone, anyway.

"There's no need for that. Your dad and I, we just wanted to double-check that everything's okay."

"Of course it's okay." She winced at a sudden avalanche of guilt. But she was only asking for a few more days, she reminded herself—just until Levi was gone. "It's fine, good."

"Okay. Tell Bax we said hello."

"He says hi, too."

"'Night, honey."

Baxter was shaking his head when she hung up, but his phone went off before he could voice his thoughts. "Here we go."

"What?"

"It's Kyle."

"Answer it."

His dark eyebrows drew together in a frown. "I don't want to answer it."

"You have to!"

"Shit!"

"Hurry!" she prodded.

He punched the talk button and immediately put his cell on speakerphone so she could hear. "Hello?"

"Why didn't you tell anyone you and Callie were taking a trip together?" Kyle asked without preamble.

Baxter cleared his throat. "Didn't think of it. She was…she was supposed to come out here over a week ago, for lunch, but we decided that…you know, to make a day of it instead. It's summer, after all, and neither of us really has a vacation planned."

"Hi, Kyle!" Callie chipped in to let him know she was in on the conversation.

"Why haven't you two been answering your phones?" he asked.

Baxter fielded this one. "We were out sailing, so we left them in the car."

"Sailing."

"That's right."

Callie wondered if Levi was still at Kyle's. "So what's going on with you?"

"The rest of us have been *working*."

If he only knew what she'd really been doing….

"Hang on," he said. "Someone wants to talk to you."

Levi came on next. "Callie?"

She pressed her fingertips to her temple. "Hi."

"You couldn't have told me you were leaving town?"

Hearing the pique in Levi's voice, she relied on what she'd told her mother. "I'm sorry. I planned to be home tonight, but…we just got off the water, so…"

"The water?"

He hadn't heard the sailing part. "Baxter has a friend here who owns a sailboat. We spent a…a beautiful afternoon on the bay. It was so…peaceful." She couldn't even guess what the weather might really be like. The Bay Area wasn't far, but San Francisco weather seemed independent of every other place. It could be cold and rainy there right now, but he wasn't any more likely to know than she was. And she could imagine a day like she'd described; in fact, she planned to have one exactly like it if she lived long enough.

"I see." His words were stilted, as if he wasn't pleased.

"I should've been clearer. I'm sorry. I really didn't think it would matter to you one way or the other."

"Wouldn't matter if something happened to you?"

"I didn't think you'd assume the worst," she hurried to say. "Anyway, since it's so late, we're going to grab dinner and stay until tomorrow, if that's okay. Do you—do you think you could look after Rifle for me?"

"Of course."

"And the glass company. They're coming out to fix the window in the morning."

"I'll be there." But he didn't sound happy about it.

Fortunately Baxter jumped in. "You'll have to come sailing with us next time, Levi. I think you'd enjoy it."

He'd contributed at the perfect time, made what she'd said convincing enough that Levi seemed to fall for it. Or else he didn't want to reveal any more of his displeasure with Baxter listening in. Either way, Baxter had just gotten her out of a tight spot. She flashed him a grateful smile.

"Thanks," Levi said. "Maybe someday I will."

As she expected, his response was noncommittal, but it ended the conversation on a polite note. They all said goodbye, then Callie closed her eyes. "I hate this," she grumbled.

Apparently no longer frustrated with her, Baxter took her hand. "You're going to get through it."

Not without a new liver she wouldn't.

22

Callie was home by noon the next day. She was looking forward to seeing Levi. He was all she'd thought about. But she didn't have a travel bag, which she would've packed had she really taken a trip to San Francisco. With her hair barely combed and no makeup on, it was also pretty obvious that she hadn't showered as she would've done had she been on vacation in the city. She had had none of her stuff—just a toothbrush and a few other necessities that Baxter had gone out and purchased before leaving the hospital last night. It wasn't as if she'd had time to prepare before rushing to the emergency room. There were a number of details that could've given her away.

But her concern over whether or not Levi would notice turned out to be unwarranted. Although Rifle greeted her when she let herself into the house and she could see that the window had been fixed, Levi wasn't around. He'd put a note on the fridge where she'd left hers.

"Working at the Gas-N-Go. See you tonight." As soon as she spotted it, she recalled Joe's messages. He must've figured out how to get through to Levi on his own. She hadn't remembered to tell Levi when they talked so briefly while he was at Kyle's, and she'd had no way to contact him after.

"Everything okay?" Baxter came into the kitchen behind her.

"Great, actually. Levi's in town."

"That gives you some breathing room, huh?" They'd been discussing how to handle the various questions he might ask.

"Now I can settle in, rest a bit more and shower before I see him." She'd also have time to call her parents, assure them she was home safe and chat as long as they wanted. She'd had to keep their conversations brief when she was in the hospital in case they overheard a doctor being paged on the intercom or something.

Rifle whined to get her attention, so she crouched to pet him. "I'm home, buddy. Everything's okay. For the moment, anyway."

"I've got to go," Baxter said.

Callie stood to give him a hug. "Thanks, Bax. For everything."

He held her a second longer than usual. "I'm glad you told me what you're going through. I'm grateful I get to spend this time with you."

She knew what he was saying about the other people in her life. He was telling her they'd feel the same way. But then he added something she didn't expect.

"Still, I have to admit…if I had the chance to be with Noah the way you've got this chance to be with Levi, I'd take it," he said. "You have every right to do what makes you happy. So enjoy it and don't feel guilty."

"What made you change your mind?" she asked as he let her go.

"I couldn't understand how he could mean so much

to you in such a short time, but—" he kissed her cheek "—you've made a believer out of me."

Levi was anxious to return to the farm. He hadn't seen Callie since he'd carried her to bed from the shower. He'd thought of her, though—almost constantly—but not for the reasons he'd expected to. Surprisingly, he felt no remorse for getting involved with her. The opposite was actually true. It was as if he'd finally broken free from everything that had held him captive for the past two years, as if the soldier he'd been in Afghanistan had died.

He wanted to bury that much younger man and never look back. He knew Behrukh would want him to go on without her and be happy. But he'd known that all along. So what had changed? Was he merely giving himself an excuse to do what he wanted?

Maybe. Believing that Behrukh would approve certainly seemed convenient. But he'd already slept with Callie once. He didn't see how stopping would change anything. He doubted he'd be able to keep his hands off her, anyway. That one encounter had been far too brief....

He saw her in the kitchen window as he turned down the drive. At the sound of his motorcycle, she looked up and smiled—and he was hit with a deluge of testosterone.

Heart pounding in anticipation, he got off his bike and strode to the house.

She met him at the door. "How was work?"

"Fine. I made another two hundred dollars."

"Good news. You need some clothes."

Right now, he felt like the only thing he needed was her.

She stepped back to let him in, as if she wasn't quite sure how to greet him.

He wanted to touch her, to draw her into his arms. But he'd been fixing cars all day, and although he'd washed his hands with the special soap at the garage, he had grease on his clothes.

He offered her an apologetic smile. "I'm dirty."

"I can see that," she said with a chuckle, but then her eyes locked with his and he knew she didn't want to wait a second longer.

Fortunately, neither did he.

"It seemed like you were gone forever," he told her and, taking her hand, led her into the bedroom.

They showered together, only this time they both peeled off their clothes before getting in. Callie laughed as Levi hurried to scrub up. He managed to get mostly clean before she gave him somewhere else to put his hands. She didn't care if he'd gotten every last smudge. She figured a girl who didn't have very long to live was justified in her impatience. What did a little grease matter in the face of that?

"Anxious, huh?" he teased with a laugh. But he quit laughing when she arched a challenging eyebrow and lathered up their stomachs. As soon as he felt her against him, he sucked in a breath and said, "Okay, you win."

After that, everything moved fast. They were out of the shower and kissing up against the wall, the vanity, the door, before they reached the bed.

There, she tried to pull him down on top of her, but

he resisted. "I owe you something first," he told her. Then he smiled as he nudged her legs apart and lowered his head.

Callie was determined to live in the moment. She refused to think about anything else—the stint in the hospital that had come before or everything that would likely come after. For now, she felt completely content and fulfilled and didn't want the slightest detail to change.

"What's going on in that pretty head of yours?" Levi murmured.

They'd been in bed since he got home nearly three hours ago. They hadn't even bothered to get up and eat. At one point, she'd finally gone to the kitchen to remove their dinner from the oven, but by then it was too late. They could still smell the charred remains of the roast she'd been cooking, despite having opened all the windows.

But even the loss of her great meal did nothing to tarnish her happiness.

"Callie?"

He'd asked her a question. Pulling herself out of her thoughts, she briefly pressed her lips to his chest. *"The Thorn Birds."*

"The *what?*"

"It's a novel, a sort of epic historical. My mother gave me a copy when I was in high school. It's one of her all-time favorites."

He lifted her chin so he could look into her face. "What made you think of it?"

She admired the thick fringe of lashes that framed his eyes. "There was something in that book about a mythical bird that spends its whole life searching for thorn trees. When it finds the perfect thorn, it impales itself."

"Why would it do that?"

"I don't remember, but it's while dying that it sings its most beautiful song."

He covered a yawn. "Sounds depressing."

"In a way, but sometimes pain and loss are worth a moment like that, don't you think?"

He shifted so he could nuzzle her neck. "Let's just say I'm not tempted to read it."

She smiled at his response.

"Why did you think of suicidal birds right now, any-way?" he asked.

Closing her eyes, she tried to commit every detail of how he felt to memory. She was going to need those positive associations later, to sustain her through the hard times. "I really liked the book."

He leaned over her. "I have bad news."

Instinctively, she stiffened. Was this where he said he was about to move on? That he'd be leaving in the morning?

She knew it was coming....

"Whoa, relax," he said, obviously noticing her reac-tion. "I shouldn't have put it like that. I was just going to say that now we've let our dinner burn, I'm hungry."

She chuckled. "I'm not surprised."

"What about you? Any interest in food?"

"Not too much. I have some peanut butter and jelly, though. I can make sandwiches."

She started to get up, but he pulled her back. "You're not trying to lose weight, are you?"

This time she was more careful about hiding her reaction. "Not really. Why?"

"You look thinner than the pictures I've seen of you. And most of your clothes are fitting pretty loosely."

She shrugged as if it was nothing to be concerned about. "I had a few pounds to lose."

"So you're okay?" he asked.

"What do you mean?"

"Sometimes...sometimes you seem so tired."

She caught her breath. "We've missed a lot of sleep in the past couple of weeks."

"This is different. It's more like...weariness. When I see it in your face, I get the feeling that...I don't know... that something might be wrong. Like that time I saw you leaning on the kitchen table right after I got here."

Callie knew if she was ever going to tell Levi about her liver, now was the time. But then it would ruin her moment, which she'd sworn to preserve. She was still clinging to the dream that he'd drive off and never have to find out.

"I'm fine." She pecked his lips. "Let's get those sandwiches going."

"What are you doing?"

Callie forced a smile as Levi came into the room. After dinner, he'd gone into the bathroom while she'd gone to the linen closet. "Just making up your bed."

He came closer. "That's what I thought."

"It's okay if you sleep here, isn't it?"

"The question is why would you want me to?"

Because she didn't dare let him sleep with her. Thanks to the sandwich she'd eaten, she wasn't feeling well again. She didn't want to risk being sick in front of him. She'd be embarrassed after all the lies she'd told. But, more than that, she already cared too much about him, didn't want him to suffer the same loss her parents and friends would. That meant she had to be careful to maintain some distance. "I thought…since you're only here for a short time we probably shouldn't risk getting *too* close."

His eyebrows slid up. "Sharing a bed is too close, but having sex isn't?"

She didn't know what to say to that. "We just…need to keep our…relationship in perspective," she said, trying again.

He propped his hands on his hips, which made him look sexy and displeased at the same time, since he was wearing no shirt and his hair was standing up on one side. "What exactly does that mean?"

"It means I don't want to hurt you in the end."

"You're shutting me out now so you won't hurt me later?"

"Who knows how this will go? Life is uncertain, right? I'm also protecting myself. I don't want my heart broken when you drive off." It was too late for that, but at least she'd reconciled herself to reality. He didn't know what her reality was.

"So that's it. We're back to goodbye again."

She could no longer meet his eyes. "Not for a few days, I hope."

"Why do you always have to talk about the end? And how I can back out if I want? Or get with another woman? Why can't we just…be where we're at and go from here?"

"Because I think we should prepare for the inevitable, don't you?"

He came over and took the blanket she'd been putting on the sofa away from her. "Is that why you haven't pushed me to tell you my name? Because you see our relationship as being so brief, so temporary?"

"I asked you what your real name was."

"Once. Immediately after you learned that the name I'd given you wasn't correct."

"You didn't want to tell me. I'm guessing you still don't."

"True, but something's wrong if you don't *want* to know."

"I respect your privacy."

"So…now that we're done making love, you've had enough of me?"

"We have to separate sometime! We'd both be better off keeping that in mind!"

"Why?"

He was so endearingly disappointed, the compulsion to kiss him became almost overpowering. It didn't matter that they'd already made love. She wanted to be with him again. And he seemed to feel the same.

Dropping his gaze to her mouth, he put a finger under her chin as if he'd bring his lips to hers, and she automatically swayed toward him. "See that?" he murmured.

She remained mute as she stared up at him.

"This—" he motioned to the bedding "—is bullshit. I'm not sleeping on the couch."

"Excuse me?"

He ran his lips lightly over hers. "Tell me you don't *want* me in your bed."

She couldn't think of anything except getting a real

kiss. "It's not that, it's…it's that I think we should be careful."

"To hell with careful!" he growled. "Love and war don't work that way."

"How do they work?"

"It's all or nothing," he said, and carried her into the bedroom, where he took off her clothes again.

Somehow Callie didn't get sick that night. Having Levi beside her might've helped. His steady breathing was soothing, and she loved the springiness of the hair on his legs as they brushed against hers almost as much as she liked to touch the smooth skin covering the muscles of his arms and chest. At one point, when she allowed herself to snuggle closer, he rolled toward her to scoop her into the curve of his body.

"You okay?" he murmured.

When she pretended to be too groggy to answer, so he wouldn't feel he had to wake up, he fell back asleep, and she smiled as she turned to study his face in the moonlight. That rawboned look he'd had when he first appeared on her doorstep, when he'd reminded her of an alley cat, was already changing. She liked that he seemed so much healthier but admired all the things that hadn't changed just as much—the high arch to his nose, the golden stubble on his cheeks and chin, the small scar on his lip, which he'd probably gotten in some fight. She wanted to get her camera, to capture him on film to help her preserve these memories, but she doubted he'd appreciate being photographed in the middle of the night.

Around four, she finally drifted off, convinced that she'd gotten what she'd asked for. The universe had granted what she'd most wanted to experience before she died—to know what it felt like to be deeply in love. Given that, she felt greedy asking for anything else so she simply braced herself for the worst. She knew the happiness they'd found together couldn't last but, God, was it good while it did.

Nothing terrible happened in the next three days. The week continued to pass in the same idyllic fashion as that perfect night. She and Levi got up early and laughed and talked while they gardened, and occasionally had a water fight. After that, they showered together, sometimes they made love if they had time, and Levi went to work at the Gas-N-Go. While he was gone, she cleaned, visited her parents, met with the insurance adjuster about the barn and ran errands, which included a trip to the mall to get him some clothes and a trip to the grocery store. But she was always home and had dinner waiting for him when he got off. Then they slept in each other's arms, making love whenever the desire struck either one of them.

Maybe it was because she was so careful to take her medicine at the correct intervals and to watch what she ate, but she didn't get sick in all of that time. She was feeling so good she was almost convinced that she'd taken a turn for the better, that her liver was somehow regenerating like the livers of healthy people. Medical miracles happened occasionally, didn't they?

She wanted to believe she might be one of those lucky few, was *determined* to believe. But she feared she'd been leading them both down a path destined to end in misery when, on Friday, Levi came home early with a gift for her.

"What's this?" she asked as he thrust a plush blue box into her hand.

The grin he gave her made her heart skip a beat. "Open it and find out."

"I hope…" She cleared her throat. "I hope you didn't spend a lot."

"I'm only making two hundred dollars a pop, so—" he laughed "—you don't have much to worry about."

But when she opened the box she could tell he must've spent at least one day's labor on it. Any necklace from Hammond and Son Fine Jewelers, a store located not far from her studio, wasn't cheap. This one had a gold hummingbird pendant with a small diamond for the eye.

"It reminds me of those birds you told me about in that book," he explained.

"I remember." He was referring to the thorn birds, the ones who sang their most beautiful song as they died…. Fortunately, he had no idea there was any kind of parallel. He just associated that story with the first full night they'd spent together and her interest in a strange bird.

"Do you like it?" he asked.

The lump in her throat made it difficult to speak. "I do."

He tilted his head to look into her face. "Hey, what's wrong?"

She took the necklace out of the box and turned, both so he wouldn't see the tears in her eyes and so he could help her put it on. "It's the best gift I've ever been given," she said. But with that little gold bird, reality had come crashing through. She'd assumed it would take him a long time to fall in love, to get past the loss of the woman he'd been with before. She'd lulled herself into believing that so nothing could ruin these precious days.

But after he fastened the clasp on her new necklace, he slid his arms around her waist and kissed her neck as she leaned back into him, making her wonder if she'd underestimated his ability to heal.

"They had other stuff, really nice stuff," he told her. "One day I'll take you there and you can pick out something more expensive."

One day? That didn't sound as if he planned on driving off in the near future.

23

"What's this called again?" Baxter grimaced as he donned his glasses. He looked good in them. He was so classically handsome he looked good in anything. But usually his vanity dictated he try to get by without them.

Callie got herself a glass of water from his fridge. "An advanced directive."

"Which is…"

"Basically, a power of attorney."

"For what?"

"So my parents can make decisions in the event that—" she tried to think of a euphemistic way to state the bald reality "—I can't make them myself."

When understanding dawned, he didn't bother reading the fine print. He dropped the paper on the table, took off his glasses and rubbed his eyes. She'd caught him on a Saturday morning, just rolling out of bed. She'd known it was a little early to show up at his place, but Levi was only going to work half a day. She wanted to take care of this while he was busy. Now that she and Levi were sleeping together as well as living together, she had less privacy than before. He overheard her telephone conversations, went into her purse for change or a pen if he needed it and was comfortable enough in her bedroom to do as he pleased. She no longer had her own space. That meant it was harder to find a safe spot to hide her meds. She'd had to take them out of the cupboard above the refrigerator and hide them in a shoebox she kept under the porch. But she didn't dare put this directive there. It needed to be in the hands of someone who knew what to do with it.

Baxter scowled at her. "And I'm the lucky recipient because…"

"I can't give it to my parents. Not yet. Just hang on to it for them until I break the news or…you know."

"If you're planning to break the news soon, like you've been talking about, you can probably hang on to it yourself."

"It's safer this way."

"You mean, in case you happen to wait too long."

"That's what I mean."

His glasses skittered across the table as he tossed them away. "Tell me what's happening with you and Levi. Somehow I like hearing about that more than when to pull the plug should you go on life support."

"We're happy," she said. "He might be a…a vagrant, a rambler, someone who's been driving around America on a motorcycle for almost two years, but…for me, he's *home*. I don't know how to describe it any better."

Baxter crossed one leg over the other. "And yet you still don't think you should tell him about your condition."

She rubbed her forehead. "Yes. I *should* tell him. I should've told him from the beginning. But it didn't seem necessary at first. And now…every time I try, the words get stuck in my throat."

"So what are you going to do? Let him be surprised?"

"No." She folded her arms to give her statement more conviction. "I've decided I'm going to get well so I won't have to tell him."

"I like that idea."

She sat next to him and covered his hand with hers. "I've felt great this week, Bax. I think recovery might be possible."

He wouldn't quite meet her eyes, which told her he was afraid that was wishful thinking. "Why weren't you at coffee yesterday?"

"It's hard to be around the gang right now. I don't like deceiving them."

"They're freaking out. After all the years we've been friends, you're withdrawing for no apparent reason. It's been all I can do to stop them from showing up at your place en masse."

"Really?"

"It all started with Kyle." He sent her a look that warned her he had something unpleasant to impart. "Callie, he blew the whistle on the friends-with-benefits thing last Sunday."

She felt her jaw drop. "He did *what?*"

"He flat out made the announcement. We were all on the phone, trying to figure out what's wrong with you, and…he said he thinks you're avoiding everyone because of him. He feels like shit."

She smacked the table. "I don't want him to feel like shit. I've told him—"

"It doesn't matter what you told him," Baxter broke in. "Your actions are speaking so loud he can't hear your words."

"But *he* was the one who didn't want to tell! Actually, *I* didn't really want everyone to know, either." She propped up her chin with one hand. "That's not the legacy I want to leave behind."

"Another reason to get well."

She braced herself. "So…what did everyone say?"

"They were understanding, for the most part. You don't have to worry about that."

"Why hasn't anyone said anything to me?"

"Besides the fact that you won't answer your damn phone?"

"Argh!" She leaned back in the chair. "I've got my life so screwed up."

He frowned in sympathy. "I need to warn you about one other thing."

"And that is…"

"My attempts to stop them from coming over have finally failed. We'll be at the farm tomorrow. They've had about all they can take."

"Wait…it's an intervention or something?"

"They want to assure you that no matter what's going on, they're still your friends and will support you through it. Whether it's sleeping with your best friend or…or suffering from liver disease," he added more softly, "but, of course, they can't say that."

"I don't want to deal with this while Levi's here!"

"Sorry. Like I said, I've put them off as long as I can. They were going to come last Monday, but that was the night I supposedly took you to San Francisco."

"When I was in the hospital."

"After that, I was afraid having them show up might upset you and cause a relapse. So I told them you were fine. That we had a blast. That you're just busy. I said to give you some time to get over the embarrassment of getting too close to Kyle. I almost had them convinced to let you be. If only you'd come to coffee yesterday...."

"You couldn't have given me a heads-up that coffee was so important?" she asked glumly.

"I didn't know! That was just when everyone started talking about you and got so worked up they wouldn't listen to me."

At least he'd done all he could.

She considered what having her army of friends show up tomorrow morning might mean—to her and to Levi. "Do they know how I feel about Levi?"

"I'm sure *Kyle*'s guessed," he said with a wink.

She flinched. She'd basically cut off all association with Kyle, which wasn't right. They'd been friends for so long, had promised each other they'd be friends for life. "I can't believe he confessed the truth. He definitely didn't want anyone to find out. I think, after marrying Noelle and getting divorced so soon after, he's embarrassed enough."

He got up to pour himself a glass of orange juice. "What he went through wasn't easy. I can see why he wouldn't want to tell anyone about this latest...whatever. But that's how worried he is about you," he said, raising his voice to be heard from the kitchen. "He's afraid you two doing the deed is at the root of the problem. He wanted us to know in case there's something we could do to assure you that we won't hate you because of it."

"Oh, dear, I need to talk to him."

"You need to talk to everyone," Bax said, returning. "And, like I just mentioned, you're going to have the chance to do that very soon."

"Tomorrow."

"That's right."

She took another sip of her water.

"Who's coming?"

He took his place at the table. "Eve, Riley, Cheyenne, Dylan, me, Noah, Kyle. The whole gang. Except Gail, of course, because she's in L.A. And Ted. He's on a tight deadline."

The mention of Ted reminded Callie of his comment about Scott from last week's coffee date. "You didn't mention Sophia."

"She wasn't on the call."

"She didn't say anything at coffee yesterday?"

The ice in his glass clinked as he took a sip. "She wasn't there."

"But she always comes."

"Not if Skip's in town."

"He's never in town on a Friday morning. If he comes home, it's usually late."

He shrugged. "Then I don't know."

She turned her glass, wiping the condensation. "I think it's what Ted said last week, don't you?"

"Could be. She's been trying to be friends with us for so long. Maybe she's given up."

"How did Ted react to her absence?"

Baxter finished his juice. "It definitely seemed to bother him. He's been acting like he hates having her crash the party every week, but his eyes went to the door every time someone opened it as if he was hoping to see her walk in. And he got sullen and quiet about halfway through when she didn't show."

"He shouldn't have been such a jerk to her," she said.

"It's complicated with them, as you know."

"Everything's complicated right now." She put her glass in the sink and dug her keys out of her purse.

"What am I going to tell Levi when my friends come over and demand to know what's wrong with me?"

He drummed his fingers on the table as though the answer was obvious.

"What?"

"At some point, you might consider the truth."

But then Levi would not only leave, he'd hate her for lying to him. What if she could beat her disease instead? What if she could get a transplant and live?

"Thanks," she said. "I'll consider that next time I want the man I love to walk out on me."

Levi found a motorcycle helmet at a garage sale as he passed through town on his way home. He thought it might be a little big for Callie, but he was willing to risk the twenty-five dollars. It didn't have to fit perfectly to protect her. At least he'd be able to take her for a ride.

After paying the ten-year-old who was collecting the money, he strapped the helmet on behind him and took off. But he didn't get far. Before he reached the outskirts of town, he saw police lights flashing in the small mirror attached to his handlebars.

"Shit," he muttered. What now? He hadn't been speeding. There was too much traffic for that.

He pulled to the side of the road, put down the kickstand and waited for the officer to approach him.

"In a hurry?"

It was Chief Stacy. Levi removed his helmet and met the steely gaze of Whiskey Creek's head of police. "Not particularly." He motioned to the road. "Are you saying I was speeding despite these stop-and-go tourists puttering through town?"

Stacy seemed to realize that would be too unbelievable. "No. You might not be aware of it, but you ran a red light back there."

Levi scowled at him. "I'm not aware of it because I didn't do it."

"Sorry. Saw you with my own eyes."

"Must've been someone else, Chief. There're only two stoplights in this town, and I'm well aware of both of them."

"You can say what you want." His lips curved into an arrogant smile. "But it's your word against mine."

When Levi swung his leg over his bike, Stacy's hand hovered above the gun at his hip. "Just stay where you are."

"Or what?" Levi said. "You'll shoot me? For getting off my bike?"

"That's no small temptation."

"Why? What have I ever done to you?"

"If I remember right, I asked you to move on."

"You mean you asked me to leave town."

His hand remained poised to grab his sidearm. "Now you're splitting hairs."

"I guess I'm not overly susceptible to suggestions you have no business making. I haven't done anything wrong, and I'm not leaving, not until I know Callie is safe."

"You don't have to worry about Callie. *I* can protect her."

Levi felt like dropping Stacy right where he stood. He knew he could do it before Stacy could draw that damn gun. But he also knew he had enough problems. In the past, he'd been far more reckless than he was now, because back then he hadn't cared if he lived or died. "The way you protected her from the fire?"

"That won't happen again. Denny and Powell are gone." He puffed out his chest. "Problem solved."

Levi couldn't believe it. "They're *what?*"

"You heard me."

But they'd been around just a few days ago. And they were supposed to be in Whiskey Creek for the entire summer. "Where did they go?"

"Let's just say…they suddenly found it in their best interest to rent elsewhere."

So that was it. "You mean you invited *them* to move on, too."

"They were better at taking a hint. No way did they want to be run up on charges for that fire."

"There was no physical proof linking them to the fire. All you had on them was motive," Levi pointed out.

"That was enough. No one else around here would do something like that."

Now he was a mind reader? Levi had no love for Denny and Powell, but he liked Stacy even less. "I'm pretty sure duress falls outside the scope of legitimate police work."

Stacy's eyes narrowed. "Who the hell are *you* to tell me that? Anyway, I'm thinking we've been too friendly, made you too comfortable here." He pulled out his citation book. "So maybe it needs to start getting a little *un*comfortable."

Levi clenched his teeth in an effort to control his temper. "That's why I'm getting a ticket? Because you don't want me here?"

Stacy didn't answer. "License and registration, please."

"You know my ID got burned in the fire."

"Your registration, too?"

"Destroyed with my wallet."

He made a *tsking* sound. "That's unfortunate," he said as he shoved the citation book back in his pocket. "I guess that gives me—well, *you*—two choices."

"And those are…"

"You can agree to leave Whiskey Creek by tomorrow. Or we can head over to the station, where I can fingerprint you to get proper ID."

Levi didn't bother hiding his disgust as he shook his head. "Neither one will get you what you really want."

Stacy seemed taken aback by this statement. "How would you know?"

"Because Callie's not interested in you."

"You think you've got more to offer her than I do?" He chuckled. "Get in the car."

Before Levi could move, the sound of tires crunching on the gravel shoulder to their left drew his attention. It was Joe.

"Hey, Chief," Joe said as he climbed out of the cab. "Something wrong here?"

Stacy pointed to the logo on Levi's shirt. "Your new grease monkey ran a red light."

Joe's eyebrows knitted. "Sucks for him. Which one?"

"Does it matter? That one right there." The police chief pointed at the closest traffic signal, only a block away.

"Are you sure it was that one, Chief?"

Stacy seemed bored when he answered. "Positive."

Joe stretched the muscles in his neck as if he'd put in a hard day's work, and Levi knew he had. "Then you must have the wrong guy."

"I know what I'm doing here, Joe." Stacy waved him off. "You can get in your truck and go on your way."

Levi could tell the police chief was irritated by this unexpected intrusion. Joe could tell, too, Levi thought. He assumed Joe would do as Stacy suggested. But he didn't.

"I'd be happy to head home, Chief," he said, "except when I came out of the hardware store right there, I saw Levi sitting at that light. Maybe he could've run through the intersection if he'd swung around all three cars that were stopped in front of him, but he was trying to make sure he had that helmet secured to the seat."

Red suffused Stacy's face. "You must be mistaken." He jerked his head toward his cruiser, indicating that Levi should get in the car, but Joe thrust his hands in his pockets and stepped between them.

"No, sir. I'm positive about what I saw."

What Joe said was the truth. Although Levi hadn't seen Joe, he'd been fiddling with Callie's new helmet while waiting for that light. Still, Levi was surprised Joe would contest what Stacy said, especially for *his* benefit. Levi got along well enough with his boss, but they'd both been so busy they hadn't talked much. It wasn't as if they were best friends.

For the first time, some uncertainty entered Stacy's manner. No doubt he realized he'd have to push the issue if he wanted to arrest Levi, and then Joe might still stand in the way. Ultimately, the police chief decided it wasn't worth the backlash he could receive because of it. "Hmm," he said, "must've been another guy on a bike, I guess. Imagine that."

"Must've been," Joe said, letting him out of it gracefully.

Stacy turned to Levi. "Looks like there won't be any need to haul you down to the station. But—" his eyes narrowed again "—you might want to consider that other alternative I mentioned."

Levi said nothing.

"What other alternative?" Joe asked as soon as Stacy got in his car.

"He's invited me to leave town."

Joe gaped at him. *"Seriously?"*

"Apparently, he doesn't want any disreputable characters in Whiskey Creek." He gazed down at his arms, at the pink lines that remained now that the stitches were gone. "My presence might cause another dog attack, or a barn-burning."

"Those things weren't your fault. And it's a free country. He can't ask you to leave. That doesn't happen in this day and age."

Levi put his helmet back on. "It just did. But thanks for your help."

24

Levi had been feeling so...*normal* for a change. It was almost as if everything in Afghanistan hadn't happened, as if it had all been nothing more than a terrible dream.

But now the past felt real again. The same resentment, the same deep-seated anger, simmered inside him, making him want to smash someone's face in. Not *someone's*. Stacy's. The police chief wasn't going to leave him alone. He'd badger him and badger him until he eventually figured out who Levi was, and then he'd make sure Levi went back to stand trial in Nevada, where he'd be facing the same odds he'd been facing a few minutes ago. If not for Joe, Levi would be at the station getting fingerprinted for a traffic violation he didn't commit.

What had he been thinking the past few days, anyway? He couldn't grow complacent. It wasn't as though he could settle down in Whiskey Creek and pretend he was someone else forever. Callie didn't own the farm, and her parents would be selling it soon. Then where would she go? Back to the apartment she'd told him she'd once rented above her studio? And what would he do—go with her?

That wasn't very realistic. Not with Stacy making

trouble for him at every turn. Callie didn't know what she was getting into, didn't even know his real name.

He needed to move on, to get out of Whiskey Creek before he did something else he'd live to regret.

"Levi?" Callie shouted above the roar of his engine.

He blinked. He'd reached the farm but was still sitting astride his bike. She stood next to him, waiting for him to notice her.

Putting down the kickstand, he cut the engine.

"You coming in?" She gestured at the door she'd left open.

Her beautiful smile made his chest tighten with the kind of emotion he hadn't felt, hadn't been willing to feel, in a long time. "Yeah," he said. But he couldn't stay.

God, she was going to be hard to leave.

Levi was hungry. His stomach rumbled at the smell of the food Callie had prepared. But eating suddenly seemed like a terrible waste of time. As soon as he crossed the threshold of the living room, he pulled her into his arms and kissed her as if he hadn't seen her in weeks.

"What is it?" she asked, startled by his intensity.

He shook his head. There was no point in telling her. She couldn't stop Stacy because she couldn't change what Levi had done. No one could. As much as he wished he could go back and live that night in Nevada over again, he couldn't. It was the same with Behrukh.

Why did mistakes always have to be so...*final?*

Anyway, even if Callie could do something about Stacy, Levi wasn't willing to hide behind her, refused to have a woman do battle for him. She'd had no problems with the people in her hometown before he came. He wanted to be sure there'd be no problems after.

"*Levi?*"

"Nothing," he breathed against her neck as his mouth moved lower. "I just missed you."

She held his face so she could look into his eyes, but he allowed that for only a second before stripping off her shirt and kissing her breasts. He was driven to possess her in a way he hadn't possessed her before, couldn't wait to escape into the completeness she'd begun to offer him.

"I missed you, too," she said, "but—"

But nothing. He wanted her. Now. She seemed to understand that when he interrupted her with a demanding kiss, then removed the rest of her clothes.

If she was surprised by his sudden aggression, by the urgency in his touch, she didn't complain. She gasped as he claimed her with two fingers but arched into him as if she completely trusted him, and that made him grow even harder.

Although he was afraid she might press him for answers about his behavior, continue to question him about whether something had happened, she didn't. She was already panting and moving against his palm, getting as swept away as he was.

"What do you want?" he whispered.

"I want *you,*" she said, and peeled off his shirt. Although he'd washed his hands at work, his clothes were no cleaner than they'd been earlier in the week, when he'd insisted on washing up before touching her. But a shower, or any other kind of delay, was out of the question. Today nothing seemed to matter except feeling her naked body against his, her softness yielding to his hardness, skin on skin.

"No one's ever made me feel like you do," she murmured.

Levi derived more satisfaction from the passion with which she'd said those words than the words themselves. It was exactly what he was looking for. But he refused to let the momentum carry them away too fast. This time their lovemaking wasn't going to blow out in a gust of energy and enthusiasm. This wasn't about meeting *his* needs. He wanted to make Callie shiver and quake and come apart in his arms again and again.

Even as that thought went through his mind, he recognized it as a juvenile, misguided attempt to ensure that she remembered him. But being able to give her pleasure seemed important, regardless.

"Again," he said after she'd already climaxed several times. He urged her to roll on top of him, in case she was getting carpet burn, but she shook her head.

"I'm done," she gasped, her chest rising and falling from exertion. "I'm too exhausted."

That was the signal he'd been waiting for. She was satisfied. Pinning her arms above her head, he enjoyed the sight of her bare breasts, completely open to his view, with the necklace he gave her resting at the base of her throat.

"That was wild," she whispered when he finally slumped over her.

He didn't answer. He was exhausted, too. Mentally exhausted, more than anything else.

Shifting to one side, so he could bear his own weight, he laid his head on her shoulder and felt her hand cup his cheek.

"Levi?"

He was breathing deeply, enjoying the scent that was so uniquely *her*. "Hmm?"

"Please tell me that wasn't goodbye."

He closed his eyes. He hated this part. He'd never thought he'd feel so strongly about a woman again. "I'm sorry," he said.

Although Levi had packed his few belongings and put them in a bag by the door, Callie had talked him into staying one more day. They'd gone for a ride on his bike this morning, had stopped in the mountains and gone skinny-dipping in a stream. Now she was getting ready while he surfed sports sites on her laptop. According to Baxter's latest text, her friends were on their way. She just had to get through their "intervention." Then she'd have the rest of the day with Levi before their time came to an end.

She couldn't believe that she'd managed to keep her condition from him, despite his proximity. Just yesterday, she'd been kicking herself for not telling him the truth. She'd been positive he was going to find out and then hate her. But now there was no reason to think anything would change before he left. She was feeling pretty good, overall, so she was glad she'd stuck to her decision. Thanks to her silence, they'd had two incredible weeks together, something that probably never would've happened otherwise. And just as she'd planned from the beginning, he'd go on with his life, untouched by what she was about to undergo.

"How do you know they're coming?" Levi asked.

She fished her mascara out of her makeup bag. "Baxter tipped me off."

"I don't get it. What do they think is wrong?"

"I haven't been returning their calls and showing up at coffee on Fridays."

"Because..."

"I've been busy. First the farm. And then you. But they're convinced I've been acting strange." No doubt she had been acting strange. She'd been struggling to cope with her own mortality, no easy thing at thirty-two. So this was one more lie...to him and to them. But after he left, she was ready to tell her friends and her family. Having Baxter's support at the hospital had been wonderful. She was ready for more of that—even if it came with a cost.

"So...you're going to blame it on me?"

She laughed. "Basically. Do you mind?"

There was a shrug in his voice when he responded. "No."

He was leaving, anyway, but neither of them wanted to talk about that. "I'll be sure to tell them you're good in bed. Will that make up for it?"

"It might preserve a bit of my male pride."

"Consider that pride preserved. So—" she paused to put on some lip gloss "—do you want to meet them?"

She assumed he'd say no....

"Why not?"

Surprised, she poked her head out of the bathroom.

When their eyes met, he said, "I'm going to miss you."

Cheyenne fidgeted nervously with her purse strap as she stood on Callie's porch with Dylan, Eve, Riley, Noah, Baxter and Kyle. They'd met at her place and taken two cars so they could all arrive at once. Ted was still on deadline for his next book and couldn't come, and no one had been able to reach Sophia.

"I hope this doesn't make matters worse," she muttered to no one in particular.

Eve was closest to her, but she probably would've been the one to respond. The guys tended to favor less intervention rather than more. Eve had all but twisted their arms to get them to participate in this. "We have to do *something*," she'd argued. "What's our other option? To just…let her drift away?"

Cheyenne didn't like the thought of losing Callie's friendship. Callie meant too much to her. But she had to admit that getting married had required her to pull back from the group just a little, to make room for Dylan and the privacy being a couple required. Maybe Callie was going through something like that, something tied to maturation and changing needs.

Before she could mention this idea, the door opened.

Cheyenne caught her breath in case Callie wasn't pleased, but Callie seemed so genuinely happy to have them all on her doorstep that Cheyenne was no longer sure they had a problem.

"It's good to see you," Callie said as she gave each of them a hug.

"This is weird," Eve whispered. They were at the back of the group and could talk amid the other voices and jostling without being overheard.

"Maybe she really has been preoccupied with getting the farm up for sale," Cheyenne whispered back.

When they were all inside, Cheyenne glanced around, hoping to see the mysterious drifter who'd come to stay with their friend, but he wasn't in the room.

"I made coffee," Callie announced while they sat

down. "And that brown-sugar cinnamon cake I served at Ted's birthday."

Noah wrinkled his nose. "Sugar so early? You don't owe us anything, but what's wrong with fruit or yogurt or oatmeal?"

"Oh, brother," she replied. "You eat those things every day."

"I gave up smoking not long ago," Dylan piped up. "That's my concession to the healthy life, so I'll take his piece."

Cheyenne squeezed his hand. "Getting off nicotine isn't easy. I'm so proud of you, honey."

He grinned at her, but Cheyenne scarcely noticed. Callie's wistful expression made Cheyenne remember what Eve had said about her wanting to get married. But whatever she was thinking didn't seem to dull her delight in the moment. "We're not watching calories or fat grams or carbs or anything else today," she said. "So forget about clogged arteries and living past a hundred. This is a celebration."

Noah propped his feet up on the coffee table. "What are we celebrating?"

Cheyenne had been wondering the same thing, but since Noah had asked, she didn't have to.

Callie's gaze moved over the group. "Friendship."

"Wait a second." Noah put his feet down again and sat up. "You just happened to have a coffee cake on hand?"

Baxter flushed so brightly, Cheyenne knew he'd told Callie they were coming. *"What?"* he said, spreading his hands when everyone turned to look at him. "It was only polite to let her know we were about to descend on her!"

Callie laughed more freely than Cheyenne had seen in some time. "It's okay. I'm glad you're all here. I've missed you."

"I'd say this is a pretty warm welcome." Riley nudged Eve, who was sitting next to him on the couch. "I guess we can't really accuse her of treating us funny now."

While several people chuckled, Cheyenne saw Callie put her hands on Kyle's shoulders from behind the low-back chair in which he sat. When he glanced up at her wearing the hurt look he'd been trying so hard to hide, Callie bent down and pressed her cheek against his. Cheyenne couldn't hear what was said, but she thought Callie whispered that she was sorry.

"Um, there's been enough canoodling between the two of *you*," Riley joked, and Callie blushed as she pulled away.

"That hasn't changed the fact that I love him," she said. "I'll always love him."

Cheyenne was afraid Kyle might start crying. She could almost see the relief that swept through him.

"I take full responsibility," he said simply.

Callie ruffled his hair. "Nice try. I participated, too. But thanks for telling everyone."

At the sarcasm in her voice, Kyle brought a hand to his chest. "That's what I thought you wanted me to do! You said so once, on the phone. You think *I* wanted to do that?"

"No. I think we both screwed up on several counts. But we're okay, the two of us, right?"

Relaxing into his chair, he smiled. "We're okay."

"Great." With a nod of satisfaction, Callie motioned to Eve. "Come help me serve the cake."

Cheyenne followed them into the kitchen. "You look

great," she told Callie. "Thinner than I've ever seen you, but…happy."

Callie met her gaze. "Thanks."

"So…you're okay? Everything's okay?"

"I feel…lucky."

Cheyenne and Eve exchanged a glance. "In what way?"

"I have a lot of good friends."

"You're completely disarming us. You know that," Eve said.

Callie slung an arm around them both. "Relax and have fun."

"Where's your…your new friend?" Eve asked.

"He's taking a shower," Callie said. "He'll be right out."

Relieved, Cheyenne carried plates of cake and cups of coffee into the living room. Everyone was talking and laughing as usual. The atmosphere was more up-beat than Fridays at Black Gold had been the past several weeks. Cheyenne was especially excited when Levi finally emerged from the bedroom. She liked him immediately. She liked the way he looked at Callie.

But then she caught a glimpse of her husband's face and realized that something was wrong. He wasn't saying anything. He was just sitting on the couch, glowering.

Slipping through the others who were returning their plates to the kitchen or getting more coffee, she sat down next to him.

"What's wrong, Dyl?" she murmured. "You don't seem happy." She couldn't imagine why. Like the other guys, he'd been hesitant to participate in Eve's little "intervention," but what he'd feared hadn't come to pass.

Callie hadn't been offended; there'd been no arguing. They were all having a great time. Except him.

He nodded over at Levi, who was busy talking to Baxter and Noah. "I know that guy," he said.

"What do you mean you know him?" Noah asked but only because he beat Baxter to it. Dylan was driving his Jeep. Cheyenne was in the passenger seat and Noah sat in the back with Baxter. Riley and Kyle had left with Eve in her 1994 Mercedes convertible, so they hadn't heard the bomb Dylan had dropped just as they turned out of the farm's driveway.

"I mean, his name's not Levi McCloud." Dylan glanced in his rearview mirror, but he was wearing sunglasses, so Baxter couldn't tell if he was looking at him or Noah. "It's Levi *Pendleton*."

Cheyenne rested her head against the window. She was obviously listening, but she wasn't looking at her husband. In the mirror attached to the sun visor, Baxter could see the frown that tugged at her lips as she watched the scenery pass by. She didn't like what he was saying any more than they did.

"How do you know?" Baxter asked.

Dylan shifted into a higher gear. "Because he's one of the best ultimate fighters I've ever seen."

Cheyenne turned away from the window. "Callie seems *so* happy. Just the expression on her face when she looks at him tells me she's in love. Are you *sure* you're not mistaken?"

He placed a hand on her leg. "I'm positive."

So many questions were going through Baxter's mind he didn't know which one to ask first. "Where did you see him before? And...and when was this?"

"It's been years, back when I was fighting myself."

"But you met a lot of fighters back then." Cheyenne still seemed to hope she could create some doubt so she wouldn't have to accept what her husband was saying.

Dylan's mouth was a straight slash beneath those mirrored glasses. "Like I said. He was one of the best. We all watched him. Carefully."

"Sounds to me like he has a lot to be proud of," Noah said. "So why would he say his name is McCloud? And why would he be wandering around without a home or family or friends?"

Dylan hesitated as if he didn't want to respond. But he eventually came out with it. "Because he's wanted for assaulting a couple of police officers in Nevada."

"Shit," Noah said. "How do you know *that?*"

"Everyone in the MMA world heard about it. It happened a couple of years ago. He put those two officers in the hospital." His voice dropped. "One with fairly severe injuries."

"And he got away with it?" Baxter asked.

"Far as I know, he was never caught."

Noah slumped in his seat. "I can't believe this. Callie finally falls for someone, and he's lying to her. Kyle was worried about that guy from the beginning. He's going to freak out."

Baxter knew more than any of them just how much Levi meant to Callie. "What was Levi doing with those cops, anyway? Were they trying to take him in for something else?"

"Seems like he was drunk and causing trouble. But I'm not sure exactly what went down before the fight broke out."

"Why didn't the policemen use their guns?" Noah asked.

"He disarmed them before they could get a shot off," Dylan replied.

Baxter didn't like boxing, let alone ultimate fighting. He didn't care for sports in general. If he'd heard about this incident he hadn't paid enough attention to remember it. "This happened two years ago?"

"I think it was the summer before last. He hadn't been fighting for a while—it'd been six or seven years since his last fight and a bit longer than that since I saw him—but it was still news."

Noah shoved Dylan's shoulder. "Did *you* ever fight him, Dyl?"

"No," he replied. "I'm glad I never had to. I started cage fighting with very little training. Desperation—that was all I had on my side. I had to make some money or Child Protective Services would come in and take my brothers away. He grew up being groomed for the sport."

"Come on, don't you think you could've taken him?" Noah asked.

"In all honesty, he probably would've kicked my ass," Dylan said. "He rarely lost a fight. Trust me, he was something special."

"So instead of being able to feel Callie's okay, we're back to worrying about her," Cheyenne said. "What are we going to do now?"

"We have to confront her," Noah replied. "We can't let her go on thinking she's found Mr. Right. He's wanted by the police. Assaulting an officer is serious. He could go to prison."

Baxter wanted to speak up, to tell them they shouldn't

say anything. If Levi left town like Callie expected, he wouldn't have to know about her, and she wouldn't have to know about him. As far as he was concerned, that was fair and a blessing to them both. But he had to think of some kind of logic to back up his opinion, since they didn't have any idea about Callie's illness.

Dylan shoved a hand through his hair. "That may be true, but I don't want to narc on him."

"Even to protect one of our best friends?" Cheyenne seemed surprised, and that made Dylan shift uncomfortably in his seat.

"I don't want anything bad to happen to Callie. That's why I'm telling you guys. But I can't turn him in. Maybe that would be the right thing to do, but... maybe not. It's just not in me to decide his fate like that. I've been in trouble too many times myself, and only a fraction of them were really my fault."

Baxter liked where he was going with this. With luck, he wouldn't have to talk them out of telling—if Dylan did that for him. "So what are you saying?"

He lowered the volume on the radio. "I'm saying we don't know what happened that night with those two cops. We weren't there."

"Um, *hello?*" Noah said. "They were *cops*. Doesn't that make them right? Sounds to me like they were trying to enforce the law, maybe take him in for drunk-and-disorderly, and he handed their asses to them instead of going peacefully."

"Not necessarily," Dylan grumbled. "Wearing a badge doesn't make you perfect."

Seeing his opening, Baxter spoke quickly. "If he's on the run, then he won't be staying here for long. Why not just…let it go? Let Callie enjoy her love affair while it lasts?"

Cheyenne twisted around in her seat. "Are you *kidding* me? You have no way of knowing how long he might stay or how that might affect Callie! He might have anger management issues. Maybe they haven't come out yet, but that doesn't mean they won't."

With a sigh, Baxter rubbed his jaw. The way Noah was looking at him, he'd guessed something was up. That wasn't really a surprise. Noah knew him better than anyone. Well, in some respects. In others, Noah didn't know him at all—or he just didn't want to see what was right in front of him. As long as they didn't talk about Baxter's sexual orientation, as long as they didn't acknowledge that he felt more than he should, their relationship could go on as it always had.

Loosening his seat belt so he could lean forward, Noah arched his eyebrows expectantly. "Well?"

"Well, what?" Baxter said.

"Come on. Out with it. You're hiding something."

That was true. He was hiding the fact that if Callie didn't get a liver transplant, it wouldn't matter who Levi McCloud was. She wouldn't be around to see him go to prison. And what he'd heard her doctor say last week at the hospital led him to believe she didn't have long.

"What is it?" Noah asked. "What aren't you telling us, Bax?"

It was time they learned the truth. All of them. But Baxter couldn't divulge Callie's secret. It wasn't his place to tell them she was dying.

"Call her," he said. "Call her and tell her about Levi and see what she says."

25

When Kyle called, Callie was happy to hear his voice. The past few weeks had been rough as far as "they" were concerned. She knew he'd been worried about her, that he'd blamed himself for her odd behavior. But this morning they'd gotten past all that. She hoped they'd now be able to resume their friendship. When he was at the house a few hours ago, he hadn't seemed to mind Levi's presence. As a matter of fact, he'd been friendly.

So she was surprised by the gravity in his voice when he said, "Can you go someplace where we can talk? *In private?*"

She glanced over at Levi, who was busy making dinner. He wanted to try his hand at a Mexican dish a friend of his father's had introduced him to. He was slicing up the meat he'd been marinating while she sliced the onions he planned to grill with it.

When she hesitated, he nudged her elbow. "Who is it?"

"Kyle. He, um, wants to talk about something that's going on with Eve. I'll be right back."

She was pretty sure Levi watched her leave, but he didn't follow. As soon as she reached the living room, she said, "Okay, I'm alone. What's wrong?"

"There's something you need to know," Kyle replied.

She swallowed a sigh. What now?

"Are you sitting down?"

"Is it *that* bad?" she asked.

"It's not good."

"Then why didn't you speak up this morning, when you were here?"

"I didn't know. None of us did."

Us. That had to refer to the rest of her friends. What could they possibly have found out since leaving her place? Had Baxter *told* them?

"What is it?" She wanted to get back to the kitchen. She'd been enjoying herself. Not only had she and Levi been cooking, they'd been talking and laughing and savoring their last night together. His bag sitting by the door made the "last night" part all too clear. So did the fact that Joe had called earlier to see if he could work the coming week, and he'd said he wouldn't be available. She hated the thought of goodbye. And yet…she was relieved at the same time. She didn't want Levi to endure something that would set him back. What if she didn't get a transplant? Her doctor hadn't called with any promising news so far, meaning she had to face that probability. And Levi had made such progress. She preferred to see him continue to heal. She wanted that even more than she wanted to keep him with her.

Once she reached her bedroom, she closed the door behind her but not before Rifle squeezed inside. "So tell me."

"Hang on," Kyle said. "I'm going to put you on speakerphone. Eve, Baxter, Noah, Dylan, Chey and Riley are with me."

"You're putting them all on?"

"I am. I don't want to be the one to break this to you."

He was going to break something to *her?* But she was the one with the secret....

"Baxter, what's going on?" she demanded when she could hear the others.

"I think it's time, Cal," he replied. "I'm sorry."

Time to be honest. That was what he had to mean. For the most part, she felt the same. But this scenario wasn't playing out the way she'd expected. "All right. So...what is it that Kyle has to say?"

She heard Eve's voice next. "Callie, when we were there earlier..."

"Yes?"

"Dylan recognized Levi."

Callie sank onto the bed. "He what?"

"He's seen Levi before, Cal. He just didn't realize it until we came over this morning."

Absently, she petted her dog, who was resting his snout on her lap. "*Where?* Where has he seen him before?"

"At a tournament in Arizona about eight years ago."

She jumped up so fast Rifle darted away. "So? That's no surprise. I know Levi used to fight."

There was an awkward silence. Then Eve tried again. "Did you also know his name isn't Levi McCloud?"

Yes! She knew that, too. But it made her nervous that her friends did. They wouldn't like the idea that he'd been using a fake name. No one would. Did they also know why?

As she wondered how to respond, Dylan spoke up, brisk and to the point.

"Callie, his name is Levi Pendleton. He's wanted by the police for assaulting two officers in Nevada."

Assaulting two officers? That was even worse than she'd imagined, worse than the far more innocuous scenarios she'd come up with to justify his use of a false name. "How bad…how badly did he hurt them?" she asked.

"One ended up in the hospital with a broken jaw. If several guys hadn't pulled Levi off, I don't know how things would've gone. The other cop was out cold."

She couldn't picture Levi acting out to that extent. He wasn't a violent person. Although she hadn't known him long, he'd been so kind, so gentle. "When was this?" she asked.

"Two years ago."

He'd just returned from Afghanistan. She knew what kind of shape he must've been in, knew that had to account for what'd happened. She wanted to tell them, to explain the degree of his loss and what his childhood had been like. But why bother? He'd be gone tomorrow. She just hoped the authorities would take the extenuating circumstances into consideration when they caught him.

"Thanks for telling me," she said softly.

"That's it?" Kyle said. "Callie, he could be dangerous, like I've been saying you all along. He could—"

"Kyle!" she broke in.

Out of patience, he came right back at her. *"What?"*

"It doesn't matter!"

"What do you mean it doesn't matter?" Eve sounded even more scandalized. "You want a family, don't you? What kind of life can you build with a man who's wanted for a violent crime? Who might get violent again? What about any children you might have? What about your parents, who'd be heartbroken to see anything happen to you? What about the rest of us who care—"

She squeezed her eyes shut in an attempt to block out the words that seemed to be hitting her like bullets from a machine gun. "Stop! I can't build a life with anyone."

Dead silence.

"What are you talking about?" Noah asked. "You're a beautiful, smart, funny woman. You'll find the right guy. Don't settle for this one."

She drew a deep breath. "Noah, Kyle, Eve…all of you."

"What is it?"

That was Cheyenne's voice. Callie recognized the fear in it. She'd had such a hard life. Callie hated that what she was about to say would only add to what was already a long list for Cheyenne. And not just her. They *all* knew something terrible was coming.

"Baxter can confirm what I'm about to tell you, because he was at the hospital with me earlier this week."

"The hospital?" Kyle echoed.

"Yes." She prayed her voice wouldn't crack even though she could feel the threat of tears. "My liver's failing. If I don't get a transplant in the next few weeks, I'll be dead before the end of summer."

Levi dropped his hand. He'd been about to knock so he could tell Callie that dinner was ready. But he'd paused to see if he'd be interrupting something important and heard her say she'd been in the hospital earlier this week. That Baxter had been with her. That she was *dying*.

At first, the words floating to him through the door sounded so preposterous he almost laughed. There had to be some mistake. She was young, beautiful, perfect. She'd been functioning as well as he had. He would've noticed if there was something wrong, wouldn't he? They'd just been laughing with each other in a beautiful mountain creek this morning.

But there was that time he'd found her lying on the floor in the bathroom, so sick and weak she couldn't get up. And she'd disappeared for two days earlier in the week. He'd thought that was odd, even at the time, but Baxter had said they'd gone sailing in San Francisco. Sure, she'd been short of breath or occasionally seemed tired. She'd lost a few pounds, too. But he'd questioned her about those things. She'd told him she was fine!

Heart pounding so hard he felt it might leap right out of his chest, he stood perfectly still, listening to the other voices coming from inside the room. Her friends were all on the phone with her. Except for Baxter, they hadn't known she was ill, either. There was crying, and anger at having been deceived. Then Callie was trying to convince them she'd had a good life, as short as it was, that everything would be okay and she didn't want anyone to be too upset.

After that, she asked them something that made Levi go numb. "Please, if…if you happen to see Levi again as he passes through town or whatever, don't mention this to him. I doubt you'll run into him, but just in case. I don't want him to know."

"Why?" someone cried. "You're obviously in love with him. And he might be in love with you. He has a right to know."

She was having none of that. "No," she said, adamant. "I don't want him to see me die."

* * *

The moment she heard Levi's motorcycle start up, Callie knew. He was supposed to be in the kitchen, fixing dinner. He had no reason to be outside. Unless…

Feeling sick in a whole new way—sick at heart—she promised to call her friends back and hung up in the middle of Kyle saying…*something*. Then, hoping to catch Levi, she ran out of the house, but he was already turning from the drive onto the road. She wanted to shout his name, beg him to come back and let her say goodbye, to see that he was okay, but all she saw was a glimpse of his back.

"No!" If only she hadn't taken that call. But what would her friends have done if they couldn't express their concern?

They might've gone to the police.

With a sigh, she sank onto the top step, next to the pink helmet Levi had bought for her. If only she'd waited to tell her friends about her illness. One more day. That was all it would've taken. She'd *planned* to wait! But she'd gotten too caught up in trying to convince them that they didn't need to do anything about Levi's past, that they could just…leave him be.

Rifle's cold, wet nose nudged her arm. She'd left the door open and he'd wandered out. Hooking her arm around his neck, she let him bathe her cheek with his warm tongue. "It's okay, isn't it, boy?" she asked. "Levi was going, anyway."

The dog whined, but she doubted he could be as sad as she was. This changed everything. Now she couldn't imagine Levi as happily oblivious whenever she thought of him. And he probably wouldn't want to think of her at all.

"Shit, Rifle. I really screwed up."

Suddenly so tired she felt she'd never be able to get up again, she lay down right there on the porch and rested her head on her arms. The sun was sinking behind the chicken coop. Rifle sat beside her, his tail thumping the wooden planks. As she watched the shadows stretch toward her, the exhilaration of the motorcycle ride she'd taken with Levi passed through her mind. His body had felt so safe and secure as she'd clung to his waist. Then there was the memory of his devilish smile when they'd stopped and he carried her kicking and screaming into that cold stream. After that came the moment when he'd walked out of the bedroom to meet her friends and she'd been so proud to show them she was with someone she loved so much. And last but not least was the comfortable, quiet companionship of cooking dinner together after her friends were gone. It all filtered through her mind, frame by excruciating frame, until finally, mercifully, the relief of sleep washed over her and dragged her into oblivion.

Kyle called Callie back several times. He, or one of the others, tried every few minutes for the next two hours. When there was no answer, they wanted to return to the farm to see what was going on, but he talked them into letting him go alone. He desperately wanted to speak with Callie, tell her how sorry he was now that he really understood. All along he'd thought she was making a bigger deal out of the fact that they'd slept together than she needed to. He'd been worried that, as a consequence, she might ruin their friendship and tear apart the group. He'd had no idea she was actually wrestling with something much bigger and felt guilty for not guessing, not somehow knowing intuitively. He'd spent the most time with her recently. He'd been out to the farm more than anyone else. And instead of simply being a good friend and listening to her—maybe she would've told him about her diagnosis—he'd taken her to bed and complicated everything. The biggest irony was that he knew she'd felt bad about his divorce and had been trying to help *him*.

"Sometimes I think I am in love with you," he muttered as he punched the gas pedal and barreled down the country road to the farm.

When he arrived, all seemed quiet. Rifle ran out to greet him as soon as he turned in at the gate, which was odd, since it was getting late. Callie's dog was usually inside by now.

It didn't look as if anyone was home. Callie's car sat in the drive, but he couldn't see Levi's motorcycle and the house was dark.

Intending to knock, just in case, he parked. But as he was about to get out and approach the house, he spotted an odd shape on the porch and realized it was Callie. She was lying there, staring back at his headlights.

What the hell?

Leaving his keys in the ignition, he hopped out. "Callie?"

Panic gripped him when she didn't answer. Maybe she wasn't just staring back at him. Maybe she was dead.

Hoping it wasn't too late, hoping he could still get her some medical help, he jogged the last few steps. But then she blinked and he clutched his chest as he took a ragged breath. "Shit, you scared me. Are you okay?"

There was no response. But tears gathered in her eyes. One slipped over the bridge of her nose.

He glanced around, once again looking for Levi's bike. "Where is he?"

"Gone," she said.

"I see." With a curse, Kyle bent and scooped her into his arms. "Come on. It's chilly out here. Let's get you inside."

"It's just us again," she said as he whistled for Rifle to join them and put her on the couch.

He covered her with a blanket, then smoothed the hair away from her face. "So we'll work with what we have."

"How?" She managed a brief smile as she wiped her tears.

Kneeling before her, he clasped her hands between his. "I'm going to take better care of you than I did," he promised.

"What's that supposed to mean?"

He brought her fingers to his lips. "I'm sorry about before. How I handled your loneliness. That was... selfish of me."

"You were lonely, too," she pointed out. "And I don't remember complaining."

That made him feel more confident that the past had really been forgiven. "Things will turn around. You'll see."

Her chest lifted as she breathed deeply. "And if they don't?"

He didn't like the thought of that. But it was a fair question. "Then I'll be with you every step of the way."

"You're a good friend, Kyle," she said and tucked the blanket up under her chin.

* * *

Levi couldn't have stayed in Whiskey Creek even if he'd wanted to. There was no point. How could he be any kind of support to Callie when it was only a matter of time before Chief Stacy or someone else figured out who he was? The moment that happened, he'd be hauled back to Nevada to stand trial. So there was nothing to be gained by sticking around and watching her suffer, nothing to be gained by going through more of the same hell he'd endured when he lost Behrukh—especially because dying of illness was often a long, protracted affair. He preferred to remember Callie as she'd been this morning when they made love on the muddy bank of that stream.

So he had nothing to feel guilty about, right? He'd had no choice; he had to leave. And not saying goodbye? He'd done them both a favor. They'd had a fabulous final day together. Why ruin the memory of it? Now it was just him and his bike and the wind, like it had been for the two years since he'd returned from Afghanistan. This was how he coped. This was how he'd gotten through.

But somehow his life felt even emptier and more aimless now.

For the first time in a long while, his thoughts turned to his father. As much as he hated his old man, there were instances when he yearned for contact, when he missed having some type of anchor. Leo was so authoritative, so autocratic and demanding and controlling. But few things had ever felt more satisfying than achieving his hard-won approval. As a child, Levi had lived for those rare moments.

He guessed it was that better part of his father he

was missing now. Not that he'd ever go back to see what had happened to Leo. The night Levi had come home from Afghanistan and they'd had that big blowout was enough contact to last him for *more* than two years.

And yet…as the miles passed and the night wore on, he found himself heading north, toward Portland.

Maybe the mistakes he'd made were Leo's fault. But that last night…Levi had to admit he'd been responsible for the argument that ensued. Although his father had seemed eager to see him, grateful he'd returned, Levi had been filled with so much anger and resentment he'd been looking to take it out on someone or something, and his father had provided the perfect target.

26

All the changes Callie had been expecting—and dreading—came to pass in the next few days. Once she told her parents about her illness, her time at the farm was over. Diana and Boone insisted she move home.

It was only Wednesday, three days after Levi had left, when her father drove out to help her pack and close up the house. They no longer trusted that she was capable of taking care of herself, which was annoying and restrictive even though she knew it stemmed from their desire to keep her with them as long as possible.

Her parents weren't the only ones making life more difficult. Her friends were also struggling to accept what was coming—and that included her assistant, Tina. Visitors came by often once she was back in town, but seeing them wasn't the same kind of fun it had once been. And to make it all that much worse, Levi's departure had left as big a hole in her life as she'd known it would.

The only positive things about having told everyone she was dying was that her parents finally met her doctor, she didn't have to hide when she took her medication or feel guilty about deceiving anyone and if she was tired she didn't need an excuse to nap. She was also rid of Chief Stacy, it seemed. When he found out she wasn't long for this world, she stopped being a viable alternative for his future wife and he lost interest. She could tell when she spoke to him, briefly, about Levi. Oddly enough, he still seemed relieved that Levi was gone, even though her friends hadn't revealed Levi's true identity. Callie wasn't sure why Chief Stacy had felt so threatened by him.

"You're looking good," Baxter told her when he came by on Thursday night after work.

They were sitting on the back patio not far from her father's large garden, watching Rifle chase bees.

"Thanks," she said. But she knew he was lying. He had to be. She was doing worse than ever. Since word got out and Levi had gone, she felt as if something inside her had caved in—like a dam washed downstream—and given her illness free rein. It was almost as if, by telling, she'd accepted her fate and could no longer avoid it.

The silence grew awkward. "How's work?" she asked in an attempt to fill the void.

Baxter yanked at the tie he'd already loosened. "Fine. I should have a good month."

They'd discussed this type of thing before. A good month meant he'd make fifteen to twenty thousand dollars. She smiled at his success. "I should've become a stockbroker."

"Why? You're an amazing photographer."

"After all the work I put into my business, I never netted twenty thousand dollars in one month."

"But you love what you do."

She hadn't even picked up her camera since she'd

moved home. "Tina will do a great job with Reflections."

Before he could object to what her statement implied, her mother called from the back door. "Callie?"

She twisted around. "Yes?"

"You've been up for quite some time. Don't you think you should come in and rest, dear?"

Callie wanted to say she could rest when she was dead, but she knew that would only upset her mother. "In a minute."

Baxter managed to unfasten another button on his expensive shirt. "Tell me something."

"What?" she said.

He waited to make sure her mother was gone before continuing. "Has Dylan ever mentioned seeing me with…"

"With…"

"A guy?"

At this, she sat up straighter. "What do you mean?"

"I mean what you think I mean. I was on a date once. We went to Jackson to avoid running into anyone around here. But Dylan came into the bar with some fighter friend. I'm pretty sure he saw me. I'm equally sure he recognized me. And I'm convinced he knew exactly what was going on."

Callie took a sip of the ice water she'd brought out with her. "When was this?"

"Before he got together with Cheyenne—a couple of years ago."

"He's never said a word. At least, not to me. Maybe he mentioned it to Cheyenne, though."

His thumb moved thoughtfully over his cleft chin. "Dylan's a cool dude."

"He's perfect for Chey. Really good to her. But what makes you ask about that now? After so much time? Wouldn't you know if he'd outed you?"

He stared across her father's carefully manicured lawn toward the cinder-block fence. Their yard wasn't large, but her father's landscaping was meticulous. "Noah's been acting strange lately. I'm afraid he's guessed."

Alarmed about what this might mean for Baxter, for their group, Callie shifted in her seat. "Strange in what way?"

"Going from one woman to the next. Sleeping around and telling me every sordid detail. I think he's trying to let me know he'll never be interested in me." He laughed bitterly. "As if I didn't know that already."

"That could be a subconscious reaction," she pointed out.

"I'm not sure. It's almost as if…as if he flinches when I come anywhere near him. It was never like that before."

"Callie?" her mother called again. "Honey, you really need to rest."

"Mom——" she started, but Baxter shook his head.

"I have to go, anyway," he said, standing.

Callie didn't want him to leave. But she knew he was probably eager to get out of his suit, and maybe he had plans. She'd never realized he was dating, but, of course, that made sense. She couldn't expect him to remain celibate his whole life just because he wasn't ever going to be with Noah.

"Thanks for coming."

He gave her a hug. "Are you missing Levi?"

Her hand went automatically to the bird pendent at

her neck. She was glad Levi had given her a keepsake to remember him by. "I'm happy he escaped this part."

"I wonder if *he* is," he murmured, but Callie pretended not to hear it.

Levi had to be happier wherever he was—or he would've come back.

His trophies were still on display. Levi hadn't really thought his father would put them away. They meant too much to Leo, were more *his* badges of honor than they were Levi's. But it was a shock to see that so little had changed in eight years. When he'd returned home after being discharged from the army, Levi had spoken to his father—or, rather, berated him—before taking off again. He hadn't been here since he was nineteen and training every day.

The front desk sat empty, but there was a class going on. Levi stood just inside the doorway, watching children six to eight years old follow the motions of their instructor. Although Levi didn't recognize the man in charge, he guessed the guy was a student from one of his father's advanced classes. Leo often hired his black belts to teach the beginners.

When the teen caught sight of Levi in the mirror that ran along one wall, his eyes widened and he stopped teaching. "We have a special treat today," he announced to the class. "Look behind you. This is Sensei Pendleton's son, Levi, who was one of the greatest fighters in the world. Do you recognize him from his picture right there?" He pointed to a plaque on the far wall. "He has a black belt in tae kwon do *and* jujitsu, and he won practically *all* of those trophies in that case over there."

Levi heard a ripple of "That's *him*?" and "He's back!"

and "Sensei told me about him." As the children turned to stare, he almost walked out. This wasn't what he'd come for, to bask in the admiration of all those who'd like to achieve what he'd achieved. After what he'd done to those police officers in Nevada, he didn't deserve their admiration.

He wasn't sure exactly *why* he'd come. It'd taken him well over a week to make his way slowly up to the city where he'd been raised. Some days he didn't want to arrive here at all, so he'd headed back or traveled inland; others, he couldn't resist the tug of homesickness that eventually won out.

"I'll get your father," the instructor said, and hurried into the back.

Leo walked out a second later, chewing, as if Levi had interrupted his lunch. No doubt it was food he'd brought from home. Chances were slim that Leo would be eating restaurant fare. He was too careful about what he put in his body.

Although Leo had started shaving his head, possibly to hide the gray, he was fit and toned and younger-looking than other men his age. But he was favoring his right leg. That old injury had always given him trouble.

"I'll be damned," he muttered. Then he focused on Levi's arms and the pinkish bite marks that weren't quite healed. "What happened to you?"

Levi didn't answer. He was asking himself what he'd hoped to gain by confronting his father again. He was crazy to expect any kind of peace with Leo, wasn't he?

It would just be more of the same. He shouldn't have made the effort.

He took a step toward the door, but his father hurried after him.

"Wait! At least sit down and talk to me for a minute."

And say what? What could they say that would change anything?

Yet Levi hesitated.

"Come on. There's a good—" Leo seemed to be scrambling to come up with something appealing "—a good restaurant down the street. I'll take you there."

"Looks like you were already having lunch," Levi said.

"I just started. We'll go there instead."

Why not? He'd come this far. Besides, he was curious to see what restaurant his father would deem good enough for a champion's body.

Levi waited as Leo gave the young man teaching the class some instructions. Then he followed Leo out into the sunshine and down the street to a dimly lit pub that served burgers and fries and draft beer.

"You're willing to eat here?" Levi raised his eyebrows in surprise.

"If it'd give me a minute alone with you, I'd eat dirt."

Levi had no idea how to respond to that. His father wasn't typically forthcoming with such comments.

"How have you been?" Leo asked.

Lost, Levi realized. He'd been lost for so long he didn't know if he'd ever find himself. And it was difficult not to blame his father, who'd been so damn overbearing. "Fine."

He indicated the scars on his arms. "Those marks are…"

"I was attacked by dogs a few weeks ago."

"Why?"

"Shit like that happens when you're out on the road," he said with a shrug.

The waitress came by and Leo asked for a veggie burger. The curvy blonde almost laughed. "Sorry, no veggie burgers here."

"What do you have?"

"As far as vegetables go, we have iceberg lettuce, pickles and tomatoes. Unless you count ketchup and fries."

"Give me whatever you think is good. Levi?"

Levi ordered a half-pound burger, onion rings and a shake. He actually preferred to eat healthy, too. His father had trained him well. But he didn't want Leo to know that his training had been so effective.

Surprisingly, Leo didn't complain about his selections. "I—I've been worried about you," his father said.

Slinging one arm over the back of his chair, Levi struck an indifferent pose. "Why would you worry about me?"

Leo lowered his voice. "Come on, that incident in Reno was all over the news. What happened, Levi? Why'd you do it?"

He'd just left his father's house a few days before. The residual emotion from that was part of the reason. He'd also been drinking, which didn't help. "The one cop, the older one, was a seasoned officer. He was showing off for the rookie."

"And?"

"I barely touched the rookie."

Leo slid the beer menu to one side. "What made you go after the other guy?"

"I was sitting on the ground, resting outside an office building. Hungry, tired. He came up and told me to move on. It could've ended there. But he kicked me when I didn't get up fast enough."

"He didn't realize you could defend yourself."

"No. I think that was kind of a shock."

His father cursed. "When I didn't hear anything from you after that, I thought maybe they'd caught you, put you in jail somewhere."

"Not yet."

"I wish that incident hadn't happened," he said, rubbing his face.

"So do I," Levi admitted.

His father straightened the ketchup and mustard and the napkin holder in the center of their small table. "You might be interested to learn that...I found Ellen a few months ago."

Levi blinked at him. "My *sister?* How?"

"I hired a P.I."

"Don't," Levi growled. "Don't do that. Leave her alone. Her and Mom."

The waitress returned with two ice waters and Levi's shake. When she was gone, Leo said, "I just...I wanted to see her, to assure myself that she was okay. That's all."

Levi had no interest in his food. How would he get it down now that he'd ordered it? "And? Is she? Okay, I mean?"

A distant smile curved Leo's lips as he nodded. "She's beautiful. Looks exactly like you. Just graduated from Oregon State in advertising and marketing."

The urge to deck his father came out of nowhere, proving that the anger was still there, lurking beneath everything else.

Purposely shifting his gaze to the dark wood paneling and lighted beer signs surrounding them, Levi told himself to calm down. His father had cost him a lot—a normal childhood, a relationship with his mother and sister, a sense of home and belonging. But there was nothing to be done about that now. Life was what it was. "Where's Mom? Did you hire a P.I. to find her, too?"

"No. And Ellen wouldn't tell me much. Shelly still wants nothing to do with me."

"Does that surprise you?" Levi asked with a bitter laugh.

He winced. "No."

Levi scratched his arms. Due to the healing process, they were always itching. "She remarried?"

"Your mother? Yes."

"Does she have other kids?"

"Two, according to Ellen."

Levi supposed Shelly deserved another family. It wasn't her fault she'd married the wrong guy the first time around. But as defensive of her as he felt, Levi couldn't help resenting the fact that she'd abandoned him. "Good for her."

"You've had no contact with her?"

"None." He drank some of his shake. "And I don't want any. What about Ellen? She married?"

"No. Got a boyfriend, though."

"And you?"

"I was married to one of my students, for a brief time."

This didn't surprise Levi. There was always a woman in Leo's life—but never one who stayed very long. "You mean since I was here last?"

"Yes."

"You said *was* married."

He shrugged. "She left a month ago."

In and out. There'd be a new girlfriend tomorrow. "Another failed relationship."

"I don't pretend to be easy to get along with, Levi," he said. "But right now I have one thing going for me."

From what Levi could tell, he had a business that was marginally successful and that was it. "The dojo and those damn trophies in the case?"

"No. This lunch."

"This lunch doesn't mean shit," Levi said.

"It's what I've been praying for."

Levi couldn't imagine that. "Why?"

"Because it gives me the chance to plead with you to get your life in order. Stop running. Turn yourself in. Pay the price it's going to take to wipe away the past and build a decent future."

"And you feel you have the right to say this to me? Why?"

"I know I've screwed up. So do yourself a favor and live your life better than I've lived mine."

Levi thought of Callie. If she were healthy, he'd have the incentive to do whatever he had to. But without her…there didn't seem to be much point.

"I'll keep that advice in mind."

Their meals came. Levi picked at his food. Leo didn't even pretend to eat. His gaze never moved from Levi.

"What?" Levi snapped, uncomfortable at his father's unrelenting attention.

"I've missed you," Leo said, his voice cracking. "You may not think I care about you, but I do."

Levi couldn't cope with all the contradictions. Maybe his father loved him, but he loved himself far more. That seemed to be a common theme with both parents. He could say the same about his mother. "I don't want to talk about whether or not you love me."

His father sighed. "Then why'd you come?"

Levi chuckled without mirth. "I don't even know." He'd certainly fought the impulse. There just didn't seem to be anywhere else to go.

Leo grasped his arm. "Stay in Portland."

After he'd spent the past eight years trying to get away? "Why would I do that?" The hamburger was tasteless in his mouth.

"You could become my partner at the dojo. Teach. It'll keep you in martial arts, which you love. And you can live with me until you get on your feet."

Levi stuck a French fry in his mouth. "I don't need your help."

"Then what will you do? You're not going back into the army."

"No." *Definitely* not. He wasn't sure what to do next. He'd thought he'd stumbled on a place he could call home when he found Whiskey Creek. But without Callie it wouldn't be any different from all the other towns he'd passed through.

"So what, then?" Leo asked.

Levi worked to swallow what was in his mouth. "There're still a lot of places I'd like to see."

His father frowned but said nothing.

"You don't approve?"

The effort Leo was making to be pleasant fell away like scaffolding. "I want more for you than rambling around like…like some *vagrant*."

Levi shoved his plate into the center of the table. "You need to start living your own dreams."

His father sat without responding for several seconds. Then he said, "At least I have dreams," and tossed some money on the table before walking out.

Leo's words echoed in Levi's mind as he drove along Oregon's Pacific Coast Highway. With his bike thrumming beneath him, giving him a greater sense of freedom than he'd ever experienced with any car, he'd drive around a curve and suddenly pop out of the cool shade of some giant trees to see the ocean in full sunlight. The waves would be slamming against black, craggy rocks, mist flying high in the air. The scenery was breathtaking, but didn't have the same soothing effect it usually did.

At least I have dreams....

That was true. Leo had sacrificed everything for his dreams, had even tried to make Levi the vehicle of bringing those dreams to life.

But that didn't mean striving to achieve something wasn't important.

So forget Leo and what he had or hadn't done, Levi told himself. His father had made his choices. What did *he* want?

It used to be escape. To show his father that he would not be controlled. But now? Leo had lost all the power he'd once possessed. Their visit a few hours ago made that clear. The only thing Levi had to fear was his own bad choices and limitations. So why wasn't he creating a better life? Because of Leo?

The more he tried to hurt his father, the more he'd hurt himself.

A scenic view sign with a turnout for motorhomes and tourists came up on the right. Levi pulled into it and shut off his engine. Then he sat and listened to the caw of seagulls as he breathed in the briny scent of the beach. As much as he loved Oregon, he knew he didn't want to live in Portland or work with his father. It was going to take a lot more than two years to overcome what he felt toward Leo. He was afraid he might never get beyond it.

But there was one place he desperately wanted to be. He hadn't allowed himself to consider returning, had shoved the desire out of his mind every time it broke upon his consciousness. He knew the price he'd pay if he went back to Whiskey Creek. He didn't want to watch Callie die any more than she wanted him to. He wouldn't be able to stand seeing her suffer.

Not only that, sooner or later Chief Stacy would make sure he was arrested and charged for what he'd done to those officers in Nevada. If he went back, he'd essentially be turning himself in. And for what? How much time did Callie have left? *Weeks?*

That was the impression he'd gotten when he'd overheard her on the phone.

He'd made the right decision when he left. The cost of staying with her was too high.

But what if she needed him? What if he could make the end a little easier for her? After all, it wasn't his practical side that was drawing him back to Whiskey Creek. It was some other part. A part of him that was willing to pay any price for just one more day....

27

On a Friday morning almost two weeks after Levi drove off, Callie sat with her friends at their customary large booth at Black Gold Coffee. It felt like one of a thousand other days, except for the surreptitious glances she received from her friends. They were worried about her, couldn't help wondering if this get-together might be her last.

She could understand why they'd feel that way. It was odd, but ever since Levi's departure she'd gone downhill fast. She could barely eat, had no energy, spent most of her time resting at her parents'. Every morning her mother would call the doctor to see if he'd arranged a transplant, and every morning he'd tell her not to call again, that he'd be in touch if a liver became available. Then she'd quickly wipe her eyes and force a smile before turning her wheelchair around to face Callie, as if Callie wouldn't notice that she'd been crying.

"I tried to go there," Ted said. "I couldn't get her to answer the door."

They'd been discussing the fact that Sophia hadn't shown up since Ted had made that comment about Scott.

"Maybe she wasn't home," Eve said.

"I think she was," Ted insisted. "Where else would she be? She hardly leaves that mausoleum they call a house."

"Did you check to see if her car was there?" Noah asked.

Ted scowled. "How could I? They have a five-car garage but every single door was down."

"She would've answered if she was there." Cheyenne always stuck up for the underdog. But Callie had to admit it was a little ironic that anyone could consider Sophia an underdog. She and her gal pals had been merciless to anyone less fortunate when they were all in high school. As the daughter of their former mayor, she'd had the power to get away with just about anything, and she'd exploited it to full advantage. No wonder they had difficulty believing her transformation.

"Not necessarily," Ted muttered.

"Give her a call," Callie said. "Maybe you can reach her by phone."

"I'm not going to keep bugging her," he said. "If she doesn't want to hear my apology, I won't bother with it."

Noah added cream to his coffee. "We're just going to ignore the fact that she isn't joining us anymore?"

The look on Ted's face suggested he didn't like this question. "What else can we do? It's her choice whether or not to come."

Callie felt like pushing their cups and plates aside so she could lay her head on the table. Instead, she took a deep breath and used a spoon to fish an ice cube from her water, hoping that might ease the nausea roiling in her stomach—a constant companion these days. "So you're happy to be rid of her?"

Ted wouldn't meet her eyes. "It doesn't matter to me one way or the other."

Callie nodded but she was unconvinced. She suspected that Kyle, who'd picked her up and brought her here, remained skeptical, too. It was hard to tell. He sat next to her, but he was too busy watching her, looking concerned, to really participate in the conversation.

Callie ignored him. She hated the way they all seemed to be waiting for the moment she might keel over.

"I sort of miss her," Eve said. "She was always very supportive."

"Always?" Ted let loose a preposterous laugh. "Oh, how quickly they forget. She's been nice the past couple of years. But only because her father has no more power in this town, and she doesn't have any other friends. She's always nice when she wants something."

Baxter was eyeing Noah. His gaze strayed in that direction so many times Callie was afraid Noah would notice that this wasn't the type of attention typical of a best friend. She didn't feel well enough to keep up with the conversation, but for Baxter's sake she spoke to distract them, especially Noah. "Has anyone seen Skip lately?"

No one cared about Skip, so it was a pointless question, but they didn't call her on it.

Kyle shook his head. "He's never home these days."

If Callie had her guess, he came home often enough to knock his wife around, but she had no proof of that, so she kept her mouth shut.

"I bet he'll be here for the Fourth of July next week." Ted rolled his eyes. "He wouldn't want to miss the parade."

Every year, Skip followed the high school marching band, the Rotary Club float and the Kiwanis Club float down Sutter Street in one of his rare Ferraris while his daughter sat in the passenger seat tossing candy to the crowds lined up to watch. Callie could picture the expensive sunglasses he chose for the occasion and his Ivy League attire. His parents, also some of the wealthiest people in the area, drove a Lamborghini in the parade, while Sophia rode atop the Bank of Gold Country float, dressed in a sparkly evening gown and looking like Red, White and Blue Barbie. Riley, Noah, Baxter and Kyle used to mock her Miss America wave. Callie had even laughed along. But once Sophia started joining them for coffee, everyone soon realized how much she hated being put on display like that. Apparently, it was Skip who insisted on this "family tradition." He was showing off. First his expensive car and pretty daughter. Then his wealthy parents. And last, his lovely wife.

"I wonder if she'll ever leave him," Noah mused.

"Maybe. I certainly get the feeling she wants to." Eve sounded slightly wistful.

"She won't do it." Ted spoke decisively. "No one else can keep her in such grand style."

Callie was sure Ted was wrong about Sophia's motives for staying in the marriage, but the hurt Sophia had caused him in the past blinded him. She didn't attempt to correct him. Right now, she felt as if someone could cut off her right arm and she'd be too sick to protest.

"Hey, are you okay?"

This came from Kyle. She opened her mouth to assure him that she was fine. She said that a dozen times a day, especially since she'd moved in with her parents. But suddenly she felt so extremely ill she couldn't form the words. Something had given out on her. She wasn't sure if it was her kidneys—she'd been having more and more trouble going to the bathroom—or another organ, but she had a feeling this might be the end.

Fleetingly, she thought about trying to scoot out of the booth so someone could take her to the hospital. But without a working liver, what was the point? They'd only be prolonging the worst misery a person could imagine.

Let go, she told herself. *Don't draw this out.*

Terror engulfed her along with a sudden darkness. She was struggling just to breathe. But her last thought was how much she loved these people so she did her best to smile a goodbye.

As soon as Levi drove into town, he stopped at the Gas-N-Go and learned that Callie was in the hospital. She was fading as fast as she'd indicated she would, and that scared him, made him hyperaware of the minutes that were passing by. He had to see her immediately, before it was too late. He just hoped he'd have the chance to say goodbye....

Joe, who'd told him where she was, also gave him directions to the hospital. Once he got there, he jogged down the corridor to the intensive care unit, heart pumping erratically, afraid he was already too late.

Let her be alive... Please, let her be alive...

Kyle saw him first. All her friends were crowded around two chairs, half blocking the hallway. There was a nurse's station across from them. Levi would've expected anyone who manned that station to be upset. Callie had far more visitors than the two specified by the rules. But the young blonde behind the desk seemed too preoccupied to complain. She kept sending them excited glances.

What was going on?

"You're back," Kyle said.

Levi could hear the accusation in that statement. Kyle was mad that he'd left in the first place. Levi didn't blame him. "Where is she?"

At the sound of his voice, Noah, Baxter, Riley, Ted and Dylan turned. So did the famous actor, Simon O'Neal. Levi had never seen him in person, but like most other people, he'd watched at least a couple of his movies. That made it easy to recognize his face—and to understand the nurse's reaction. No one was going to ask Simon or anyone with him to leave, even if it *was* a hospital. Maybe Simon had promised to finance a new wing in exchange. He definitely had the money to do whatever he wished.

Eve, Cheyenne and the redhead from the photograph in Callie's studio—Simon's wife—pushed through the men to be able to see him.

"She's in Room Four," Cheyenne said. "But the doctor is—"

Levi didn't wait to hear the rest. He had to reach her. But he also had to slow down. There wasn't enough space to move quickly, not unless he wanted to bowl over the equipment in this section of the facility and get himself kicked out. He didn't know whether the preferential treatment being extended to Simon and friends covered him, as well, so he tried to navigate carefully.

It wasn't until he stood right outside Callie's room and could hear the quiet murmur of voices within that he began to feel uncertain. Was she awake? In pain?

Was there anything he could do to make her happy before she died?

Staring down at his shaking hands, he closed them into fists. Then he opened them again, drew a deep breath and went inside.

Her parents were there. At least, he assumed the woman in the wheelchair was Callie's mother. He'd never met her. The doctor was with them. When they glanced up, surprised by his intrusion, Levi felt so conspicuous he almost backed out of the room.

But then Callie saw him.

"Levi!" She tried to sit up but didn't have the strength. At that point, he would've forced his way through all of them if he had to. Slipping between them, he reached her bedside and took her hand.

"Hi. I'm so glad—" he swallowed against the sudden tightness in his throat "—I'm so glad you're hanging in there. I'm sorry I left. I—I shouldn't have. I panicked."

"It's okay." Her eyes closed briefly, as if she had to summon the energy just to open them. "They took my...my necklace."

Her necklace? He was so busy noticing all the changes in her, and handling the shock of how quickly those changes had occurred, that he didn't know what she was talking about. Then he remembered the hummingbird pendant he'd given her. Obviously, she was upset over its loss. "I'll find it for you, okay? Don't worry."

That seemed to please her. She nodded slightly and let her eyes close again.

"The nurses took her necklace off before we got here," her mother explained. "She—she collapsed at the coffee shop two days ago and one of her friends

called an ambulance, so the emergency room person-
nel did what they had to. She keeps asking for it, but
they won't let her have it. They say it'll get in the way,
and we don't want anything to stop them from giving
her the care she needs."

Callie didn't find it easy to talk, but she tried again.
"It's *mine*," she whispered, letting Levi know she
wanted it back regardless of their reasons for denying
her request.

"Can't we get it for her?" he asked the doctor.

"It's standard procedure to remove all jewelry," he
replied as if that was that. Then he stuck out his hand.
"I'm Dr. Yee, Callie's hepatologist. And you are…"

"Her boyfriend." He was afraid that might sound
presumptuous. They'd never made a verbal commitment to each other. But it was there in the subtext of
everything they'd done together, in the strength of their
feelings for each other. And he feared that if he didn't
acknowledge what he felt, he'd be denied access to her.

If her parents were taken aback by this announcement, they didn't say so. Maybe they could tell by Callie's reaction that he was as significant to her as he
claimed.

"Nice to meet you," Dr. Yee said.

"Likewise," Levi responded. "So back to her necklace…"

Dr. Yee shook his head. "Like I said—"

Lowering his voice, Levi broke in before the doctor
could finish. "I heard that bit about standard procedure.
But it's a small thing to ask, right? I mean…you're dealing with human beings in this hospital, and that means
some exceptions should be made, depending on the circumstances. Wouldn't you agree?"

Yee looked to her parents. They'd given in to him so far, but now they seemed to think better of it. "It obviously means a great deal to Callie," her mother said.

"And we've asked if she could have it many times," Boone added.

With a thoughtful frown, the doctor collected his clipboard and started out of the room. "I guess there could be worse things to work around should surgery become imminent. If it's that important, I'll see what I can do."

Levi followed him out. "And, Doc?"

Dr. Yee turned. "Yes?"

"What can we do to get her a transplant?"

He seemed genuinely concerned when he said, "Nothing, except pray that a liver becomes available. I've categorized her as status one. That gives her the highest priority."

"How much more time do we have?"

"Maybe a few days," he said.

The Fourth of July came and went with Callie mostly unconscious. Her parents were at her bedside constantly through those days. She knew that. Her friends were often there, too, especially Kyle and Baxter. Even Gail and Simon had pulled themselves away from their commitments in Los Angeles. Several of the nurses had asked about her connection to the big movie star. But the person whose presence meant the most was Levi, probably because having him there was such an unexpected gift. She could hear him talking to her parents or her friends, and it brought her a measure of peace to know he cared enough to come back to her, that he was committed to what they'd shared, despite her situation.

She wished she was stronger and found it ironic that her female vanity hadn't deserted her even at such a dire point. But she made a conscious effort not to worry about how she looked. She had so little time left. She figured she might as well enjoy the pleasure of having Levi there, holding her hand. Although the hospital had relented and given her the necklace, it didn't seem nearly as important now that she actually had him with her.

"Hey, you. How are you feeling?"

Callie managed to lift her heavy eyelids to see Baxter. He'd come at a time when she had no other visitors. Her father had driven her mother to a doctor's appointment, and Levi had left to get a shower and something to eat. Her parents had given him the key to the farm, so he was staying there and taking care of Rifle. That seemed fitting somehow. Callie wished more than anything that she could go home with him and see her dog, but at least the two of them got to stay at the farm for a while longer.

"Fine." She tried to smile for Baxter's benefit.

"You look good," he told her.

She knew he was lying. She *couldn't* look good. But he did—as always. He smelled good, too.

"Do you want me to read to you?" he asked.

Ted had been coming to the hospital and reading his latest book. Even his editor hadn't seen this one. She loved his stories, but she also liked it when Baxter read from various magazines. In keeping with his personality, he focused on sensational tidbits, like the mother who beat off three robbers with a broom, or the reality TV star whose cosmetic surgery didn't turn out quite as planned.

She nodded. But then she realized that she hadn't spent any time alone with Baxter in the eight days she'd been in the hospital and decided she'd rather talk—if she could.

"Wait…"

"What is it?" he said.

"How're…things with…you?"

"Busy."

"You…seeing anyone?"

"Not right now. But Noah is. She's another groupie, loves professional cyclists."

"I think…he knows," she said.

"That I'm gay? Maybe."

"So why…why not address it? Just you…and him. Privately."

He didn't answer for a few seconds. Then he said, "I'll promise you this. You get well, and I'll tell Noah that I'm madly in love with him. Fair enough?"

She attempted a laugh. "Now I know…you don't think I'm going…to make it. Or…or you wouldn't commit…to that."

"I'm trying to motivate you to keep fighting."

Levi had given her enough motivation already. She was hanging on with everything she had, hoping that a liver would become available. "Okay. I'll keep… fighting."

He looked as if he was about to say something else, but Gail and Simon came into the room.

"Mind if we crash the party?" Gail asked.

Callie was so tired, but she mustered a smile. "Giving…the nurses another…thrill, Simon?"

He grinned at her. "I've told them I just look like Simon O'Neal, but they're not buying it."

"How are the kids getting along without you?" Baxter asked.

"They're doing great," Gail said. "We have a fabulous nanny. She may bring them out here in a few days. Once Callie gets a liver, she'll be in the hospital another week or two, so it makes sense."

If Callie gets a liver, Callie thought, but she didn't have the energy to say it. She knew they wouldn't want to hear her talking negatively, anyway.

"What about Simon's work commitments?" Baxter asked.

"Hey, he's not the only one with work commitments," Gail teased. "But we're managing. Callie's more important than anything going on in our professional lives. We're all pulling together. Right, Cal? We're going to hold out until we get what we need."

Callie gathered her strength. "Hope it comes…soon."

"So do we." Gail sat on the other side of the bed, across from Baxter. Simon stood behind her and massaged her shoulders while she talked. "About that guy who's been hanging around."

The reference made Callie smile. She knew Gail was joking, that she remembered Levi's name. "Yes?"

"He's handsome. And devoted. I think you did well when you caught his eye."

She hoped Dylan hadn't said anything about Levi's past. She didn't want Gail or Simon or anyone else who didn't already know to find out about the fight he'd had with those two officers. She knew he felt bad about it. He'd said as much yesterday while her parents were at lunch and they'd had a few minutes to themselves.

Fortunately, she sensed that her friends were willing to let his past go, at least for the time being. As a matter of fact, everyone was acting as if Dylan had never told them he'd recognized Levi. Even Kyle hadn't mentioned it.

"I love him," she said.

Gail squeezed her arm. "I can tell. Joe thinks he's great, too. Wants him to come work at the Gas-N-Go when you're all better."

Callie imagined moving back to the farm and taking up where they'd left off. They'd been so happy during those two weeks. It was that vision that kept her clinging to life. "Nice of him."

"Joe told me he's never seen a more talented mechanic," Simon added. "I guess he fixed some BMW Joe was having trouble with."

"So it was…the main computer?"

Callie must've spoken too softly. Gail leaned toward her. "What?"

The comment wasn't important enough to repeat. "Never…mind."

Her parents joined them next. "Where's Levi?" Diana asked, sounding slightly disappointed that he wasn't in the room.

Callie took a breath. "Showering."

Diana wedged her wheelchair into a spot at the foot of the bed. "He's such a nice young man. Don't you think so, Gail?"

Gail nodded. "I was just telling Callie the same thing."

They continued to talk—about Simon's next movie, more improvements to Baxter's Victorian and Gail's new PR clients. Callie listened to what she could. But it wasn't long before she had to give up and rest. She wanted to speak, especially when she heard her father murmur something to Simon, and Simon responded with, "No word yet." She worried that they were doing exactly what she'd told Baxter she didn't want them to—using Simon's power and influence to put her ahead of everyone else who needed a liver transplant.

But there was nothing she could do about it, even if they were. At the moment, she was too weak to say a word.

The farm wasn't the same without Callie. Levi showered and ate and slept there when he wasn't at the hospital. He also fed and cared for Rifle, since her parents weren't up to it. But he wanted her back home, wanted another chance at what they'd had. He certainly had other problems to work through, but he couldn't address them, or anything else, until he knew what was going to happen to Callie.

"Hey, boy." Sitting down on the porch with Rifle, he stared at the damaged barn. He wanted to rebuild it. He wanted to paint the chicken coop, too. There was so much to do here. Her garden was getting ruined since he hadn't been around to care for it. He hated the thought of that, especially because she'd put so much work into it.

"I don't know if she's going to survive," he confided to the dog.

It was such a hot day. Rifle seemed to be feeling the heat. He panted as he rested his muzzle on Levi's lap.

"She's getting worse," Levi told him. "I can see it every day, almost every hour." He squinted into the distance, not wanting to face the truth but unable to escape it. "The doctors are doing everything they can, but it's not enough."

Rifle whined, and Levi toyed with his ears, wondering what would happen to him and the dog when this was all over. Callie provided the foundation they both needed, somehow brought sense and order to their worlds.

They shared a few minutes of commiseration. Then Callie's cell phone went off. Her parents had insisted Levi take it so they could stay in touch.

His heart in his throat, Levi dug the phone out of his pocket. Even Rifle seemed agitated. He sat up and barked as Levi frowned at the display. It was her parents, all right. The screen read Daddy and had a picture of her father.

Although they'd asked him to carry her phone, they'd never actually tried to reach him on it. They wouldn't be calling him now unless something had changed. That meant one of two things.

Levi feared he knew which one it had to be. Callie's doctor hadn't given them much hope.

Closing his eyes, he said a brief prayer. He'd never been a religious man, but he'd said a lot of prayers in the past few days. Then, standing, he punched the talk button. "Hello?"

Her father was crying. He could barely talk.

Was Callie gone?

Levi's stomach twisted at the sound of Boone's broken words. Until they began to make sense....

"They have a liver," he said. "It's on its way to the hospital from Southern California. Get over here as soon as possible. They'll be taking her into surgery the moment it arrives."

28

When the surgery had lasted fourteen hours, Levi grew so anxious he could only pace. The doctor had said it would take ten to twelve, so he'd been expecting a lengthy wait, but the extra time frightened him, made him wonder if something had gone wrong. Had the liver been damaged in transport? Was Callie holding up? What was taking so damn long?

The doctor hadn't had a chance to explain the procedure to him in detail. By the time he arrived, they were well into getting her prepped. But her parents knew all about it. They told him and her other friends that the doctor would make an incision in her abdomen, detach her liver from the blood vessels and common bile duct and clamp them off. Then they'd remove her liver and attach the donor liver. If necessary, they'd also put in a few temporary tubes to drain blood and excess fluids and check bile production. Provided all went well, she'd go to the anesthesia recovery area after surgery and then back to intensive care until she stabilized. After that they'd take out her breathing tube and catheter and, although she'd be carefully monitored to make sure her body didn't reject the new liver, she'd likely get to recover in a regular hospital room. After a week or so, if all went well, she'd be released.

"Do you think we should be worried?" Diana murmured to Boone. There'd been a lot of talking at first. Callie had a huge crowd waiting to hear how the surgery went. But in the past hour they'd all fallen silent. Of course, it was after six in the morning. Most of them, including Levi, had been up for twenty-four hours. That meant the doctor had been up a long time, too....

Was Dr. Yee alert enough to do the job? Was he almost finished?

Levi watched Boone put his arm around his wife, trying to comfort her. Callie's father didn't have any answers, but he kept telling her he was sure everything was all right.

Callie's friends, too tired to talk anymore, lounged in chairs in the waiting room, most of them sitting close together. There was one woman named Sophia, however, who sat off by herself, while a guy named Ted shot surreptitious glances in her direction.

Levi wondered what was going on between them, but he was too concerned about Callie to think much about it. The news that they'd found a liver had changed everything in his mind, given him more hope than he probably should've allowed.

What if she died, anyway?

He had her necklace in one pocket, carrying it around like a good luck charm—the doctor had brought it to him before surgery, said it definitely wasn't going in there with her. But Levi had never had a lot of luck when it came to the people he loved. He was afraid he couldn't count on luck now.

"Okay, I have to ask."

Everyone turned to look at Baxter, who was addressing Simon.

"Ask what?" Simon sat on one of the couches, his wife leaning against him.

Baxter slid forward. "Are you responsible for this?"

Simon seemed confused. "For what?"

"Did you make this happen? Pay someone or...or use your influence or whatever to get Callie a transplant?"

Gail lifted her head. "We tried, Bax," she said. "The moment we learned of her situation we started calling everyone we know who might be able to help."

"And?" The conversation had drawn Noah's attention from the TV playing in one corner.

Gail shook her head. "They told us there was nothing we could do."

"So it's just a coincidence that she got a liver after you found out she needed one?" Baxter clarified.

Simon hid a yawn. "It's just a coincidence."

Raking a hand through his hair, Baxter sat back. "Good. When she comes out of this, she'll be happy to hear it was legit."

If she pulls through. Levi didn't add that, but he was certainly thinking it. He didn't know how she could endure such a long and intensive surgery. She'd been so sick this week.

Come on, babe. You can do it. Hang in there. For us.

They deserved a chance to explore what they felt for each other, didn't they?

He pulled the necklace out of his pocket and examined the little bird pendant. "Thorn birds," he muttered.

"What'd you say?"

This came from Dylan, who'd spoken less than anyone. Levi shoved the necklace back in his pocket. "Nothing." He walked out of the room to the vending machine in the hall and slipped a dollar into the slot. He needed a drink. For the first time in a long while, he wished he could drink something stronger than water but, other than an occasional glass of wine, he didn't drink any-more—not since that night in Nevada.

A bottle fell to the bottom of the dispenser. As he retrieved it, he heard footsteps behind him.

Dylan had followed him. Thinking Cheyenne's hus-band had also come for something from the vending machine, he stepped to one side, but Dylan stopped him before he could go back to the waiting room.

"I saw you fight once," he said.

A burst of alarm shot through Levi. He understood what Dylan was trying to tell him. Dylan knew who he was. "Small world," he said.

Dylan nodded. "No shit."

"Did I win?"

His lips curved into a smile. "Didn't you always?"

"Some things come easier to me than others." He jerked his head toward the room. "Does everyone else know?"

"Not her parents. I told most of the others the day I recognized you at the farm."

And yet no one had let on. That confirmed how wor-ried they were about Callie. It also suggested that they might be willing to forgive his mistake. He found that hopeful.

"What did they say?"

"We told Callie but no one else."

"Not Chief Stacy."

"No."

The condensation on the water bottle made his hand wet. "When will you do that?"

Dylan studied him for a second. "We're going to leave that up to you."

Levi remained in the hall as Dylan walked back to the waiting room. He might've interpreted Dylan's words as a subtle threat that he had to turn himself in or they'd eventually come forward. But he knew that wasn't the intent. Dylan was telling him that whatever he chose to do about that night—it truly was his decision.

After twisting off the cap, Levi took a long drink. He had to get through Callie's operation before he could even think about any other problem, he told himself.

He was just heading back to join the others when he saw Callie's doctor coming down the hall.

"How is she?" he asked, suddenly finding it hard to breathe.

"I think she's going to be fine." Dr. Yee gave him an exhausted smile. "All the signs are good. She came through it like a champ."

It'd been several days since the surgery. Callie couldn't believe how much better she felt. Already she was in a regular hospital room and her doctor was talking about letting her go home after the weekend. The difference a healthy liver could make was astonishing. She only hoped her body wouldn't reject the transplant, but so far so good.

"What is it?" she murmured.

It was the middle of the night. Her parents and friends had gone home much earlier, leaving her and Levi alone.

"I'm just thinking." He stood over by the window, looking out into a moonlit courtyard.

"About what?"

He came back toward the bed. "The future."

"What about it?" she asked.

"Dylan knows who I am."

She felt a measure of concern. She wasn't sure she wanted to discuss what he'd done in Nevada; she didn't see how that could offer any solutions. If he didn't turn himself in, he'd be looking over his shoulder for the rest of his life. But if he *did,* he'd probably go to prison. "Yes."

"I'm thinking of turning myself in."

"No!"

"I don't have any other choice. If I don't, that night in Nevada will always stand between us."

She knew in her heart he was right. But could she face the alternative? She'd just reclaimed her future, wanted to spend it with him. "But they could put you away for…years."

"That's true. There'll be a trial. And a punishment."

"Prison, like I said."

"Most likely."

She swallowed hard. "Are you prepared to deal with that?"

"If that's what it takes to be the kind of man I should be, I am."

When she reached for him, he moved closer. "But prison, Levi?"

"I can't live under a false identity forever. What if we have kids? What if this comes back to haunt us at an even worse time?"

Her hand automatically went to the necklace he'd given her, which he'd put back on her the day after the transplant. "You want to handle it now."

"I think so." He bent over her, kissed her forehead.

"Will you wait for me if I do? Will you be patient until I can get my life in order so we can have a future together?"

They hadn't talked about marriage. But that was exactly what Callie wanted. The long hours they'd spent getting to know each other in her hospital room, when they could do nothing of a sexual nature, had convinced her that she felt far more for Levi than lust.

She touched his face, saw the uncertainty in his eyes. He'd lost so much in his life that he had a difficult time trusting anyone or anything to be there for him, but she planned to show him that he could trust *her*. "How about if we get married first?"

He rubbed his cheek against hers. "Are you sure you don't want to wait until you see how I'm going to come out of it? Now that you're healthy, Chief Stacy might come back into the picture. He has that pension and all."

She smiled at his teasing. "Chief Stacy wasn't an option even before I learned about Nevada."

"I know, but you might be committing your life to someone who could be locked away for several years."

She captured his face between her hands and stared into his eyes. "I'd wait for you forever."

He kissed her lips. "Then I'm going to do it," he said. "I'm going to turn myself in. But, for your sake, we'll marry *after* that."

Callie had wanted Levi to pick her up from the hospital on his bike. But he'd insisted on bringing her SUV instead. He said she had too much medication to bring home—she'd be taking nineteen pills a day until her doctor changed her regimen. But she knew there was more to his reasoning. He felt it was too soon for her to be on the bike. He was almost *too* protective of her.

Still, the day she returned to the farm was one of the best of her life. She'd never thought she'd see it again, never thought she'd see Rifle, either. When her dog came bounding down the lane to greet her, barking in excitement, tears immediately welled up. She'd made it through the past few weeks. Somehow she was going to survive the summer—and maybe many more years. She found it a bittersweet thing to realize that her life had been spared while someone else's had been lost. That sometimes created mixed emotions. But the generosity of the gift a stranger from Southern California had given her brought such overwhelming gratitude. Her parents and friends didn't talk about that aspect, at least not to her. She knew they didn't want to point out the obvious for fear it would make her sad. But there were times, when she was alone in the hospital, that she'd raised her gown just to see the stitches and to marvel at the difference in how she felt and her excitement about her future, which was now restored because of the magnitude of this gift.

"I love it here," she murmured.

"I'm glad." Levi threaded his fingers through hers with one hand while steering with the other. "Because... I have some good news."

She turned to look at him. "What kind of good news?"

"Your parents are going to let us buy it from them."

She grinned. "I was hoping."

"I talked to them about it while you were in the hospital. I can make a living, Callie. I'm capable enough. If you can just hang on until...until I clear up my past, we'll be able to afford this place. We can stay here as long as you like."

"We'll be okay," she assured him. "I still have my photography studio."

"Is it making enough that you can get by without me? Even while you recover? Or should I wait to—"

"No, we already discussed this. We need to put a definitive end to that part of your life so we can move on with ours."

"Okay." He stopped to let Rifle in the car, but held him back so he couldn't be too aggressive with her.

"She's a little fragile right now, bud," he told her dog. "Take it easy."

Rifle made an effort to calm down. He whined, as if it was a challenge because he was so excited, but he settled for licking her face.

"That's a good dog. We're all home," she said. "We're all home together." She sent Levi another smile. "Where we belong."

Three weeks later, once Callie got clearance from her doctor to take a week-long trip, they left for Reno. Levi asked Baxter to come with them. In case they arrested him on the spot, he wanted someone to be able to drive her home.

When he parked at the police station, he looked over at her. She could tell he was nervous. She was nervous, too. The thought of not seeing him for months, possibly years, had her so worked up she could feel her heart beating in her throat.

"Let me go in with you," she said.

He gave her a halfhearted grin that did little to hide his true feelings. "And what are you going to do? Tell them I'm a good guy?"

"Yes!"

"I don't think they're going to take your word for it.

Anyway, there's too many germs in there. You know you have to be careful."

"I'll go in," Baxter said.

Levi twisted around to address him. "I'd rather you stayed here. Take care of her, okay? They should allow me one call. I'll let you know if…if you need to leave without me."

When he leaned over to kiss her, she clung to him. "We should've gotten married first."

"It'll be better when I don't have this hanging over my head. Just stay well until I can get out. Then I'll come back to you."

Forcing herself to let him go, she nodded. Then she watched him get out and walk through the station doors.

"We should've stayed in Whiskey Creek," she told Baxter. "Of course they're going to put him in jail! There's a warrant out for his arrest."

"He's got balls. I'll say that for him."

She blew out a shaky breath. As if the past few months hadn't been hard enough, now she had to deal with possibly losing the man she loved for an undetermined length of time. It was so easy to understand how Levi had done what he'd done, but she didn't expect the police to see it that way.

Baxter reached over the seat to squeeze her shoulder. "You going to be okay?"

"No."

"Come on, don't talk like that."

"My liver's working fine. It's my heart I'm worried about."

"You'll get through this just like you did the surgery."

She shifted so she could see him. "That reminds me."

"Of what?"

"You said you'd tell Noah how you feel about him if I made it."

His eyes slid away from hers. "No way."

"So now you're reneging?"

"I can already tell you how it would go, Callie."

She didn't argue with him, because she suspected he was right. Noah had been dating more than ever, going from one girl to the next. "He's out of control."

"I think he's reacting to what he knows but doesn't want to face."

"Where does that leave you?" she asked.

"I'm trying to get over him."

"Meaning you're dating other people?"

"When I'm in the city."

"You don't spend many weekends in the city."

"Yeah, well, I said I was trying. I didn't say it was working."

They fell silent. Callie knew he'd have to be committed to whatever he chose to do and didn't want to interfere too much. But she wasn't sure what else to talk about. She was too nervous to make small talk.

Baxter made an effort to keep her focused on other things. "Levi told me that before your operation, Chief Stacy tried to strong-arm him into leaving town."

She wrung her hands as she watched people—other people and not Levi—walking out of the police station. "Can you believe it?"

"Not really. He can be an egotistical ass, but cops can be that way."

"Once I get past this, I'm going to file a complaint."

"Do you think it'll do any good?"

"Maybe not. He has a lot of friends in Whiskey

Creek, but I want to let him know he can't push people around without some sort of resistance."

Baxter propped his hands behind his head and scooted lower in the seat. "He can't be all bad. He did get rid of Denny and Powell."

"But the way he went about it was wrong."

He arched his eyebrows at her. "So are you going to complain about *that,* too?"

She thought about the relief she felt to have Denny and Powell and Spike—whom they'd reclaimed before hurrying off—gone, and managed to smile. "No."

"Nothing will happen to Stacy."

"I know."

For the next thirty minutes, she watched the entrance to the police station, hoping she'd see Levi walk out. When he didn't come and he didn't come, she started to fidget. "I'm going inside," she said. "I have to find out what's happening."

Baxter got out when she did. "No, Callie. He said he'd call us. Give him a chance to deal with this."

Feeling torn, she rubbed her hands over her face. But before she could get back in the car, Levi emerged from the station and hurried toward them.

"How did it go?" she asked.

He grinned. "You're not going to believe this."

"What?"

"The cop I beat? The one I put in the hospital?"

"Yes?"

"He was fired for misconduct six months ago. Apparently, after what I did, several people came forward to say he got physical with them, too—with no provocation. Even the rookie he was training, the other guy I hit to keep him from drawing on me, testified against him."

Callie glanced at Baxter to see if he was hearing the same thing she was. "So what does that mean?" she asked Levi.

"It means the chances of the district attorney prosecuting me for that incident are slim. He knows I'd have a great case. Other than that, my record is clean. I was honorably discharged from the army. A good attorney could probably get me off with probation and a little community service."

"You're kidding." He was right; Callie couldn't believe it. This was the last thing she'd expected.

"I'm not kidding. I actually spoke to the rookie who was there that night. He said he'd tell the truth, tell the D.A. that Officer Howton kicked me twice before I reacted."

Relief flooded through Callie as she slipped her arms around his neck. "That is such good news."

He kissed her temple. "We have a fresh start, babe. Let's make the most of it."

She pulled back to smile up at him. "And how do we do that?"

"I think it's time to plan the wedding."

"So, will I be Mrs. McCloud or Mrs. Pendleton?"

"Pendleton. It'll be great to use my real name again."

With his arms loosely around her waist, he jerked his head at Baxter. "Bax, will you be my best man?"

Baxter laughed as he nodded. "Hell, yeah! Are we going to Vegas?"

"No," Callie said. "I want a small ceremony at the church where my parents were married—right there in Whiskey Creek."

Epilogue

It was a perfect October afternoon, with a butter-yellow sun shining outside and flowers adorning every pew of the old church. Callie *almost* wished she could photograph the event. She was that impressed with how it had all come together. But she'd spent plenty of hours photographing other people's weddings. Today it was her turn to be escorted down the aisle, and Tina was behind the lens.

Her assistant would do a great job. Callie wasn't worried about that. She was too happy to worry about anything, except maybe Kyle. Along with Ted, Baxter, Riley, Noah, Dylan and Simon, he stood in front, next to Levi. She could see the whole line—including Gail, Cheyenne, Eve and Sophia on her side—when she poked her head out of the small antechamber where she was waiting for the wedding march to begin. Dressed in tuxedos or lovely champagne-colored dresses, they were all smiling in anticipation. Kyle, however, looked slightly uncomfortable, and she knew he had reason to be.

She probably shouldn't have hired his old girlfriend to plan the wedding, Callie thought. Kyle wasn't over her yet. Callie had known that, of course. She'd considered trying to find someone else, but there were too many other factors. Everyone in Whiskey Creek hired Olivia. It would've seemed like an intentional slight to go with someone else. Not only that, but Callie had photographed Olivia's wedding. How could she not return the favor?

Besides, Olivia honestly deserved the business. She was quick and efficient and personable. With only eight weeks to pull off an event of this magnitude, she'd done an outstanding job.

"You nervous?" Her father was waiting for her. He kept straightening his tie and shifting on his feet as if this were the biggest moment of his life.

Callie slipped her arm though his in an effort to calm him. "No. You?"

"A little," he admitted. "But seeing you so in love… This is one of the best days of my life."

"Mine, too." Callie could see Olivia slipping through the guests crowded along the side of the church, carrying her clipboard and wearing a purposeful expression that indicated they were minutes away from starting. Olivia's sexy husband, Brandon, watched her with a proud grin. Although they didn't have any children yet, he'd given up extreme skiing to settle down and have a family. Word had it he was going to open a ski shop in town. There'd even been some recent talk that he might simply go into business with Noah and expand Noah's bike shop to include items for other sports. Callie wondered if he realized that his stepbrother was still in love with the woman who'd become *his* wife.

"You two all set?" Olivia asked, entering the vestibule.

Her father stepped out to take a look at how things

were going. "I think the whole town has turned out," he said.

It certainly felt that way. Besides the people pressed up along the sides of the church, there were rows and rows of guests standing at the back. Callie should've been overwhelmed, but she wasn't. She knew these people, loved them. They'd been part of her life since she was born. The only person she didn't know was Levi's father. At first, she hadn't been sure that encouraging Levi to invite Leo was the right thing to do, but now she was glad. Mr. Pendleton, who sat in the front row next to her mother and Godfrey and Mina, had thanked them both for letting him come at least three different times.

"I'm all set," she said.

Olivia gave her arm an encouraging squeeze. "You're one of the loveliest brides I've ever seen."

Callie smiled. She'd bought a long white gown with a fitted bodice at Miosa's Bridal in Sacramento. "Thank you."

"And the ceremony is going to come off without a hitch," Olivia added with a wink.

It wouldn't matter to Callie even if it didn't. She felt fortunate just to have the opportunity to promise herself forever to the man she loved. So what if they ran out of candy in the candy decanters? She had her life back, and she had the person she wanted to spend it with waiting to say "I do."

"I know it will," she said. "Thanks again for everything."

The swell of organ music signaled that it was time to walk down the aisle. She glanced up at her father, saw tears sparkling in his eyes and felt the lump grow in her own throat. Three months ago she'd been lying in a hospital bed, fighting for each breath. And now, thanks to what was, to her, a miracle of generosity on the part of a stranger, she was getting married.

"Here we go, Callie girl," her father muttered, and they started off.

Her friends waited at the end of the aisle. She could see them blinking to hold back tears or actually wiping them from their cheeks. And in the center of the people she'd always loved the most was Levi, looking more handsome than she'd ever seen him.

He grinned at her as she came toward him and she grinned back.

"Take good care of her," her father murmured.

Levi's warm hands gripped hers. "Yes, sir. I'll do everything I can to keep her safe and make her happy," he said.

* * * * *

New York Times Bestselling Author

CARLA NEGGERS

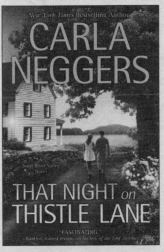

Librarian Phoebe O'Dunn deals in stories, but she knows that happy endings are rare. Her life in Knights Bridge, Massachusetts, is safe and uneventful…until she discovers the hidden room.

Among its secrets is a cache of vintage clothing, including a spectacular gown—perfect for the gala masquerade. In the guise of a princess, Phoebe is captivated by a handsome swashbuckler who's also adopted a more daring persona. Noah Kendrick's wealth has made him wary, especially of women: everybody wants something.

When Noah and Phoebe meet again in Knights Bridge, at first neither recognizes the other. And neither one is sure they can trust the magic of the night they shared—until an unexpected threat prompts them to unmask their truest selves.

Available wherever books are sold.

www.Harlequin.com

MCN1420

REQUEST YOUR FREE BOOKS!

2 FREE NOVELS
FROM THE ROMANCE COLLECTION
PLUS 2 FREE GIFTS!

YES! Please send me 2 FREE novels from the Romance Collection and my 2 FREE gifts (gifts are worth about $10). After receiving them, if I don't wish to receive any more books, I can return the shipping statement marked "cancel." If I don't cancel, I will receive 4 brand-new novels every month and be billed just $5.99 per book in the U.S. or $6.49 per book in Canada. That's a savings of at least 25% off the cover price. It's quite a bargain! Shipping and handling is just 50¢ per book in the U.S. and 75¢ per book in Canada.* I understand that accepting the 2 free books and gifts places me under no obligation to buy anything. I can always return a shipment and cancel at any time. Even if I never buy another book, the two free books and gifts are mine to keep forever.

194/394 MDN FVU7

Name	(PLEASE PRINT)	
Address		Apt. #
City	State/Prov.	Zip/Postal Code

Signature (if under 18, a parent or guardian must sign)

Mail to the **Harlequin® Reader Service:**
IN U.S.A.: P.O. Box 1867, Buffalo, NY 14240-1867
IN CANADA: P.O. Box 609, Fort Erie, Ontario L2A 5X3

Want to try two free books from another line?
Call 1-800-873-8635 or visit www.ReaderService.com.

* Terms and prices subject to change without notice. Prices do not include applicable taxes. Sales tax applicable in N.Y. Canadian residents will be charged applicable taxes. Offer not valid in Quebec. This offer is limited to one order per household. Not valid for current subscribers to the Romance Collection or the Romance/Suspense Collection. All orders subject to credit approval. Credit or debit balances in a customer's account(s) may be offset by any other outstanding balance owed by or to the customer. Please allow 4 to 6 weeks for delivery. Offer available while quantities last.

Your Privacy—The Harlequin® Reader Service is committed to protecting your privacy. Our Privacy Policy is available online at www.ReaderService.com or upon request from the Harlequin Reader Service.

We make a portion of our mailing list available to reputable third parties that offer products we believe may interest you. If you prefer that we not exchange your name with third parties, or if you wish to clarify or modify your communication preferences, please visit us at www.ReaderService.com/consumerschoice or write to us at Harlequin Reader Service Preference Service, P.O. Box 9062, Buffalo, NY 14269. Include your complete name and address.

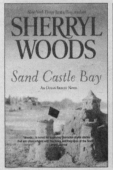

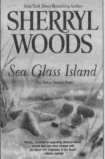

BRENDA NOVAK

31351	WHEN LIGHTNING STRIKES	___ $7.99 U.S.	___ $9.99 CAN.
31371	WHEN SNOW FALLS	___ $7.99 U.S.	___ $9.99 CAN.
32993	INSIDE	___ $7.99 U.S.	___ $9.99 CAN.
32904	WATCH ME	___ $7.99 U.S.	___ $9.99 CAN.
32903	TRUST ME	___ $7.99 U.S.	___ $9.99 CAN.
32886	DEAD GIVEAWAY	___ $7.99 U.S.	___ $9.99 CAN.
32831	KILLER HEAT	___ $7.99 U.S.	___ $9.99 CAN.
32803	BODY HEAT	___ $7.99 U.S.	___ $9.99 CAN.
32725	THE PERFECT MURDER	___ $7.99 U.S.	___ $8.99 CAN.
32724	THE PERFECT LIAR	___ $7.99 U.S.	___ $8.99 CAN.
32667	THE PERFECT COUPLE	___ $7.99 U.S.	___ $8.99 CAN.
31244	IN SECONDS	___ $7.99 U.S.	___ $9.99 CAN.
28858	DEAD SILENCE	___ $7.99 U.S.	___ $9.99 CAN.

(limited quantities available)

TOTAL AMOUNT	$ _____
POSTAGE & HANDLING	$ _____
($1.00 for 1 book, 50¢ for each additional)	
APPLICABLE TAXES*	$ _____
TOTAL PAYABLE	$ _____

(check or money order—please do not send cash)

To order, complete this form and send it, along with a check or money order for the total above, payable to Harlequin MIRA, to: **In the U.S.:** 3010 Walden Avenue, P.O. Box 9077, Buffalo, NY 14269-9077; **In Canada:** P.O. Box 636, Fort Erie, Ontario, L2A 5X3.

Name: _____
Address: _____ City: _____
State/Prov.: _____ Zip/Postal Code: _____
Account Number (if applicable): _____

075 CSAS

*New York residents remit applicable sales taxes.
*Canadian residents remit applicable GST and provincial taxes.

HARLEQUIN® MIRA®
www.Harlequin.com

MBN0213BL